# THE FRENCH BRIDE

*Also by Evelyn Anthony*
*in Thorndike Large Print*

Albatross
The Avenue of the Dead
The Company of Saints
A Place to Hide
Voices on the Wind
The Scarlet Thread

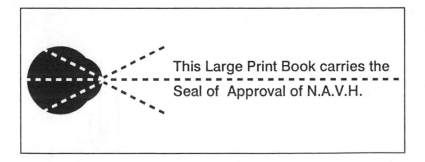

This Large Print Book carries the
Seal of Approval of N.A.V.H.

# THE
# FRENCH
# BRIDE

## Evelyn Anthony

Thorndike Press • Thorndike, Maine

Library of Congress Cataloging in Publication Data:

Anthony, Evelyn.
    The French bride / Evelyn Anthony.
        p.   cm.
    ISBN 1-56054-315-9 (alk. paper : lg. print)
    1. Large type books. I. Title.
[PR6069.T428F74        1991]                    91-36617
823'.914—dc20                                    CIP

Thorndike Press Large Print edition published in 1991
by arrangement with Doubleday, a division of Bantam
Doubleday Dell Publishing Group, Inc.

Cover photo by Alan LaVallee.

**The tree indicium is a trademark of Thorndike Press.**

This book is printed on acid-free, high opacity paper. ∞

# THE
# FRENCH
# BRIDE

# Chapter 1

"M. le Chevalier, your son!" Sir James Macdonald of Dundrenan, Chevalier of France and assistant to the Marquis de Monteynard, the Minister of War, took his wife's hand in his and pressed it gently. He looked down at her, into the lovely face that had changed so little after nearly thirty years of marriage, and said quietly: "Try to be patient with him, Katherine. He'll agree."

"I shan't speak to him at all; this last episode is too much to forgive!"

Sir James turned and spoke to the servant who stood by the door. They had their own apartments in the grounds of Versailles, which they occupied while attending the court, and a small château at Compiègne which had been given them by King Louis XV in one of his rare moments of generosity to the Scottish and Irish exiles who took refuge in France.

There were many like James Macdonald and his wife, exiles as a result of the last Stuart rising in the Highlands in 1745; most were penniless mercenaries and adventurers, living on their wits and on the charity of any rich nobleman who could be persuaded to take an interest in them. But the Macdonalds had prospered; James had distinguished himself in the Seven Years' War against England and Prussia, and the charm and beauty of his wife made powerful friends for them, including King Louis' mistress, the Comtesse du Barry. They were in favour and in receipt of a handsome pension, the latter they owed to the good offices of the Du Barry. Lady Katherine had been too well mannered and too politic to snub her when she had first made her appearance at Versailles and nobody imagined she would hold the King for more than a few weeks. The Macdonalds were twenty thousand livres a year richer as a result.

"Admit M. Charles," Sir James said.

Their only son had been waiting in the anteroom for nearly twenty minutes while his parents discussed what he knew to be his last and worst indiscretion. They were used to his women; he could remember the disgust and anger on his mother's face when she had discovered that two of her little chambermaids were pregnant by him at the same time, and he was only just sixteen himself. He had accepted her reproaches in the same mood in which he waited for them now; bored, impenitent, and mocking. He was leaning back against the wall, glancing at his own reflection in the mirror on the opposite side of the room; once he made the reflection a little bow.

The image in the glass showed a very fashionably dressed young French aristocrat, from the fine lace at his cravat to the embroidered coat and breeches and the diamond buckles on his shoes. But the face was not French; the features were thin and arrogant and the pale-green eyes belonged to the past; they were as much a part of that past as the perpetual mocking grin which never left his mouth unless he was angry or drunk. The face in the mirror was the face of a dead man. Charles was the double of his uncle Hugh Macdonald, who had lost his infamous life at the Battle of Culloden in the Highlands, long before Charles was born. He took out his watch and swore. Twenty minutes; it was his mother of course, who kept him waiting outside as if he were a lackey. She had always hated him. It almost made him laugh aloud to think of how much angrier she would be when she knew the exact amount of money he owed De Charlot. . . .

If it were not for that debt he would have gone to keep his appointment and let his parents go to the devil. He had often consigned them there in the course of his twenty-five years.

"M. Charles, will you go in, please?"

Charles walked past the servant without looking at him, he never looked at servants; even when he kicked his own valet for some fault, he hardly bothered to glance at him. If the menservants at the château and Versailles detested him, the women responded only too well to a kind word or gesture. . . .

"My dear father; madame, my mother." He bowed low to both his parents. They were standing side by side and, as usual, his mother was holding his father's arm. Their fidelity to each other bored their son; he was only more bored by people who asked him if the story of their escape and marriage were really true. . . . Had all members of his mother's family perished in the attack the Macdonalds led upon their castle and had his father actually come on her with a drawn sword and then eloped with her instead . . . ?

Dear God, he thought, how dull and smug and virtuous they were. He met his mother's eye, that blue, cold eye which had never once looked on him with maternal feeling. He rather admired her for that. Whatever she was, his mother was no fool. It was his father who spoke to him.

"I suppose you know why we've sent for you?"

"I can guess. You've read my note asking

10

your assistance, and not unnaturally you want to know how much?"

Sir James's very dark eyes narrowed angrily.

"Yes, my son," he said. "We want to know how much you owe the Marquis de Charlot and we also want to know why you expect us to settle the debt for you. Before you took the trouble to write me, I was informed by De Charlot that you had refused to pay him. Is that correct?"

"It is," Charles answered coolly. "Since I had no money to my credit and other — er — rather pressing bills, I couldn't do anything else. I did ask him to wait, though."

"Not according to De Charlot," his father cut in. "I understood from him that you had threatened to kill him if he pressed you for the money. He came to me in some alarm."

Charles laughed. "The miserable little cur! I daresay he *was* alarmed . . . I told him if he came pestering me for a few paltry thousands, I'd take him out and cut his throat!" There was no grin on his face now; his father appreciated only too well why the Marquis de Charlot had sought him out, stuttering with fright and indignation and ending the interview by threatening to complain to the King.

"Did he tell you how much I owed him?"

"Ten thousand livres!" Lady Katherine spoke for the first time. "Ten thousand livres lost in a night at faro. Do you know how much your father and I possessed to live on in our first years here? Less than half that! And when you lose it, you behave like some common cutthroat and threaten the man! James, tell him what we've decided and let's get the business over before I lose my temper with him."

"My dear mother," Charles said calmly. "You are always losing your temper with me. If you don't tonight, I shall be quite disappointed. I played cards, I lost the money. I also lost my temper as a result of being dunned. Other nights I usually win, but no one mentions that. Are you going to pay it for me, or shall I carry out my threat to De Charlot? I wouldn't have asked you so soon again except that I heard a rumour he was going to the King."

"It's no rumour," Katherine retorted. "That's why we sent for you. The last time was six months ago and your father and I swore we'd never pay another gambling loss for you whatever the consequences. But things have changed since then. James, you tell him."

She turned away and walked to the other end of the room. She was so agitated that she couldn't trust herself. Her son, the child of their consuming love, the result of a passion which had survived the hazards of war, of clan feuds, even of murder itself, still bound them

12

indivisibly after twenty-seven years, their son and now their heir to the impounded estates in the Highlands, was the reincarnation of one of the most evil men that she had ever known, the cruel and pitiless Hugh Macdonald who had killed her own brother and once tried to murder her. From the moment she saw that resemblance in the child she held in her arms, all love for him had disappeared. He had proved to be like his uncle in more ways than his looks. He gambled, he fought, he seduced without mercy or moral considerations of any kind; at the age of nineteen he had killed three men in duels over women and cards, and one unhappy creature who had allowed herself to be involved with him committed suicide when he told her to go back to the husband who had turned her out.

Thank God, Katherine thought, thank God we have Jean. They both loved their daughter, happily married to a gentle, scholarly French nobleman and the mother of three small children. Thank God, she thought again, that we have Jean.

"As your mother said," Sir James began, "we told you last time we would never settle another debt for you. As far as we are concerned, De Charlot could go to the King and you could learn a very salutary lesson in the Bastille for a month or two. I wouldn't lift a hand to interfere except for just one thing. The English Government have agreed to restore our estates in Scotland. Not to me, unfortunately, they've got long memories; but to you, my son."

"Really?" The light eyes gleamed and then he half closed them as if he were a little bored; it was a trick which had once brought his father's hand down on the side of his head with such force that he had sprawled on the floor. He had been a youth then; not even James would dare to strike him now.

"You mean that I am the heir to Dundrenan and Clandara?"

"You are, or at least you will be as soon as I accept the terms and surrender my own claims and your mother's. You are the future chief of the Macdonalds of Dandrenan and the closest blood heir of the Frasers of Clandara. You can bring the two clans together and give them the leadership they've lacked for twenty-seven years. That means more to me than your miserable debts; that's why I shan't let De Charlot go to the King and accuse you, and your mother feels the same."

"I'm very grateful," Charles said. "I can't see myself as a chief in the Highlands, but if the lands are good and the property . . . I daresay I'll pay a visit and see what can be done with it."

"There's a condition." Katherine came back and put her arm around her husband. "No debt will be paid and no inheritance accepted unless you meet this, Charles. Refuse, and you can take your debts and your difficulties out of this room and never enter it again. We'll ask the English to transfer your rights to Jean. I'm not sure we shouldn't do that anyway!"

"What is the condition?" Charles asked softly.

His father answered. "That you marry your cousin, Anne de Bernard, and settle down to a reasonable life. And that you undertake to live at least six months of the year in the Highlands and have your sons educated and brought up there as befits Macdonalds. Believe me, your mother and I will not allow our peoples to be cheated. Do this, and your debt will be paid by tomorrow. Refuse, and I feel certain that De Charlot and his friends will persuade the King to throw you into prison until it is. It's up to you."

"How much time have I?" he asked them. Marry. Marry Anne de Bernard. He looked from one to the other of them. He was already late for his appointment with Louise; he needed Louise tonight. If he delayed much more, the Du Barry might send for her to play cards or sing. She had a pretty voice, among her other considerable accomplishments, and the King liked music. He enjoyed nothing better than to sit with the Du Barry half naked on his knees while another pretty woman sang or played.

"You have no time at all," his father said. "You decide now."

"Marry my rich cousin and inherit eighty thousand acres and two chieftainships or else kill De Charlot and risk prison or not kill him and probably go to prison anyway. My dear father, and madame my mother, I accept your conditions — unconditionally. May I leave now . . . ? I have a pressing engagement."

"I can imagine with whom," Katherine answered. "Of all the women at Versailles you have to choose the most vicious and depraved. That will stop too, after you are married."

He did not answer her, but she saw the mocking defiance in his face, and she could not pretend that it was not a very handsome face. Even if he had been ugly, he would still have possessed the same dangerous charm, the fascination of the heartless and the wholly bad.

"You will settle the debt?" He addressed his father, and Sir James nodded. "By tonight, I told you. I am going to ask the King's permission for the marriage; it's only a formality and we'll announce it as soon as we've been down to Charantaise."

He remembered the splendid château; he

16

used to go there as a child and stay with his mother's relations, the De Bernards. There used to be a little marquise, very talkative and overdressed, painted up like a Parisian whore, with the mincing manners of an age that reflected the King's last, great mistress, Madame de Pompadour. The little marquise with her passion for scandal and mischief was dead now, and only her daughter Anne and an old uncle who was her guardian remained. He hadn't seen his cousin since she was a child and all he knew about her was that she was immensely rich. He bowed to his parents.

"I wish you both good night. Excuse me; I know you wouldn't want me to keep the lady waiting." As he went out of the room, he laughed.

Katherine turned to her husband.

"James, James, all I can think of is that poor child Anne. How can we marry her to him . . . even for the sake of Dundrenan and Clandara — it's twenty-seven years since the Rebellion; how do we know what state the clans are in or if there's anyone left in the glens at all?"

"The two houses are in ruins but our people are still there," he answered. "They need a leader; they need Anne de Bernard's money to rebuild and replenish the land. She'll fare well enough. How do you know marriage won't change him . . . it changed me."

"My darling," she said gently, "if he were anything like you, I'd love him with all my heart and she'd be the luckiest woman in the world to marry him. But there's none of you in him, and none of me either. Only the very worst of both families — that's all I see in him. You are determined on this marriage, aren't you?"

"Absolutely," he said quietly. "Don't ask me to change my mind because I can't. I'm Scots to my bones in spite of living here. I must do what is best for my people."

"So be it then," she said. "At least I can try to protect her from him when they're married."

"When they're married," James answered slowly, "we both can. Come, my darling, I'm going to seek an audience of the King."

Louise de Vitale was a very beautiful woman, even in a court where beautiful women were in abundance and pretty women too numerous to be counted. At twenty-three she was a widow; her husband, the Baron de Vitale, was already an old man when she married him, and having lived a life of excess, his constitution did not survive the strain of being married to his young and lovely wife for more than two years. When he died he left everything in his possession to the woman whom he described as the most perfect *compagnonne de nuit* any man could wish for. By the time she was twenty, Louise was rich, well connected, and very bored with living in the country on her husband's estates and carrying on intrigues with the husbands of her neighbours. She had exhausted them all during her year's mourning and she left her estates in the hands of a bailiff and set out for Versailles. Almost at once she attracted the attention of the Duc de Richelieu; it was not only advisable but a pleasure for Louise to become his mistress. He was attractive and charming and he enjoyed intrigue as much as she did. Also he was an intimate of the King's new mistress, the Comtesse du Barry, and that opened the door to many things.

In a court where everyone powdered, two women were conspicuous for wearing their hair naturally. One was the royal mistress, whose hair was a ravishing golden red as fine as silk, and the other, the Baroness de Vitale, whose beautiful hair was so dark that in some lights it seemed touched with blue. With this sable hair, she possessed a skin as pale and smooth as milk, and her body was of the same texture and colour as her face. Her eyes were very large and black with heavy, painted lids above them, and a mouth which was full and red. She was beautiful and she dressed superbly, and she had been Charles Macdonald's mistress for over a year. He was the first man to whom she had ever been faithful, and while she waited for him that night, she was so restless that she walked up and down like an animal in a cage. She had a maid who had been in her service since she married, a sharp-eyed little Breton who shared all her secrets.

"Don't worry, madame. M. Charles will come."

"What time is it?" Louise demanded. "He's never as late as this!" That was another oddity, Marie thought, taking out her watch. He often kept the baroness waiting, whereas all the other gentlemen would sit outside her door for an hour before she was ready. Marie did not like Charles Macdonald. He was a foreigner for all that he was born and bred in France; there was an arrogance about him, a brutality, which she had seen in his quarrels with her mistress, that was definitely not French. Once he had come to the baroness' apartments drunk, and when she reproached him, he struck her and dragged her into the bedroom and locked the door. When he left the next morning, her mistress was more abjectly in love with him than ever. Marie had a lover of her own; he worked as a footman for the Duchesse de Gramont and together they were saving every sou to get married and open a small shop in Paris.

"It is nearly eleven o'clock, madame. Perhaps he isn't coming this time?"

"He would have sent a note, some word," her mistress said. "He'll come, he's been detained by something, that's all it is." Louise went to the looking glass on the wall and examined herself in it. Charles was the only man she had ever met who made her unsure of her beauty; she stared at herself anxiously. Her dress was pale yellow and made of the soft, thin silk which the Du Barry had brought into fashion; worn without panniers it clung to the body and it showed every line of her beautiful figure; her breasts were almost exposed, only a gauze fichu covered them. She was one of those rare women who looked as beautiful in déshabille as she did in the most magnificent ball gown.

From the beginning of their relationship, when they had met at a card party given by the Duc d'Aiguillon who was at that time Du Barry's lover and political protector, Louise decided that it was useless to expect him to behave like other men. She had begun the intrigue because he was attractive and at first he had paid her no attention. The moment he took her in his arms, he established an absolute mastery of her; in bewilderment she submitted to a sexual domination she had never imagined could exist. Its power over her was such that as she waited for him, she was trembling.

"Madame," Marie whispered, "I hear him coming!" Louise heard his voice, talking and laughing to another man as they walked down the corridor, and then the other set of steps went on, and the door opened and he came towards her.

"Charles!" She ran to him and for a moment he held her off, mocking her eagerness. Then he pulled her to him and kissed her. After a moment he looked up at the maid.

"Get out!"

Marie curtsied and vanished through the door in the wall; she slept in a small closet where she could hear the baroness' bell if she were needed. It wouldn't ring tonight.

"You're so late," Louise whispered, avoiding his mouth for a moment. "I have supper prepared for you. . . . Darling beloved, you're tearing my dress . . . come and sit down for a moment."

"I don't want supper and I'm not going to sit down. Come to bed, Louise; to hell with the dress. I'll buy you another one!"

"What with?" she whispered. He picked her up and kicked open the bedroom door. A table was laid for supper in one corner of the room;

there were candles and flowers and the bed was turned down. The rooms were very small and in the upper regions of an outer wing, far from the main buildings. Louise was lucky to have secured them. "How can you buy me a new dress when you're always in debt?" She looked up at him from the bed. He had flung off his wig and stripped off his coat. "I'll be a rich man soon. No more questions now!" Louise held out her arms to him.

"Silence me then," she said.

Louis XV was sixty-one years old and he had been King of France for fifty-six years. Those who wished to see him privately knew that the quickest means of entry was through the rooms of Madame du Barry, and the best way of ensuring a sympathetic audience was to talk to her first.

In spite of her reputation, Sir James Macdonald found it impossible to dislike the King's mistress. She was common and inclined to be familiar; more than one disdainful nobleman and many haughty women had felt the sting of the comtesse's urchin sense of humour, but in a court where morals were a scandal and the inhumanities practised as a matter of course, the Du Barry was no more vicious than anyone else and far better-natured than most. She injured nobody and tried to help many;

her greatest wish was to be liked and accepted. Her extravagance and lewdness were part of the day-to-day life at Versailles, and those who wished for the King's favour, accepted both without comment. She was sitting in her boudoir when Sir James came in. She looked exquisitely pretty in a loose gown of pale blue, sewed with pink and silver lover's knots, and a fortune in pink pearls shining on her neck and breast. Her famous hair was gathered up by more pink and silver bows and an enormous pink diamond winked and blazed out of the mass of curls. The comtesse was ready for His Majesty; she had found a street juggler in Paris and, being delighted by his tricks, brought him to Versailles to perform before the King. A select group of Du Barry's friends had been invited; after the juggler there was a singer and some musicians. The King was growing old so rapidly that it was necessary to stimulate him with songs and plays of such lasciviousness that even the court was shocked. But the gay and pretty little courtesan knew better. She was no prude and they made her laugh. If they made the King affectionate and he wanted to sit and fondle her in public and recapture some of his old vigour afterwards, why should a few sour faces grudge it to him. . . .

She gave her hand to Sir James to kiss and asked him at once what he wanted.

"I know you want something, monsieur, you have the look . . . I've been here long enough now to recognise it a mile off. What can I do for you — or what can the King do?"

"Something very simple, madame," he answered and in spite of himself he smiled into the lovely, impudent little face. "Something very simple which won't cost His Majesty a sou."

"By God, that'll be a change." Du Barry giggled. "Everyone who comes in here has his hand out; it hardly leaves enough for me. How do you like my pearls, monsieur? I've told your dear wife before that I really can't pronounce your name; it's quite impossible for a Parisienne. How is she, by the way? I wish she'd come to see me, but I know it's no use inviting her to one of my evenings. . . ."

"She'll wait on you tomorrow," he promised. Du Barry winked at him. "Very skilfully avoided, monsieur. Don't worry. I won't embarrass her or you by inviting you to see my little play tomorrow. I think it's so amusing, I almost split my stays the first time I saw it. . . . Now, what is this favour that isn't going to cost the King any money?"

"His permission for the marriage of my son Charles."

Du Barry glanced up at him and made a face.

"I know of your son, monsieur, and if you don't mind my saying so, I don't envy the bride, whoever she is. There's a dear friend of mine who's attached to him. I think she's mad and I've told her so. But never mind, never mind. Go and wait in the anteroom; the King will be here in a minute. I'll call for you as soon as he's ready and before he sees my juggler. Don't worry, he'll give his permission. He adores to think of women being made to suffer. Poor little wretch. Until a little later, monsieur."

"I knew the girl's mother very well," the King said. "One of the biggest mischief-makers in France. From what I remember of Anne de Bernard, she doesn't resemble her mother in the least. Is she agreeable to this marriage?"

James nodded. "Her guardian assures me that she will follow his advice, sire. If you consent to the match, the engagement will be announced next month after my son's return from Charantaise."

"She's very rich," the old King said. His very black eyes looked past Sir James towards Madame du Barry. She blew him a kiss and for a moment the long, melancholy face softened and he smiled.

"Very rich and wellborn; a quiet and modest creature, if I recall her properly." He frowned, trying to remember. "Ah yes, delightful, very pretty. Your son is lucky, monsieur. Very well, your arguments about your estates have decided me. You have my permission. You may go, M. Macdonald." As Sir James bowed, he saw Louis yawn and hold out his hand to the Du Barry. He hurried out of the second-floor apartments which were the official quarters of the mistress, and went back to tell his wife that now the marriage could take place. He was also in a hurry to arrange the payment of Charles's debt.

"There's no need for you to marry this woman! Why didn't you come to me, I would have mortgaged my estates, done anything — I would have found the money for you somehow!"

"I told you," Charles said. "There's more to it than the debt. I'm going to inherit my family's lands in Scotland — I need a rich wife; besides, my dear Louise, by the time you gathered the money together, De Charlot would have had me sent to the Bastille, and you know how easy it is to get out of there!"

He closed his eyes for a moment; he felt sleepy and relaxed and rather hungry. He wished that she would stop harassing him about his marriage. He reached out and brought her close beside him; he had only to touch her to feel his strength and his desire surging back like the blood tide in his veins. He kissed her shoulder and began to pull her down with him, caressing her; to his surprise she struck his hands away and sprang off the bed. He opened his eyes and looked at her and laughed.

"You look very beautiful when you're jealous. Jealous and naked; both suit you to perfection. Stop being such a damned fool Louise! If you won't make love with me, then at least give me some supper. I'm hungry now."

"You weren't when you came in," she said.

She covered herself with a long satin robe; her hands were shaking. Lying beside him, drowsing and whispering, he had suddenly told her that he was going to marry one of the richest young women in France. She hardly listened to his account of his interview with his parents, or the cynical way in which he spoke of the match itself. All Louise knew was that another woman would have legal title to him, a woman she had never seen, a woman who was young and a great heiress.

"How can you expect me to be anything but jealous?" she demanded. She reached over and began tying the laces of his shirt; her eyes were full of tears. "You know I love you more than anything in the world. Don't do it, Charles, don't, I beg of you! I'll go to the

Du Barry, she'll help me, she'll intercede with the King. He won't listen to De Charlot. And I'll find the ten thousand livres for you! You've no need to marry her!"

Charles took her hands away and finished fastening the shirt himself. He looked down at her with an expression she had seen once or twice before, a look of cold, irritated boredom that could develop in a moment into the kind of anger that silenced a nagging woman with a blow.

"If you think that being your lover is more important to me than inheriting my rights in my own country, then you're a very stupid woman. Do you suppose I'm going to be an exile, living on French charity all my life, just because my mistress doesn't want me to take a wife . . . ?"

"Don't be angry with me," she said quickly.

She turned away to arrange her hair before the dressing table and control herself. One more tactless word and he would walk out of the room, perhaps never enter it again. She had often amused herself by teasing and provoking her lovers for the pleasure of seeing them come crawling back. Now it was her turn to abase herself, and she wanted him so much that she had long since lost all sense of shame. She pulled out the chair for him and without speaking he sat down in it and began to help himself to the cold meats and pastry dishes. She poured out two glasses of wine and sat opposite to him.

"I won't mention it again," she said softly. "You know what's best."

He put down his glass and smiled at her. "You've no reason to worry," he said. "She's my *cousin* . . . nothing will change between us. She'll learn to do what she's told."

The Château of Charantaise de la Haye had been built in the fifteenth century by the Sieur de Bernard, who designed it as a fortress in command of his vast lands. Little of the original building remained; his descendants, notably the fifth marquis, rebuilt it on the scale of an elegant palace, inspired by the splendours being carried out by King Louis XIV in his palace at Versailles. The beautiful stone building was set in a valley; behind the park of more than a hundred acres, including woods, formal gardens, fountain walks, and a fine orangery; land stretched out as far as the eye could see. Every farm, every field of grain, every tree, stream, and bush, and every living creature belonged to the Seigneur of Charantaise.

For the last twelve years the great estates had been owned by a woman. There were two hundred rooms in the château and one hundred and fifty indoor servants, excluding gardeners, grooms, messengers, woodsmen, and gamekeepers. There was a banqueting hall with a ceiling painted by Vernet, a library containing over a thousand books, and a magnificent private chapel. The woods were full of game, for the De Bernards were great hunters; unlike most of the nobility of the period, they preferred to live on their splendid estates and make only token appearances at court. Apart from her formal presentation at Versailles, Anne de Bernard had stayed at Charantaise.

A group of horses raced across the green parkland, and a sound of a huntsman's horn sang through the autumn air. Ahead of them a deer fled for its life, bounding over the ground, pursued by a dozen hunting dogs in full cry. One horse galloped faster and jumped more recklessly than the rest and it was ridden by a woman in a green riding dress. As she had said to her uncle, Anne de Bernard saw no reason why she should miss an afternoon's hunting even if her future husband was coming to Charantaise that day.

When the riders came back to the château, the light was beginning to fail; the deer had reached the shelter of the woods where the horses could not follow it and the hounds were called off, yelping and barking with disappointment. Their mistress stopped at the foot of the entrance stairs and patted them, laughing. She adored the excitement and the danger of the chase, but she was always glad when the quarry escaped after a good run. A footman came to take her gloves and whip; the enormous doors of the château were opened wide, and inside the marble entrance hall with its palisades and statues, servants were carrying boxes up the staircase, and her own steward of the household came running down the steps to meet her.

"Madame, your guests have arrived!"

"So I see — have they been here long?"

"About an hour, madame; Monsieur, your uncle, asked you to come to him as soon as you returned."

"Where is my uncle?" Anne asked him. She paused in the entrance and looked round. There were faces that she did not know, wearing strange livery, and a very thin, grey-haired little woman in a brown cloak, shouting directions about the luggage in such a bad accent that even Anne could hardly understand her. But she recognised her; it was her cousin Lady Katherine's maid, Annie, and Annie was very much a part of their extraordinary story. She had been found a year after their escape from Scotland, the only survivor of the massacre which had killed all her mistress' family, and brought over to France to join her.

"Your uncle is in the Long Salon," her steward said. "With your guests, madame."

"Very good, I'll join them there." She walked over to the little Scotswoman and touched her on the shoulder.

"Good day, Annie. Do you recognise me after all this time?"

"M. la Marquise!" Annie's reply was made in lilting Scots. "Och, how ye've grown; I'd hardly know ye now from the tiny lassie I used to play with down here!" She curtsied, and her sharp, lined face turned pink. She would never have recognised the shy, ordinary child of years ago in this tall, beautiful girl with her dazzling smile. The change was unbelievable.

"Have you brought my future husband with you?" Anne asked her.

The old woman's smile disappeared; "Aye," she said shortly. "But don't hurry now — it'll do him no harm to be kept waiting! I can't believe my eyes, madame, ye're so much altered."

Anne laughed. "I always knew I was an ugly child. I'd best go and change my dress." She looked down at her skirt, it was streaked with dirt where the dogs had leaped at her affectionately. "If there is anything you need for your master and mistress or yourself, go to my steward Henri; only don't speak to him in English. He doesn't understand it. Good afternoon Annie. And welcome."

She ran up the wide stairs; like the hall they were made of the finest Carrara marble, exported from the Italian quarries at enormous cost. There were alcoves along the wall where her ancestor had placed the early Roman sculptures he had collected. As a very small child, Anne used to amuse herself by skipping down the staircase, making faces at the figures as she passed. The man her guardian wanted her to marry had been a little boy who used to join her in that game; it was one of the few things she remembered about him except that he was older and she much preferred his younger sister. She and Jean Macdonald de Mallot were still close friends who wrote regularly to each other though they seldom visited. She could remember very little indeed about Charles.

She walked quickly along the upper corridor that was really a fine gallery hung with portraits; generations of De Bernards looked down at her, some in hunting dress with their dogs beside them, others in armour mounted upon rearing horses, others with their wives and children in stiff groups. The ancestress, who had married a Scottish earl and gone to live with him at Clandara in the Highlands, was one of the prettiest of the pictures in the gallery; Anne was her great-niece and Charles Macdonald was her great-grandson. At the far end of the gallery she almost knocked into a man; he had been standing with his back to her, staring at the picture of the dead Countess of Clandara, Marie Elizabeth de Bernard at the age of twenty, wearing the costume of Diana.

"Monsieur!"

Charles turned and bowed. "I beg your pardon, madame. I didn't see you."

"Nor I you," she answered. He was staring at her coolly, and to her annoyance, she blushed. There was something about him, some mocking look that was familiar. "I was just admiring this picture," he said. "She's the only pretty one among the whole gallery; the De Bernards are not an attractive family; don't you agree?"

"No," Anne said, "I'm afraid I don't. I happen to be Anne de Bernard!"

He turned back to her and smiled. "I know," he said lightly. "I recognised you the moment you bumped into me so clumsily. Even as a child you were always bumping into things or rolling on the lawns with your dogs. As soon as I saw someone in a riding habit covered in mud to the eyes, I knew it was you. I'm your cousin Charles. Did you recognise me? I hope *I've* changed!"

"Not very much," she answered. "I don't remember much about you except that you always made me cry. You haven't altered at all. Excuse me, I'm going to change my dress and go down to greet your mother."

He stood and watched her as she ran down the rest of the gallery and disappeared through the door at the end. He lied when he said he had recognised her at once; as a child her hair had been brown and her face quite unremarkable; there was no distinguishing feature to identify her twelve years later. Now the mousey hair was the colour of the burnished beech trees in the park outside, and the eyes which had filled with tears at his rudeness were large and very blue. She was quite beautiful, but it was not a beauty that appealed to him in the least. He did not know what he had expected and he had not really cared; he was determined to dislike her because she was not his choice. But this naïve, unsophisticated gentlewoman who blushed and blundered into him like an awkward schoolgirl. . . . He put his hands in his pockets and began to walk slowly down the gallery. He was being made to pay a heavy price for his debts and the estates in Scotland he had never seen. Louise need have no fear. He had hardly been in the house before he was counting the days till he returned to Versailles.

"What dress will you wear, madame? I've put out three for you, but you left no instructions this morning and I didn't know. . . ." Anne had two maids to look after her. She often felt that one was quite sufficient, but the De Bernard ladies always had two women of the chamber, and after they were married, they had three.

She went into the dressing closet and pulled out the dresses one by one. There was a yellow silk trimmed round the sleeves with gold lace, a crimson velvet with cuffs and hem lined in imperial sables, and a peacock blue — the petticoat covered in silver embroidery. After a moment Anne pointed to the blue dress. "I will wear that; bring out my jewel boxes."

She had said nothing about meeting her cousin; she allowed the maids to undress her and bathe her, but when they tried to talk about the visit and her fiancé, she told them to be quiet. The laws of obedience to the mistress were very strictly enforced at Charantaise; nobody dared to say a word. After she was laced into the blue dress and sitting before her dressing mirror while one of the maids dressed her hair, Anne opened the jewel boxes one after another, taking out this piece and that and rejecting it. Her mother had been passionately fond of jewels; many of the lovely rings and ornaments were given to her by her lovers. Her husband had been a stern and solid man, devoted to his estates and his sports and accustomed to the vagaries of his frivolous wife which he ignored. Anne had inherited the splendid family jewels of the De Bernards and the sentimental trophies of her imprudent mother. It was a set of these which suited the brilliant colour of her dress. They were pale sapphire, surrounded by large diamonds and exquisitely set in a necklace and a brooch. It was the custom to change four times a day, when one went walking or driving out, hunting, receiving visitors in the afternoon, and again when she dined at night, even alone.

The only difference was in her choice that night, the blue gown was very formal; her reflection in the mirror dazzled with diamonds and the flash of silver embroidery. She would have given anything in the world to have met her cousin Charles for the first time, looking as she did at that moment.

"My fan," she said. The maid put a pale-blue one in her hand. "Ring for my uncle to escort me."

"Immediately, madame."

When the old Comte de Bernard came into her boudoir he opened his eyes wide and made her a low bow.

"My dear Anne! Why, you look simply brilliant, simply dazzling!"

"Uncle, before I go down I want to tell you something. I don't like my cousin and I'm not going to marry him."

The comte was genuinely fond of his niece. It was his ambition to see her suitably married before he died and the future of Charantaise secured by several children. He could think of no more sensible match than between the two cousins. He had hardly seen the young man himself, but he was handsome enough to please any woman and, in the comte's estimation, his reputation was not a disadvantage. The old roué would never have wished an inexperienced prig upon his niece. Equally, his greatest anxiety had been the advent of some smooth-mannered fortune hunter; but Charles Macdonald had excellent prospects and the Scots were notoriously independent. Anne and her great possessions would be safer with him than with any of the degenerate scoundrels he lad seen loafing around Versailles.

"How do you know, my darling child, when you haven't even seen him?"

"I have," she retorted. "I met him in the gallery. I had been out hunting as you know, and my dress was dirty . . . he said he knew me immediately because I was covered in mud as usual! Well, be can't say that now. You really think I look well?"

"I've never seen you look more beautiful," he answered. He came up to her and kissed her gently on the cheek. "If you dislike him so much, my dear, why are you so piqued . . . and why all the trouble to dress up? Come now, don't be so sensitive . . . I'm sure he only meant to tease you. You're not used to it, that's all. You have all the young men for miles around sighing at your feet and telling you you're a goddess, and you don't understand one who doesn't say the same. Perhaps he will say something different when he sees you tonight."

"Perhaps . . ." she turned away from him, opening and closing the fan until the comte begged her to stop. He could not bear the small, clicking noise.

"You won't make me marry him if I really don't want to, will you, Uncle . . . I'm simply terrified of marriage."

"Only because you've had too much of your own way," he said gently. "But I've never made you do anything against your will ever since your parents died. I won't do it now. But I would like you to marry your cousin if you can. I know it's right for you and it would make me happy. Wait for a few days and we'll talk of it again."

40

"I am so happy to be here again," Lady Katherine said. She glanced across at her husband and smiled. It was the first time she smiled since they had sat down to dinner. She turned to Anne.

"You know that I met James while I was staying in this house with your mother? You can imagine what wonderful memories it brings back to me dining in this room again."

"And to me," James said. "Now, young people are spoilt; I doubt if any of them would survive our difficulty." He gave an angry look at his son who smiled crookedly back at him and went on sipping his wine.

Charles found his parents' sentimentalism quite nauseating; he had heard the story of their first meeting and every event that followed since he was old enough to understand, and he was intensely bored by it. He looked across at his cousin Anne who sat at the head of the table in her sparkling blue gown that was a year behind the fashions Louise wore, and decided he had better not yawn. Her face was very flushed and she was listening to his mother without really hearing a word that was said. He had spoken once to her after she came downstairs with her uncle, and not a word had passed between them during dinner. Her embarrassment and his parents' irritation amused him very much. Even the old comte was silent; he had given up all his attempts to bring his niece and Charles together and devoted himself to the food and wine.

"Charles," his father's voice was curt, "we will excuse you from sitting on with us. You may escort your cousin into the salon."

Anne gave the signal and they rose, leaving Sir James and the count behind them; Charles looked from his mother to his cousin and made them both a low bow.

"Which of you charming ladies will take my arm," he said. "I confess I can't make up my mind between you."

"I am going to bed," his mother snapped. "The journey tired me. You and your cousin will be glad to be alone."

He held out his arm and Anne placed her hand on it. They followed his mother out of the dining room and in the hall she turned and kissed the girl.

"Good night, my dear child. Don't let my son weary you." She went up the stairs without speaking to Charles.

"What a pity I always put my mother into such a vile temper," he remarked. "I'm glad she wasn't hypocrite enough to kiss me."

"She is a wonderful woman," Anne said quickly. "I can't think of anyone I admire more than your parents."

"Perhaps that's because you're not their child. Personally, they bore me intolerably."

"As much as I bore you?"

She stopped in the middle of the salon and faced him. To her surprise he laughed.

"I haven't had time to find out whether you bore me or not, but I expect you will. Most women do after a time. Why don't we sit down and make conversation as we've been instructed, or are you going to try and quarrel? You'll get the worst of it if you do; I'm not chivalrous I warn you."

"I can see that," Anne retorted. "You're not even good mannered either! Why did you come here? You don't want to marry me any more than I want to marry you!"

"Don't you want to marry me?" He smiled down at her, his eyebrows raised. "I'm not such an unattractive fellow surely . . . or perhaps there's some noble country gentleman you fancy. . . ."

"There's no one," Anne said slowly. "But I still don't want to marry you."

"I'm glad to find it's mutual." Charles sat back on one of the elegant gilt sofas. "Don't tell me that old dotard is forcing you into it; he hasn't the spirit of a sheep."

"He's my guardian," she answered. "He told me tonight his heart was set on it; he said he was sure I'd be happy with you."

43

"Then he's more of a fool than I thought him," Charles retorted. "You know why I'm here, don't you? You know why this marriage is being arranged?"

"No," she said. "I know nothing about it; your father and my uncle have been writing to each other and I was told it had been agreed between them. I thought you had agreed to it too."

"I have, my dear Anne. Considering the alternative was being sent to the Bastille for a debt I couldn't pay, I hadn't much choice. . . . Why don't you sit down. Don't worry, I shan't come near you, if that's what you're afraid of; not until I have to, as part of my duties as a husband."

She sat down a little way from him; she was very pale.

"I'm sorry," she said at last. "I had no idea that I was being forced upon you. I understand now why you've been so rude. I'm sure I should have done the same."

"That's very understanding of you. Are you going to refuse your uncle and let me go to prison or shall we play out this little game for them and then make the best of the marriage afterwards?"

"What do you mean by the best?" she asked him. The pale-green eyes glinted back at her; there was no softness in them, only the old jeering look that somehow hurt her more and more. She thought suddenly that she had never seen anyone who could look so cruel when he smiled.

"This will be a marriage of convenience," Charles said. "Neither of us want it, neither of us are even imagining that we love each other, though I don't place much value on that . . . I have to marry you because you're rich and my estates in Scotland will benefit by your money. Apart from the little matter of that debt and going to prison. Incidentally, my father has paid half of it; he's clever enough to hold the rest over my head in case I tried to break my promise. Your uncle wants a marriage between cousins and he likes the thought of my inheritance in Scotland. Those are the terms, are they not? Well then, we haven't any choice but to accept them. That doesn't mean to say we can't lead our own lives as we please afterwards. You can stay here, where you're happy, and I can go where I'm happy. Is that so impossible?"

"And is that what you want?" she asked him. "Is that your idea of marriage?"

"Marriage isn't my idea at all," he answered shortly. "I've no mind to burden myself with any woman permanently. Be sensible with me and you'll find I'm very accommodating."

Anne did not speak for a moment. Only a

month ago the young son of their neighbour, the Vicomte de Bré, had knelt in that same room and begged her to marry him on his knees. She had refused him gently, feeling quite sad that his love meant nothing to her and could only cause him pain. Nothing would hurt the man sitting opposite to her; no woman's tears would touch that heartless nature to a moment's pity. She should refuse the match while she had time, implore her uncle, weep and beg and persuade him to release her, and she knew that in the end he would. And Charles would go to prison. She sensed that neither his father nor his mother would forgive him if he failed to keep his part of the bargain they had made.

"Is there anyone you love?" she said at last. "Is that why you resent me so?"

"Love? My dear cousin, I don't understand the word. If you are trying to ask if I have a mistress, then I have indeed. She's a most admirable woman, and she's never been stupid enough to ask if I loved her. . . . Besides, I don't like answering personal questions. Don't ever try to pry on me . . . I won't on you."

"Then it's a bargain," Anne heard herself saying it, and could not stop. "But there is one condition."

"Oh, really?" he said. "I don't like conditions."

46

She looked at him and tried to smile.

"You must be nice to me until the wedding," she said. "Pretend to like me a little. Spare me the humiliation of tonight. It isn't much to ask."

Charles went to a side table and poured out two glasses of wine.

"What a damnable condition; how can I endure being nice to you for one whole month? Tell me, Anne my dear, what must I do? Pay you little attentions, follow you around, compliment you on your clothes? The first thing you had better do is send for a good modiste from Paris; that dress is a year out of date!"

"You just can't stop tormenting me, can you? It's no good, I've changed my mind. I won't marry you!" She put down her glass and her hand was so unsteady that she spilled the wine; she tried to get up but he caught her wrist. The grip was so hard that it hurt her.

"Stay where you are," he said. "I like tormenting you. You should learn how to retaliate."

"The only retaliation I know is to box your ears," Anne turned on him angrily. "Let me go, you're hurting my arm." She had not meant to struggle with him; he was so strong that he had forced her back onto the sofa and imprisoned both her wrists before she had time to cry out. Instinct made him do something he had never intended or thought that he could want to do. He bent her head back and kissed her.

She kept her mouth closed, trying furiously to free herself, but it was useless; if she struggled he hurt her and the pressure of his mouth was forcing hers to open. Suddenly she submitted and her senses reeled under the shock. Her eyes closed and she felt as if she were falling.

When he released her and she opened her eyes, she saw him watching her with the same mocking smile on his face.

"I think you'll marry me, won't you? Is that what you meant by being nice?"

She sprang up and ran out of the room without a word. Anne ordered her maids to wait outside, and shut herself in her bedroom; she sank down on the bed, trembling violently, her hands pressed hard against her outraged mouth. It was bruised and aching, and yet the memory of that kiss was still so strong it made her head swim. Others had kissed her, but theirs were gentle kisses, tender and respectful. He had kissed her as if she were a common whore, mercilessly and brutally, and then laughed at her because she had succumbed. After a moment she got up and went to her dressing mirror. Carefully she wiped her face;

it was deathly pale under the rouge, and she sat deliberately still and composed herself before ringing for her maids. They undressed her in silence, put away the heavy jewels, and helped her into her nightgown. The blue dress, its embroidery glittering in the candlelight, was folded up over the senior maid's arm when Anne spoke over her shoulder.

"Don't put it back in the closet, Marie-Jeanne. I shan't wear it again; you may have it."

"Oh, thank you, madame, thank you!"

Marie-Jeanne held up the dress for a moment with an exclamation of delight and then curtsied deeply before she hurried away with it. Her mistress was always generous to her servants; she often gave them clothes and shoes when they were scarcely worn, but this dress was only a few months old and she had only put it on three times.

"Is there anything else you need, madame?" the younger girl asked her. Anne noticed that she looked a little crestfallen and said kindly, "Nothing, thank you Marie-Thérèse. And you may have the shoes. I'll snuff the candles myself."

When she climbed into the canopied bed, she lay back exhausted, fighting the desire to lie and recapture the feel of his mouth enclosing hers and the pressure of his hands. For

49

a moment he had touched her throat and breast, and suddenly she turned round and hid her face in the silk pillow, overcome with shame and passion and bewilderment at what had happened to her. But it was not so sudden or so miraculous. The seed of it was there in the picture gallery, it was there during dinner when he didn't speak to her and she could not forbear to look towards him. It had made her change her dress for the newest she possessed and deck herself out in her mother's sapphires. It had been there from the moment she had first met him, and there was nothing she could do about it. Even if he had never touched her, and that kiss was just a jeer and an insult in another form, she knew that she would still have married him. Later there was a knock on her door; she had been lying very still, not sleeping, hardly thinking, and she had cried a great deal as people do when they are faced with the inevitable and are afraid of it.

"Who is it?"

"Katherine, my dear. May I come in?"

Anne sat up and lit the candles by the bed. The door opened and Charles's mother came into the room, holding a candlestick. She was dressed in a long velvet night robe and her hair hung down her back. She looked very young and beautiful in the soft light.

50

"I hoped you might be awake," she said. "I did want to talk to you so badly, my dear Anne. I'm sorry to disturb you."

"Please sit down, Cousin Katherine," she said. "You're not disturbing me at all. What can I do for you?"

"I want to talk to you," Katherine said. "I want to talk to you about my son. If James knew this he would be very angry with me but I felt I had to come to you, even behind his back." She put her hand out and touched Anne's gently. "I want you to think well before you agree to this marriage," she said. "First I must tell you that his father and I are forcing him into it."

"I know," Anne said. "He told me."

"You're my cousin," Katherine went on; "I knew you as a little child; I've always had great affection for you and my dear Jean is devoted to you. I can't let you be tied to my son without knowing what you're doing. Be careful; he's the most heartless scoundrel I've ever met, save one. Hugh Macdonald was my brother-in-law. He was a murderer, and a libertine. My son is exactly like him and I tremble to think what kind of husband he will make you. That's what I came to say. Think well, and if you decide you cannot do it, I'll support you."

"And let your son be sent to the Bastille?"

51

Anne asked her quietly. Her cousin's fine blue eyes were hard and angry; it was as if there was some old deep hate in her heart that was reflected by her hatred for her son.

"People said evil things against his father when I met him," she said. "But I knew James was good; James loved me, and loving changed us both. There is no love in my son; he cannot feel it. It has broken my heart to see him growing up to grieve and disappoint his father. It will break my heart if he makes you suffer and I stand by and let him. I don't care one jot if he goes to the Bastille. It would be the best place for him."

"That is the most terrible thing I have ever heard," Anne said. "I feel very sorry for him. I'm grateful to you for trying to warn me. But I'm afraid it won't make any difference now. I've fallen in love with him."

For a moment neither spoke; then Katherine got up off the bed and picked up her candlestick.

"In that case, I'll go," she said. "But if ever you need help, remember you can come to me. Good night, my dear. Sleep well."

# Chapter 2

September was a particularly beautiful month; there were days so mild that it seemed as if a late summer had come to Charantaise, and Anne entertained her guests with picnics in the château parklands. There were evening receptions twice a week, and Madame Louet, the famous harpist, came down from Paris to give a special recital. All Anne's neighbours were invited to that party; it was also the public celebration of her engagement to her cousin Charles and the great house was filled with distant relatives and friends; to Anne's joy, her childhood confidante, Charles's sister Jean came to stay for the occasion with her husband and their three small children. It was such a pleasure to see Jean again; when Anne embraced her she almost wept. They had arrived late; she explained — in between kissing Anne and calling the nurse to bring her children and looking over her shoulder for her husband — that their coach had broken down on the road, and really Paul was so angry with the postillions for taking so long to put it right, he must be abusing them still — there wasn't a sign of him. Then he came in and was dragged forward by his laughing wife to kiss Anne's cheek and agree that she never changed except to look more beautiful.

Anne had been about to change for the reception before the concert when the De Mallots had arrived and Jean rushed into her bedroom. She was profoundly glad that Charles was not there to make fun of their meeting and chill the little glow of human warmth that her old friend's affection had lit in her heart. A splendid new dress was laid out for her; in her closet there were dozens more, part of the magnificent trousseau she had ordered, and at least he could not sneer at them for being out of fashion. She had sent for a modiste from Paris, and secured the woman who made dresses for the Duchesse de Gramont and Madame de Conde, two of the noblest and smartest women at Versailles. She looked up into Jean's round, pretty little face and smiled. Jean had not changed, and it was four years since they had last met. She was a small, gay, lively girl with bright-red hair, freckles that she lamented as the curse of her life, and dark eyes like her father's; her husband was a studious Frenchman who had married her when he was forty and she nineteen; he was rich and a man of unusual intelligence with a serious interest in chemistry and science which his wife airily dismissed as a means of making smells. He adored her and indulged her as if she were one of his children, and she had been pregnant and in rosy health every year since their marriage.

"Darling Anne," Jean said. "It is so lovely to be back at Charantaise again and to see you. . . . Do you think I'm looking well? I have a new dressmaker and she's really very clever at disguising the fat places." She turned round, pulling off her cloak as she did so. The lively and noisy children, dragging at their nurse's hand and trying to catch their mother's eye, had taken away Madame la Comtesse de Mallot's little waist and rounded out her dainty figure. Anne said, quite sincerely, "I have never seen you look prettier in your life. And I don't see anything to disguise, my silly Jean. Oh, it's so lovely to see you all again! I'm really overcome, I'm so happy at this moment!"

Jean kissed her hand to her husband, and with a nod, he made his excuses and left for his own rooms.

"Take the children out, they must be famished and exhausted, poor little lambs; come, kiss me my sweetest ones, and go with your nurse now. Gerard, don't you dare to disturb

Madame la Marquise by crying like that! You are a man now — all of five years old! Be off and I'll come later and kiss all of you good night . . . I must look at this wonderful dress, my dear Anne. Where ever did you get it; surely there's no one at Charantaise who can style like that? And the embroidery. . . ."

She picked it up and held it out, examining it. It was pale-pink satin, the material woven and dyed at the great silk centre at Lyons, and the pearly pink colour was the very latest fashion; at Versailles it was known as Du Barry pink. The favourite, in defiance of tradition, matched the exquisite shade with her red hair and porcelain skin, and looked so ravishing that everyone rushed to copy her. The neck was low and cut straight, with a deep frill of delicate Mechlin lace, and the bodice and petticoat were a mass of pink-pearl, *diamanté,* and crystal embroidery. Jean had never seen anything like it since she left Versailles after her marriage.

"I had it made specially. Charles thought my clothes were old fashioned and I followed his advice. I have a dozen better than that one."

"How is Charles?" Jean asked; she was still looking at the dress and now she was pretending to examine it. They had never got on, the brother and sister. When she asked about him, her tone was almost curt.

"He's very well," Anne answered. "I think I've kept him amused since he's been here."

Jean dropped the dress down on the bed.

"Whatever made you do this, Anne? When my mother wrote to me, I couldn't believe it! I know he's my brother, but I'm certain he's not the sort of husband you should have. Forgive me speaking my mind, but you know me, I always do."

"Everyone says that," Anne answered. "Everyone belonging to him comes and says to me that he's the wrong person for me, that he'll make me miserably unhappy. Tell me something — don't any of you love him?"

"He's not very loveable," her friend answered. She stared hard at Anne and her mouth opened in horror.

"Anne, don't tell me you've fallen in *love* with him! Oh no, I couldn't bear it. . . . What in God's name has happened to you? You used to loathe him!"

"I was a child," she said quietly. "And children grow up. I fell in love with him; I can't tell you why it should have happened, but it did. The marriage was arranged, you know all about that. I hadn't seen him for twelve years and when we met again . . . Jean, I shall have to get ready; you can take as long as you like but he will expect me to be down to receive our guests."

"Oh, he'll expect a great deal, if I know Charles," Jean said sarcastically. "Tell me one thing. Does he love you?"

"No." Anne drew near her mirror and picked up a big swansdown puff and began powdering her throat and shoulders. "But I think he will in the end. I'm gambling everything on that. And now you must forgive me, Jean. Marie-Jeanne, come and begin dressing my hair please." She blew her friend a kiss. "I'll see you later at the reception." As Jean went to the door, the little maid held it open for her; she turned round and shook her head.

"Anne, I think you're mad. If he does anything to hurt you after what you've told me, he'll have me to reckon with. I'm going to have a few words with my dear brother. Until later!"

Charles had been given his own suite of rooms at Charantaise and he was waited on by the De Bernard servants, all of whom hated him because he cuffed them and swore at them; they took the intolerable arrogance of their own aristocracy for granted; the valet expected to be kicked on occasions by his master, but all the servants at the Château resented this foreigner who ordered them about like dogs. But he was obeyed and he was feared;

he was the future master of the château and everyone in it. When he married the marquise he would inherit her power over them all. He could have the servants thrown out to starve, dispossess the tenants of their lands, hang them for theft or refusal to obey an order. A lackey tried to stop Jean at the outer door.

"Monsieur is not to be disturbed, madame. Those are his instructions."

Jean gave him a look which quelled her own servants and had silenced her own husband on occasions.

"Get out of the way. I am monsieur's sister."

Charles was lying on a couch reading when she walked into his bedroom.

"I told that oaf outside I was not to be disturbed," he said. "This household needs a lesson in obedience; I'll take a cane to him for letting you in here."

"Oh, no you won't," Jean said. "You'll control your temper and pretend that you're glad to see me after all this time. You might at least get up!"

"I have no intention of getting up," Charles remarked. "I've spent the morning hunting with my charming fiancée and I'm tired. Why don't you go away?"

Jean walked over to him and sat down.

"I want to talk to you, Brother, and you're going to listen to me. Put that book down or I swear I'll knock it out of your hand!"

"Poor De Mallot," he mocked. "Fancy being married to a bad-tempered bitch like you, Jean. Thank God, my wife will know how to behave with me after we're married."

"You're not married yet," his sister snapped. "That's what I want to talk to you about. Why are you going through with this? Have you any feeling for Anne at all?"

"What feelings am I supposed to have? It's a marriage of convenience, surely you know that . . . don't you approve of me as a husband for her?"

"I know about your debts and the scandal you've caused," she answered. "As for approving of you, I think you're beneath contempt. Why did you agree to marry Anne — wasn't there another rich woman you could victimise?"

"She was our parents' choice," Charles retorted. "You should blame them, not me."

"I have no influence with Father; all he's thinking about are the estates in Scotland. If they weren't being restored to us, he'd have let you go to the Bastille and rot there! All I'm concerned about is Anne. I've just left her."

"Ah!" He swung his legs to the ground and sat up. "And what has she said to bring you here like an avenging angel — has she com-

60

plained of me? How miserably disloyal — I see it's not only the servants I shall have to discipline."

"She's in love with you," Jean said slowly. "That's what has horrified me more than anything. Did you know that, did you know she loves you?"

"It depends what you mean by love." He grinned at her. "I imagine I compare rather better as a lover than these country idiots she's been accustomed to. Does that answer your question, my dear sister, or must I elaborate?"

"I don't want to discuss her feelings," Jean interrupted. "I want to find out about yours. You don't care for her at all, do you?"

"What a boring little provincial you've become," he mocked. "Care for her . . . I don't care whether she lives or dies, if that's what you want to know. I'm marrying her because I have no choice. After that she can go to the devil!"

"I see." Jean stood up. "That's what I suspected. What are you going to do after you're married?"

"Go back to Versailles as quickly as possible. She can stay here; I told her that. Oh, I haven't deceived her! I shan't interfere with her; she can amuse herself as she pleases. It'll be an admirable arrangement. She won't suffer anything from me if she's sensible."

For a moment Jean hesitated. As children they had quarrelled bitterly; he had bullied her and jeered at her and many times she had flown at him with her fists and teeth. She was not afraid of him and he knew it. She could afford to lower her pride for the sake of her childhood friend.

"I've never asked anything of you in my life," she said at last. "Perhaps I should have done. If we hadn't been so strong willed, we might have understood each other better. Charles, will you promise me something?"

"Certainly. I never keep my promises."

"Will you be kind to Anne? She's good and gentle and she really loves you. I beg of you not to hurt her. It isn't much to ask."

"You really are fond of her, aren't you?" he said. "It must cost you a great deal to say 'I beg' to me. I shall promise you nothing, my dear Jean. I told you, she can go to the devil for all I care. But if you want to protect her, then give her good advice. Tell her to keep out of my way. Then I assure you she'll be safe enough."

"Very well." Jean's eyes were very narrow. "I've spoken for Anne, now I'll speak for myself. If you harm her, I swear before God I'll find a way to have you killed. And you know I mean that."

"We're not in the Highlands now," he reminded her. "You might find it more difficult to murder me here than you would in Scotland. *You* should inherit the estates, my dear Jean. You're a Fraser to your fingers' ends. What a pity you have Mother's red hair without her looks! Go away now, before I lose my temper and throw you out into the passage. And don't forget to kiss me when we meet in public."

Half an hour later, Charles went down to meet his fiancée and their guests. The lackey who had admitted his sister was still on duty outside the door. He paused for a moment, adjusting the lace handkerchief that hung from his sleeve, and with the same movement brought his right hand up and struck the servant across the face.

"Next time," he said, without even looking at him, "do what you're told."

The dinner was over, and even by court standards, Charles had to admit that it was magnificent. There were a hundred guests seated in the enormous dining room at two long parallel tables, and fifteen courses were served to them. Quail covered with light pastry, salmon and river trout, pigeons cooked in herbs and wine, venison and hare and duckling, fruits swimming in brandy, suckling pig stuffed with chestnuts and apples, sweetmeats and desserts that would have done credit to the King's table at Versailles. The banquet lasted for four hours, and at the end of it, Anne and Charles led their guests into the Marble Salon for Madame Louet's recital.

"I am constantly surprised at how rich you are," he whispered to her. "Such a pity to waste all that magnificence on these provincial bumpkins. How long is this woman going to play?"

"Until I give the signal. Does music bore you?"

They were sitting together at the head of the salon in two gilt chairs. He had to admit that she was not only beautiful — the dazzling pink dress would have excited the acquisitive Du Barry's admiration — but she also knew how to entertain. When he spoke to her she blushed; he glanced across at his sister and smiled. "When I'm bored, my dear Anne, I leave. Give this an hour and no more."

"As you wish." She sat very still, listening to the recital; one or two of the male guests were asleep. Whenever she looked across at Jean she saw her watching Charles, her face pale and expressionless. It was surprising that such a soft, gay woman could look so implacable; she reminded her suddenly of Lady Katherine on the night she had come to her bedroom to dissuade her from marrying her son. Charles leant towards her.

"The hour is up," he said. "Stop her before some of your audience break into snores." Anne gave the signal and led the applause. The harpist came up to them and curtsied.

"A wonderful performance, madame," Anne thanked her. "We have been enchanted. There will be dancing in the Long Salon. Be kind enough to join us."

"You keep late hours for the country," Charles said. "Hunting half the day, eating and drinking for hours on end. No wonder all your neighbours look so gross. Will we have to go through this again on the wedding night? I'm afraid I may have to retire early if we do. . . ."

"When a De Bernard marries, certain things are expected," Anne said quietly. "I'm sure in your own country you had obligations to your neighbours. Ah, M. le Vicomte de Bré — may I present my future husband, M. Macdonald!"

Charles noticed the young man's fair face flush a deep red as he kissed Anne's hand. They bowed to each other and he saw the hostility in the younger man's eyes.

"My felicitations, monsieur," the vicomte said stiffly. "You are the most fortunate man in the world."

"So I hear on all sides," Charles answered. "I only fear that my good fortune is ill fortune for others. Anne, my dear, I'm sure M. de Bré wishes to claim you for a dance. I relinquish her to you, monsieur."

He watched them move away, and the old Comte de Bernard came up to him.

"This is a sad night for that young man," he remarked. "He's been Anne's suitor for years."

"So I guessed," Charles said. "I wonder she refused him."

"She took my advice." The old man smiled. "I told her to wait for a better. There was not much hesitation about you after you arrived. You've made her very happy, my dear boy."

"I'm glad to hear it." Charles bowed. "I'm sure she deserves all the happiness I can give her."

Anne danced the figures of the minuet, smiling mechanically into the face of her partner, watching for Charles whenever they turned.

"I wish you happiness," De Bré said to her quietly. "You know I would give anything in the world to be in his place, but I wish you all possible joy."

"I know you do," she said gently. "And you will have that joy yourself one day. I pray that you'll find it quickly. Excuse me, my dear Michel, but I think my fiancé is looking for me. . . ."

She left him as soon as the dance ended. Charles was drinking wine in a corner, making conversation with an elderly lady who claimed to have known his parents when both were visiting France before their marriage.

"How little your mother has changed," she was saying. "Still as beautiful as ever. I'm surprised you don't resemble either of them more."

Charles gave her a disarming smile.

"I'm told I take after my uncle Hugh," he said. "He was a famous rapist. I beg your indulgence, madame; I see my delightful fiancée approaching."

He bowed low over the astonished old lady's hand and kissed it. He came up to Anne and he was frowning; he caught her arm and forced her towards the door.

"I'm intolerably bored," he said. "I've decided to go back to Versailles until the wedding."

A lackey sprang to the door and opened it wide for them, bowing low as they passed through. In the empty corridor Anne turned and faced him.

"Are you sure you intend to come back for the wedding?" She spoke very quietly. "Please, Charles, tell me the truth. If you're going to defy your parents, at least give me warning. I promise I shan't speak a word to them."

"No." He shook his head. "I shall be back to marry you, depend upon it. By God, so many people are against it, it's almost a challenge to me now. I'm going to bed. I'll start at dawn tomorrow. You can make what excuse you wish to my family." She began to walk up the staircase with him; at the entrance to his suite of rooms she touched his arm.

"I must speak to you, just for a moment."

"Everyone wants to speak to me just for a moment," he sneered. "My dear sister came bursting in upon me, just to speak for a moment. Now it's you . . . what do you want? Do me the favour of being brief. I'm bone weary."

"I don't know what Jean said to you but I can guess. What I have to say is brief indeed. We began this engagement in the worst possible circumstances; let us review it before it is too late. Charles, I don't want you to marry me against your will."

"And what exactly did you think I was doing, except that?" he demanded. "Didn't I make it clear to you that I was being blackmailed into this marriage?"

"You did indeed," she said. "But even so, I hoped — I thought that you might change. Now I can see you haven't. You're unhappy here; nothing I've done has pleased you. I don't please you, I doubt I ever shall. Charles, I cannot force you into this. Let me give you the money to pay that creature De Charlot, and I willingly free you from any obligation to marry me, or pay me back."

She was very pale; it had taken all her courage to offer him his escape when all she wanted in the world was to keep him by her at any price. To her surprise he laughed.

"Very noble of you, my dear Anne. Is it possible that you have changed your mind and seek to buy me off? By God, there's no end to the subtlety of women, even the stupidest! Do you think my father would be balked of his desire to bolster his Highlands with your money? Do you think my lady mother would allow you to frustrate her plans to fetter me? De Charlot would have his money and I should be a penniless outcast, disinherited from my Scottish rights!" He stepped close to her and caught her arms; the grip was so tight that she winced.

"You agreed to have me and now I've grown used to the idea. I'm going to marry you, my little cousin, whether you want it or not."

"Don't judge me by the strumpets at Versailles," she said. "I made the offer out of decency — and pride, if you like. Women have pride too. I admit I haven't shown much in the last few weeks, but that was only weakness. If you wish to humiliate me further I'll oblige. I still want you, detestable as you are! But if you want your freedom, you can have it!"

"Generous, honourable Anne," he mocked. "To hell with your generosity!" He was still holding her and there was something in his face that made her shrink away and struggle to release herself. He laughed and forced her arms behind her back.

"Go down and console that poor oaf De Bré," he sneered. "And don't forget, I shall be back the night before the wedding." He thrust her away from him and disappeared into his rooms, slamming the door on her.

The wealth that Charles left behind him at Charantaise did not extend to the villages and towns on the estates as he travelled back towards Versailles. Anne's people at the great château were well fed and properly cared for; her stewards and bailiffs treated the servants and the estate workers with the consideration due to pedigree animals. Unlike the majority of the peasants, undernourished, sullen, frightened, and dirty, the staff were intelligent and trained. Charles had heard a great deal about the poverty of Scotland and the wretched conditions to which the Highland people were reduced by the oppression of the English.

As he rode through the French countryside, he doubted if anything he encountered on his return to Dundrenan could be much worse than the windowless hovels and half-naked creatures who ran after his coach, yelling for alms. It was a country endowed with enormous natural wealth; its soil was productive, its climate superb, but the fields were tilled as they had been three hundred years before; men drew the plough and women sowed and reaped by hand with the crudest tools. There was no proper drainage system; outbreaks of plague ravaged the countryside. What little profit the farmer managed to produce was swallowed up by the extortionate taxes from which his aristocratic master was exempted, and by the corruption of the fiscal officers.

Speeding back to the most luxurious and extravagant court in Europe, Charles was less interested in the conditions that were eating away the internal prosperity of France, than in the problems facing him in his native Scotland. He had begun to think a little more of Dundrenan and Clandara since his stay at Charantaise. God knew there was nothing else to interest him. . . . The year after the wedding it was planned to return with his bride and take possession of the estates. Sir James had warned him that he would find the people sunk in the deepest poverty, the two great houses lay in blackened ruins, and many of the old clan ways were abandoned altogether. At the time he had shrugged and betrayed no interest, but later he began to think about it. The size and complexity of Anne's huge estates were closely paralleled by his own but only in acreage. French money would have to water the poor Highland soil and build up the mansions destroyed by war and clan feud. He had never seen Scotland, and one of his favourite means of exasperating both parents was to dismiss it as a land of penniless barbarians. Now he was becoming curious; when he returned he would own something, and something more than land, as his angry father had so often tried to tell him. He would own his Macdonald people, not as the irresponsible and wastrel French seigneur bodily owned his peasants, but with a spiritual ownership. He would cease to be the son of an emigrant Scots revolutionary, tolerated by the French nobles because of his father's favour with the King. He would be the Macdonald of Dundrenan, lord over the unwilling Frasers, for he was the last who carried their blood.

Sitting back in the coach, he thought of the woman whose wealth would bring all this about; her money would re-stock the vanished herds of sheep and cattle for his people, raise a great house on the site of his clan's ancient home and fill it with fine furniture, silver, and plate. She was responsible for his inheritance becoming a reality. For that alone, his pride would never permit him to forgive her. He thought of his sister's threat and laughed. They were a fierce breed, the Scots; however much you tamed them with European manners they still turned on you like wolves if you pricked them. The women were no better than their men; the sister, who hated him and snarled like a lioness in defence of her friend, would have died sooner than submit to a man who had abused her as he had done to Anne. "Good and gentle," Jean had called her, as if those cloister virtues were a recommendation in a wife. If Anne had thrown him out of her house, he might have tempered his dislike of her with a modicum of respect. But she loved him, just as Louise loved him, because of the power he exercised over their bodies. He had despised women from the moment he discovered how much of their lives was governed by sexual greed. He leant back against the cushions and settled down to sleep for the rest of the day's journey.

Louise de Vitale was a very good horsewoman, even though she lacked the brilliance of Anne whose horses were half broken by the standards of Versailles. She and Charles had joined the royal hunt, and at the end of a long morning's chase, they were making their way slowly back in the wake of the King and his attendants. There were dozens of coaches following the hunt, filled with ladies from the court who were not able to ride, and with onlookers from all over the country who had driven for miles in order to follow the King. In a conspicuous vehicle with gold carving and painted door panels, drawn by four magnificent grey horses, the Comtesse du Barry was a spectator of the King's triumphant pursuit and kill of the deer. The comtesse did not know how to ride well enough to expose herself to the ridicule of her many enemies, all of whom would have been enchanted had she fallen off and, best of all, broken her exquisite neck. She waved to her lover like a pagan goddess from her golden chariot, her masses of curling hair dressed round her shoulders, sparkling with diamonds and silver lace. Louise drew her horse level with Charles, and touched him with her little ivory switch.

"Let's walk awhile now; I'm beginning to feel tired!" He looked round at her and laughed. She was extraordinarily handsome in her riding habit of blue velvet, and her face shaded by sweeping plumes from the brim of her velvet hat. He had spent a long and arduous night with her; they had seen the dawn come up, and still there was no end to her craving for him, or to her passionate abandonment to his demands.

"You deserve to, my dear Louise. I've never known anyone so improved by a little absence! I must go away again. . . ."

"Why must you, when you can be so happy here?" she said softly. "Didn't I please you? Didn't I drive all thought of that dull creature out of your mind?"

"She was never in it," Charles said. "I have been intolerably bored. But I am returning for the marriage at the end of the month."

"You are determined, aren't you?" Louise said angrily. "I've told you again and again there's no need for it. I'm not badly off —" She managed to laugh as if it were a joke. "If you're that desperate for money, why don't you marry me?" He did not see her face; it was in shadow, and her tone betrayed nothing of the desperate anxiety in her heart. After last night when they lay in each other's arms, she had experienced a tenderness that was entirely new to her, a warmth towards this selfish, unscrupulous man that was an undiscovered side to love. And that was when the idea came to her; he wanted money. He could have every sou that she possessed, if only he would give up Anne de Bernard.

Charles turned and looked at her, his pale

eyes full of mockery. "Only a fool marries his mistress. And you're not a tenth as rich as my wife-to-be. Her wealth is beyond counting — she lives like a princess of the blood. If she wore some of the jewels she owns she'd rival that glittering whore over there! Do you see how ridiculous a comparison is between you? Oblige me, my dear heart, and don't mention it again!"

"As you wish." Louise answered him lightly; she had turned pale. "But one day I shan't receive you back. One day when you're bored to the point of death with your rich wife and her possessions, and come hungry for a little pleasure to me — then, Charles my love, I shall send you away!"

"I doubt that," he mocked. "Besides, I don't intend to spend a long honeymoon away from Versailles and all its diversions. I can accomplish my duties in regard to her quickly enough and return to you. Why aren't you content with that?"

"I am content so long as I see you," she said slowly. "God knows, I'm in no position to make the terms with you."

"You're an incomparable mistress and a clever woman." He bowed to her from the saddle. "I adore you. Hurry, Louise, we're being summoned."

"One of the King's personal guards," she

pointed out. "I know who it is — it's De Legnier, he's a captain of musketeers and a great favourite."

Louis had halted his horse, and the whole company of huntsmen, gentlemen and ladies in waiting, and the rest of the field were waiting for His Majesty to move on. In her gold coach the Du Barry leaned out of the window; she had stopped in a clearing by the roadside, and some of the royal household were riding among the carriages of the ordinary spectators, ordering them to halt.

The King waited without speaking for the two riders to come up to him. He looked far older than his age; under the plumed hat his face was sallow, the dark, sad eyes half hidden by pouches of skin, the legacy of years of vicious indulgence; he was worn out with debauch and the furious pursuit of pleasure that eluded him more and more, the harder he searched for it and the viler the avenues he explored in the course of that search. Yet he governed his kingdom, held audience, and hunted every morning of his life; his energy was like a fever, driving him to the limit of his weakened strength, urged on by the challenge of his youthful mistress who had not got the wit to see that his health was as necessary to her survival as any of the boisterous amusements she arranged for him. Like many libertines, he was a prude concerning the moral attitudes of other people.

"M. Macdonald, sire, and the Baroness de Vitale."

Charles dismounted, and Louise bowed low from the saddle.

"M. Macdonald." The deep voice was irritable. "Where is the Marquise de Bernard?"

"She is at Charantaise, Your Majesty, preparing for our marriage."

"Then may I ask why you are not there with her? Are you aware, monsieur, that I gave special permission to your father for this alliance? I am not pleased to find you neglecting your duties even before your marriage. Be good enough to leave Versailles and return to the marquise."

Charles bowed low. "As Your Majesty commands."

"And you, madame." The King's heavy eye considered Louise with such displeasure that she turned white. "You will oblige me by joining the Duchesse de Gramont and riding the rest of the way with her."

He touched his horse and moved away.

Those few words had ended Charles's stay at Versailles and made it impossible for him to see or speak to Louise again before he left. The penalty for disobeying Louis, when Louis gave a personal order, was exile to some isolated country village. If the King was really irritated, the culprit might find that his destination was a fortress.

When De Charlot had threatened Charles with a *lettre de cachet,* he was invoking a weapon from which no man or woman in France was safe. In its minor form it was an order of banishment or house arrest until the offender was forgiven, but the signed order, obtained in secret from the King, sentenced its victim to a lifetime of imprisonment in the Bastille. That was the terror and the virtue of the *lettre de cachet.* It was procured in secret; whoever's name was on it was arrested in secret and taken to a prison where he vanished from the world without trace. No one knew what became of him; no one dared to ask. Men had fallen victim to the *lettre de cachet* for crimes as varied as speaking against the King, pressing a nobleman for a debt, attempting to marry a girl above his station, or merely exciting the jealousy of someone with a friend at court. Imprisonment without trial was often no worse than coming before one of His Majesty's judges who by custom bought his appointments and interpreted the law according to the prisoner's ability to bribe him.

Injustice, for so many centuries the lot of the common people of all nations, was meted out with equal vigour to the middle classes in France. Medicine, the law, the army and navy, and all court offices were closed to those not born of the nobility; some of the finest brains wasted their capacities in menial positions or took to the arts as protégés of the very class who had refused to admit them upon equal terms. Writers and philosophers abounded as they had always done in that country of singular genius, and they served to put into words the seething discontent of the masses of the people of France. Privilege: it was spat at the nobility and the clergy like an oath, and in its abuse of power and its blind injustice, it had indeed become obscene. Since the reign of Louis XIV, the final degradation to which the French monarchy lent its authority was the dreaded *lettre de cachet,* empowering arrest and imprisonment without trial or hope of release. Charles rode away from the forest at Versailles, rebellious and angry, and his mistress spent the rest of the day in tears, unable to reach her friend, the Du Barry, and ask her to soften Louis' anger. The favourite was shut up with her lover, dissipating one of his moods of fearful depression.

Charles rode back to Charantaise and there was nothing Louise could do but send a messenger after him. He stopped the coach on the main road some miles out of Versailles and passed a package through the window.

Charles unwrapped it and found there a diamond pin. The note in which she had wrapped it was short and ill written; Louise had never been interested in the finer points of education. As a young girl she had amused herself by seducing her tutor and ignoring his lessons. Charles lit the small wax taper in the side of the coach; he turned the pin over in its light, and the large diamond flashed and sparkled. He knew that jewel; it had belonged to her husband the baron. It was a fine diamond. He fixed it in his cravat and glanced at the note she had written.

"My Beloved. I send you this in tender anticipation of your return. Accept the diamond; you already possess the heart and soul of her who sends it. *Adieu,* my tears will flow until I see you once again. Louise."

He screwed up the letter and threw it out of the window.

On the twenty-fourth of October, Anne de Bernard was married in the chapel at Charantaise. The chapel was two centuries older than the great château; it was small and dark, and full of white and yellow flowers that came from the splendid greenhouses. The marquise's family maintained their own priest and assistant but there was only room for a hundred guests in the little chapel, and

Charles's parents, his sister, and Anne's guardian knelt immediately behind the bride and groom, while the rest of the chapel was filled with close friends and some of the more privileged servants, such as Lady Katherine's Annie Fraser, and the marquise's old wet nurse who could hardly walk.

Outside, the sun was streaming down; it was a perfect day, cloudless and warm; within the cool chapel, Anne felt almost cold in spite of the weight of her wedding dress. It was made of white brocade embroidered with silver, and white ermine lined the long train that fell from her shoulders. The veil in which many generations of De Bernards had been married, covered her face, and a circle of enormous diamond and pearl flowers held it in place. It had taken nearly three hours to dress her after her hair was powdered, from the glittering dress down to her white satin shoes with buckles that blazed with diamonds as she walked. Jean and Lady Katherine had spent most of the morning with her; she wore her husband's wedding present round her neck. The chain and the locket with its single sugar-pink diamond was brought to her by Charles's valet, with a formal note in his writing, but the exquisite jewel belonged to his mother, and Anne knew it.

They were already married, both had taken

their vows: she so quietly that it was done in a whisper; Charles in a clear, almost arrogant voice. He had put his ring upon her finger, sworn to love and cherish her in fidelity until death, and she had promised to obey him and serve him as long as she lived. She had lost her name, her title, her identity; the Marquise de Bernard had entered the chapel, now Mme. Macdonald stood in her place with a husband beside her who had not once looked at her during the ceremony. Charles wore a white tunic; a vivid sash of tartan crossed his breast, caught on the shoulder with a cairngorm brooch, and his breeches were silk tartan. Sir James Macdonald and his wife were both in Highland dress; in his bonnet he wore the eagle's feather of the chief.

The nuptial Mass began and bride and groom knelt in front of the altar; while the service proceeded Anne hid her face and prayed. Her parents had been married in this same church, the pretty, frivolous little mother she hardly remembered and the unbending father who was only a name to his child. They had not been happy; perhaps her father had loved his bride as passionately as she loved her bridegroom, perhaps he too had prayed for happiness as she was doing, and not known that he would never touch his wife's heart.

When Charles came back almost immediately from Versailles, she had not dared to question him, his mood was so savage. He had been curt with her in public, ignoring her plea that he should observe the conventions before others. The night before the wedding he excused himself, and the gossip all over the château was that he had got drunk and struck his valet while the man was trying to put him to bed.

Now it was done; she had accepted the challenge of his hatred, risking all on her determination to change it into love. She glanced at him and saw that he was staring straight ahead, unmistakably bored and in an ill temper, his handsome face as hard as stone. Now the power was his; power to spend her fortune, power to go where he pleased and regulate her movements accordingly. She had no redress against any restrictions he chose to place upon her, no claim upon the law which recognised only the husband's rights and regarded the woman and all her possessions as his chattels once she married him.

At the end of the Mass they knelt again to receive the priest's blessing: "And now, my children, leave this holy place in the unity of God's blessing and the sanctity of your married state; love one another and obey God's laws. I will pray for you both."

The priest had known Anne since childhood; he was a kindly old man, singularly uncorrupted by the reverence paid him. For a moment the shrewd brown eyes smiled at her, and then they glanced keenly into the face of the man she had married, searching for some sign of emotion. She could tell by the way in which he turned from Charles that he had seen nothing.

At the door they hesitated; there was a long line of servants and tenants waiting for them and Anne blinked in the bright sunshine.

"Come, madame. Let us run this gauntlet as quickly as possible." They were the first words he had spoken to her that day. There was a long wedding banquet; Anne ate almost nothing. Her steward fussed behind her chair; he had served Mme. la Marquise since she was old enough to sit at table and he was worried that she might faint after the long ceremony. She looked as white as her dress. Suddenly Charles looked up at him over his shoulder. "Your ministrations to Madame are disturbing me. Go away!"

"Charles," Anne whispered. She saw the steward turn red and still he stood behind her as if her husband had not spoken. "Charles, please. I need some wine. . . ."

"You need a new steward," he remarked. "I shall find one for you in the morning. I told that one to go and he's still there. He must be growing deaf. Have a little command of yourself even if you haven't over your servants. You can cry as hard as you wish when we're alone." He raised his glass to his sister who was sitting further down the table, watching them and unable to hear what had been said. He did not look at his wife again; his head ached and he felt tired and furiously angry, angry with her because she was beautiful enough to rouse in him a kind of irritable desire, angry with his parents who had married him against his will, angry with everyone sitting round them, celebrating and smirking and wishing them well.

"James." Katherine touched her husband's arm. "Have you been watching them?"

"There's little point to it, the thing is done." He smiled at his wife, trying to give her reassurance. "It was a splendid wedding, and if my son can resist a bride like that, then he's no Macdonald!"

"He won't resist her," Katherine said. "Poor child, I only wish he would! James, James, what have we done? Even for Dundrenan and Clandara, isn't the price too high for that unhappy girl to pay?"

"Her heart was set on it," he answered. "You know it was; she loves him. She was determined to have him, in spite of you and

Jean," he added. "Nothing was forced upon her and our son certainly revealed himself in his most unattractive aspects long before today. We're going back to Paris tomorrow and we'll leave them to themselves. Nothing will make Charles behave worse to her than knowing you are watching!"

"I cannot bear him," Katherine said slowly. "Can you imagine what it means to a mother to detest her only son? To look at him on his wedding day and not find a single warm feeling towards him in my heart. . . . Why couldn't he have been like you?" she demanded. "Why must he take after your brother? Whenever he looks at me, it's Hugh I see; whenever he laughs, it's Hugh I hear. . . ."

"Yet he's your son, my love," Sir James reminded her. "There must be some of you in him, he can't be all Macdonald."

"If there is, it's too well hidden for anyone to find it," she said bitterly. "I'm not sure we ought to go to Paris; perhaps we should stay for a time in case Anne needs us."

"We are going tomorrow," Sir James said gently. "It will be best for Anne, I promise you."

"And where is my eager bride? In bed already — not *asleep*, I trust?"

Anne had been waiting alone in her room

for three hours after they had retired from their guests. She had been dressed by her maids in a white nightgown trimmed with four layers of priceless lace, her hair had been brushed out over her shoulders, and she had spent the first hour walking up and down her room, waiting for the sound of steps, waiting for him to come. At last she climbed into the big canopied bed and wept as she had not done since the night after her mother died. Worn out with tears and emotional fatigue, she fell asleep and that was how Charles found her when at last he came into her bedroom. She looked very childish and innocent lying in the middle of the ornate bed, holding one side of the satin pillow in her arms. He stood beside her, and as he watched she moved uneasily, and the movement exposed her pale breasts under the thin gown. He was in his dressing robe and breeches, and he was just drunk enough to be dangerous to anything or anyone that crossed him.

"Wake up," he said loudly. Anne's eyes opened and then she sat up, drawing the sheets over herself. She looked into the pale mocking face and the narrowed green eyes, and she flushed to her hair.

"I have waited hours for you," she said slowly. "Now, I hope you'll be gentleman enough not to disturb me. I am very tired!"

"Oh, really so?" The narrow eyes became slits and there was an angry glitter in them. "I married you this morning, my dear cousin, don't you remember? And I've a *mind* to disturb you, as it happens!"

She made a movement to escape him but he was too quick for her. For a few desperate moments she tried to fight him, and he felt the scorching pain of her nails on his skin. "You little vixen," he said. "You damned shrew —" He tore the magnificent nightgown from neck to waist and ripped it off her. Then the full weight and strength of his body stilled her struggles and she submitted and was mastered, the tears streaming down her face as the moment of possession came, bringing with it unbearable pleasure and pain. She lost consciousness for a few seconds, and then the crushing arms released her. When she opened her eyes his hands were in her hair, not hurting her except when she tried to turn away.

"You're my wife," he said softly. "I'll trouble you very seldom, but when I do, by God I hope you've learned not to say no to me!" Then he withdrew from her and turning on his side he went to sleep.

There were no tears left in her then; she was bruised and hurt, trembling with weakness; exalted and horrified at the same time at the nature of the lesson he had taught her.

Before the dawn came, the touch of his hands awoke her again, and she knew better now than to draw back from him. His second love-making was so different from the first that she could hardly believe the lover who possessed her then was the same man as the jeering violator of some hours before. Not a word did he speak; he took her in silence and he subjected her to the expertise gained in the arms of many women until her senses swam and incoherent cries came from her lips as they were opened by his own. When the culmination came it was a shared ascent, explosive but controlled, completely different from that other brutal act of domination.

Anne put her arms around his neck and fell asleep against his breast, not daring to speak for fear of breaking the spell that seemed to have encompassed them. In his arms she felt very soft and light, very pliable compared to the stiff, resistant body that he had overcome by force the first time. She was different from Louise; Louise entwined herself like a serpent when they were in repose together, unwilling to lose the slightest contact or abjure the last faint sensation of enjoyment. His wife slept in his arms like a child who had been loved and comforted. He felt content himself at that moment; surprised, but contented and very much inclined to hold her close and sleep. All his life he had taken what the moment offered. She was a change after Louise. While the month's honeymoon lasted, she would serve well enough.

"Madame is very happy," the little maid Marie-Thérèse whispered. The senior girl frowned at her. It was not proper to discuss their mistress but she could not resist it that morning. She had helped to put the pale-faced bride to bed; she and the others had listened for hours in the anterooms for the bridegroom who had not come. And when he did, the word had already reached them through his servants that he had been drinking. And yet this morning the marquise was transformed. Her beauty bloomed; she smiled and sang as they dressed her.

"Yes," Marie-Jeanne whispered back, "yes, she is happy; how it is possible with that foreign brute, God knows. At least we can be glad for her. For me, I'd as soon lie with the devil!"

When Anne awoke he was gone; it was already late and the sun was streaming through the curtain cracks. She had slept on for hours; his pillow was cold when she touched it. She slipped out of bed and saw the ruined nightdress lying on the floor; she hid it in a drawer and put on another. It was the only time in her life that she had dressed herself without help. The thought made her smile, but then everything was touched by the overwhelming happiness that filled her heart. She had forgotten nothing; there were marks on her arms and shoulders that would take many days to fade, but of what consequence were they when she had gone to sleep cradled in his arms, nursed as gently as if she were a little child. . . .

"Marie-Jeanne, where is monsieur?"

"I do not know, madame. But Madame his mother and sister have been asking for you. They would not permit us to disturb you, and so they left an hour ago."

"Oh." She was disappointed; she would have liked nothing better than to tell them both how wrong they were when they feared for her happiness. All had come right, and sooner than she had ever dared to hope. She had dressed with great care, having chosen one of the simple morning dresses that had been made by the Versailles dressmaker. It was of pale-blue broadcloth, severely cut with a crisp frill of white linen outlining her throat and circling the narrow sleeves. A short pelisse lined with dark fox made it a dress in which a great lady could walk comfortably through her gardens or take a drive out through her park.

"Marie-Jeanne, go down and see if Monsieur is in the house."

"Yes, Mme. la Marquise."

"One moment," Anne said. "You must remember not to call me that. I am Mme. Macdonald now."

The girl curtsied; "Yes, madame, I will try to remember."

It seemed a very long time to Anne before she returned but it was only a few minutes. One of the hall footmen had answered her question with a grimace. Monsieur had been out riding early. He was in the library if Madame wanted him.

Charles was reading when she came in; he was sitting on top of the tall library steps, turning the pages of a book.

"Charles."

He looked up and then turned another page.

"I am reading," he said curtly. "What do you want?" For a moment she could not answer him; she felt her colour changing and all her happiness disintegrated in the second when she looked up at the cold, disinterested face.

"You have a very good library," he remarked. "Thank God, I shall have some means of passing the time here. . . ."

He put the book back and came down the steps; he was still in riding dress, his boots were covered with dust and the crop was thrown on a chair. "That and your horses," he went on. "I've taken the black gelding for myself. No one is to ride him in future."

"No," she said at last. "No one will, if that is your wish."

"It's my order," he snapped. "Well, I asked you what you wanted?" She came towards him; she felt sick, sick and desperately near to tears, and she knew instinctively that it was not the moment to cry in front of him.

"Has nothing changed between us then? Last night — you meant none of it?"

He sat down and stretched his legs out and laughed at her. It was not a pleasant laugh and there was no humour in it.

"What exactly do you mean by that; to which incident are you referring? The little lesson in obedience I taught you?"

"No," she said desperately, "I accept that, it's past. But the other time. You were so gentle, I thought . . ."

"My dear Anne, I am not responsible for what you think," he sneered. "Are you so ignorant of men that you suppose they always behave in the same fashion? One must have variety, even with one's wife. Come, don't let's embark on a sentimental scene; it would bore me to death. And I'm an unpleasant fellow when I'm bored. I shall see you at dinner. There's a letter for you from my mother and one from Jean. I opened them, naturally, in case there was anything of interest to me. Both made me feel profoundly glad that they had the tact to take their leave so quickly."

"How dare you! You have no right to open my letters!" There was no danger of tears now; she was angrier than she had ever been in her life, her anger was that of a woman whose will had never once been thwarted, hereditary mistress of herself and the great château and its thousands of acres of land. Not even her guardian, the comte, had ever committed such an outrage. She came very close to him.

"You have the manners of a lackey," she said. "If I were not your wife, I'd call my servants and have you whipped out of the house. If ever you do such a thing again, that's exactly what I shall do!"

Before he could answer, she picked up the letters and left the room, slamming the door after her. For a moment Charles stayed on in the chair; he whistled a little tune to himself and smiled. Bad-tempered. Spoilt. But quite helpless in spite of her threats. She could do nothing and he could do what he pleased. If any servant laid hands on him he had the power in law to have the man hanged. He laughed out loud. His insults hadn't roused her, any more than his indifference, or his brutality. But the infringement of her privacy —

at least she had some spirit in her. It would be amusing to see how much she had left at the end of the honeymoon. Still whistling, he climbed the library steps again and resumed his inspection of her books.

# Chapter 3

The atmosphere in the Salon d'Appollon was stifling; the King held his evening reception in the magnificent hall, one of the most splendid in all the superb salons and halls of the *grand appartements* of Versailles, but much of its beauty was hidden by the crowd of more than three hundred courtiers, who pushed and trampled their way into it, fighting for place at the front where they could see the King and be seen by him.

The same scenes were repeated every day, beginning at the Salon de l'Oeil de Boeuf, which was the antechamber to the royal bedchamber; to be received by Louis while still in his shirt was a mark of outstanding favour. Ladies and gentlemen elbowed and trod on one another from the moment the King rose in the morning until the hour when he retired on the Du Barry's arm at night. To be at Versailles without being noticed was nearly as bad as not being there at all. Hundreds flocked to Versailles every day from their homes in

Paris and the surrounding country, enduring the nightmare roads in the early dawn, risking the attacks of thieves who waited in the woodlands, and suffering the rigours of a particularly bitter winter rather than miss the court for a single day. Others, richer and more privileged, lived in Versailles itself, but so many were the applicants for rooms, that even the vast palace could not accommodate them with any degree of privacy or comfort. Comtesses and marquises fought like cats over the smallest chamber with a bed and a chair in it; owners of great châteaux contented themselves with sharing a room with two or three others; their servants disposed themselves as and where they could; nobody cared about them when the plight of their masters and mistresses was so miserably uncomfortable.

The life at court was incredibly arduous; the highest standard of dress was required, and there were few who could lay legitimate claim to a cupboard in which to keep their clothes. Etiquette was pitiless. The King's courtiers witnessed every moment of his day; he sat and gave audience, hunted, went to Mass, and amused himself in public, but spectators stood while he sat, and it was nothing for great ladies to find themselves ten hours or more on their feet. The highest mark of royal favour was to be given a folding stool on which to rest while in attendance on His Majesty, and it was not a privilege that he gave to many.

As compensation there were the entertainments: splendid hunting in the park of fifteen thousand acres which was well stocked with game; boating expeditions down the Grand Canal on which the King delighted to sail to one of the smaller châteaux, such as the Trianon or its tiny counterpart, the Petit Trianon, there to disembark and enjoy a play or a firework display, or go to the *ménagerie* where the wild animals were kept. There were the suppers, where everyone gathered to gossip and circulate and indulge in the general occupation of intrigue. Fortunes were made, offices obtained, friends advanced, and enemies undermined, and life rushed past on a tide of excitement that made the slower pace of living away from Versailles, no matter how luxuriously, seem intolerably dull to those who lived in attendance on the King.

Everyone who wished for a position or a favour made his way to the palace and began by bribing the servants for entry to the antechamber where the King was likely to pass, and then his ministers or intimates if they could afford it, in order to secure an audience. Among the crowd of hundreds waiting in the Salon d'Appollon for Louis to appear that night was a man who had travelled half across Europe for the chance to speak to him.

Francis O'Neil was twenty-eight years old; he had been an exile from his native Ireland all his life, and, since he was sixteen, a soldier in the army of anyone who paid him. Europe was full of his compatriots, English and Irish and Scottish Catholics, outlawed by the government of George III, disinherited and penniless, ready to do anything in order to exist as gentlemen should. War was their only trade; the profession of mercenary was the only one open to them. Francis O'Neil had spent most of his youth fighting in Germany in the Seven Years' War, and then in sporadic service after it, until the German prince who employed him disbanded his forces and made peace with his rivals.

It was always the lot of the money soldier, as the mercenaries were contemptuously called. If the mercenary survived the campaign, he was packed out of the country as quickly as possible, and with as little reward as his employers could give him. He was beloved by no side. Francis had taken his pay and sold off what loot he had managed to collect and equipped himself with enough clothes and two good horses for the journey to France. He had brought a one-eyed Bohemian grenadier with him as a servant. Like himself, Hans

Boehmer was without family or friends and he, too, had been fighting since he was a boy. He followed Francis like a dog, and on that long journey he had stolen food for them with the expertise of an old campaigner who could make off with a couple of chickens as silently as he could slit a sentry's throat.

Francis was tired of wandering, and even more tired of serving the unpredictable Germanic war lords. He had come to Versailles to beg a commission in the King's Army. If it was refused, then he would set off in the direction of whatever war was being waged. He wore a plain coat of dark-blue silk and white breeches, stockings and buckled shoes. His lace cravat was adequate, a single sapphire sparkled in it, the legacy of his dead father, whose family had owned land in Ireland since the Norman Conquest, and been torn from their possessions by the English and driven out to starve or beg.

Sir John O'Neil of Clonmere had joined the Catholic Stuarts in Rome and sailed to Scotland with Bonnie Prince Charlie in 1745 to win back his rights in the only way he knew. Defeat and disaster overtook the Prince and the Highlands; O'Neil survived and sailed back with him into a life of blighted hopes and bitter reproaches for the chances that some insisted had been wilfully lost. Francis was too poor to remain in that small unhappy circle; when his father died, he inherited nothing from him but his hatred of the English and the sapphire pin. He had buckled on his sword and sold himself to the highest bidder in the field. That had been the sum of his life until then.

His hair was unpowdered, it was thick and very blond, tied back by a dark blue ribbon; the face that turned so anxiously towards the door, watching for the King, was handsome and stern-featured, with the Celtic blue eyes and the sensitive mouth of his unhappy race. He looked in that company exactly what he was; a poorly dressed adventurer of noble birth, scarred by many battles and not unfamiliar with an empty stomach. As a natural consequence, no one considered speaking to him for a moment, though one or two of the women paused to look at him again. Personally, Francis saw them all and paid them as little attention as they did him. He was not impressed by the magnificence of dress, the flashing jewels, the affected voices and insufferable arrogance that surrounded him. He was not ashamed of his plain coat; in his own eyes he was the equal of any man there in breeding, and the superior of most of them in courage. He could only hope that His Majesty, King Louis, would evaluate him by the same standards.

The heat was intense; the candles in the enormous ormolu chandeliers above their heads dripped hot wax on to the company, some of the women were leaning exhausted against the painted walls; two women, both duchesses, were perched upon their precious stools near the door fanning themselves.

Francis had eaten nothing since the early morning; he had not known where the midday dinner was dispensed in the palace, and by the time he came to the Salle de Venus, everything was cleared away, and the servants would not give him so much as a cup of wine. He felt empty and tired, and for the third time someone bumped against him as that person in turn was pushed by someone else. He turned with a frown, and was just quick enough to catch a young woman as she stumbled and nearly lost her balance. A very pretty face was turned up to him; she had large blue eyes and an exquisite complexion, more dazzling than her jewels, and for the first time in twenty-four hours, someone smiled at him.

"Thank you, monsieur; my heel was caught and for a moment I felt sure I should sit down on the floor!"

"I'm afraid I pushed against you, madame," he answered. "I do beg your pardon. It's like a battlefield in here."

"You must have only just arrived or you'd be used to it," the lady said. She was not only beautiful but very rich; her rubies were enormous, her crimson dress blazed with gold embroidery. Her hair was powdered and dressed rather high in the new fashion adopted by the Austrian-born dauphine, Marie Antoinette. Francis bowed to her.

"Captain O'Neil, at your service, madame."

"Mme. Macdonald, monsieur." Anne smiled at him; he looked very lonely and thin standing there, a petitioner if ever she had seen one in that pitiless jungle of self-seekers. And not French. Definitely not French.

"I know that name," he said. "I've known a good many Macdonalds in my time; there are no fighters to compare with that clan."

"None except the O'Neils of Ireland," she said gently. "My husband is a Macdonald; I am French-born."

"My compliments to your husband, madame. Is he here?"

"I believe so." For a moment the smile faded. "It's only too easy to lose one another here."

It was a poor excuse, made to this strange young man, and she could see by his eyes that it did not deceive him for a moment. Charles was indeed at Versailles; he had been there for the past three months and she had followed

104

him in despair, unable to obey and stay behind at Charantaise, and now enduring the agony of his indifference and the positive proof that he was being unfaithful to her. She flushed and turned away from the penetrating eyes of the man beside her.

"I expect he will come here to find me," she said. "Everyone will go to the supper room after the King's reception."

"Is your husband in the King's household, madame?" he asked.

"He has an appointment in the Foreign Ministry," Anne answered.

The office was granted Charles soon after their marriage; she had not understood its significance at the time, supposing his parents had secured it for him; only now, when she knew the means by which such posts were filled, did she realise that Charles's mistress had obtained it for him in order to keep him at Versailles. Once only she had seen Louise de Vitale; here in the Salon d'Appollon, standing by the window with her hand on Charles's arm, laughing up into his face. And Anne had known who she was and what they were to each other even before a malicious whisper from her neighbour told her. "The Baroness de Vitale, the friend of the Du Barry. And her lover who had just married a rich, plain little heiress who was buried in the country. . . ."

Anne had not approached them.

Later that night Charles came to visit Anne, for her wealth and position had secured her a tiny suite of two rooms, a privilege that made a hundred enemies in a moment among the less fortunate who had been at Versailles for years. Charles had seen her in the Salon, and his mockery had been unbearable. Thinking of it all again, she felt as if her heart would burst with pain. With an effort she turned to the Irishman.

"Are you waiting to see the King?" she asked. He smiled and shrugged; it made him look nearly as young as his age.

"Madame, I've been travelling for weeks and I've spent my last louis in the hope of seeing him. I want a commission in the army. I shall just have to wait until he speaks to me, that's all."

"But you could wait for weeks, months, perhaps for ever, and he might never notice you! Monsieur O'Neil, you can't just *wait* at Versailles!"

"I know that." Again the engaging smile flashed at her. "I've laid out a little money to help catch His Majesty's attention. There's a gentleman here who's a member of the King's bedchamber. He's promised to call the King's attention to me."

"Oh, I see." Anne had been at court long

enough to know exactly how much that promise was worth. Whoever had taken the captain's bribe was most likely an upper servant who would pocket the bribe and forget who had given it within five minutes. Duping strangers to the court in this way was common practice among the household; many a hard-pressed nobleman had played the same trick upon a newcomer.

"You're a professional soldier then," she said.

"Thank you for that, madame," O'Neil said gently. "I'm a common mercenary with a mind to settle in French service. I've neither land nor money in my own country — indeed, they'd hang me if I ever showed my face there. I'm for sale, my dear lady, and my only trouble is to find a buyer!"

"Let me help you," Anne said suddenly. To her surprise the handsome face flushed. "No thank you, madame. I appreciate it, but I've never cared for favours from women. It should be the other way round."

"Don't be angry," she said. "I didn't mean any hurt to your pride. But I know this place; I must tell you, you'll never have a word with the King and you've just dropped your money into a rascal's pocket. I'd like to help you if I can, and I can't promise anything. But if the King should speak to me at any time and you're near, I'll present you to him. That's all."

Francis looked down at her. He had met a great many women in his travels, women of all classes and conditions, and until that moment, his only experience of the wellborn was one of selfishness, arrogance, and lack of morals. He had never received a kindness at the hands of any of them. Now, something insisted that this woman was not to be compared with the others. She was not inviting an amorous adventure or seeking to put him under an obligation for a sinister purpose. One Bohemian countess had used her influence to secure him a lieutenancy once, and then asked him to murder one of her husband's political enemies. Francis had little faith in the charity of the great of either sex.

"Please forgive me," he said. "I should be everlastingly in your debt if you could speak a word for me. Indeed, my dear madame, I can't afford to wait for more than a week or two."

"Let us hope the opportunity comes then," Anne answered. "But don't hope that it will be tonight. When the King is late he usually hurries through the salon."

A few minutes after she had spoken, the doors opened and the King was announced, preceded by his gentlemen ushers, the Constable of France and a train of gentlemen in waiting and his Minister of the Government, the unpopular, enigmatic Fleury.

Fleury was beloved of his sovereign because he had the same disinclination to do anything positive in the government of France as the King himself. The King disliked disturbance as much as he disliked decisions. Fleury took care not to trouble him with either. Louis passed through the double line into which the crowd had divided itself, pausing to speak to less than half a dozen, and his words to them were brief. He looked tired and irritable and he passed within a foot of Anne and O'Neil without glancing at either of them.

"Bah!" exclaimed a young man on Anne's left. "Three hours waiting here, all this morning in the antechamber, and not even a flicker of his eye towards me! What a misery life is!"

"It is indeed," she agreed. "Is your need so pressing then?"

"Pressing?" The young man stared at her in astonishment. His eyebrows were outlined in black like a woman's and he wore a huge diamond in each ear. "My dear madame, what village have you come from? I am the Comte de Tallieu . . . I have no need of anything except that His Majesty should know that I am here!" He gave her a look of contempt and turned his back on her.

"You may be the Comte de Tallieu, sir," a quiet voice said in his ear, "but you have the manners of a dog, and dogs get kicked when they misbehave. Apologise to this lady before I show you what I mean!"

The Comte swung round with a gasp; it was so feminine that Anne almost laughed. His painted eyes narrowed as he met the furious glare of the O'Neil. "Whoever you are, and obviously —" He stared contemptuously at the captain, from his plain buckled shoes to his unpowdered head. "Obviously you're *no one*, you should be careful who you offend with your taproom manners, monsieur. A De Tallieu does not fight with inferiors or I should teach you a very unpleasant lesson!" Before Francis could reply he had vanished into the crowd.

"The cowardly little coxcomb! He's run off!"

"Yes." Anne smiled. "And just as well. If he's the Comte de Tallieu, then he's a very important person; you mustn't make enemies here. But thank you for defending me. . . ."

"It wasn't much of a defence; I got no apology from him," he answered. "But I daresay I'll see him again. Madame, I see the supper room is opening. May I escort you?"

"With pleasure," Anne answered. He made her a little bow and offered his arm. They went into the supper room together, and he guided Anne quickly to a window seat.

"Wait there, madame, I shan't be long."

The trestle table stretched the length of the wall, covered with an embroidered cloth, and servants in the royal livery served from behind it; Francis had never seen such a quantity of food. Every kind of fowl was displayed, whole sides of meat, enormous pastry dishes filled with fish and savouries, ices and cream sweets in fantastic shapes, and mountains of sweetmeats and *pâtisseries,* for which the royal kitchens were famous. Unlimited wines and sweet cordials were being served in the Salon d'Abondance. He came back to Anne with enough food for four people, and sat beside her on the window seat.

"I congratulate you," she said. "I haven't eaten so quickly here for the past month."

"I have sharp elbows." He laughed. "And I'm hungry."

"Where are you staying?" she asked him.

"God knows," he answered. "Anywhere I can find a bed. I have a servant with me, he's a resourceful fellow; I've no doubt he'll have reserved a place for me. You live here, madame?"

"I have two rooms," she admitted. "It's a great honour; very few people are given apartments."

111

"You must be as important as the Comte de Tallieu," he said gently.

"No," Anne shook her head. "Not important, Captain O'Neil. Just rich. Sometimes I wish I weren't."

"Wealth has never been one of my burdens." He smiled down at her. "Why does it weigh so heavily upon you? Or is that an impudent question? Please forgive me if it is."

"It's not impudent at all." He was extraordinarily easy to talk to. It was a very long time since there had been anyone in whom she could confide. Four whole months, since the day she married Charles.

"I was married for my money, you see. I haven't become accustomed to it yet."

"Not only for that, surely. You underestimate yourself."

"On the contrary. I was aware of it from the beginning; I was stupid enough to imagine that my husband's feelings towards me might change."

"I'm not sure I wish to meet him, then," Francis said. "It's bad enough that he should leave you here alone to fend for yourself. I didn't care for that as a start. Why did you marry him?"

"Because I loved him," she answered. "This is a very odd conversation, Captain O'Neil, I don't know what you must think of me for speaking to you of such things . . . I'm afraid it's a long time since anyone has been so nice to me and taken trouble to look after me. It's made me a little foolish, I suppose. Please excuse me."

"I will not excuse you, if you withdraw your confidence," he said quietly. "I'm only a stranger here, madame, a poor beggar from the Palatinate Army, looking for a post. You've done me a great honour in supping with me, and talking to me as you have. Don't spoil it for me now."

His eyes seemed a darker blue, and suddenly she looked away from him and flushed.

"How selfish and petty this must seem to you, when you have real troubles," she said. "My story is only too common, and I brought it on myself. I came to Versailles in defiance of my husband. He didn't wish me to follow him; he can't be blamed for neglecting me as a result."

"Allow me to blame him if I wish," he answered. "Where is your home, madame?"

"Charantaise, near Blois," Anne said. "Do you know it?"

"No." Francis shook his head. "But I've heard of it. It's one of the greatest châteaux in France. Why don't you go back there, and let M. Macdonald go to the devil!"

"Because I am his wife," she said. "And

I am not beaten yet. I hate this place, and everyone in it. Look at them, pushing and shouting like a herd of animals; there's no dignity or grace in Versailles, it's like a zoo. But Charles is here and I won't leave him. Do you despise me, Captain? I haven't much feminine modesty, forcing myself upon a man who doesn't want me."

"I only despise the man fool enough not to appreciate you," he answered. "If I do come face to face with him, I shall probably knock the head off his shoulders."

"No, you won't," Anne said slowly. "My husband is no court fop; if you so much as looked awry at him, he'd kill you."

"At least he's a man, then," the O'Neil said. "That's one comfort. How long do you intend to stay here?"

"Until he agrees to come back to Charantaise with me," she said quietly. "I have a house in Paris. I shall open it up; I can't bear living in these dreadful cramped rooms at Versailles. I shall open my house and entertain. Perhaps if I can offer him some amusement, he'll come there. I hope that you will, too."

"If I have my commission." He smiled. "All the more reason for wanting it now. Will you walk out in the gardens with me for a while? This room is like an oven and the noise is worse than a battle."

114

"I think not," Anne refused. "I'm tired today; there was a play last night which the King attended and it went on till two in the morning. One has to be up for the levée at eight and the public Mass at ten. Would you walk with me to my apartments? It's far, I'm afraid."

"It would give me more pleasure than anything else," he said. "And the farther the better. I've no wish to lose sight of you so soon. Dare I ask you to meet me tomorrow?"

They were walking down the long corridors, out through the Galéries des Glaces, where the wall of mirrors threw their own reflections back at them; down longer passages still, where a few lackeys dozed at their posts, and up the north staircase leading to the upper rooms.

Here Anne paused, while he waited for her answer. It was the classic situation, repeated over and over again with a thousand variations in society, in books, and on the stage; the neglected wife and the enterprising stranger, the first meeting, the second already assuming the guise of an assignation. And the man was a foreigner, an Irish mercenary officer without a position or a sou to his name. She could imagine how her friends would exclaim at her folly, and her husband Charles would jeer, and laugh about it with his mistress.

As if he read her thoughts, Francis said quickly: "Don't misunderstand me. I ask nothing of you, Mme. Macdonald but your company. I am not seeking favours, money, or introductions. I came here without the hope of any of them and I shall probably leave as I came. Will you spend some part of tomorrow with me?"

"Yes," she said. "There's a hunt tomorrow morning at midday. Bring your horse and servant and we'll ride together. Good night, Captain."

She gave him her hand and he bowed very low and kissed it.

"Good night, madame." He turned away and walked very quickly down the corridor. At the foot of the steps of the Cour de Marbre, his servant Boehmer sprang up and called him.

"Captain, here!"

"Did you find me a bed?" Francis asked him.

"A corner in one of the pavilions down there, Captain. I got some straw; there's not an inch in the place for a gentleman to lie."

"Straw will do," Francis said.

It was a fine night and the sky above them glittered with stars, but it was cold and he shivered as he walked across the great open expanse of courtyard towards the balustrade and the steps down to the pavilions in the distance.

"Did you see the King, Captain?" Boehmer ventured.

"I saw him, but he did not see me. No matter; we'll gain something here. I'm sure of that."

With his coat collar turned up, Francis began to whistle, half running against the wind. He felt unaccountably happy, as if the King had given him a regiment and promoted him to colonel with a handsome pension. He fell asleep very quickly, and as he slept, he smiled as if his dreams were sweet.

"That material, my dear Louise! It's exquisite! Where did you find it, I insist on knowing!"

The Comte de Tallieu picked up the skirt of Louise's gown and examined the pale-yellow silk. It was cleverly shot through with palest green; it changed colour as she moved and the effect was very elegant.

"There's a silk merchant in the rue de Lyons in Paris," she explained. "He has some excellent stuffs; you ought to go there, my dear comte."

"I shall, at the first opportunity. I need some new stuffs for waistcoats and bed gowns. Unless the Du Barry discovers it and buys up everything as usual. The cupidity of that creature grows worse every day!"

Louise laughed, and so did the small group of courtiers in the room with her; she was giving a small reception before the supper and a performance in the Trianon theatre in which the dauphine and the Duchesses de Gramont and de la Rochefoucauld were among the principal performers. It was to be a gala occasion; the Dauphine Marie Antoinette was a favourite with the King and she was fast making amateur theatricals fashionable.

The court was perfectly prepared to see the plays of Molière poorly performed by amateurs, provided that they were the future Queen of France and princesses of the blood. It also amused them to witness the boredom of Mme. du Barry who found the programmes far beyond her understanding and spent the time yawning behind her fan and whispering into the King's ear. Louise might be her protégée, but she did not consider it necessary to be loyal when among intimates.

"You should be careful, comte," she admonished the simpering De Tallieu. "You know she is a friend of mine. . . . Besides, I've no intention of revealing the secret of my little merchant to her. There'd be nothing left for me either!"

"She's like a magpie," De Tallieu continued

spitefully. Nothing aroused his perverted malice more than the favourite's exaggerated femininity; her habit of exposing her breasts in fancy costume made him hysterical with disgust. "She has no taste, no discrimination, nothing but her gutter greed. Her apartments here are crammed with ornaments, furniture, valuables of every kind. As for that house at Louvieciennes, it's a treasure store! It makes one weep to see such avarice being indulged."

"The King can refuse her nothing," a certain Mme. Lalage interposed. "They say she's supplying him with different girls for the Parc au Cerf, chosen by herself."

The notorious house within the grounds of the palace had been the inspiration of the late Mme. de Pompadour. Unable to satisfy the inordinate demands of the King herself, the delicate and frigid mistress had encouraged him to instal a brothel within reach of the palace where his appetites might be satisfied by girls who could never rival the supremacy of the Pompadour. She had provided him with a brilliant variety of entertainments in which the Parc au Cerf had its place in company with the finest productions of opera and the drama seen in France at that time. Du Barry had inherited her management of the house in the grounds, and when Louis showed signs of flagging with her, she procured some novelty and made him a present of the woman. His interest never lasted more than a night or two and he returned, content and grateful for the Du Barry's efforts on his behalf.

"Speaking of wealth," Toulouse remarked, "I saw your dear friend Charles's wife driving out this afternoon. What a magnificent equipage! What footmen, what horses!" He watched the smile leave Louise's face and he continued, enjoying her discomfort. "She's quite a handsome creature, too. From your description, my dear, I imagined I should see something big-boned and ugly. You shouldn't be so grudging. She's quite exquisite in her way!" Louise turned towards him, and her dark eyes glittered.

"How you surprise me," she said sweetly. "I never thought a woman's beauty could possibly interest you, dear Comte. . . . This is a miracle! I must see that Mme. Macdonald knows you are an admirer."

"There's no necessity," he said smoothly. "She has one already and she seems very content with him. I almost thrashed the creature a week ago in the Salon d'Appollon. He was insufferably rude to me on her behalf. I remember snubbing her a little for a ridiculously gauche remark she addressed to me; not knowing who I was, of course. As a matter of fact, the admirer was riding beside this splendid coach I was describing. Looking a great deal poorer than her footmen. It might be amusing to know who he is!"

"It might," Louise said casually. "But I doubt if Charles would be interested; he's completely indifferent to her."

"Of course," the comte agreed. "I'm surprised he isn't here by now — does he often keep you waiting, Louise? You should insist on punctuality, it's the least tribute he can pay you. . . ."

Louise turned away from him without answering. She detested the malicious, painted creature when his capricious spite was directed at her, but at other times she found him amusing and a source of useful scandal. He was also a persistent and vindictive enemy. Charles was late; she had been expecting him for the past half hour; they had agreed to go to the play at the Trianon together. She had manoeuvred this arrangement very carefully, for nothing would humiliate Anne Macdonald more than his appearance at such a function, publicly escorting his mistress. If Anne remained at Versailles after that, she would be a laughing stock. It might even be thought wise in high circles that she should be asked to retire and avoid further scandal.

Louise had been planning this and watching

her plan mature with growing confidence. She had hardly expected the unwanted wife to present herself at court; she had even enjoyed her humiliation and made as much a parade of Charles as he would let her. But she was still uneasy at Anne's presence. Incidents like that unpleasant exchange with the comte always irritated her and undermined her feeling of security. And there had been many like it; remarks made in her hearing about the beauty and wealth of the lady and the number of people who were seeking her company. Louise had many enemies, and Charles had more. There were always those eager to inflict a little wound when they could, and her jealousy of her lover's wife made her painfully vulnerable. If one wish could have been granted Louise, she would have asked that Anne Macdonald be removed out of her sight and that she need never hear of her again. Perhaps after this evening that wish would be granted.

"It is late," she said. "I have only two hours in which to dress. I must beg you to excuse me, my dear friends. We will meet again at the play this evening!"

"I look forward to it," the comte bowed over her hand and made a pretence of kissing it. He detested physical contact with women. "I believe the charming dauphine has more enthusiasm than talent. However, we shall see!

*Au revoir,* my dear Louise!"

Marie was waiting to dress her; the yellow dress was hung away and Louise stepped into a petticoat stiffened on each side with whalebone; her waist was pulled in by a corset so tight that she gasped for breath as her maid pulled on the laces. Petticoats trimmed with lace and ribbons went on over the boned hoops, and an underpetticoat of cerise brocade, heavily embroidered with silver. The overdress, which opened at the skirt to reveal the cerise petticoat, was plum-coloured velvet, silver lace cascading from the sleeves and round the low neck. Louise had spent a great deal more than she could afford on this dress; even the dark-red shoes with silver heels and diamond buckles had cost a fortune. But to-night was significant; she must look more beautiful, more richly dressed than she had ever done before, when so many important people's eyes would be upon her, and she would inflict such a brutal defeat upon her lover's wife. Anne's diamonds would profit her nothing; she would be alone at the Trianon, escorted by friends or even by the mysterious admirer that poisonous De Tallieu had mentioned, though if he were really poor, he was unlikely to have been invited. The great heiress of Charantaise might have rooms at Versailles and rival the Du Barry with her jewels and carriages, but she could not command the attentions of her own husband, and the entire court would be able to dismiss her with contempt.

"Marie, go and look down the corridor; see if you can see M. Charles coming!"

"There's no need, M. Charles is here in person!" He was standing in the door, and she ran to him with an exclamation and held out her arms. To her surprise he ignored them and stepped past her into the room. He spoke one word to the maid. "Go!" With a curtsy she fled, closing the door behind her.

"Charles, you missed my reception," Louise said. "I was so disappointed. Come, my love, what do you think of my costume?"

"Magnificent; you have exquisite taste. I regret the reception but I was with my wife."

"Oh?" She turned round quickly, her displeasure showing on her face.

"Don't scowl," Charles remarked. "It doesn't suit you. What is so surprising about what I said?"

"Nothing," Louise retorted. "Nothing except that you have seen her once or twice since she came here and tonight we had a special arrangement because of the play. I gave the reception to please you."

"I forgot," he said. "And I haven't time to argue with you, my dear Louise. I only came to tell you that I cannot escort you to the Trianon tonight; I'm taking my wife!"

Louise went so white that the rouge on her face stood out in livid relief. She stared at Charles for a moment unable to speak, and a mad impulse came over her to slap her open hand across the mocking face.

"You are taking your wife. . . ." She repeated it slowly. "You agreed to escort me, and now you humiliate me in this way, leaving me no time to find another escort or join a party, telling me half an hour before we leave for the Grand Canal that you are taking your wife instead! It's unbelievable, I won't allow you to do this!"

"Don't be ridiculous," he snapped. "Why must you always forget that you're only my mistress? I didn't realise the protocol for tonight when I said I'd take you. The dauphine is performing, it's almost a state occasion. Of course I cannot sit with you and ignore Anne. Control yourself, Louise, before you choke with all that temper. If I choose to insult my wife, that's my affair and I'll do it in my own way. I don't care for these little schemes of yours. If you'd succeeded and I'd gone with you, I should have broken your neck for you afterwards. I should send a note to some of your odious friends to come and join you. Perhaps that nasty little pederast De Tallieu will oblige. Good night!"

As he left her, he heard the crash of something striking the door and smashing in pieces, and he laughed. Clever though she was, she still made mistakes, and the discovery of how he had been tricked into committing himself for that night had made him very angry. She was lucky he had no time to waste with her; his first impulse had been to go to her rooms and box her ears for what she had dared to try and bring about.

His wife had come unwanted to Versailles and the King had intimated that her presence was desired. Charles could not order her to leave or employ force to make her, as he could have done in other circumstances. And however Louise sneered and raged about her, Anne had behaved with perfect dignity. He began to hurry up the side staircase towards her apartments. He had sent her a message, peremptory enough, telling her to be ready to embark in one of the barges on the Grand Canal at six o'clock. When he came into her small room, she was ready; Marie-Jeanne from Charantaise had come to Versailles with her, and as soon as she saw Charles, she backed out of his way and shut herself in the tiny anteroom where she slept on the floor near her mistress. Anne was dressed from head to foot in brilliant turquoise; a cockade of white

126

and turquoise ostrich plumes was fastened in her hair by an ornament blazing with diamonds; her throat was on fire with the same stones, and they were festooned over the bodice of her dress. He stood where he was and considered her. Not a word had been spoken.

"Turn round," he said. She did so, moving slowly because her panniers were very wide and there was little space.

"Very good," he said at last. "A harsh colour, but you carry it well. Your taste improves every time I see you. Come, we shall be late."

"I had made other arrangements," Anne said quietly. "I had no reason to suppose you would take me to the play."

"What a pleasant surprise it must have been for you," he mocked. "I imagine you have cancelled your other arrangements and will not refuse to come with me?"

"I have never refused you anything," she said quietly.

"Perhaps you should," Charles said. "Try one day, and see what happens. Hurry now."

She fastened a long velvet cloak of the same vivid colour over her dress, and together they joined the growing stream of people making their way to the coaches for the drive to the Grand Canal. The crowd was very gay; people called and waved to each other, and the atmosphere on the deck of the richly ornamented barge was as informal as it could ever be at Versailles. They took their places near the prow, Anne with her hand in his arm, holding on to him as the boat began to move away from the bank into the middle of the artificial canal, the oars dipping and rising in the water. It was a cool spring evening, and the barges were lit by torches; a small fleet of them were moving down towards the Trianon, glittering like fireflies in the dusk, led by the splendid state barge, carved and gilded and hung with silken awnings, where the King sat on a dais on the poop deck, with the Du Barry wrapped in ermine and silver lace beside him.

It was an anxious evening for the favourite; even she, the spoilt, indulged darling of the most powerful monarch in the world, was subject to worries and distresses, albeit of the most trivial kind. The Du Barry was constantly hurt by the refusal of the Austrian dauphine to recognise her existence by speaking a single word.

Marie Antoinette was very young; she was also very proud and inclined to display her moral rectitude at the expense of the old King and his disreputable mistress. And the mistress yearned for one friendly word from the young princess, one nod of the head, one passing sentence which would relieve the tension that arose whenever the two women chanced to be in the same room. A little gesture from the dauphine could still the spiteful tongues and malicious laughter of all Du Barry's enemies. On this trifle a whole conspiracy was built; those who sought the mistress' patronage promised to intercede with Marie Antoinette, ambassadors and ministers approached the intractable princess with angry messages from the King himself, and still she made no sign that the Comtesse Du Barry inhabited the same planet. And on the opposite side, those who hated the favourite, encouraged and lectured the princess on her duty to ignore her and give a good example to the court. Sitting beside her lover, the Du Barry fidgeted with her fan and sighed and wondered if that night, perhaps, her enemy might relent and even smile at her after the performance. She had already determined to send her a gift of jewels to see if greed could succeed where diplomacy had failed.

At the Trianon the King and his immediate party entered the theatre and took their seats in the royal box which was hung with tapestries and decorated with hundreds of spring flowers. The audience clapped the King vigorously, and from the orchestra pit the first strains of introductory music sounded and the rustling, whispering crowd became quiet.

Anne and Charles were seated on a narrow

bench in the upper gallery, so crushed by others that there was scarcely room to move. He had seemed in a curiously good mood during the trip, keeping her arm within his, helping her to disembark with great courtesy. He looked extremely handsome and, as usual, very elegant, wearing the Macdonald sash across his breast, and a fine diamond pin in his cravat. She had remarked on the stone once, and he had begun to laugh at her. "One day," he had said, "perhaps I'll give it to you!"

The curtain rose on the first act of a well-known comedy by Molière, and there was more clapping for the appearance of the dauphine in the principal part. Anne leaned forward to see her better; she was a pretty girl with a beautiful complexion and rather protuberant blue eyes of fine colour. Her red hair was hidden by a towering grey wig covered in feathers and jewels, and she spoke her lines clearly and enthusiastically so that all could hear her. She had little acting talent and no comic sense.

"There's a rumour that she may speak to the Du Barry tonight," Anne whispered to him. He glanced away from the stage for a moment; "I'll wager a hundred louis she does nothing of the kind. She's as stiff-necked as a mule, and an Austrian mule is the worst of the breed. She'll never acknowledge the woman; I don't know why the devil the Du Barry can't ignore her and let the damned business drop."

"She feels the slight, I believe," Anne murmured. "I've been told many things about her, and they say she's quite sensitive."

"There's a lot of the country simpleton about you still," he said under his breath. "Come to one of her evening soirées and see her sitting half naked on the King's knees like a drunken whore in a bawdy house; then tell me how sensitive she is! Keep these judgments to yourself, my dear Anne. You're only a child and you don't know the world. Let's listen to the noble princess and her ladies murdering Molière's lines!"

Charles sat through the remaining acts without paying any attention to the action on the stage. He felt relaxed and benevolent; he had not the least regret that Louise was not beside him, whispering and sparkling and demanding his attention. He enjoyed his wife's scent, and in a strange way he had also enjoyed the looks and comments that had followed them from the barge to the Trianon itself. She looked very beautiful; in the dim theatre she glittered when she moved and her magnificent diamonds caught the fitful candlelight from the walls. She was a restful creature to be with at times and he was off his guard that night after his quarrel with Louise. He was not bored, as he had so often taunted Anne in the past; she neither wearied him nor distracted him, and he was perversely amused to imagine that somewhere in the auditorium Louise was sitting through the interminable performance consumed with jealousy and rage; at the same time distracted with fear that she might lose the man who had treated her so badly. Charles knew every twist in her character, every devious impulse, every flash of temper, and every spit of jealousy. She stimulated him; he would go back to her in a day or two when she had time to cool and her anxiety made her pliable. If he left it long enough she would be on her knees to him when he returned. She needed a lesson. Thinking of the humiliation she had planned for his unsuspecting wife, he grew angry again. Anne had not recognised the significance of the Trianon play or what it would cost her in pride to he seen in the same company as her husband and his mistress. The court was full of men and women engaged in public liaison, but they did not indulge them openly in the presence of the King. She would have had to leave Versailles if Louise had succeeded.

And whatever there was between them, Charles did not permit his wife to be exiled by his mistress. It was a matter of pride. She bore his name and he alone had the right to abuse her if he chose. When the play was over, they went back to the barges and the whole glittering procession set out for the main palace and a late supper. The King had remained behind at the Trianon with Marie Antoinette and a circle of friends especially invited. The Du Barry had not been included in the dauphine's invitation to join her supper party, and while the King went back to congratulate her and the company, he declined to dine without his mistress, and the court set out again for Versailles. Everyone was talking about the Du Barry's disappointment and the snubs exchanged between Louis and the dauphine. Only Anne was silent; she had been happy for those few hours, happier than at any time since her marriage. It was the first time Charles had been nice to her without the interjecting of a single wounding sneer or curt rebuff. Now it was ending; as the boat drew into the landing stage, she felt tears in her eyes.

"Will you have supper with me?" he asked her suddenly. They were standing together at the top of the steps leading up from the Cour de Marbre; people were pushing past them, talking and laughing, and the lackeys were leading away the carriages below.

She could see nothing in his face; it was quite cool and expressionless as he looked down at her.

"Yes, I would be glad to." She had completely forgotten that Francis O'Neil was waiting for her in the Salon d'Appollon. He had not been asked to the Trianon, and after that week he had told her he would be forced to leave Versailles as his money was finished and he was no further advanced in his search for a commission than the day he arrived there. Only as they passed into the supper room did Anne remember and she saw him standing in the distance, looking for her. He was her constant companion now; her shield against the attentions of the men who knew she was to all intents alone, her companion, her provider, her hunting partner. They had grown very intimate in those long days and she knew all about him, from the bleak childhood in Rome with the exiled Stuarts, to the dirt and privations suffered by the mercenary soldier. Not a word of impropriety had passed between them; he had never done more than kiss her hand, and yet she sensed that there was something more.

"Oh, Charles, I forgot; there's poor Captain O'Neil. I promised to have supper with him and we thought perhaps the King might speak to me and I could present him . . . can't we

134

ask him to join us? Please?"

Charles looked across at the man standing half turned away from them, searching among the crowd streaming in; one of the Irish mercenaries, no doubt, hanging about in a pathetic search for favour from a singularly ungenerous King. He saw the handsome face at that moment, and the fine breeding in the features, and turning to Anne, he said coldly: "No, my dear. You may pick up with what rag tags you choose when I'm not with you, but I don't care to eat with money soldiers. He must find someone else to sponsor him tonight."

They supped in the long room, where Francis had sat with her the night they first met, and in spite of herself she felt happy; the moment of coolness was gone; she could force herself to forget the unkindness in that refusal; instead, she held on to the precious time they spent together, and her heart ached and yearned for this to be the normal way of life between them. Perhaps she bored him still; it was so difficult to tell, that thin dark face was such an impossible page to read except when it was full of mockery and illumined by his savage temper. The eyes which considered her said nothing either, occasionally they grew light as he smiled, but it was not a change she trusted. And yet he was all she wanted, even the uncertainty and fear of being with him was more than the tenderest attentions from any other man.

When the supper was over, there was dancing in the Salon d'Appollon and the King made an appearance with the Du Barry, whose little doll's face was flushed with wine and her voice a tone above its usual pitch. When she was bored or unhappy she drank, and she had been both that evening. She was ready to burst into tears and shout a stream of fishwife language at the smirking courtiers who had witnessed yet another snub delivered by Marie Antoinette that night. For a moment Anne thought again of Francis O'Neil, but though she looked among the crowd, she could not see him, and again the King passed quickly through the company and spoke to hardly anyone. When he left, Charles turned to Anne.

"It grows late, and I grow weary," he said. "It was an interminable play, intolerably acted. I pray to God we shan't have to sit through another for a very long time."

"I enjoyed it," Anne said unsteadily. "I wasn't bored at all." For a moment the pale eyes gleamed at her, with laughter, with contempt — it was impossible to tell. He lifted her hand and kissed it. "As I said, there's much of the country about you still. Good night, madame."

She made her way out of the stuffy room

and when she came to the corridors beyond the Galérie des Glaces, Anne began to run, and as she ran, the tears were flowing down her face. At the doorway to her rooms, she paused; in all her life she had never so far forgotten herself as to cry before a servant; none but her old nurse had ever seen her weep. With an effort she composed herself and opened the door. The maid, Marie-Jeanne, was dozing on her stool; she sprang up, blushing and stammering at being caught asleep.

"Undress me quickly," Anne said. She felt intolerably tired. Her legs ached from standing and she now felt the full weight of her heavy dress. The dress, the petticoats, the corselet, the panniers, at last they were laid aside and a lawn nightgown, warmed by the fire, was slipped over her head. The jewels and false-hair pieces were taken off and Marie-Jeanne brushed her long hair as she had done since her mistress was a child.

The bed was warmed by a pan filled with hot coals; there was a hot brick wrapped in flannel at the bottom for her feet. Anne lay back and closed her eyes while the maid drew the covers up and tucked them in. Then she curtsied.

"Good night, madame."

"Good night, Marie-Jeanne. Blow out the bedside candle." She fell asleep immediately;

not long afterwards, she woke with a sensation of someone touching her, and found that it was not a dream. She tried to sit up with a cry of fear, and Charles's voice said out of the darkness: "Lie still! Who did you think it was — your Irish money soldier . . . ?"

# Chapter 4

The Hôtel de Bernard had been closed for many years; after the old marquise's death, the great Paris house had been shut up, its furniture shrouded in sheets, its treasures packed away, and Anne had never intended opening it again. Now it was full of servants cleaning and polishing and re-laying the Aubusson carpets and hanging the priceless tapestries. Gold and silver plate, superb porcelain, and some of the loveliest furniture — made by cabinetmakers to the King at the beginning of the reign — were arranged in the reception rooms. Anne had engaged a steward to supervise the large staff of servants and he had secured one of the best chefs in the city. Horses were brought up from Charantaise for her stables, and she had ordered a magnificent new town coach with special springing to withstand the abominable cobbled streets of Paris. Versailles was full of rumour and speculation about the ball that Anne was giving to celebrate the opening of her hôtel; it was predicted that the King himself would honour the occasion and there was much jealousy and angling for invitations.

The appointment of Captain O'Neil as her agent, added a delicious spice of scandal to the whole affair, and some of the more malicious, including the Comte de Tallieu who was revelling in the gossip, insisted that Mme. Macdonald shared her favours between the handsome captain and his hideous, one-eyed servant Boehmer.

Only one person betrayed no interest in the hôtel or the ball, and that was Charles. He neither discussed it nor permitted it to be discussed. He was not interested in whether his wife opened her house or pulled it down. He preserved a stony silence which discouraged comment to his face and caused a furore of talk behind his back. What was even more extraordinary about this most tantalising situation was the rumour, gained from the indiscretion of Mme. Macdonald's simple little maid to another servant, that the husband was in the habit of visiting his wife, entirely capriciously, and staying the night with her.

It was this last rumour, coupled with Anne's preparations to make her stay at Versailles and Paris permanent, that tortured Louise as effectively as if she were being subjected to the rack. She and Charles were reconciled again, but it was an uneasy reconciliation; there were times when it took all her considerable skill to hold his interest and all her charm to keep him in a good humour. On the surface their relationship was unchanged; he spent most of his spare time with her, he made her presents of jewels and dresses bought with his wife's money; they appeared in public together and they made their rendezvous as usual. But all Louise's female instincts sensed a withdrawal in him, and she loved him so intensely that she was not deceived by what he irritably insisted was his contempt for and indifference to his wife. One night, driven by jealousy and suspense, she had unwisely asked him whether he indeed made love to Anne, and the curt answer made her bitterly regret having asked the question.

"I need a change from you and she provides it. You don't own me, and I shall sleep with whom I please!"

And yet she had allowed him to make love to her after he had said it, hating him and needing him and despising her own weakness. Marie, the stolid maid who had been through so many phases of her mistress' life and watched the course run by all her love affairs, considered that the baroness was bewitched. Marie was not only her maid, she was now her closest confidante, the recipient of Louise's fears and disappointments and outbursts of jealousy; the one to whom every word and gesture of Charles, the most intimate secrets of their relationship were poured out by her mistress.

"She's going to stay here," Louise said again. "And he has encouraged her! He could have ordered her to go away, I know he could. Now this hôtel in Paris, a ball to which the King will go. . . . She is established at court! I shall never be rid of her!"

"Perhaps it is the Irishman who keeps her here," Marie suggested. "If they are lovers, all this must be to please him, madame."

"I wish I knew," Louise turned round to her. "If it were really that: if I could prove that she was this mercenary's mistress. But in my heart, Marie, I don't believe she is, I think it's to make Charles jealous!"

"And is he?" Marie asked her.

"No." Louise almost spat the word. "Because he doesn't believe it either! But if it were so — Ah, my God, Marie, he may not want her, but I should hate to be in her place if he found out that she were deceiving him with that beggar! She'd leave Versailles soon enough then!"

"It should be easy enough to find out," Marie said. "All you need is a servant in that household who can watch them. I could ask Pierre if he knows anyone, preferably a woman, who could take employment at the Hôtel de Bernard. You would have to pay her, madame. These people are not cheap if they're going to be reliable."

"Find someone," Louise said quickly. "I'll pay whatever they ask. And tell Pierre there'll be twenty pistoles for him if he can arrange it."

"One of the Duchesse de Gramont's maids would be perfect," Marie said. "She would be sure to get a place in any household coming from there. I will try and send him a message this evening, madame. He may slip away from his duties for a little time."

"Marie." Louise went to her bureau; she spoke with her back to the maid. "I'm very grateful to you. You're a clever girl. Here, take this. . . . I'll double it the day I can show M. Macdonald proof that his wife and that fellow are lovers."

She threw a little purse towards Marie who caught it and made her mistress a deep curtsy.

"You shall have the proof, madame. Even if it doesn't exist." And she laughed.

"My dear Anne, how nice it is to spend a few moments together away from all the crowds of people."

Lady Katherine turned to her daughter-in-law and smiled. Both ladies were walking through the ornamental gardens towards the magnificent Bassin de Neptune fountain in the palace grounds. It was a beautiful spring day, and they wore light cloaks over their dresses and carried muffs made of lace and ribbons. They walked slowly, bowing to people they passed who were also promenading in the sunshine. Two little page boys trotted at a distance of twenty-five paces behind them as it was considered improper for ladies of rank to walk anywhere unattended.

"Privacy is impossible," Anne answered. "How I long to move to Paris to my own house. You can come and see me often there, dear Mme. Mama."

"James will be very grateful," Katherine said. "He grows more and more oppressed by living here. You may find we visit you much too often!"

"That could never be," Anne said. "You're like my own parents. You will dine with me before the ball, won't you?"

"We'll be delighted. Everyone I meet is talking about it, and quite a lot of people are hinting to me about invitations." She laughed. "You know, my dear, for someone who has spent her life at Charantaise, living far away from the court, you have caused more sensation in the last two months than anyone I can recall! You will invite the Du Barry, of course?"

"Of course. I very badly want the King to come. I wanted to ask you, Mme. Mama, will you present me to the Du Barry soon — I've never met her and I know you're on friendly terms."

"I will with pleasure. I only advise you to be extremely pleasant but not to get too intimate. She's a deplorable creature in many ways, though quite kindhearted in others. Certainly her friends are not fit companions for you. Tell me something, why have you decided to launch yourself so spectacularly at court? I imagined you'd tire of it after a few weeks and hurry back to Charantaise . . . I'm delighted, my dear Anne, but still a little surprised."

"You cannot guess why?" Anne asked her. They turned off the main promenade path down towards the enormous shimmering fountain, its jets sending a cloud of water and spray into the air.

"No," Katherine said. "I cannot. Unless you have grown to like court life, and I find that very out of character."

"I detest Versailles," Anne said quietly. "I detest living in two dingy little rooms like cupboards, standing for hours on end, being hungry and thirsty — cold when it's cold, and baked when it's hot; I hate fighting for food and drink and spending my time running from

145

one salon to another in the King's wake and running upstairs to change my costume ten times a day. I hate every moment of it. As for living in Paris and coming here at the same time — it will be a nightmare. But if I am going to please my husband, then I must be where he is and do what he likes doing. If my parties are lavish enough, he'll come to them instead of other peoples'; if I have a splendid house, he will visit me there. That's why I am doing it. I shan't keep him by living at Charantaise, however much I love it."

Katherine stopped abruptly.

"You are doing all this for Charles?"

"Yes, and for myself too. I want him with me."

"And you really think that all this will bring him? Anne, will you forgive me if I ask you how things really are between you? I've been so worried ever since your wedding; James has forbidden me to interfere or I would have sought you out and asked you long before now. But I've got to know the truth. I hardly see my son; I seldom speak to him if I can help it. But I hear all the rumours just the same. He hasn't left his mistress, has he?"

"No," Anne said. "But he hasn't left me either. That's what gives me hope. He still comes to me at times; I never know when or why, but he just comes."

"And otherwise he just ignores you," Katherine said. "He pays you no attentions, never escorts you, spends all his time with that creature, and then *visits* you. . . . Is that what you mean, Anne?"

"He has taken me to the Tuileries, and once we went hunting together. Otherwise he comes at night." She blushed and looked appealingly at her mother-in-law. "Try not to despise me. It's all I have of him."

"And you still *love* this scoundrel?" The older woman stared at her; suddenly she shook her head. "Of course you must, to submit to it. If you take my advice, you'll put a knife under your pillow and the next time my son comes near you, you'll welcome him with that!"

"I'm not like you, Mme. Mama," Anne said quietly. "I couldn't hurt Charles, whatever he did. Don't you see, if he didn't care for me at all, he wouldn't come . . . it's not from duty. It must be because he has some feeling for me."

"Is he tender to you?" Katherine asked her. "Does he tell you he loves you?"

"No," she said. "He hardly says a word to me. Sometimes he's gentle, sometimes — not. It depends upon his mood. I'm used to it now. But if he stops coming to me, I shall know that all is really lost. And whatever it costs me, I'm going to keep what little hold on him I have."

"I see." Katherine began to walk on and Anne followed her. The two little boys marched on behind them keeping the regulation distance. At the edge of the great fountain they stopped; the fine spray whirled above their heads in clouds of wet mist, blown away from them by the breeze. On the other side of the huge marble basin, the paths were quite damp.

"I see," Katherine said again. "Well, my dear, that answers the other question James forbade me to ask you."

"And what was that? Please ask it, I shan't mind. I haven't any secrets from you."

"Whether this Captain O'Neil is your lover. Everyone is sure he is, especially since you've taken him into your household."

"Well, they're wrong!" Anne said shortly. "Really, the minds of the people here are as low as their morals. Francis O'Neil is a dear friend of mine and all I've done is to give him employment as my agent to enable him to stay at Versailles until he can get an audience with the King. I need an agent; this house and the staff and my horses are all too much for me to manage alone. I always had a steward and a comptroller and my uncle at Charantaise. Francis has done everything wonderfully well for me. I'm not giving him charity, I promise you. If you think he'd take it from a mistress or anyone else, you don't know him!"

"No, I don't know him, my dear," Katherine answered gently. "I don't think I've ever seen him. And don't misunderstand me. If he were your lover, I should be delighted for you. It's just that it seems a pity to suffer a bad reputation when he's not."

"There's not one woman at court who *has* any reputation, whether she's virtuous or not. If it weren't Francis they were gossiping about, it would be someone else. The moment he gets a commission from the King, he'll leave. That ought to satisfy them."

"One thing surprises me," her mother-in-law said. "Knowing what my son is like, I wonder he hasn't picked a quarrel with your captain out of pride. Be careful he doesn't, Anne. There's nothing would please Charles more than to fight a duel with someone and kill him when he knew he was innocent. I should be careful for this young man's sake."

"There's no need," she said quickly. "Charles knows I'm faithful to him. And I'm afraid I don't believe he's as evil as you say. Shall we turn back now?"

"If you like; don't be angry with me. I'm only trying to protect you. As for being faithful to my son, if you ever decide to deceive him, you can be sure of my blessing!"

"Mme. Mama!" Anne looked at her for a moment and then began to laugh. "I'm glad I'm your daughter-in-law and not your son. . . ." They walked back to the palace arm in arm.

The Hôtel de Bernard was completed by the end of April, and while keeping her apartments at Versailles, Anne moved into her house in Paris. Francis O'Neil was at the door to meet her when her coach stopped and she came up the steps. The shabby clothes had been replaced by fashionably cut coat and breeches, and the captain wore a powdered wig. He looked very much the descendant of twenty generations of Norman-Irish aristocrats, as he bent over Anne's hand and kissed it.

"Everything is ready; we have been working since dawn to have everything in place for you. I only hope you'll be pleased with it."

"I know I will." She smiled at him, and for a moment he held her hand longer than he needed. Behind him there were ranks of footmen headed by the steward; the marble hall was full of candles, blazing from fine ormolu *torchères* and from the massive bronze and gilded chandeliers hanging from the ceiling. He gave her his arm and together they walked into the house and up the magnificent staircase, it's polished steps inlaid with different-coloured woods in a delicate design, past paintings and sculptures, and slowly through the main reception rooms, all of which were splendidly furnished, their tapestries and hangings glowing against the white and gold walls.

Anne stopped at the dining salon.

"This is different, Francis — it's magnificent!"

She had chosen the furniture and ornaments for all the main rooms herself, leaving the final placings to Francis, but the dining room was not as she had ordered it. The table was golden, from the elegant, carved legs to the mosaic top; it stretched down the room, its soft jewel-coloured surface shimmering in the candlelight. The chairs were gold, too, upholstered in silkwork with a delicate design of exotic birds. There were no tapestries on the walls, but painted murals of an idyllic landscape scene with lovers; trees and waterfalls and vistas of flowers against a background of azure-blue sky and drifting clouds gave the room a magical beauty and perspective.

"Francis, it's unbelievable! That table and the chairs are beautiful enough, but these paintings. . . ."

"Boucher," the captain said, smiling; "He's

done much the same for the Du Barry at Louvieciennes. I thought you'd like his work."

"But the cost," she murmured. "He's the most fashionable artist in France!"

"Not a penny above what you told me to spend," he said triumphantly. "I'm a mean man when it comes to paying out. I had enough left and more, to make this room a complete surprise for you. But I hope you like it, or I'd best go out and shoot myself!"

"I love it," she said warmly. "I shall be the envy of Paris; everyone will fight to come and dine here. Dear Francis, how clever of you to have done all this!"

"I wanted to please you," he said gently. "I wanted to give you a surprise. If I had had the money I'd have paid for it myself. But it was little enough to take a bit of trouble for you — after all you've done for me!"

"I've done nothing for you," she said quickly. "All I've done is secure myself the best friend any woman ever had. Thank you, dear Francis. I've never seen anything so lovely."

Impulsively she reached up and kissed him on the cheek, and at once he flushed deeply. "If you do that, Anne, I may forget my place."

She touched her breast. "Your place is here, with all the people who are dear to me. Come, show me the rest!"

Neither of them noticed the maid who was trimming the lights just outside the open door of the dining room. She had been engaged the week before, after suddenly leaving the employment of the Duchesse de Gramont, with an excuse that she was getting married. Her references had been in order and she was among ten others taken on at the hôtel at the same time. Pierre, the footman at the duchess' house, had already given her five pistoles and the rest would be paid when she had collected the proof required. It was also suggested that what she failed to discover might have to be manufactured. From what she had just seen pass between the mistress of the hôtel and her agent, she wouldn't need to invent anything.

Alone in her bedroom Anne threw aside her cloak and muff and sat down on the little gilt seat by the window. This room too was beautiful in decoration and proportion, dominated by the tall, canopied bed, the yellow satin drapery caught at the top by carved wood cupids holding a wreath of painted flowers. The dressing table, the low seats, the splendid ormolu and satinwood chests were pieces specially made for her mother; it was a coquette's room, its ceiling painted with cupids surrounding a half-nude goddess, discreetly veiled by clouds.

She would have gladly exchanged all of it

to be back at Charantaise among the familiar rooms and the well-loved furnishings, to hear the excited barking of her dogs as they raced across the hall to welcome her. She did not enjoy hunting at Versailles; it was too formal, too bound by etiquette. There was nothing to compare with the wild chase across the fields and through the woods of her own lands, side by side with the huntsmen who had taught her as a child, and be able to spare the stag if she wished. For a moment she felt very tired; her mother-in-law's face haunted her, the expression of pity and surprise mocked all her hopes when she thought of Charles and laid her plans to draw him to her. Katherine did not believe she would succeed. Katherine considered his visits an insult, prompted by cold-blooded lust instead of the signs of sentiment she imagined them. She was his mother; she was probably right.

"Madame?"

Marie-Jeanne was so close to her that Anne jumped.

"I beg your pardon, madame, I didn't mean to frighten you. I knocked, but you didn't hear. A messenger brought this. He is below, waiting for an answer."

Anne saw the Macdonald seal on the note and tore it open.

"My dear daughter, I have arranged for you

to be presented to Mme. du Barry at tomorrow evening's reception in the Salon de Mars. I have also arranged for her to receive Captain O'Neil. Accept this small peace offering for my tactlessness the other day. Your affectionate mother, Katherine Macdonald of Dundrenan."

"Marie-Jeanne!" Anne sprang up; she had forgotten her depression in her relief that at last she could give Francis some hope — no, more than hope. What the Du Barry asked, the King granted.

"Marie-Jeanne, go and find Captain O'Neil — tell him to come here at once!"

"I can't believe it," he said; they were both in Anne's boudoir, chaperoned by two footmen who served them wine and stood with their backs to the wall, still as statues.

"This is the introduction everyone dreams of getting — to the Du Barry herself. Mme. Anne, I will be offered a marshal's baton!"

"And you'll deserve it." She laughed at him. "But it's all my mother-in-law's doing, not mine. Wait until you meet her, Francis; she's a great beauty, even now."

"Why should she help me?" he asked. "Did you mention it?"

"Only in passing," Anne admitted. "I spoke about the King, not the Du Barry; she's almost as difficult to approach. I had some idea that on the night of my ball I might be able to introduce you, but this is much better. We can go to Versailles tomorrow. Dear Francis, aren't you happy?"

He didn't answer her for a moment. He would probably get his commission; it was the first chance of security he had ever known, a chance to settle in the service of one monarch and adopt France as his country. If he had never met Anne he could have asked for nothing more in the world.

"I am very happy," he said gently. "Except that I shall have to leave you."

"I know," Anne said. "I don't know what I should have done without you. I don't know what I shall do without you. But it's what you wanted, isn't it?"

"It is." The blue eyes smiled at her and there was an expression in them that was suddenly very gay. "And if I get it, I'm going to come and ask you something, one more favour before I say good-bye."

"Ask me now," Anne said. "I hate secrets. What is it?"

He shook his head. "Not now," he said. "Now is not the time. But I'm going to ask it, no matter what happens. The time will come."

The Salon de Mars was part of the *grands*

*appartements* at Versailles, and it was here that the King settled down to play cards after dining. His companions were always carefully selected; princes of the blood, a Rohan, a Guise, a Condé, bearers of names as proud and ancient as that of Bourbon itself; squeezed in among them was occasionally someone the King liked, like the reprobate Marquis de Chauvelin who accompanied him to the Parc au Cerf and even managed to make the monarch laugh.

When Anne, accompanied by Katherine and followed by Francis O'Neil, entered the salon she sank in a deep curtsy in the doorway and after proceeding a few steps into the room, turned very slowly towards the table where the King was seated at play, and curtsied once again. The King looked up and acknowledged her with a slight nod. Walking past him sideways so as not to turn her back, Anne followed her mother-in-law into the far end of the salon where a group of people were standing paying a great deal of attention to someone in their midst.

Over her shoulder Anne smiled at Francis. He was in a coat of deep-blue satin with white satin breeches and fine lace, and on Anne's advice he wore his thick yellow hair unpowdered. "She will remember you better if you don't look much like everybody else," she had told him, and he had taken her advice. It was good advice because every woman in the room paused to glance up at him as he passed. The King, who made a point of noticing no one who was not a pretty woman, kept his eyes on his cards.

They stood together while Katherine made her way into the little circle. After a few moments she beckoned to them. The group had dispersed, revealing the charming figure of the Comtesse du Barry seated in an armchair, with her exquisite ankles crossed on a footstool, looking as fresh and lovely as a newly opened rose in her famous pink-coloured dress, wearing a wig dyed to match. She smiled at them, as nonchalant as a duchess and quite indistinguishable from one except that the neck of her gown was so low that it exposed her breasts to the nipples.

"Madame, may I present my daughter-in-law, Mme. Macdonald." Anne made a slight bow, exactly right in proportion to her own rank and the importance of the favourite who responded by smiling broadly at her.

"I've seen you, madame," she said. "I've often admired your jewels; they've made me look to my own, I can tell you."

With difficulty Anne kept her eyes on the lovely face and above the level of that outrageous décolletage.

"Comtesse, you don't need jewels. Nature has already adorned you enough."

Du Barry laughed; it was a gay sound and the King looked up for a moment, pleased to see that his mistress was being amused.

"Thank you, madame; one doesn't often get a compliment from another woman. Your mother-in-law, Mme. Macdonald, tells me you have a magnificent hôtel in Paris which you're going to open for our entertainment. What a good idea! I'm sure it will turn everyone green with envy."

"I am giving a ball to mark the occasion," Anne said; the favourite was very easy to talk to. She affected none of the chilly and majestic airs that had made her predecessor, Mme. de Pompadour, so hated. "It would do me great honour if you consented to be present. I shall send you an invitation if that is agreeable to you."

"Very agreeable," Du Barry responded. "If it suits His Majesty, of course. Depend upon it, madame, I shall be there if he allows me — if he goes himself, I mean. I am dying with curiosity to see your new house. This place stifles me! I shall be delighted to get out of it for an evening."

She nodded to Anne and Anne withdrew. The introduction was over; she saw Katherine smiling at her; she had done well. The favourite liked her. Louis would come to the ball and her place as one of the most important hostesses in Paris was assured. As she moved away she looked at Francis; the same expression was in his eyes as on the previous evening, a look of boldness, even of recklessness which she had never seen before. As they passed each other, Anne's lips moved.

"Be nice to her."

He gave a tiny nod, and then she saw him bending over the Du Barry's hand. Francis had seen many beautiful women; he had seen the King's mistress as often as he had seen the King, in those long weary weeks while he kicked his heels at Versailles and went hungry to make his meagre money last. But he was unprepared for the power of her attraction at close quarters. He was a man and he knew too what was expected of him. He gazed deliberately at the beautiful bosom and then raised the look until it reached her lovely face. The bright eyes sparkled into his with the coquetry that was as natural to her as breathing. Her appraisal was as bold and as admiring as his, and she showed it by laughing; she was one of the few women at court whose teeth were perfect.

"Captain O'Neil, my daughter's agent, madame," Katherine said. "He has waited a long time at Versailles for an opportunity to meet you."

"What do you want, monsieur? I can't make you *my* agent, unfortunately. The King wouldn't like it, even if I might! How long have you been here?"

"Two months, madame," Francis answered coolly. "If it weren't for the charity of Mme. Macdonald in giving me some employment, I should have been forced to leave after the first fortnight. I find court life very expensive."

"I'm glad you found someone to befriend you," the Du Barry winked. "Now tell me, Captain, whose name I can't possibly pronounce, what is there to know about you?"

"Very little, madame," he answered. "My family were exiled from Ireland by the English after fighting for the Catholic House of Stuart. I have neither lands nor fortune; I have been a soldier all my life, fighting for whomsoever would pay me. I came in the hope that I might offer my sword to His Majesty."

"Have you any friends here?" she asked him.

"None, but Mme. Macdonald."

"I'm tired of sitting down, monsieur. Give me your hand and escort me to the other side of the room." The Du Barry got out of her chair, moving as gracefully as a dancer, and a mischievous look at Katherine, she walked away on the arm of the O'Neil. They paused

161

by a window. To his surprise he saw that the mocking little face was quite serious.

"If you haven't any friends, monsieur, you already have enemies. I've heard a great deal about you and Mme. Macdonald. I like her and I like you. If you want a commission from the King, I'll get one for you. But you know you'll lose her?"

"No, I won't," Francis said very quietly; there was no pretence, no flirtation between them now. "Once I've a position of my own, I'll take her with me."

"Good," she said. "I'm glad of that. Her husband's a swine."

"There's no reason in the world why you should help me, but I'll be grateful to you for the rest of my life if you do."

"I've never done anyone a bad turn." The Du Barry smiled up at him. "Sometimes I like to do a good one if I can. I can remember what it was like to be without friends and without money. I've a sharp instinct for Versailles, my dear Captain, and I smell the wolves gathering about you two, I can't tell why. There's been too much talk about you and Madame there. It will be better for you both to go away together as soon as you can. I'll get your commission out of him —" She nodded towards the King. "You'll have it within the month. Take me back to my chair now

162

before he looks up and sees us. He gets more unpredictable every day."

Francis gave her his arm once more and handed her into the armchair with a bow as low as he would have given to the dauphine herself.

"Madame," he said as he kissed her hand. "Consider me your devoted servant — for life."

"If I ever need a strong sword arm, I'll remember you," she said gaily. "*Au revoir,* Captain."

"I must congratulate you," Katherine said to him as they walked down the corridors together. "You made exactly the right impression on her. I'm sure she'll help you."

"I believe she will, madame." Francis looked directly into the beautiful face and the penetrating blue eyes that were openly examining him. "I must thank you with all my heart for your kindness in arranging that introduction. First so much kindness from Madame herself, and now from you too. I wish I could repay it."

"You can, Captain," Katherine spoke very quietly; Anne was a little ahead of them and she began to walk more slowly so that the distance widened between them. "You can repay any small favour I or Anne have done you by insisting that Anne is more discreet with you. Please!" She saw the angry flash in his eyes and she held up her hand. "I know perfectly well your friendship is entirely innocent; what I do know is the amount of gossip that is spreading about you, especially since you entered my daughter-in-law's service. Everyone says you're her lover, Captain, whether you are or not. I'm only afraid that my son may decide to take the rumour seriously. Having met you, I feel you might well be a match for him, but I tremble to think what he would do to Anne. For her sake, get your commission and leave us quickly as you can. In the meantime, I wish you'd resign your position with her and move out of the hôtel!"

Francis walked on slowly side by side with her. "I have never met your son, madame," he said at last, "but from what I've heard of him, I agree that it would go very hard with Anne if he suspected anything. For that reason alone I have no intention of leaving her alone. As for my commission, I believe I shall get it, and I shall leave Versailles at once. As for your son, I warn you, if he accuses me or molests Anne, I shall certainly kill him!"

"Yes," Katherine said quietly. "Perhaps you will. That would be a happy solution for everybody. I will leave you both here." She came up to Anne and kissed her. "Good night, my child." Then she turned to Francis and gave him her hand. "I know you will see my daughter safely back to Paris," she said. "Good night, Captain."

Outside in the long avenue leading to the Cour de Marbre, two carriages passed each other, one setting out for Paris, the other returning from a trip to the Trianon; Louise leant forward and looked out of the window as they passed; the postillions carried torches, and the arms of Anne de Bernard Macdonald were clearly visible on the panels of the coach that swung away from them. She could also see the outlines of two people sitting together inside it. She leant back and looked at Charles who was sitting with his eyes closed. They had been gambling at the Trianon and he had lost rather a lot of money, while she had won. He was not in an agreeable mood, but she felt the opportunity must not be missed. The spy at the Hôtel de Bernard had not sent any information and Louise was beginning to suspect the woman of prolonging her employment and withholding what she knew.

"What a pity you were sleeping," Louise said. "You have just missed seeing your wife and her lover driving back to Paris!"

The pale eyes opened and in the dim light they glittered at her. "My wife and her lover . . . is that what you said, or was I dreaming?"

"That's what I said," Louise persisted. "I've

no doubt you know all about it — everyone else in Versailles does!" She looked down at him, and though she was afraid, she went on, slightly mocking him. He would probably hit her, but it wouldn't be the first time and it would be worth it.

"I must say, you surprise me, Charles. I never imagined you'd allow yourself to be made a cuckold so openly! There they were, driving away together in her coach for all the world to see. Still, it's no affair of mine. I suppose she's entitled to amuse herself, even if she is being very indiscreet about it."

"Are you by any chance jeering at me, my dear?" he asked her. "Or is this some joke in your peculiarly bad taste? Do tell me, before I do something you might regret. . . ."

"I'm not jeering," Louise said. "I'm telling you the truth. I've hinted at it often enough and you never took any notice. Now it's the talk of Versailles; he's been dancing attendance on her for weeks and she's taken him into the hôtel to live with her; she calls him her agent! Everyone is convulsed at the effrontery of it. I'm sorry if you're angry with me, but I really thought you knew what was common knowledge everywhere."

"Well, I'm going to surprise you. I didn't!" He made no move towards her; it was impossible to tell what he was going to say or

166

do. But she, who knew him so well, sensed the intensity of his anger as if it were lightning that flickered and darted in the coach. After a moment he pulled on the string in the roof and the panel slid back; the second coachman's head appeared above them.

"Stop the coach!" Charles snapped. The coach pulled up, the horses stamping a little in their harness. He turned to Louise. "Get out," he said.

"What! What do you mean, get out?"

"I mean that I'm going to Paris and I haven't time to waste taking you back to the palace. You must pay the penalty of your unpleasant tongue. A walk will do you good. Get out."

"It's nearly a quarter of a mile," Louise protested. "Charles, you know I can't walk . . . my shoes will be ruined; if I'm seen I'll be a laughing stock! Please, I beg of you, let me come with you if you won't take me back!"

"If you're a laughing stock, then you'll be keeping company with me, if what you've said is true. I'm not prepared to argue with you. Open that door and get out before I throw you into the road."

He leant forward and flung the carriage door wide. One of the postillions sprang down, and after a moment's hesitation, Louise gave the man her hand and climbed out. She stood in the road looking up at Charles; her face was terribly pale and her mouth trembled.

"I will never forgive you for this," she said. He pulled the door shut and shouted up through the roof panel.

"Drive on! Take the Paris road and hurry!"

The porter at the gates of the Hôtel de Bernard was half asleep when the carriage drew up in front of them, and the postillion jumped down and pulled on the bell rope. Grumbling, the porter came out of his shelter, demanding to know who asked entry at such a late hour. It was past two o'clock and his mistress had only just returned. He had been told to close the gates for the night.

"Open up, you old fool," the postillion shouted. "Your master, M. Macdonald, is outside! He'll have your hide if you keep him waiting!"

"I serve the marquise," the old man retorted. "Macdonald means nothing to me!" But he opened the gates, still grumbling loudly, and then sprang back as the carriage swept through, almost knocking him to the ground. At the door of the hôtel the same scene was repeated; after some delay a sleepy footman let them in, and Charles stood in his wife's house for the first time. He gave one swift glance round him, and then turned to the footman.

"Where will I find Madame at this time?"

"Upstairs, monsieur, in her boudoir. She ordered us to shut the house for the night."

"Take me there," Charles said. "But open your mouth to announce me or make any commotion and I'll run you through on the spot!"

He followed the footman up the wide staircase; the house was very quiet. At a door on the first landing the man paused.

"Wait by the head of the stairs," Charles ordered. "I may need you again."

He turned the handle of the door very quietly and then flung it open so hard that it crashed against the wall. He stepped forward into the little yellow and white boudoir; it was empty. The next moment a door at the far end of it opened, and he saw Anne standing in her nightdress, staring at him and turning very pale.

"Charles! Whatever is wrong . . . ? You terrified me!"

"I wanted to surprise you," he said softly. "And I have a feeling I've succeeded. We'll shut this door, shall we, and open that one a little wider. . . . You were in bed, I see?"

"I was." She came out into the boudoir, and he walked past her and into her bedroom. It was empty, and one glance assured him that Anne had been alone. The pillows were arranged for one person; there was not a sign of disorder in the room, not a suggestion that any male had ever crossed the doorway. He did not trouble to open cupboards or show his suspicions because he knew for certain that they were baseless.

"Would you please tell me what you are looking for, and why you burst into my room at this hour like a thief?"

"Don't take that impudent tone with me," he snapped. "I came here to talk to you. Sit down!"

"You came to search my room," Anne said coldly. She was beginning to feel angry, and angrier with herself because her inclination was to accept his behaviour in the hope that he would stay the night.

"Isn't that a husband's privilege when his wife's reputation is in question?" he demanded.

"Wouldn't it occur to a husband to defend her," Anne countered. "Instead of believing she was guilty! And who did you expect to find with me tonight? Who have you ever found at Versailles when you came upon me unexpectedly? How dare you insult me like this. This is my house, and I ask you to leave it immediately!"

"How independent you've become," he mocked. He sat down on one of her little fragile chairs, balancing backwards on two legs. He watched her with a thin smile.

"People are gossiping about you and that mercenary," he said curtly. "The rumour is that you're his mistress. He's employed by you, isn't he, my dear . . . a single man, a gentleman too, and living with you in this splendid hôtel. Hardly wise, hardly the way a respectable woman of position should compromise her husband's name, is it?"

"It is perfectly innocent," Anne insisted. "I befriended Francis because he had no one to help him; and I had no husband to help me! He's my agent, but he's not my lover! Now will you please go?"

"Francis," Charles mimicked her. "How very intimate you two must be — tell me, does he call you by your Christian name?"

"Yes, he does," she retorted. "But not in public. We're friends, Charles, that's all. I'm lonely; I haven't seen you for the past month!" She stood up and turned away from him; she was very close to weeping.

"If I *had* betrayed you, you couldn't have blamed me," she said. When he moved, he moved very quickly and with little sound. He was beside her in a moment, and he caught her by the wrist so fiercely that she winced.

"Don't ever try me," he said. "You're my wife, you're a Macdonald now. If you smirch my honour and my name, I'll kill you, and I'll kill your lover first, in front of you."

She turned so that she faced him and she looked quite calmly into the dark, angry face above her.

"If you don't interfere with me, I shan't interfere with you, you can live as you please, you said that to me before we were married, do you remember, Charles? What's become of that promise now?"

"I've changed my mind," he said. "I shall do as I please, my dear Anne, and you will do what I tell you and what befits my wife. You did insist upon becoming it, you know," he added. "Now you must pay the penalty. No more acts of friendship to penniless young men, no more flouting the conventions and causing scandal." He lifted her hand and examined the red marks where he had held her wrist.

"I don't believe you've been unfaithful; only stupid and naïve. You're still a country simpleton. How much money have you given this adventurer?" She tried to draw away from him but his fingers closed tightly over her arm again. "Don't do that, stay where you are, and answer me!"

"The wages agreed for his services and not a penny more! If you knew Francis O'Neil, you wouldn't ask that question."

"Ah, then he's a man of principle, a nobleman too proud to take favours from a woman. . . . Really, what a little fool you are! Do you know how these mercenaries live? Do you know anything about this gallant gentleman with whom you've compromised yourself and made a laughing stock of me?"

"Mercenaries fight for pay," Anne answered. "There's no disgrace in that!"

"The pay isn't what attracts them," Charles said. "It's the sacking of captured towns, the loot and rapine after a victory — that's what draws them, like wolves from every corner of the world! How many women and children has this money soldier murdered? Did you ever ask him?"

"What do you care what he's done?" Anne countered. "Your honour is safe, that's all that matters to you! If I consorted with thieves and trollops, what difference would that make to you?"

"You do consort with them," he laughed unpleasantly. "What else abounds at Versailles, hiding under noble names and the King's patronage? That brings me to another point. I hear my mother presented you to the Du Barry. I must speak to her about it. I object to my wife consorting with the most notorious whore in France. Next time, you imitate the dauphine and turn your back, do you understand?"

"Charles, don't be ridiculous. I did no harm;

it's unlikely I shall ever speak more than a word or two to her. Besides, you can't forbid me, when your own mistress is one of her intimates. You cause some scandal yourself, I might say, and I have never reproached you!"

"It wouldn't be wise if you did," he answered. "Louise de Vitale is my mistress. That doesn't give you licence to enter a circle of whores. Nothing I do concerns you except to obey my instructions. Now tell me where I can find Captain O'Neil!"

"Why?" Anne demanded. She was free of him now and she turned to him and touched him in a gesture of appeal. "Please, Charles, please don't hurt Francis — don't go and pick a quarrel with him!" Her mother-in-law's words came back to her: "Nothing would please Charles more than to kill an innocent man in a duel. . . ." "I'll do what you want me to do; I'll tell him he must leave, I won't invite the Du Barry to the ball, I'll do anything, only don't do him any harm. He's done none to you!"

"Not for the want of trying, or the want of wishing, I'll swear to that. Where is he, Anne? Tell me and stop arguing or I'll take you down with me in your nightdress to find him. That should provoke this quarrel you're so anxious to avoid. Are you afraid I'll kill

174

him? Or are you thinking of me, by any chance?"

"I'm thinking of you both," she said desperately. "He could just as well kill you as the other way about — he's an expert swordsman."

"How interesting," Charles jeered. "You whet my appetite to try him. Once more, where is he?"

"Probably downstairs working at the accounts; that's where he said he was going when I said good night. Please, I beg you, don't go down. Let me dismiss him in the morning."

For a moment Charles considered her. "Go and dress in something," he said suddenly. "You will dismiss him in my presence. That should be interesting. Hurry, or I'll do it alone. And I think you know what that will mean."

At the door of her room she turned and looked at him; her eyes were red with tears.

"Is there not one jot of human feeling in you?" she asked him. "Are you so completely cruel and merciless that you must punish both of us by making me do this?"

"Cruel and merciless!" He grinned at her, pretending to be surprised. "'When I've been moved by your pleas! I'd really intended to have him beaten by my postillions and thrown into the gutter outside the gates. . . . How ungrateful you are, my dear! Come, I'm waiting!"

175

Francis was in the small closet on the ground floor which he used as an office; there were two candles burning on the writing table and he was so intent on the heap of papers in front of him that he did not look up at once when the door opened. When he did so, and saw Anne, deadly pale, with Charles beside her, he sprang up with an exclamation. As Charles moved into the room, he stood very still behind the table. He had never seen Anne's husband before. The man who moved towards him, drawing Anne by the hand, was as tall and sparsely built as an athlete, fashionably dressed in brocade and laces, with the fierce, cruel face of a leopard, under his powdered wig, and one hand on his sword. His expression of arrogant contempt was so insufferable that even before he spoke, Francis stepped out into the middle of the room.

"So you are Captain O'Neil, my wife's agent?" The drawling tone was as insulting as the look that went with it. Francis flushed an angry red. Watching him, Charles recognised the quality that made Anne say that he might just as well kill him if they fought. This was no worthless libertine; he had met men of O'Neil's mettle before. To his surprise he felt the same sharp pang of annoyance as on the first evening when he had seen the handsome young man waiting for his wife in the

Salon d'Appollon. Charles had never been jealous of anyone before; he found the emotion difficult to sustain even for a moment. He was about to lose his temper.

"I am, sir," Francis said. "Who, may I enquire, are you?" Generations of proud and insolent O'Neils spoke through their descendant's mouth at that moment. It was an answer delivered in a manner worthy of any Macdonald at his worst. Anne pulled her hand away from her husband and came quickly forward.

"Francis, this is my husband. We — I have something to say to you."

"Yes," Charles said. "My wife has no further need of your services. You are to leave the hôtel."

Francis turned away from him and came face to face with Anne.

"Is this what you wish?" he asked quietly. "Don't be afraid. If you want me to throw him into the street, I'll do it. I won't let him harm you. Just say the word."

"I told you," Charles cut in, and now there was no pretence between any of them. "Leave the house, or by God, I'll have my servants strip you and whip you through the streets! Anne, go upstairs to your room . . . your money soldier doesn't like being dislodged, I see."

Francis looked over his shoulder at him. "No servant of yours will lay a hand on me before I've thrashed the master with the flat of my sword if he's too much a coward to try it at the proper end!" He spoke gently to Anne. "Do as he says. Go upstairs and leave this to me."

"No." Desperately she faced him, moving between him and Charles. "No, Francis, I'm not going. My husband is right. I want you to leave. I'm not being forced; I realise it's necessary. My honour is in question and so is yours. Please, for the sake of our friendship, I implore you to go."

"Take her advice," Charles sneered. "She knows I'll kill you if you don't."

"You flatter yourself." O'Neil almost spat the words at him. "Whether I leave the house or not, you haven't done with me, sir. Once more, Anne, this is your wish?"

"It is," she said. "If either of you fight, it will break my heart. For my sake, do as my husband says and go away."

Francis came up to her and took her hand. "I am your servant, madame," he said quietly. "In every sense of the word. I shall go because you ask it. If you need me, just send word." He turned away from her and as he did so, she covered her face with her hands and began to weep. He came and stood very close to

Charles and there was a look of murder on his face.

"You'll account to me for those tears," he said. "You haven't won. I'll take her away from you yet!" He pushed past him and the door slammed shut.

"You haven't saved him, you know," Charles said softly. "Only for tonight. I'm going to seek him out. . . ."

"Don't trouble," Anne burst out; she was trembling and near hysteria. "He'll seek you! Now you see he's not a coward! At least you can't despise him, however much you try!"

"Dear me." The mocking voice was unbearably smooth. "What a beautiful relationship I have disrupted — what mutual esteem you have for one another! A poverty-stricken exile, living by cutting throats, and my stupid, moon-struck wife with more money than intelligence. Go upstairs; you're making me quite sick! Go on, do as you're told, damn you, before I give you the thrashing you deserve and send my men out after that beggar to teach him a lesson. . . ."

She ran up the stairs, past the frightened servants who had come out and now shrank back into the shadows; only Marie-Jeanne rushed after her weeping mistress and closed the door. For a second she hesitated. "Pig," she said fiercely to herself. "Savage! Let him do what he likes to me; he shan't get in here tonight." Then she turned the key in the boudoir door, and following Anne into the bedroom, she locked that too.

But though the maid stayed awake until morning, watching her exhausted mistress sleep, no one came to disturb her until the chambermaid knocked with her tray of chocolate, and the second maid followed her with hot water for Madame's toilette. On the chocolate tray there was a note. Sitting up in bed, her eyes swollen with crying, Anne recognised the handwriting and tore it open. A single sheet of paper contained a few short lines, written by Charles and dated early that same morning.

"If you persist in remaining in Paris, you must conduct yourself in a proper manner. If you see or communicate with anyone of whom I disapprove again, I shall petition the King to exile you to Charantaise for flagrant immorality with an inferior. I shall also have the person concerned killed." It was signed with the initial C.

As Anne read the note, she looked up suddenly, and found the chambermaid, who brought her bath water, still lingering in the room. The woman was watching her intently.

"What are you doing?" Anne demanded; she had seen the same servant once or twice before and there was something about her she disliked. "Put down the water and go. Marie-Jeanne, close the door!"

The chambermaid curtsied without saying a word and slipped out. The next moment Anne had forgotten her completely. She tore the note into pieces and threw them away.

"Madame," Marie-Jeanne said anxiously. "Madame, you look so pale. Is it bad news?"

Anne looked into the worried face of the girl who had attended her for so many years; it was almost the first time she had noticed her as a human being. Kind, conscientious Marie-Jeanne was actually fond of her mistress. There was not one other person near her whom Anne could trust.

"I am forbidden to see Captain O'Neil," she said. "Monsieur threatens to have him killed if I so much as write to him. Marie-Jeanne, I owe the captain money — I can't abandon him like this!"

"I can find him for you, madame," the little maid said. "I can carry messages between you, if you like. I'm not afraid of Monsieur." It was such a pity, she thought, in agreement with the other servants, that Madame and the captain were not lovers. Such a pity that that sinister husband who treated her so badly was not getting the cuckolding he deserved. Everyone liked the captain; he was exacting but

181

he was fair, and everyone with eyes in their heads could see that he was passionately in love with Madame.

"I will do anything you ask, if it will help you and the captain," she said. "You can trust me."

"I know I can," Anne said. "I'm very grateful to you. You're a good girl, Marie-Jeanne. I also know you locked the doors last night."

"Yes, I did. I told you," she said stoutly, "I'm not afraid of him. Besides, he must be very jealous of you to care about the captain. All my friends among the maids at Versailles told me that their ladies' husbands were completely indifferent to them and allowed them to do as they liked. It is strange that Monsieur should be so strict with you."

"Yes," Anne said slowly. "Yes, it is strange. But Monsieur is a harsh man where honour is concerned. He is not French."

Marie-Jeanne nodded; she was a simple girl and her mind worked in simple ways.

"If it were not Monsieur," she said, "one would have said he was jealous because he was in love with you himself. But alas, madame, it can't be so. Shall I prepare your bath?"

For the rest of the morning she puzzled over the change of mood in her mistress. In spite of the captain's dismissal and her husband's strictures, Madame seemed curiously happy.

# Chapter 5

"My dear Louise, he must be madly jealous of her! Rushing to Paris and turning out her lover in the middle of the night!" The Comte de Tallieu leant back and laughed in his high-pitched way.

"Why, *mon Dieu,* I can't think of a husband at Versailles who couldn't have at least waited till the morning! Whatever possessed you to draw his attention to it?"

"I don't know why I confide in you," Louise snapped at him. "You're so malicious! Why do you say Charles is jealous — I told you she means nothing to him; he was only furious because he felt he was being laughed at!"

"Ha, he and a thousand others! What would happen if every husband took that view?" The comte sat forward and smiled at her. It amused him to see her so angry. And already she knew that what he was saying was the truth. "Perhaps you're right — perhaps it was outraged pride that sent him racing off into the night. In any case, I don't see what advantage you've gained from it, except to deprive his wife of her lover. She'll only replace him."

"I thought he'd catch them together," Louise admitted. She regretted bitterly the impulse which made her tell De Tallieu what had happened. It was extraordinary why she trusted him when she knew he was not to be trusted. They had little in common except their dislike of Charles's wife, and the comte's pathological spite towards O'Neil, who had threatened to teach him manners. He had never forgotten the incident and he often referred to it. If he could injure O'Neil or harm the woman he loved, then De Tallieu was prepared to give Louise or any other enemy the full benefit of his remarkable intelligence.

"And obviously he hasn't, otherwise he'd have killed that upstart. What do you suggest now?"

"Why should I suggest anything?" Louise demanded. She was walking up and down, twisting the ribbons of her dress in and out of her fingers. Charles was jealous of Anne. She could cheerfully have murdered De Tallieu for putting her most secret fear into words. Jealous. He couldn't be jealous of Anne without having some feeling for her. . . . She felt as if her aching head would burst. "Why should I suggest anything?" she repeated. "Things between us have never been happier."

This was true on the surface; Charles had returned to her as usual, offering no apology for that nightmare walk in which she had crept up the back entrance to the palace, carrying her torn shoes in her hand, and luckily had seen no one who recognised her. She had not mentioned it, though in a strange way it rankled more than any of the many cruel and hurtful things that he had done to her. They were still lovers as much as before, but he had told her nothing of what had happened when he went after Anne and the Irishman. The story had come back to her from the spy she had placed in the Hôtel de Bernard, and thanks to her own tongue and the servants' gossip, the story was soon flying round the city and Versailles itself.

"If all is well between you, why are you pursuing his wife so vigorously?" De Tallieu asked. "Come now, my dear Louise, you fill my ears with all these stories, and then, when we come near the truth of the matter, you take refuge in lies." He stood up, picking up his gold and mother-of-pearl cane. "If you can't be honest with me, then I refuse to listen to another word. Besides" — he glanced at her slyly — "I don't know why you bring me into this at all."

"Because you're a hundred times cleverer than anyone I know, and because you seem to have a little score to settle yourself," she retorted. "Sit down, please. You're a detestable creature and I swear you enjoy tormenting me. But I need you. Is that reason enough?"

"Admirably honest even if it is unflattering." The comte sat back again. "I am an unpleasant person because nature made me so," he said sweetly. "Also, I dislike my fellow men and I enjoy their misfortunes. It's almost my only amusement in life. You are a wicked bitch, my dear, and far more wicked since you fell in love with your lover. I always thought the tender feeling was supposed to soften and improve. . . ." He giggled, his eyes as bright as a snake's. "You're not sure of him, are you? Isn't that the truth? You're not so sure that this convenient marriage means nothing to him. . . . You want to be rid of the woman by some means or another, so that you can devour M. Charles, like those charming female spiders."

"I am going to say something to you which may surprise you," Louise said quietly. "I don't want to *devour* Charles, as you put it. I love him. I would do anything in the world for him. But as I am only his mistress, I am at a disadvantage. I have nothing to offer him but myself. She, on the other hand, has a great deal as time goes on. She has beauty — I'm not as blind with malice as you think." She smiled bitterly. "She has wealth — she is his wife, and she is here. If she had never followed him, I don't believe he would have thought of her from one year's end to the next. But proximity and patience; those are the two things that can take him away from me. And if he leaves me I shall die. I'm sure you find this very funny!"

"I find it astonishing," he remarked. "The intensity of passion you people inspire in one another — whereas I, with my little pages . . . I have all the pleasure and none of the pain. When I have tired of one, I buy another. Poor Louise; stop tearing those exquisite ribbons, you've ruined them. Do you want my advice?"

"Yes," she said desperately. "What shall I do — how can I get her to leave Versailles and go away, far away, back to her damned château in the country?"

"I don't see how you can," he said. "At least, not at the moment. I don't see there's anything you can do, because you allowed your jealousy to bungle that affair with the mercenary. You should have consulted me. I'd have arranged that your Charles caught them properly! I'm afraid you must just be patient, my dear, and use your wits and talents — whatever they may be — to keep him happy with you. An opportunity will present itself, it always does if one waits."

"I shall try," Louise said. "Have you been invited to this ball she's giving?"

The comte's rouged face changed colour a little.

"No," he answered, "no, I've not been asked. Everyone I know has received an invitation except me. And you, I presume."

Louise nodded.

"That's another little debt I owe Mme. Macdonald. She'll find that it was most unwise to leave me out! I must go, Louise. If you hear anything interesting, send me a message."

"I will."

Louise gave him her hand and he made his usual pretence of kissing it. When she was alone, Louise rang for her maid.

"Marie, come and help me change. I'm riding in the park with M. Macdonald in an hour. Afterwards I want you to send a message to that woman at the Hôtel de Bernard. She's to keep the sharpest watch possible upon her mistress."

As she spoke, she stepped out of the overdress Marie had unfastened and stood in her petticoats before the mirror on her bedroom wall. She watched as her maid stripped off the long, full skirts and unhooked the small, boned pannier; she stood in her shift and the narrow steel corselet that gripped her waist so tightly that Charles could span it with his hands. The same corselet pushed her breasts high so that they came well above the neck of her dress. She looked at herself critically, anxiously, as she had done so often since she met him.

She was very beautiful; it was not vanity or self-deception to claim that. Her features were arresting, her brilliant eyes and pale skin were matched by the shining blackness of her abundant hair. Her body was as smooth and graceful as a young girl's; even so, she could offer him more than the physical beauty that had brought so many men in pursuit of her. Her sensuality was as fierce as any man's and as capable of infinite variations of mood, so that Charles was never bored and never quite knew what to expect. She could have been a king's mistress, and she knew it. And yet every instinct quivered with anxiety when she thought of Anne Macdonald, and all her logical arguments and Charles's contemptuous rebuttals could not make that sense of uneasiness quiescent. The wife was a danger to her; she could not really say why or how, but she knew it was so. One day, he would go to his wife and stay, and she would have lost him forever. When that day came, as she told the comte, she would not want to live.

Dressed at last in her blue cloth riding habit, with a hat covered in emerald-green ostrich feathers, she examined herself once more and could find no fault. Carefully she composed her face, forcing away the lines between her eyebrows, turning her red mouth up into a smile. That must be her face when she was with him. At the door she turned again to Marie.

"Don't forget that message. The strictest watch! I have a feeling something's going to happen!"

It was only three days before the ball, and Anne was so busy that she stayed at the hôtel supervising the preparations. The King had expressed his intention of honouring Mme. Macdonald by coming to her ball; it was un- thinkable that the monarch should be directly invited by a subject. Mme. Du Barry would be coming with him, and the list ran on through dukes and princes of the blood, even including the dauphin and Marie Antoinette herself who rarely went to anything not given by a personal friend.

Everyone's curiosity was aroused; older people spoke of the magnificent parties given by Anne's mother, the marquise, who had de- lighted to appear at them in fancy dress, glittering from head to foot with diamonds and escorted by her latest lover. If the De Bernard hospitality was being offered on that scale, life in Paris and at court would be all the more amusing.

The great rooms were ready at last, and a dozen chefs and twice that number of assistants were busy in the huge kitchens, baking and roasting and decorating tons of food for the supper, while more still were in the cellars, perfecting cordials and fruit drinks. When the cellar was opened up there were enough fine wines to satisfy the most exacting guests, and Anne engaged a group of Italian musicians who were touring France at the time.

The reception would begin with supper, followed by a ball; there were rooms set aside for gaming; the dauphine was notorious for sitting at the gambling table until dawn; the great salon had been turned into a ballroom with a special dais for the orchestra, and another, with throne and canopy, where His Majesty could sit if he wished and watch the dancers.

The rooms were banked with masses of flowers; Anne's steward had cleared the Parisian markets, and upstairs her bedroom and boudoir were full of boxes, ribbons, wrappings, and paper. Rows of wigs of various heights dressed in different styles were put out on stands in her powder closet. A big walnut cabinet the size of a small chest stood in her bedroom; there were three sets of drawers above a deep, fitted interior and it contained Anne's famous collection of jewels. The day before the ball had been spent having last fittings of her dress, consulting the wigmaker about which style suited her best, and submitting to the tyranny of Marie-Jeanne who was determined that her mistress should outshine even the dauphine herself at the ball.

To Anne's delight her sister-in-law, Jean, Comtesse de Mallot, had arrived in Paris and was staying at her brother-in-law's hôtel in the city, accompanied by her husband. On this occasion she had left her brood of children with their nurses in the country. In her letter of acceptance she told Anne that by some miracle she was not pregnant and was about to order the most expensive dress in Paris. They had not seen each other since the wedding at Charantaise, and knowing how Charles disliked his sister, Anne had not mentioned her.

Now all the people Anne was fond of were coming to the ball: Katherine and Sir James, Jean and Paul, and old friends from Charantaise, cousins and neighbours and the highest level of court society from the King downwards. It would be an occasion to remember, and it astonished her to think how shy she used to be and how disinclined to give parties at the château. And yet she was still in the cruelest suspense because the letter she had sent to Charles at the War Ministry had not been answered. She had begged him to come, writing and rewriting it several times in her determination to avoid a pleading tone that would irritate him, and yet show him that the ball and all it represented would mean nothing to her if he were not there to share it with her. It would break her heart if he refused. She had only to think that he would send a curt refusal, or worse still, not trouble to reply at all, and she was ready to cancel everything and make her way back in defeat to Charantaise.

The thought of Francis troubled her too; Marie-Jeanne had not found him and Anne had received no word. Though she looked for him at Versailles, she never saw him or could discover anyone else who had. He might have disappeared from the face of the earth. She owed him money, she owed him above all an explanation for that dreadful dismissal; she would have risked the consequence of Charles's discovery just to see him for a few minutes and heal the wound that her husband had forced her to inflict upon him. But there was no word and no sign.

She had been waiting in her little boudoir, tired out and yet unable to take her maid's advice and rest because she was waiting and listening for a message. . . . "I am coming . . . I will join you. . . . The prospect bores me, I have other plans. . . ." Some word must come; only one day was left. Not even Charles could inflict such a wanton insult on her. When the door opened she opened her eyes; when she saw the maidservant with a letter in her hand, she sprang up. "Give it to me! Quickly!" She was too agitated to notice that the girl was the same one who brought her water in the morning, the silent one who watched her and whom she often curtly told to go away.

The maid curtsied, and withdrew; deliberately, she neglected to quite close the door and in the empty corridor outside she stood and peered through the crack. She saw her mistress tear the letter open, noted the trembling hands and fading colour, saw the look of intense disappointment that passed across her face for a moment, and then watched while the note was re-read. A quick glance behind her assured the spy that she was still alone; no one was coming, or she would have heard steps on the marble floors long before anyone came in sight of her. She stooped to the door again. Mme. Macdonald was at her writing desk, her back to her, answering whatever was in that letter. She had taken the job out of greed; the pay offered by the Baroness de Vitale was high enough to tempt anyone; by this time her jealousy and dislike of her victim made the task a pleasure. Rich, arrogant, spoilt; she spied on the marquise avidly, hoping to do her some harm in retaliation for her impatient manners and disapproving looks. Bringing the bath water to her room every morning, the girl often felt tempted to make it scalding hot so that the high-born whore would burn the skin off her body. She saw her close the desk; there were two letters in her hand. She rang her little hand bell, and Marie-Jeanne came hurrying out of her closet. Flat against the door, the spy strained to catch what was said. "Take this to the comtesse. . . ." The last word eluded her as it often does with a new name. She swore under her breath. "And this one to the captain!" That was what she had been waiting for! That was who had sent that letter. . . . They were still in contact with each other but no one knew where or how; he had certainly not entered the house since the night he left it, like a beaten cur with his luggage on the back of that horrible one-eyed Bohemian brute, Boehmer. If she could but get that letter, the one she had so foolishly delivered without daring to steam it open first, then she could have the proof Baroness de Vitale wanted. She ran down the corridor and slipped into an empty bedroom, hiding again behind the door until she saw Marie-Jeanne hurrying past, wrapped in a cloak. That was one out of the way. If only that other pampered bitch would go into her bedroom and lie down, she could slip into the boudoir and try the lid of that desk. . . . That note was still inside it; she was certain that if she could once get in and open the desk she would find it.

She came out and made her way back to Anne's apartments; unfortunately the door was properly shut; though she listened hard, she could hear nothing. She rubbed her hand across her face; she was sweating with fear. Even the money wouldn't have made her take the risk, nothing but primitive jealousy of her mistress gave her the courage to open the door very quietly and look in.

The boudoir was empty. The bedroom door was shut; she could hear sounds behind it. Her mistress was in there, not resting, moving about — she might come out at any second; if she heard a sound she was certain to do so. The maid crept across the floor towards the little desk, one eye on the bedroom door, her hearing as sharp as a predator's seeking its prey in the forest. She reached the desk

196

and the tips of her fingers touched the lid. It moved; as she expected, it was not locked. She half turned away from the door to Anne's bedroom, and very slowly drew the lid back until it rested against her. She waited a second more; the woman in the room was pulling out some drawer, she could hear it distinctly. Like a flash, the spy went through the few papers in the desk; what she was looking for was under a half sheet of blank paper. She stuffed it into the neck of her dress; gently, very gently, she closed the lid again and, with a last glance at the shut door, she fled from the room.

"Anne! Anne, my dearest, let me embrace you!" Jean de Mallot held out her arms to her old friend. Anne's hood fell back, her hair was loosely drawn up with ribbons; under her cloak she wore a boudoir gown.

"Jean, did you get my note? I beg you to forgive me, but you were the only one I could trust!"

"Of course I got it; that fool of a maid of yours didn't wait or I should have told her it was quite all right."

"She had another to deliver," Anne said. She blushed suddenly. "Jean, it isn't what you think."

"He's here," her sister-in-law said gently.

"He's been here for half an hour. What is it that I'm supposed to think, by the way?"

"It's not an assignation," Anne said. "He's a friend, I owe him a great deal — I had to see him for a moment. I'm not being unfaithful to Charles."

Jean looked at her and laughed.

"More fool you, then. I've seen your handsome captain, and by Heaven, I wouldn't like to trust myself with him for long! Unfaithful to Charles! What a sweet idiot you are; I should hope you've betrayed him a dozen times by now! Who is this captain? Do tell me, I'm dying of curiosity."

"We met at Versailles," Anne said. "He was friendless, and at that time I knew hardly anyone and I was grateful for his company. He's a mercenary soldier; he hoped the King would give him a commission. The time went by, you know how it is at court, the King comes, he passes, and those without influence can stand in front of him for years without being seen or spoken to — I asked Francis to be my agent when I re-opened the hôtel. He did everything for me, miracles of organisation. I could never have accomplished it alone or without being robbed twice over. Then Charles broke in one night and made me send him away. He accused us, can you imagine it?"

Jean nodded. "Only too clearly. What a re-volting hypocrite — whose bed had he crawled out of, that whore Vitale's I suppose. Sorry, my dear, go on. I didn't mean to say that."

"There's nothing else to tell," Anne said. "Francis was turned out of the house like a dog. I searched for him but I had to be careful. Charles threatened to have me exiled and Francis killed if we saw each other again. Then, not two hours ago, I got a note from him, begging me to meet him. I sent to tell him to come here; it was the only place where we'd be safe. Oh, Jean, please believe me, we are both innocent. But I couldn't let him go without a word, without explaining what had happened."

"Are you in love with him?" her sister-in-law asked her.

Anne shook her head. "No. You must be-lieve that too. Where is he?"

"Downstairs in the library. Go to him and don't worry. No one will disturb you."

He had his back to her when she opened the door; he was standing by the window, holding the curtain and looking out onto the dark Paris street, one hand in his breeches pocket in the attitude she knew so well. Even before he turned, Anne wondered why it was that she was not in love with him, and whether if Charles and she had never met, her whole life might not have been quite different.

"Francis!"

"Anne!"

When he took her in his arms she did not try to draw away; he held her and she felt him tremble, his cheek pressed against hers. Comfort, tenderness, safety. His love enveloped her, freed at last of the restraints he had put upon it. He didn't speak a word, but turned her face to his and kissed her on the mouth. It was not what she imagined it would be; romantic, almost deferential. It was the kiss given by a man to the woman he loves, and for a moment the force of his passion communicated itself to her; the masculine demand for submission was so strong and her nature so naturally responsive to it that for a moment she weakened in his arms. But it was only a moment and it was not what she felt in the arms of Charles, who kissed her and made love to her and did not care for her at all.

"Francis, I beg you, let me go. . . ."

"I've waited months for this," he whispered. "I've thought of it and lain awake, knowing you were in the room above me, and fought the temptation to get up and go to you. I love you, Anne. I love you more than anything in the whole world."

He released her a little and looked down at her.

"I've got my commission from the King," he said. "I'm going to Metz tomorrow to join the third regiment of musketeers. At last I've got something to offer you now; the King gave me a permanent commission with the rank of captain. My darling, will you come with me?"

"I can't, I can't." She shook her head, stammering, and still he held her and his bright-blue eyes were full of his love and his triumph at having her within reach at last.

"That's what I've been waiting for," he went on. "A commission. I told you I'd have something to ask you, do you remember? I told you the time would come for it. Come away with me! I love you, I've always loved you. I'll make you happy, Anne. Come to Metz."

"And my husband," she said. "Have you forgotten him?"

"No," he sad quietly. "I'm not likely to forget him or that night when he dragged you into the room and made you send me away. I knew you had to do it; I understood. I should have killed him there and then. But I'll do that when he comes after us to get you back. And he'll come, don't doubt it! He's not the man to let you be happy with anyone else. And I shall kill him, my love, I know it. Then we'll be free to marry."

"Let me go," she begged him. "Please, I've

got to talk to you."

"I know what you'll say," he interrupted. "You don't love me, do you?"

"No," Anne said. "No, I don't love you. I should, God knows, I ought to love you. But I don't."

"I knew that too," Francis answered. "Your love will come. Give me the chance."

"I can never love you, Francis." Gently she drew back from him and at last he let her go. "I can never love you because I am still in love with him. I told you that a long time ago, when we first met. Nothing he does to me can kill that love; nothing will ever kill it. I shall love him until the day I die. That's why I cannot go with you to Metz. I can only ask you to forgive me. Even a moment ago when you kissed me . . . I knew it was useless. I still belong to Charles Macdonald, and I always will."

He did not speak for a moment; they stood looking at each other and Anne made a little helpless gesture.

"Forgive me," she whispered. "Please forgive me."

"No," he came back to her and took her hands. "There's nothing to forgive. I should be asking you to pardon me; Anne, if I've distressed you . . . if I've taken advantage of you — I didn't mean it. You may love him

202

for the rest of your life — I don't believe it. I know I shall always love you. Don't cry, my love. I'm going now and I don't want to remember you in tears. Take this — it belonged to my father and it's all I have to give you. If ever you need me, send it back and I promise I'll come to you. Even out of the grave."

He took the sapphire pin out of his cravat and fastened it to her dress. Gently, Anne reached up and kissed him.

"I'll keep it always. May God go with you."

"Remember," he said, and his voice shook, "if ever you need me. . . ."

The door shut after him and she was alone in the room; she waited, and the tears she had held back while he was with her began to flow at last, but they were for him and his disappointed love, not for herself.

"I can't understand how you could be such a fool," Jean said. "He asked you to run away with him and you refused because you loved my *brother!* Mother has told me how Charles treats you; truly, Anne, I think you're mad."

"I don't love him," Anne repeated. "Not in the way he loves me. I can't; Charles has taken it all. He gave me this, Jean." She took off the pin. "It was his father's and the only thing of value he had." The small blue stone flashed in the light. Jean examined it and gave it back.

"How could you have sent him away," she said slowly. "How could you have refused him everything like that, even if you wouldn't go to Metz . . . ?"

"Have you been unfaithful to Paul?" Anne demanded. "Why should you expect me . . . ?"

"You asked a question," Jean said calmly. "Wait for the answer. Yes, I have. The last child isn't his; but it's all over now. He's dead. He was a soldier too."

"I'm sorry," Anne said slowly. "I had no idea. . . . I thought you and Paul were so happy."

"We are." Jean smiled at her. "He knows nothing about it, and he's too good a man to hurt. It won't ever happen again; I made up my mind to that. Don't let's discuss it any more. Sit down and tell me about this splendid ball; I can't wait to wear my new dress for it!"

"You'll look lovely," Anne said. "I know what an extravagant minx you are when it comes to clothes. I've spent a fortune on my own and now I don't know whether I like it or not."

"What colour?" Jean asked. Her voice was normal, even gay, but her pink cheeks were pale and there was a drawn look about her pretty face that Anne had never seen before. Her last child was only two years old, a plump, brown-haired little girl with her mother's hazel eyes.

"It's a secret," Anne said. "You must wait till tomorrow."

"I suppose it's tactless to enquire, but is your husband dining with Mother and us tomorrow at the hôtel? I shall have to try and be civil to him, but I don't know how I'm going to manage it!"

"I don't know," Anne said slowly. "I don't know if he is even coming to the ball. I haven't heard a word or seen him since he burst into my house in the middle of the night."

"All the better," Jean's eyes narrowed angrily, but she smiled. "It will be far pleasanter without him. You shouldn't have invited him at all!"

"I am giving it for him," Anne explained. "I don't want all this expense and trouble for myself; I'm not interested in impressing these creatures at Versailles or living the life at court at all! But I told your mother; it's what Charles wants. He's always sneered at me for being a country simpleton. He won't be able to say that after tomorrow!"

"No, he won't," Jean agreed. "You'll be one of the first ladies in France, hostess to the King and the royal family . . . my dear, you'll be so sought after — he won't be able to get near you! And I hope someone will succeed where that poor young captain failed!"

"I doubt it." Anne smiled. "I must go now; there's still so much to be done. God bless you, Jean, you're the most understanding woman in the world."

They kissed and the little comtesse squeezed her affectionately. "Bah, I did nothing. As you've discovered, I'm not such a country simpleton either. Good night, my dear sister. Take good care of that little pin; it's worth more than all your diamonds."

"Did you find him?" Louise demanded.

"No," Charles said. "He left for Metz this morning; that's all I could find out. Stop asking questions, you're beginning to bore me!"

She shrugged and smiled. Louise was not hurt by his insults or frightened by his bad temper. She had never seen him so angry since she gave him that letter the night before; his dark skin had turned grey as she watched him reading it.

"I beg you to meet me; the time has come when I can ask my favour of you. Send word where we can meet in privacy, or if you wish, I'll come to you. Ever your devoted O'Neil of Clonmere."

He had folded it up very carefully, and this surprised her, until she saw that his hands were trembling.

"You damned, spying whore," he had shouted at her. "Where did you find this?"

"In your wife's desk," she had answered him. "Why call me a whore — it's not written to me!" Even when he had slapped her hard across the face, she did not really mind. And the next day he had sought her out before she had had time to seek him, and she knew at last that she was very near to winning him for good.

She came up to him then and put her arm through his.

"Don't trouble about it," she murmured. "If he's gone, then that's all that matters. The affair must be over for the moment. Forget it, Charles. Ignore it."

He looked down at her and smiled unpleasantly. "Is that why you went to so much trouble to collect the evidence?" he asked. "Because it's not important? You're being very obvious, my dear, not your subtle self at all!"

"It was important to prove to you what she was worth," Louise said quickly. "That was all I wanted. Now you know, you can forget about her."

"Oh, I shall," he said softly. "But only after I've taught her not to disobey me. I warned her what I would do. . . ."

She twisted round until she was facing him, and she locked her arms around his waist. She

207

reached up and began to kiss his mouth; it was a particular trick which always excited him and she performed it with consummate skill and subtle variations.

"Forget her," she whispered. "Think what you'll do later. Come to bed now — there's plenty of time."

He looked down at her, mocking and half smiling, and began to caress her shoulders; only the pale-green eyes were cold and glittering with rage.

"You're a great comfort to me in many ways," he said. "Perhaps I don't appreciate you. I struck you last night, didn't I? Let me make it up to you, my dear Louise. I feel I should start playing the gentleman with you for a change."

"Make it up to me now," she whispered, leaning against him, her eyes closed.

"Oh, I shall," Charles said. "And I'll do more. I'll take you to my wife's hôtel this evening. You know how you enjoy these affairs. It would amuse you, my love, wouldn't it, to make an entrance with me."

"Charles!" She began to exclaim in her excitement but he took her into the inner room and her cries of triumph were soon silenced. When he turned away from her, he lay very still, looking upwards at the canopy above their heads. She was too happy to speak.

"If she's been unfaithful to me," Charles said suddenly, "I shall kill her."

There was a large crowd outside the gates of the Hôtel de Bernard; word soon spread through Paris that the King himself, the dauphin and the dauphine, Marie Antoinette, were coming to attend a ball in the De Bernard mansion, and several hundred people collected round the entrance and the surrounding streets.

A great many beggars had taken up their station by the gates very early, and though Anne's porters drove them off with sticks, they crept back, dragging their stumps of limbs, their frightful deformities of face and body illumined by the torches flaring at the gates, until it seemed as if the entrance were a glimpse of hell, peopled by the whining, cursing, pushing monstrosities, some of whom carried blind or mutilated children as part of their trade. For a trade it was, run by the strongest and cruelest in the community of beggar brethren, and many of those, particularly the weak, the children, and the very old, had been sold to the community, deliberately mutilated and then hired out to beg.

The ordinary citizens of Paris kept a little apart, and the cutpurses moved stealthily among them, picking pockets and snipping the strings of the women's bags. Prostitutes, too, joined the crowd, some of them pitifully young, offering themselves for a few sous. A sweetmeat seller and a woman with a tray of little cakes and rolls did quite a trade among the hungry watchers, and when the first carriages began to roll up to the gates, there was a fearful outcry from the beggars who clutched at the horses' heads and tried to climb the carriage steps, yelling for alms. Sometimes a window opened and a few coins were flung out; fierce fighting broke out on the stones below and the coach passed through the gates and into the inner courtyard. More often the postillions and running footmen cleared a way for the carriages with sticks and whips.

Inside the gates, the great façade of the hôtel was blazing with torches and there were lights pouring out of the windows. It was separated from the gates by a large courtyard, but some swore they could hear distant sounds of music, and there were many who insisted they could smell the rich food, their senses sharpened by hunger.

Anne stood at the head of the staircase welcoming her guests. The long stream of them crept up the stairs like a glittering, many-coloured snake, the women s wide skirts brushing against the walls, swaying like ships as they took a step upward, and above them their hostess sparkled and shone in the many lights in a dress of cloth of silver, the skirt and bodice encrusted with embroidered silver flowers and leaves, the hearts and stems of which glittered with tiny emeralds and diamonds. A short train of silver lace fell from her shoulders, and she carried a fan decorated to match her dress. The wigmaker had surpassed himself with a creation so elaborate that Anne was afraid to move her head. Pure-white ospreys flared out from the centre of a mass of grey-powdered curls, and the hair rose high above them, falling in more curls down her back and across one bare shoulder. Strings of pearls and diamonds were festooned in the headdress, and a single enormous emerald blazed from the heart of the delicate ospreys. There were emeralds and diamonds round her neck and glittering on her wrists and fingers; their size and colour caused much comment and a good deal of envy. Their magnificence obviously annoyed the Duchesse de Luynes, who greeted her hostess with coolness and whispered angrily to the duke that she would have worn her own famous sapphires had she expected such an ostentatious display. Anne's face was very pale, and the pallor was accentuated by a single heart-shaped patch she wore high on one cheek.

When Charles first came in sight of her beneath the staircase, he hardly recognised the lovely, fresh-complexioned girl, who had married him in Charantaise, in the sophisticated beauty, gowned and painted in the extreme of fashion, wearing the fantastic emeralds which she had always sworn she hated. He felt a pressure on his arm; Louise had seen her too. And in spite of her preparations and her beauty, the mistress could not compete with the wife. Her scarlet velvet gown was cut with elegance and flair, its skirts enormously wide, her bosom as white as the lace that fell in delicate fronds around it, and she wore no jewels but diamonds, and they were the best she had. A single scarlet plume drooped in her jet-black hair, and a narrow chain of diamonds hung in a point to her brow, ending in a single pear-shaped stone. Beauty and elegance she had, and for his purpose he was pleased with her. But there was no comparison.

Charles snapped his fingers and one of the lackeys on duty in the hall came running to him.

"I am M. Macdonald. Tell Madame to come down." The lackey bowed.

"Your pardon, monsieur, but we have just had word that His Majesty's carriage is at the gates. Madame will be coming down to receive him now."

There was an excited buzz breaking out among the crowds in the hall, and those who had been waiting on the stairs were already turning back to line up for the King's arrival.

"Come," Charles said. "We will stand here." He could see Anne making her way down the staircase, and the shouts of the crowd outside rose to a roar of cheers as the royal carriage turned into the inner courtyard. Lackeys with torches were stationed at the lower steps and Anne's comptroller and major-domo were on either side of the entrance. She passed so close to him that the edge of her skirts brushed him, but she did not see him or the woman by his side.

At the open doorway she stepped out onto the top steps; from where he waited, Charles could see the tall, stooped figure of the King walking slowly up towards her, his gentlemen in waiting on either side, and a few paces behind him came Mme. du Barry, glittering like a firefly in a cloak sewn with precious stones. Anne curtsied to the ground and the King paused, offering her his hand to kiss, and murmured something which everyone strained to catch. From the expression on his face he appeared in a good humour. The Du Barry's gay little laugh was clearly heard as she greeted her hostess, and Charles's face hardened angrily.

As the King moved into the hall with Anne beside him, Charles stepped forward and made a deep bow.

"May I welcome Your Majesty to my house," he said. "This is a great honour."

The King did not betray surprise; the lined and weary face was like a mask. Charles bent over the hand of the favourite; his eyes flickered over the Du Barry with insulting indifference.

"Madame, your servant."

Then he turned and came face to face with his wife. He offered his arm and when she placed her hand upon it he felt that she was trembling.

"Let us escort our illustrious guests together, madame," he said. "As husband and wife should on such a happy occasion."

He was aware of Louise, her red dress blazing a few feet away from him, and some perverse instinct enjoyed the pain that he was inflicting upon her. But it was nothing to what he intended Anne should suffer for having seen the Irishman again against his orders. She did not speak a word; they led the King and the Du Barry up the stairs and into the magnificent reception room, passing between the lines of courtiers, where he was quickly surrounded.

For a moment they were alone and Anne

turned to Charles, her lovely face was flushed. "Thank you." Her voice was quite unsteady. "Thank you for coming. My heart has been breaking all day, I was so afraid you wouldn't come." He smiled at her, mockingly, angry because her beauty had suddenly so affected him that he could have struck her.

"You disobeyed me," he said softly. "You saw your mercenary again, didn't you . . . ? Oh, I know all about it. What a pity he isn't here to support you, but I know he's gone to Metz, so I felt I ought to deputise. . . ."

"Don't," she whispered. "Don't be angry with me now, don't spoil everything now. I can explain what happened. I meant to tell you. . . ."

"I'm sure you did." The light eyes glittered back at her. "You're so truthful, so obedient . . . everything a wife should be. Wait here. I have someone I wish you to meet."

He found Louise below in the hall; she was standing very near where he had left her, and suddenly he despised her for it. He held out his hand.

"Come," he said. "It's time you were presented to your hostess."

Even the arrival of the dauphin and Marie Antoinette, and her wilful disregard of the favourite, was surpassed by the effect upon the court assembled there when Charles brought his mistress face to face with his wife in the supper room and introduced her.

"My dear" — his voice was heard very clearly by dozens of fascinated onlookers — "I don't think you know the Baroness de Vitale. Louise, my charming wife."

For a moment the room swam before Anne's eyes; the noise and the lights receded and the face of the woman standing before her, holding Charles's arm, was a blur that suddenly came into focus and the moment of faintness passed. She had never fainted in her life; she had never been closer to it than in those few seconds as she saw her husband's mistress smile and for the first time heard her voice.

"I am enchanted, madame."

Everyone in the room was watching them; the Duchesse de Luynes, still smarting with jealousy over the De Bernard emeralds, gave a little laugh. Anne looked at the woman whom the fashionable world knew was Charles's acknowledged mistress.

"My apologies, Baroness, for not having invited you. As my husband's guest, I hope you will be entertained."

She turned her back on both of them and walked away.

It was dawn before the last guests left the Hôtel de Bernard, and truly everyone agreed that it was one of the best social events of the year; the King had stayed late and had even been observed to smile now and then; the feud between Marie Antoinette and the Du Barry was still flourishing; and the hostess had insulted her husband's mistress in such a manner that the baroness had called for her coach and left immediately with M. Macdonald. It had been a memorable evening and the scandal would keep everyone occupied for days.

The rest of the night was like a nightmare to Anne — in which she moved and spoke and smiled and went through the motions of entertaining and enjoying herself as if she were one of those mechanical dolls that were so fashionable at that time. Generations of breeding and the code in which she had been brought up gave her the self-control to hide the outrage that had been done to her feelings and to face the searching glances that surrounded her, watching for some word or sign to embellish the incident. It was such a small moment in her life, that minute or two when Charles came up to her and his words had been so few; hours of bitter quarrelling and a flood of brutal insults could never have hurt her as that public insult had done, deliberately delivered as it was before a large audience — and with her mortal rival as the chief participant. As soon as the rumour reached them, her mother and father-in-law hurried to her, followed by Jean and her husband, and formed a little protective coterie around her. One or other stayed beside her the rest of the evening, and it was Katherine Macdonald who put her arm around Anne's shoulders when the last carriage had turned out of the courtyard, and led her upstairs to her room.

"I've sent for James and Jean and Paul," she said. "Come, my poor child, you must be undressed at once. Marie-Jeanne!"

It had taken nearly four hours to dress Anne; in half an hour the gorgeous dress was put away, the wig removed, and her own hair brushed out. She was dressed in a warm robe, lined with fur, over her nightgown, and at Katherine's insistence she drank a little cognac.

"I'm quite all right," she said. "I promise you, I'm only tired. It's been a long night."

"You look exhausted," Katherine said. "Finish that, it'll restore you a little. Marie-Jeanne, bring Madame a rug for her knees!"

A little later, James Macdonald and Jean and her husband came upstairs; Anne's father-in-law came over to the sofa where she was wrapped up and, bending down, he kissed her.

"A most wonderful evening, a superb success! You will be the toast of the court after tonight; I heard someone say the King was delighted." Anne smiled at him; her control was weakening now, surrounded by the loving solicitude of her relations she felt the tears rising and, in the middle of the smile, her mouth began to tremble.

"Don't you think we should put Anne to bed and leave this till the morning?" Sir James asked his wife. Katherine shook her head. "No, it must be done now. Otherwise she may weaken; I'm not being harsh, my love. This is for Anne's own good. If her mother were here, she would insist upon it. I must insist in her place."

"What do you mean, Mme. Mama?" Anne asked.

Jean came over and put her arms round her. "We managed to have a family conference tonight, while the last guests were leaving," she explained. "Mama, you'd better tell Anne; I don't think she'll listen to me."

"After what my son did tonight, I think she'd be well advised to listen to anyone," Katherine spoke firmly. "We proposed this marriage, we forced Charles into it by threats, and I'm afraid we influenced your uncle to influence you. He will agree that now it is entirely our affair. Anne, after what Charles did tonight in front of the whole court, you have got to separate from him. Officially! You have no alternative!"

For some moments there was silence, the will of the older woman seemed to fill the room; as if to confirm what she had said, her husband reached out and took her hand. "We will support you," Sir James said. "We will support the petition in the courts and I will use my influence with the King. You cannot be subjected to this kind of treatment, and I know perfectly well there's no use appealing to my son. He is beyond decency."

"He always was," Jean interposed fiercely. "There's not a single human feeling in him."

"They're all right, you know, Anne." For the first time the Comte de Mallot spoke; he had very kind brown eyes and Anne suddenly thought how wise their expression was and how compassionate. In a flash of instinct she knew that he was well aware of Jean's one desperate indiscretion.

"You cannot ignore what happened tonight. If you do, you will become a laughing stock. Society is very cruel, my dear. It saw your humiliation, in many ways it sympathised, probably because your husband is a foreigner and very much disliked. But it will have no pity for you if you show weakness now. You have nothing to gain by forgiving him and everything to lose."

"Paul is right," Katherine said quickly.

"Think what this means. If he ever came to you again, would you receive him? Would you submit, after tonight?"

Anne raised her head.

"No," she answered. "I don't think I will ever speak to him again. I would rather he had killed me than humiliate me with that woman."

"I'm glad to hear you say it." Katherine came over and embraced her. Anne thought suddenly that they were all overflowing with tenderness towards her because she was agreeing to break up her marriage. She had a hysterical impulse to laugh and cry at the same time. Instead she said wearily: "The marriage is finished. I know that."

She looked from one to the other of them and at last the tears began to flow, silently, down her pale face. "I believed that in his way he loved me a little," she said. "When I saw him here tonight, I was sure of it; I was sure that he was cruel over Francis O'Neil because he was jealous. But I was wrong. His pride was hurt; nothing had touched his heart. Nothing I do will ever touch it. So he punished me with that woman, humiliating me before the world. If he had loved me, he'd have taken me up here and broken every bone in my body if he had suspected anything. But when he brought that woman here and made me speak to her . . . I knew then what a fool I'd been. I'll do as you advise. I shall separate from him."

"Thank God." Katherine kissed her. "Sir James will see him tomorrow and tell him he is forbidden to enter this house or molest you in any way; if he does so, his own father will lodge a complaint against him. The best possible thing would be for him to go to Scotland and not return. After all," she added bitterly, "the whole marriage was proposed to make that possible. Thanks to your settlement, our estates are saved. Oh, my poor Anne, can you ever forgive us?"

"Of course she can," Jean said quickly. "Just so long as she never forgives him." She bent very close to Anne and whispered. "You need a change. Go down to Metz!"

"I'm tired," Anne said. "I beg of you, excuse me now. I'll do exactly what you think I should. And I'd be very grateful to you, M. Papa, if you will see him" — her voice faltered — "and make sure he doesn't come near me . . . I don't think I could bear it."

"You can be sure of that," Sir James promised. "Come, Katherine, and let Anne go to bed now. Jean, you will come back later today when she is rested?"

"I shall stay here, if Anne wants me," Jean said. "But I'll talk about that later on. Good night, my poor sister. God bless you. And think over what I've suggested, it might be exactly what you need."

When they had left and she was at last in bed, tucked in by Marie-Jeanne, the curtains drawn to shut out the daylight, Anne lay very still. She was no longer able to cry; she felt unspeakably empty, almost as if she had been drugged and the pain which she knew was raging in her had not come through. It was all over. The poor fantasy that he cared for her, the hopes she had bred out of his selfish lust and brutal pride were dissipated like smoke. He had never loved her; he had abused her and neglected her and then tortured her by moments of happiness, like the evening at the Trianon when they saw the Molière comedy and he had come back to her later that night. He had used her too, casually, as if she were a possession, and because she loved him so, she had submitted. She had spent a fortune trying to compete in the fashionable world which was naturally alien to her, abjuring the simple life she loved at Charantaise, all in the attempt to win him from the woman who had looked into her face with dark, triumphant eyes that night, holding tightly to her lover's arm. And while he lived openly with his mistress, she had sent away the fine and honourable man who loved her, a man a thousand

223

times more worthy than Charles Macdonald could ever be.

"Go down to Metz." Jean's words came back to her in the dark room, and she repeated them aloud. Abandon the hopeless quest for the love of her husband, and find what consolation she could with Francis O'Neil. It was not a temptation; it was a decision, made with the coldness that comes from absolute despair when only pride is left. It would take a little time to close up the hôtel; she felt a sense of loathing for the great house. Once that was done and she had obtained permission to retire from Versailles, she would take Jean's advice and go to Francis. There was nothing left for her but that. At last she fell asleep, and when she woke, it was late afternoon and her pillows were quite wet with tears.

Three days later the signs of the great ball had all been cleared away and the reception rooms were being closed up once more, the furniture and pictures stacked away and shrouded in dust sheets. Some of the staff had been dismissed and Anne was already supervising the removal of her clothes and valuables. She had written, begging the King's permission to retire for a time from Versailles; she gave her health as the excuse. She received permission to absent herself from His

Majesty's presence by messenger.

Now, nothing prevented her from making the final arrangements to shut up the hôtel and go to Metz. Nothing but her own disinclination and the letter to Francis which she had not yet written. There was no reason to delay it now. She had only to go to her writing table and begin; a short note, avoiding explanations, just telling him that she had changed her mind and was coming to him after all. She could imagine his joy; she could imagine the scene when they met and how he would run forward and take her in his arms. She could imagine further still to the moment when she became his mistress. It would be different from the night Charles had come drunk into her room and taken her virginity with such violence. Francis would be gentle, tender. The thought of it made her feel oddly light-headed, as if it were all a dream and would never become reality.

Anne put the writing paper away and got up. She decided to write that evening; she was tired out and the room was suddenly stiflingly hot. As she went to open the window, her legs began to tremble; waves of heat flowed over her to be followed immediately by a sense of being icy cold. She made a last effort to get to the window, but the floor slid from under her as if the whole house were a ship rolling at sea. She fell unconscious to the floor and that was how Marie-Jeanne found her. a few minutes later.

"My dear madame." The doctor smiled down at Anne. "All you need is a little rest in bed. Stay where you are for today and make up your mind that from now onwards, you must take care of yourself."

He shook his head and made a little noise between his teeth. Anne remembered the old doctor at Charantaise doing exactly the same thing when he came to see her as a child.

"Two months gone with child, madame, and you suspected nothing? *Tiens, tiens* . . . no riding, a light diet, and regular bleeding, that's all you need. You are a very healthy woman. All should go quite smoothly. I will call again in three days' time. And my congratulations to Monsieur your husband! Your servant, madame."

Marie-Jeanne opened the door for him and they almost knocked down the servant who was cleaning the handles and escutcheons outside it.

"What do you think you are doing?" Marie-Jeanne snapped at her. Of all the household, this girl irritated her the most; she seemed to be forever hanging round Madame's apartments and the maid knew very well that her mistress did not like the girl. She had spoken once about dismissing her and then, unfortunately, had forgotten. Marie-Jeanne gave her a push. "Get out of the way, idiot that you are. I'm forever falling over you! Pardon, M. le docteur, I will show you out!"

As they went down the passage, the spy heard him say clearly: "I have reassured Madame, but with a first child, one never knows. She must take care — it would be a pity to lose it. . . ." They turned the corner and the rest was lost. The girl put her dusters back into her pocket. So Madame was pregnant! That would be news for the baroness. She hurried downstairs to compose a message and find someone willing to carry it for her to Versailles on the next trip.

# Chapter 6

The evening reception in the Oeil de Boeuf was as crowded as usual; the warm weather increased the discomfort of those who had spent all day hurrying from one part of the palace to another, and following the tireless King's hunt for the whole afternoon. Everyone was hot and ill-tempered and the plight of the women in their heavy headdresses and enormous, swaying gowns was pitiful. Even the prettiest were scarlet-faced and limp. The Baroness de Vitale, usually so cool and elegant, was fighting her way through the press of people, her face drawn and white with fatigue.

"The Comte de Tallieu," she demanded, again and again, "have you seen him?" At last someone obliged her; the comte was in a corner by one of the enormous windows, all of which were tightly closed against the dangers of fresh air. Louise saw him leaning against the wall, fanning himself wearily and talking to the Duchesse de Luynes. He saw Louise coming, without appearing to take his eyes off the illustrious lady to whom he was speaking, and he noted her extreme pallor and the shadows under her eyes and decided they had nothing to do with the foul atmosphere and the hot weather. Louise, as he often spitefully remarked, had the constitution of a horse and the energy of a man. Something was wrong. She endured a few moments of agony while the duchess, ignoring her existence, continued to talk to De Tallieu and finish her assault on a mutual friend's reputation. The duchess enjoyed the sinister creature's company in much the same way as she was amused by a pair of grotesquely deformed little pages. Both were perverted by Nature, both possessed intelligence of a high degree. Their innate malice made them the best companions in the world when one was bored.

"Ah," the comte said at last. "My dear Louise; how disarranged you look! Isn't this place infernal? I don't know why one puts up with it, year after year." And he sighed and fanned himself.

"I must speak to you," Louise said. "I've been looking for you since this afternoon when that damned hunt was finished. Something terrible has happened. Can't we go out into the corridors; it's impossible to speak a word here without being overheard!"

Together they pushed their way through the

crowds, edging along the side of the salon until they reached the doors; there still remained the Salles de Venus and de Diane which were as crowded as the Salon Oeil de Boeuf itself.

At last they were in the corridors, and there were recesses there where it was possible to speak in private; by the great marble Ambassadors' Staircase there were places more private still, covered by curtains and furnished with a couch for the convenience of lovers who needed a half hour or so alone. There had even been instances of rape carried out in these niches. As its devotees said, everything one needed in the world to be amused was at Versailles.

"Now," De Tallieu said. "Speak out, my dear, and tell me what has chased the roses from your charming cheeks." He giggled.

Louise held out a creased and dirty piece of paper. "This came this afternoon," she said.

The comte unrolled it with distaste; he was fanatically clean in his person and caused much amusement by frequent washing of his hands and regular bathings of his whole body, which as everyone knew was extremely dangerous to the health.

"Ill-spelt and ill-written, but I think I can make it out," he said. "Mme. Macdonald is in an interesting condition." He gave an exaggerated shudder. "It may revolt me, my dear, but I fail to see why you're distressed. You have the husband safe now, they've separated and the word is it will reach the courts. What do you care if she's as swollen up as a balloon or not? I suppose it's the mercenary's bastard?"

"No," Louise said slowly. "It isn't. She was never his mistress. Charles believed that and he's no fool. This child is his."

The reptilian eyes glittered at her.

"How can that be," he said softly. "If he took no notice of her, as you so often told me?"

"I lied," she said fiercely. "I didn't want you to know; I knew how you'd sneer at me. He used to visit her here. He told me. When I objected, he laughed in my face and said he liked variety. As for possessing him now —" She turned her back to him; she had begun to tear her handkerchief to shreds. "He's like a tiger since she left him. He's so difficult, so quarrelsome and cruel. I don't know how I bear it."

One thing she still kept back; no one should ever know that often when they came together now, Charles threw her off and would not touch her.

"He isn't happy, then?" De Tallieu enquired.

"No," she admitted, "he isn't. His family

have all disowned him. His father threatened him with the Bastille if he molested his wife again. I should be more patient." She was desperately trying to calm herself and recover the composure that had deserted her completely when she received that note.

"He will settle down with me eventually," she went on. "I know that. Everything would have been all right between us — if this hadn't happened!"

"And now it has," the comte said. "Tell me the truth, Louise, or I won't lift a finger to help you. No lies now, I warn you. What will this news mean to him?"

"It'll bring him back to her," she said. She turned to face him once again, her eyes blazing in her ashen face. "You want the truth, my friend? Then you shall have it. He loves her. He doesn't realise it yet himself, but I know that he does. He's lost her now, you see, and he never really meant to let her go. If he discovers this, nothing will keep him from getting her back. I told you once" — her voice was almost a whisper — "if I lose him, I shall die."

"Hmmm." The comte closed his fan with a sharp snap. As a boy, his tutor had made private reports to his parents that their son showed remarkable mathematical powers and a truly amazing quickness of mind which might well advance him in the service of the

King. Unfortunately, these gifts lay fallow, unsummoned except in the pursuit of a piece of feminine mischief or the necessity to extract money from his neglected estates. "You really need to get rid of her, don't you?" he said at last. "Before the happy news is conveyed to her husband."

"Yes." Louise swung around on him, grasping his sleeve. "Yes, that's what I want — to get rid of her! But how? I know she's leaving for her damned château, but that's not far enough away! What am I going to do?"

"Let go my sleeve, you're making horrible creases," he said, "and listen to me for a moment. I can tell you what you will have to do, but I haven't yet thought out how you're going to do it. You need Madame to disappear for ever, she and her child together, isn't that so?"

"Yes," Louise said. "For ever, where he can never find them."

"Then you must get a *lettre de cachet*."

The comte took out a little gold snuff box and inhaled a few grains. "From the King," he went on. "We must think of some favour to do him, some little kindness. . . . You dare not offer yourself, for fear that your dear friend the Du Barry might wreak her vengeance upon you, or rather that cur D'Aiguillon; he watches over her interests like a panther. It would have to be something else. Or someone else. . . ." As he talked, his mind was speeding ahead with a dozen alternatives, discarding one after the other. The woman opposite him had not said a word, only her lips formed the dreaded words — *lettre de cachet* — silently, as if they were too terrible to speak aloud. The *lettre de cachet*. The means of having her rival arrested in secret, taken in a closed coach to any fortress in France — no, not any fortress, the one fortress from which escape was impossible — the Bastille itself! The power to bury her alive in a cell, deprived of identity, without word from any living soul outside, abandoned, forgotten, her fate a secret which would never be divulged. She leant back and closed her eyes.

"Show me how to get it," she whispered. "That's all I ask. Show me how to get a *lettre de cachet* for her as soon as possible."

"Give me until tomorrow," the comte said. "I have an idea, but it needs thinking out; I don't want to spoil it." He turned and smiled at her. "What a diversion! Getting rid of that insufferable creature who had the ill manners not to ask me to her ball, perhaps even doing a little disservice to someone else whom I can think of — apart from being a kind friend to you, my dear . . . I feel like a guardian angel! Come to this place at ten tomorrow morning. I shall have something definite to propose to you by then. Now let us go back and speak no more about it. One word gets out and we are lost you know, and he will be back with the wife of his bosom. Keep your tongue still from now on, except to me."

At the entrance to the Oeil de Boeuf, he turned to her once more. "You are quite sure you have no scruples about this?" he whispered.

Louise gave him a look from blazing eyes. "Scruples? Don't be ridiculous!"

"That's what I thought," the comte said gaily. "You really are a wicked bitch, my dear." Then the crowd swallowed them and they disappeared into the salon.

The King had been suffering from one of his blackest fits of melancholy. His ill-humour lay over the court like a blight. He had yawned through the performance of the opera arranged by the dauphine Marie Antoinette and sat in gloomy silence during one of the Du Barry's most lascivious evening entertainments. Even the favourite's gay spirits were damped by his continuing refusal to be amused, and his ministers suffered from his indifference to the most pressing state affairs. Even hunting palled on him and this was a bad sign indeed. There were rumours that his daughters, the implacable Carmelite Louise in particular, were plaguing him to abandon his mistress and be reconciled with the Church. It was a situation that occurred every Easter when His Majesty was unable to receive the Sacraments because of his scandalous private life with the Du Barry, and every year it had been fraught with danger for her. Worse still, there were the times when he fell ill and her enemies crowded round his bedside, warning him of eternal damnation if he were to die in mortal sin. But now there was no religious problem and no deterioration of his health to account for the change in his relations with his mistress and his obstinate depression.

The court had been whispering for weeks that if a woman able to cure his melancholy was introduced to him, Du Barry would be sent into retirement. As the palace clocks struck ten the next morning, Louise was waiting in the niche in the long corridor by the Ambassadors' Staircase. She had not seen Charles the previous night; her maid Marie had returned with a message undelivered. She was unable to find him and no one knew where he had gone. Louise had spent the night, pacing her room in a fever of jealousy; only Marie's pleading restrained her from ordering her coach in the small hours and setting out for Paris to see if he had gone to the Hôtel de Bernard. The comte was a few minutes late and only her desperate need of him prevented Louise from berating him for keeping her waiting.

"We must be quick," he said, "or we shall be late for the royal Mass. I have thought it out very carefully and I am sure it can be done. Look over there, you see my little Gaston?"

Louise looked towards the young page boy who was the comte's latest acquisition, a handsome boy of fourteen dressed in his master's green and gold livery, his petulant face rouged and powdered like a young girl's.

"He is a treasure," De Tallieu murmured. "The best I have ever owned. I'm delighted with him. I have a special place where I purchase these little creatures, did you know that? No, well, I will tell you about it. There's a woman in the Quai d'Orée who has an establishment; not a very pleasant place perhaps, but stocked with the most interesting and — er — varied wares if one has the money to pay. That's where I found Gaston. I always go there. The Du Barry goes there too, and so do many others who have special needs. Now pay attention. The King is in a bad humour, yes? Before long, the charming comtesse will be on her way to the Quai d'Orée to find some little gift to cheer him up, some ornament for the Parc au Cerf. My plan is that you should go there first and make the purchase."

Louise gasped. "You mean find a girl for the King? You must be mad . . . how could I introduce her . . . ? It's impossible."

"Not at all." De Tallieu smiled. "I can arrange the details of the introduction. There are a number of people who would be glad to help if they thought it would harm the Du Barry. But you must choose the girl, my dear. You must go there and explain to the creature who owns the place that you have a special friend in mind; none of her ordinary little pock-marked whores will do. This must be a virgin, and worthy of her destiny. Mme. Grande-mère will understand. It will cost you a fortune, but I beseech you, do not haggle or she will palm you off with something that won't do at all."

"I have money," Louise said. "I can pay anything she asks."

"Good, good. Disguise yourself, of course. You have a great deal to do, my dear, and not much time. Go to the Quai d'Orée tonight and take a couple of strong fellows with you, armed in case of trouble. It's not a savoury part of the city."

"I know where it is — it's in the beggars' quarter, where every thief and prostitute and murderer in Paris lives," Louise said. "Won't you come with me? You'd know better who to choose."

"Ah no." The comte shook his head. "I will play my part here, and you must play yours. Besides, I have no idea what kind of woman appeals to men. I abhor the creatures myself."

"I'll go alone then," she said. "I'll buy one of these girls and keep her hidden. Then what must I do?"

"Give money to the lackeys you take with you and send them out of Paris. There must be no witnesses, no gossiping. I will arrange for you to bring the girl to the King's private cabinet tomorrow night. That much I promise you. If you have chosen wisely, you may ask for your *letter de cachet* before the morning, and I swear you'll get it. It's been done before at such an hour. No one will ever know. How you apply it and where you place Madame for safe-keeping, is up to you."

"I know where I'll send her," Louise whispered. "I've thought of nothing else all night. Why are you doing this?" she asked. "Not just to help me, surely?"

"I told you." He giggled his soft laugh. "Pure mischief. I'm bored and I get restless without some little intrigue to pass the time. I have a score to settle with Madame, remember? I told you she'd pay for snubbing me like that. And if I can help replace the dear Du Barry, I shall have grateful friends in the highest places. If your find is a success, she may stay on, who knows? One last word. Look for a girl with breeding and intelligence, if such a one exists. Otherwise, I suggest you insist on the bizarre. Come, it is late and we must go. The Quai d'Orée, and ask for Mme. Grand-mère. Such a clever name for an old procuress, don't you think?"

Charles had been to Paris that night, but not to see his wife. As a boy he had suffered from fits of restlessness that drove him out in search of trouble, in search of women as he grew older, even into picking drunken quarrels. It was a long time since the urge to lose himself in some debauch had attacked him as violently as it did that evening, and it hounded him as it had done his Scottish ancestors long ago, sending them out on cattle raids, burning and kidnapping and killing for the sheer pleasure of it.

A few friends went to the capital with him, the young Vicomte de Renouille — the companion of that fatal game in which he lost his money to De Charlot and the whole unhappy train of events began nearly a year before — and a captain of musketeers with more money than sense or morals. It was the vicomte's idea that they should visit a certain courtesan who kept a fine house near the Tuileries where rich young men were welcomed and provided with amusement. By two in the morning they had settled down to gamble; his friends were hilariously drunk, but Charles, with more wine and brandy in his stomach than any of them, was deadly sober and in an evil mood. Luck ran against him, and he pursued it savagely, losing with every hand. He already owed the mistress of the house a thousand louis, and the captain of musketeers five hundred more.

Mme. Boileau was a handsome woman in her thirties, who had advanced from common prostitution on the streets to the semi-respectable status of a kept woman, protected by several rich men of middle class. The house was the parting gift of the last of them and she was wealthy enough now to run her own establishment with a select clientele of young noblemen and officers and a choice of half a dozen girls. Madame had developed taste since her youth; there was nothing sordid or vulgar about her house. She catered with elegance and she charged accordingly, and in her own way she was not ill-natured.

"Come, M. Macdonald, you've lost enough for tonight," she said. It would never do to let the young fool run into debts he could not pay; it would give her place a bad name among his friends. "Leave the cards for tonight; they're not going to run in your favour. Come upstairs with me instead."

He looked up at her, hesitating for a moment. He knew the whores in the upper rooms; in his time he had sampled all of them. "You'll be paid, madame," he snarled, "no matter what I lose. De Renouille, deal another hand!"

The vicomte shook his head. "Too drunk, my dear Charles. Too drunk to play now. . . . Did you suggest a trip upstairs, madame? I think I can just make the most of it if we go now. . . . Poor Charles here is in a devilish state, aren't you, friend? His wife has left him and he's lost a fortune. . . . Come on, madame, see what you can do to cheer him up." He was half on his feet when Charles's fist caught him in the mouth; he fell backwards, upsetting the table, and lay, without moving, on his back. Madame put her hand on Charles's shoulder.

"He deserved that," she said quietly. "Come to my rooms, we'll leave the girls for tonight. That's not what you need."

"Tell me," he sneered, "what do I need then? What do you suggest . . . ?"

Madame's suggestion kept him until the dawn broke, and when he left her bed, the note for a thousand louis had been torn up,

242

and Madame lay sleeping peacefully, as handsome as one of Boucher's voluptuous goddesses, on her satin pillows. She was capable of such acts of generosity at times; it was worth the money to prove that she was still better at her art than the conceited strumpets she employed who were only half her age.

As the dawn came up over the city, Charles spurred his horse on the road to Versailles and as he rode, he cursed. He had never felt worse in his life. If he had met his wife along that road, he felt he would have killed her, and on his soul he could not understand why he should hate her so. It was not as if he had ever loved her for a moment.

"Madame, I beg you, let me send word to the Comtesse de Mallot. Let me send for Lady Macdonald!"

"No," Anne said. "No, Marie-Jeanne, I forbid you to tell anyone about this. The doctor says I'm perfectly well. It will be time enough to tell them when we're back at Charantaise. I couldn't bear to have them fussing over me. If anyone told my husband, I should never forgive them."

"But madame." The little maid's eyes opened wide. "He'll have to know!"

"I see no reason why he should," her mistress said. "That's all over now. The child is nothing to do with him."

She got up and walked away, repressing the tears that threatened. If Charles were told, he would imagine it a trick to get him back. She was done with making those attempts.

And now the matter was beyond her; her father-in-law had written to say he was consulting a lawyer to arrange a final settlement and begin the case for separation once they had the King's approval. This request must be delayed because the King's bad humour made him capricious where petitions were concerned. It struck her as doubly ironic that those cousins, who had been so anxious to arrange the match, were taking so much trouble to bring it to an end. And now she was content to let them. All her life Anne had been strong and independent; she had fought with tenacity and courage to win Charles's love, sacrificing pride and honour, and deeming both well lost. Until the night of that fatal ball her hopes had still run high, but those few words had crushed them finally.

"I don't think you know the Baroness de Vitale. Louise, my charming wife." Even when the words themselves had slipped into confusion, when she was an old woman and past looking for love, she would remember that dark face, so full of mockery and cruelty, and the light eyes gleaming down at her in triumph. It was all she could remember of him now. Pregnancy had sapped her strength; she was weak for the first time, weak and painfully vulnerable. If she could not have comfort, she shrank in horror from the thought of cruelty, and cruelty of the kind at which Charles was so expert. If he came near her, if she fell victim to his mockery, his callousness, she would be broken, and she knew it. The child must be kept secret; it would be all she had to live for, all that remained of the absolute ruin of her life.

"He's taken everything from me," she said suddenly. "If I have a son, he shan't grow up to be like him. He shan't take my child too. And he would, Marie-Jeanne, he would. I know that now. That would be his ultimate revenge on me for marrying him." She swung round. "No one is to know, you understand, no one in the world. In two more weeks we'll be at Charantaise and we'll be safe!"

"Thank God, madame," the maid said quickly. She waited a moment; the intimacy that had grown up between them was still new, and she blushed.

"Madame . . . what about Captain O'Neil . . . you said we would be going to Metz."

"That is no concern of yours," Anne answered, more sharply than she meant, and seeing the girl's flushed face, she instantly relented. "I didn't mean to snap at you, my child. I haven't forgotten the captain. Anyway, if I were going there, it would be no place for you." Marie-Jeanne curtsied and said no more.

The Quai d'Orée was a dark, winding street in the heart of the city; the houses leant across the narrow cobbled way until the rooftops seemed to touch. It was a place of darkness and stench, riddled with alleyways and passages like a stinking rat run, and Louise had been forced to abandon her coach some way back and go on foot, protected by the two armed lackeys. Both carried a torch in one hand and an iron-tipped cudgel in the other. Creatures, scarcely identifiable as human, watched them from the black doorways and the alley mouths, and scuttled away. Once a beggar approached them, horribly deformed in both legs, crawling along on rough crutches, whining and whimpering for alms, until the servants drove him off. The language that followed them down the dark street made Louise feel sick.

"We should turn back," the senior lackey said. "This is madness, madame. The place is crawling with cutthroats and thieves!"

"Hold your tongue," his mistress snapped. "This must be the house — there, where a lantern hangs outside the door."

De Tallieu had given her directions, and this must be the place. It was the only one that had a light; the light was only a tallow candle, guttering and spitting in its glass frame, and it swung to and fro in the cold wind blowing in from the Seine. She was covered from head to foot in a cloak and her face was hidden by a silk half mask. Most of Mme. Grandmère's clients came to her incognito. If she guessed their names, she had no proof and wanted none. Money was her only interest. Blackmail would have quickly ruined her trade and banished her to prison. Some of the most powerful people in the kingdom slipped into the house on the Quai d'Orée.

When the door was opened to Louise, the smell was almost worse than the stink of refuse in the streets. There was a scented pomander hidden in her muff and she raised it quickly to her face. A man in dirty rags led the way down a dank passage, lit here and there by more tallow candles, and finally showed her into a little room. The lackeys stayed outside the door. The room was furnished with a chair and a table and it was empty. The creature who had escorted her made a low bow. He had great thick arms and shoulders like a wrestler, and the black hair hung down almost to his eyes.

"Sit down, Highness, Mme. Grand-mère will be here in a moment."

A few moments later the door opened again and an extraordinary apparition came hobbling through it, supporting herself on a stick. It was impossible to guess the woman's age, or even to be sure it was a woman. The painted face, daubed with scarlet rouge, its sunken eyes outlined with black, was almost sexless; the mouth was a red slit, and it parted, showing gums and isolated teeth in a hideous travesty of a smile. On the head there was set a black wig, covered in shiny, black curls, with a mob cap on top of it. A black woollen shawl and a lace apron, now so dirty as to be part of the fusty dress she wore, completed the appearance of the infamous Mme. Grand-mère. Rumour had insisted once that she was actually a man; it was not so. The monster was indeed a female one. Too unbelievably ugly to sell herself, she had started early in life selling others and now she was undisputed mistress of the frightful trade in vice that flourished in the city.

Bastard children were sold to her; girls who ventured into Paris from the country without protection were often kidnapped and delivered to Mme. Grand-mère, where they were soon beaten and starved into submission and sent out onto the streets or loaned to clients

248

for a night or two. The children were the most profitable part of her trade; if they grew up to be pretty girls and handsome boys, she fed them and trained them with an eye to her special customers, such as the Comte de Tallieu. Those who proved impossible to sell into prostitution because they were ugly or defective were either murdered or brutally maimed and sold to the beggar fraternity, where they were put out to work the streets. The brute who had shown Louise to the room was one of Madame's little band of disciplinarians who kept the merchandise in order and tamed the spirits of the new recruits.

Many a noble lady or a well-off, middle-class matron who yielded to the temptation to put out her bastard child to fosterhood, actually gave it into the keeping of Mme. Grand-mère and never heard of it again. Madame dropped a curtsy to her new client; the darting black eyes noted the expensive stuff of her cloak and the ermine muff. In spite of the mask she was sure she had never seen her before, not even when parties of ladies and gentlemen visited her after an evening's entertainment when many were the worse for wine. It was easy to sell them anything then; non-virgins, boys who had been caught picking pockets on the streets. . . . This great lady, nervous and sniffing at her scented muff, had not entered Mme. Grand-mère's house before.

"I am honoured, Highness. What can I do for you?"

"I want a girl," Louise said. Her nerve was returning; she sensed a business woman in the monstrosity before her; if one forgot the surroundings, the stink and the horror of the creature herself, it would be possible to get out of her what she needed.

"Certainly madame. For yourself? I have some beautiful little girls if you prefer them very young — or a big strapping country lass, with muscles like a man. . . ."

"No, no!" Louise interrupted in disgust. "I don't want one of these creatures for myself. Listen a moment. I want a young girl, beautiful — untouched, you understand. Absolutely untouched."

Madame nodded. "For a man, then. I see. I see."

"For a man so important," Louise said slowly, "that I dare not think what may happen to me, and to you, Mme. Grand-mère, if he is disappointed. A man of sensibility and taste; a coarse girl, one who is clumsy or graceless would be useless. I want a young virgin, with some breeding in her, if that's possible — some charm. Ugh!" She shuddered. "It seems impossible that anything could exist here but the dregs. You had better let me see what you have."

"You underestimate me, madame," the old woman said softly. "My house may be humble but I have had the children of duchesses here before now. My boys and girls have gone to some of the greatest homes in France and none has disgraced their old grandmother. Come with me and you shall see. Pierre!" she yelled for the man who had been Louise's guide and he came out into the corridor, carrying a lamp.

They began a steep climb up some rickety stairs as dark as the inside of a well and on the first landing they stopped outside a door. Mme. Grand-mère found a bunch of keys in her skirts and opened the door with one of them. The room was in semi-darkness, a small rush light burned in one corner and it was furnished with nothing but heaps of straw. There were empty food bowls on the floor; it reminded Louise of a dog kennel.

"Come in," the old woman said. "Hold up the lamp, you idiot, so that the lady can see!" She stepped into the room and clapped her hands. "Stand up, my children, and come forward. One of you may be going to a new home! Look your best then, children, just as I have taught you!"

Slowly the light travelled over a line of faces; some were so young they had not reached their teens; it flashed into eyes of every colour — green, blue, black, brown — and over figures of every size and shape. Some delicate, too thin almost, some unmistakably voluptuous; others big-boned and country-bred. Skins that were fair under the dirt, skins that were swarthy; the light paused for a moment over a beautiful gipsy girl, her black hair curling over her bare shoulders, her black eyes spitting fire at them like a cat out of the gloom.

"There's a fine girl for you," madame remarked. "Look at that body; like a tigress she is too. . . . And none's put a hand on her! Does your gentleman like spirit?"

"No," Louise said. "I said breeding, charm . . . not a wild animal! She looks as if she'd knife us."

"When I first got her, a month ago, she might," the old woman chuckled. "But she's learnt better since. She's very tame now, aren't you, my little spitfire?"

The girl shrank back and animal terror distorted the lovely face. When madame inflicted a beating, it was worse than anything the inhuman brutes of men could do, and she was careful not to leave a mark on her merchandise. She had beaten the gipsy on the soles of her feet. The light travelled on. "Wait!" Louise said suddenly. "That one you passed! Show her again."

252

"Come forward," the old woman ordered, and slowly a girl stepped nearer to them and the lantern threw all its light upon her.

"How old are you?" Louise asked.

"I do not know, my lady." The voice was soft. "I was fifteen once but that was long ago."

"A year," Mme. Grand-mère said. "She was ill when she came to us, poor child. I nursed her myself."

There was no fear in the pale, exquisite face of the young girl; she looked at her monstrous gaoler with calm eyes, as if she were indifferent to her. It had never been necessary to hurt this one; she seemed to know instinctively that she was lost from the moment they brought her into the house, and she had never once resisted. She was dressed in a coarse, shapeless dress of homespun; it drooped off her shoulders and great rents showed her legs and the shape of one breast.

As if she sensed what was passing through Louise's mind, Mme. Grand-mère made a gesture. Mechanically, the girl slipped the dirty garment off.

"Well," she demanded after a moment. "Is this the one you want? You've made a good choice if it is, except for one thing."

"She's beautiful," Louise said slowly. "She has a face like a saint. What's wrong with her?"

"Lack of temperament," the old woman said. "I deal honestly, Highness, or not at all. If your gentleman wants a pretty doll with sawdust in her instead of spine, then that's the one to take. But don't say I didn't warn you first."

"Bring her downstairs," Louise said. "I want to see her again and I want to know something about her. What was this illness?"

"Fevers," the old woman said. They had begun the climb down again and once more they were in the bare reception room; Pierre kept the girl outside until they called for her. She looked into the masked face before her and winked.

"You have a good eye, Highness. You said you wanted breeding and you certainly chose it. That girl was brought to me a year ago, sick with fever; I paid for her too, ill though she was, when the foster mother told me who the real mother was. There's a certain marquise who lives near Lyons, a very handsome lady, very nobly born, and married. That brat was her one indiscretion. She put it out to foster parents as soon as it was born. Then, over the years the payments lapsed; the woman's husband was dead, she was burdened with this sickly girl and someone told her to bring her to me. I took her in and nursed her back to health; she'd been shamefully neglected, shamefully."

The black wig shook vigorously. "She's fair-skinned and blue-eyed like the marquise, according to the woman who looked after her. I've never had a moment's trouble with her. You saw how she obeyed? Good-tempered, submissive . . . if that's what you want, you have it. And a virgin, of course. They all are in that room."

"I should like to speak to her alone," Louise said firmly. Breeding, refinement, if possible; that was what the comte had advised her to look for, and there, like a pearl in a dung heap, she bad come upon this aristocrat's bastard with her delicate madonna face and perfect bodily form. Louise had an instinct for beauty; something glimmered under the dirt and the rags and she saw its fitful gleam by the lantern light, where before she had seen nothing but pretty faces and the ghastly impression of a child among the others.

"As Your Highness wishes. Pierre!" The hoarse voice rose in a yell. "Bring the girl in!"

A moment later Louise was alone with her. She felt no feeling of pity or even of human kinship with the silent girl in front of her. Too much was at stake to risk sentiment, and there was little inclination towards it in her nature. Everything depended on the success or failure of this piece of goods, for as such

255

she regarded her. She examined her as she would have done a prize mare.

"Smile!" The girl did so, showing perfect teeth.

"Turn round!" She moved well; her bare feet were small, and though the hands were rough and reddened, the wrists were delicate. Louise lifted a strand of the fair hair. A bath and some proper clothes would transform the girl into a dazzling blond beauty.

"They say you're spiritless, is that true?" The dark-blue eyes were wary. "I am whatever you want me to be; so long as you buy me, my lady, and I can get out of here."

"I thought you weren't such a fool as you pretended," Louise said. "You can make yourself agreeable to a gentleman? A great noble, powerful and exalted . . . you will take trouble to please him?"

"I have been taught a little," the girl answered, "by her outside. Your gentleman won't complain about me."

"No," Louise said thoughtfully, "I don't believe he will." On an impulse of curiosity she turned to her once more. "You have no objection to your fate; no rebellion? You accept it quite calmly?"

"My lady" — the eyes were strangely alive now — "I know who my mother was and who I am. But there's no sense in resisting against hopeless odds; I saw what was done to that gipsy girl and others. I've learnt to obey because I had no choice. Once get me out of here and I shan't be a prostitute for long. May I ask a question?"

"Hurry," Louise answered. By God, she said to herself, how fortune smiled on me when I picked her. There's brain here and ambition and no little skill, I'll swear. When she knows it's the King . . . she might unseat the Du Barry herself in the end.

"Shall I belong to you?" the girl asked her. "Or to this gentleman?"

"To the gentleman," Louise told her. "And what you make of your chances after that are up to you! Go and call that old harridan."

"Now," Mme. Grand-mère said. "You have decided on her; we must come down to the price!"

"How much?"

"Fifteen hundred louis!" The sunken black eyes watched the eyes of the woman through the mask; they told her nothing. Fifteen hundred louis was a ridiculous sum in the old woman's opinion for that pasty little aristocrat. She had only kept her for just such a chance as this, a special need, not easily satisfied. She blessed her own good sense and decided not to budge an inch when the client started bargaining. To her surprise the woman opposite

257

drew out a heavy bag from the folds of her cloak.

"You will find fifteen hundred here. Count it out."

It was the first time she had taken her hands out of the little muff; Mme. Grand-mère caught a glimpse of a curious ring on her right hand, two hearts made of a diamond and a ruby, surmounted by a stag's head in brilliants. It was a most unusual jewel. The old woman began counting out the coins. Better and better, the money was in gold. She put the rest back in the bag and gave it to Louise.

"Put a cloak on the girl. I will take her with me now."

A few moments later they were back in the inky street, Louise and her purchase muffled in a heavy-hooded wrap, the two lackeys on guard each side of them. When they reached the baroness' coach she gave the address of a lodging house in a respectable quarter of the city and they drove away at speed.

It was past midnight; the King had retired early after playing cards and his humour was not improved by losing. He seemed as much abstracted as bored; the watchers reported delightedly that he had not left his rooms to visit Mme. du Barry in her apartments on the first floor. Anxiety had driven the favourite to the wine bottle and she had gone to bed tipsy and near to tears, escorted by her friend the Duc d'Aiguillon and her niece the Vicomtesse du Barry; she was quite unsteady on her feet.

Lights still burned in Louise's room; her maid Marie had been dismissed and forbidden to leave her closet. The baroness and the Comte de Tallieu were making a last inspection of their investment, and the investment turned round for them obediently at their command and curtsied as Louise had taught her.

"I really must congratulate you," the comte murmured. "In perfect taste. All of sixteen, you say."

He peered once more at the dainty figure in a dress of simple, blue silk, the neck and sleeves sewn with fine lace. She had been bathed and scented and her thick golden hair hung down her back, tied with a blue satin ribbon. The lovely face was as serene as an angel's; the pale skin was not touched by powder or rouge and a faint natural colour gave it radiance.

"Do you know who is waiting for you?" the comte asked softly. The girl shook her head.

"No, monseigneur. I know nothing."

"Excellent. You will find out soon enough."

"You think she'll do then?" Louise demanded.

She was trembling with impatience, her nerves so overstrung that she had boxed the minx's ears that evening while she was giving her the last instructions.

"Why are we waiting, suppose he goes to sleep?"

"He won't," the comte said. "He's been well primed, his curiosity is whetted. Put on your cloak, my child, and cover your face well. De Verier is waiting in the cabinet. Everything is arranged."

They went down the long corridors and down the stairs, passing a sleepy guard on duty who paid them no attention. Versailles was a place where women came and went at night and no one questioned them. At the door of the anteroom to the royal bedchamber, De Tallieu paused and knocked. The King's valet opened it and behind it they saw the King's confidant and *valet de chambre*, De Verier. He had served the King for years; he was Louis' friend as well as his servant and the guardian of all his amorous secrets. Du Barry herself had entered the King's room through the influence of De Verier.

The comte made Louise a sweeping bow. "Good luck," he murmured. "Now it is up to you and your charming protégée. I can do no more for either of you."

De Verier closed the anteroom door behind

them, and at a signal from Louise the girl took off her cloak. She was used to being inspected now and when the *valet de chambre* had taken stock of her, he turned to the baroness.

"Does she know where she is going, what is expected of her?" Louise made a gesture and took the girl aside. She gripped her arm so fiercely that she winced.

"Through that door is the King's bedroom. *He* is the gentleman you have to please! Succeed, and your fortune is made. Fail me, and by God I'll throw you at Mme. Grand-mère's feet and demand my money back. You know what that will mean for you!"

The blue eyes opened wide, but only for a moment, and the soft colour deepened to a rosy blush.

"The King! Don't worry, madame. I won't fail you — or myself!" Then she was gone and Louise settled down on a chair to wait.

The hours went by so slowly, and yet she could not even doze. She heard the palace clocks chime through the night and there was no movement, no opening of the inner door. It was five o'clock in the morning and she had drawn back the curtain to see the dark sky turning grey, when a hand touched her and she swung round. De Verier stood before her, his thin face creased by a smile.

"Congratulations, madame. His Majesty

sends you his thanks; he is enchanted, delighted. I have his authority to grant any favour you may ask."

She gave a sigh, a long, trembling sigh of pent-up nerves and rising triumph; for a moment her knees shook under her. "You know what I want," she whispered. "The comte told you?"

"He mentioned it," De Verier admitted. "A *lettre de cachet*, madame, with the name left blank? One moment, and I will prepare it."

He went through a door in the tapestry which was cleverly concealed and held it open for her. His little cabinet was beyond it, a small room well lit and comfortably furnished, with a writing table and bed in it. She waited silently while he sat down, waited interminably while he selected a quill and tested the ink and spread out a sheet of paper, and then she saw the signature already written at the bottom of it, a new signature with grains of sand still clinging to the final stroke beneath the name: Louis, le Roi. The King had signed. The valet spoke again.

"There, madame — there is your reward. Fill in the name yourself. I suggest that you go now. I will look after Mademoiselle. You will not be seeing her again."

"No one will know?" Louise whispered. "You will be discreet . . . ?"

"If I were not, madame, I'd hardly hold my post," he answered gently. "I have never seen you, I know nothing. No one will ever know. I think you'll find that paper contains all you want."

She found her way back down the long passages, already turning light with the dawn, and shut herself into her own room. Slowly, with her hands trembling, she unfolded the paper and began to read it.

"This is to authorise the arrest of" —a blank space followed — "and their confinement in the fortress of the Bastille in strictest secrecy, that confinement to continue in perpetuity unless the King's mercy intervenes." Then came Louis' signature. The *lettre de cachet* in those terms was a sentence of imprisonment for life. The King's mercy never intervened. He did not even wish to know against whom he had signed the order. The victim would never be seen or heard of again. Louise went to her table and sat down. She wrote very carefully and clearly in the empty space the name of Anne Macdonald, Marquise de Bernard.

"Under the circumstances I think that the time is right for you to go to Scotland," Sir James Macdonald said. "You can get leave from the War Ministry for a month's absence or more."

"If you insist," Charles said. He stretched out his legs in front of him and then crossed one over the other. He was bored and he was showing it in his casual slumping in the chair. He watched his father with hostile eyes.

"I suppose I shall have to visit the god-forsaken place sometime and it might as well be now."

"You'll not only have to visit it," Sir James snapped. "You'll live in it and look after your people, or by God, you'll answer to me!"

"I don't know why you didn't give the estates to Jean," Charles retorted. "She'd fit the role of Scottish landlord far and away better than I shall. Especially since I'm deprived of my wife's services. . . ." And he laughed.

"That's your own fault!" His father gestured angrily. "I'm glad you find it so amusing, I assure you, we don't. Anne is finished with you. There's no point in discussing why. You will restore Dundrenan and Clandara on your own: perhaps a little really hard work will improve you. Personally, I doubt it," he added.

"Oh, but I know Mother has faith in me," his son sneered. "Father — don't imagine I have any complaint about the sensation; I never wanted to marry her, I never cared a curse about her. She's been a damnable nuisance to me all along. And since you only wanted her for the money, and you've got that, I don't see why you're not as satisfied as I am. And by God, I feel as if a great weight had been lifted off me! I should hate you and Mother to feel you'd done me an ill turn by encouraging the separation," he added coolly.

"We weren't thinking of you," his father retorted. "Only of Anne. You're a scoundrel, you know." He looked quite calmly at his son, appraising him as if he were a stranger. "A heartless, ruthless scoundrel. One day you'll go too far and then someone will kill you. Not one of your family will shed a tear."

"Not even Mother?" Charles asked gently, and then burst out laughing. "Am I forbidden to speak to her still, by the way?"

"She has nothing more to say to you," his father said coldly. "I only speak to you because I must, and I've nothing more to say. Make your arrangements to go to Scotland. And remember one thing; I meant what I said if you try and molest your wife again!"

"Don't worry." Charles got up and stretched; he looked so like Sir James's dead brother that it made him shiver. "I wouldn't go within a mile of her."

When his father left him, he hesitated, and a mischievous impulse sent him in search of Louise. She had been restless and on edge the last few days, quite unlike herself; she was always so cool and poised. He was surprised at how much she irritated him, even when she was trying most to please; he had accepted so much about her before because she satisfied him in so many ways. Now he found himself becoming more and more critical, more and more cruel in their relationship.

He did not want to go to Scotland; he did not know what it was he wanted, and the only thing he could imagine that might pass the time was the sport of baiting Louise with the news of his departure. He had never loved her; in the old days when they were lovers, he used to tell her so, if she became demanding or when they quarrelled, now he remarked on his absence of feeling for her at every opportunity. It pleased him to see her flush and turn away as if he had struck her, and he knew that in a sense he had; that pleased him too. When he made love to her he was deliberately selfish and abrupt, and often when it was over he felt irritable and dissatisfied. Desire between them was still hot and urgent, but a new element was creeping in that he could not understand. Even when she pleased him, he resented it. Boredom nagged at him sometimes; not only boredom but the infuriating suspicion that in some hidden way she had won a victory over him, and victory was something Charles had never permitted any woman.

When he told her he was leaving, she showed no regret; he could almost have sworn that the fleeting look in her eyes was akin to relief. He twisted the dagger a little to see if the wound would bleed.

"I may be gone for months."

"Oh no, you won't." She had come up and put her arms around his neck, standing very close to him in the way that always brought him into her arms, except that now he didn't feel like holding her.

"You'll be back as soon as you can get a passage. I know you, my love. You'll be dying of boredom in Scotland within a week."

It was the truth, and he knew it. He pulled her arms away and pushed her back.

"And when I do come back, how do you know it will be to you?" The dark eyes flashed at him and for the first time in weeks she laughed. There *was* a victory, there was something which gave her secret confidence and strength too, the strength to bear with his moods and his calculated cruelty. He caught her arms and held them so tightly that he hurt her.

"How do you know?" he demanded. "What makes you so damned sure?"

"Because there won't be anyone else left for you but me," she said, and that was all he got from her before he left Versailles at the end of the week.

He left France on the morning tide at Calais on a ship bound for Leith, and from Leith the journey was arranged to take him to the Highlands, to the ravaged lands of his forefathers. The ship was full of exiles; going home at last, he kept aloof from them; and to many bearing the name of Fraser and Mackintosh and Ogilvy, his own name was enough. They left the sullen, arrogant Macdonald to himself.

He returned to Scotland a stranger, born and brought up in France with a foreign accent when he spoke to his own people, and no man he knew to greet him. He made the slow journey to Dundrenan first, and on a wild day, with the winds blowing hard across the heather and the summer rain whipping his face, he stood in the blackened ruins of his family's great house, and from there set out on horseback for the ride to all that remained of Clandara, the gutted remains of the great Fraser stronghold, put to fire and sword by his father thirty years before.

It was not one month but three before Charles Macdonald set sail again for France.

# Chapter 7

In one more week the Hôtel de Bernard would be completely closed up; in four more days Anne herself would be on the road to Charantaise. She leant back in her coach and closed her eyes; she was tired and it was very late. She was on her way back from a music recital given by the Vicomte de Louvrier and his wife, both good friends she had made at Versailles.

It had surprised her how many people had taken the trouble to seek her out when they heard of her separation from Charles. Anne had expected to be isolated once it was known that she was leaving Versailles and closing up her house. It was only too easy to be the most popular hostess at Versailles for one night, and completely forgotten the next, once it was known that she had decided to retire to her estates. But she had friends in unexpected places; not all those at Versailles were without heart or completely ruled by what was fashionable.

The De Louvriers had been extremely kind to her, and she had enjoyed the recital as much as she was able to enjoy anything. They owned a charming little château a few miles outside the palace boundaries; it had been a hunting box belonging to the vicomte's grandfather, and it had been converted into the intimate small country house which was one of the delights of rural France. Etiquette was lax; Anne had taken her second coach and only one postillion as escort, and dressed simply with few jewels. It was almost like being at Charantaise once more, now that the unhappy struggle for her husband was at an end. As the coach jogged slowly down the country road towards Paris, she fell asleep.

The road wound onward through a small wood; the night was very dark. A lone fox barked somewhere among the trees. Four men were waiting by the roadside where the wood enclosed the roadway, their horses were tethered back in the woods. A fifth sat on the box of a small, plain carriage built like a square box and painted black; the windows were covered with an iron grille and thick blinds were pulled down over them.

"They should be coming into the wood now," one said.

"Silence!" his companion snapped. "How

the devil can I hear if you keep gabbling!"

He was the senior of the officials of the Paris police, the protectors and enforcers of the King's law in the city, and there was little enough to choose between most of them and the ruffians they were empowered to arrest and hang for breaking those laws. He went up to the silent man on the coach box.

"When we've made the arrest," he said, "I'll go inside with the prisoner and you'll drive. Wait, I think I hear them coming now!" He took out a pistol and primed it and ran back to the others waiting by the road's edge. "Take up your places!"

The first shot woke Anne; the next moment she was thrown to the floor of the coach. There was a frightful scream and the sound of men shouting; for a moment she stayed on her knees, half dazed. Her first thought was that the coach had been attacked by thieves, and when the door was wrenched open, she shrank back. When a man caught hold of her she screamed and tried to strike at him, but her assailant was quick and powerful. He dragged her out onto the road and held her, one hand over her mouth. There seemed to be men everywhere, and then she saw the postillion lying on the ground beside the coach, sprawled on his back, his face blackened with blood, his dead mouth gaping.

One of the men came up to her.

"Do not struggle, madame, or it will be the worse for you. We are His Majesty's officers. Gaston, let her speak! Are you Mme. Macdonald, Marquise de Bernard?"

"I am," she gasped. "Let go of me, you wretch! How dare you. . . ."

The words were choked back as her captor stifled them with his hand. The man who had spoken nodded to the one who held her. "This is the woman," he said. "Bind and gag her and put her in the coach."

One wild scream more rang out through the dark wood, waking the sleeping birds, but the men were experts and within a few minutes Anne lay on the ground, her wrists and ankles bound, a cloth tied over her mouth. The officer in charge pointed at the small, shuttered coach and Anne was lifted up and laid inside it on the seat. She had ceased struggling now; she lay back helpless and half fainting for what seemed hours, while the men dragged the bodies of her dead coachman and postillion clear and threw them into her own coach which was then driven on ahead, the horses bounding along the road.

The instructions were — no witnesses, no sign of any struggle. The bodies would be disposed of, the marquise's carriage sold with all signs of ownership removed. The price was one of the senior officer's rewards. He had done well out of this business, and he was in a good humour when he climbed into the dark coach and slammed the door. The woman who had given him the order for arrest had made a further contribution. There was a purse with twenty louis d'or in his pocket to make sure he showed his prisoner no mercy and left no trace of her behind.

There was a tiny candle in the coach wall, shielded by glass. He lit it and turned to his prisoner, pulling her upright on the seat. The blue eyes stared back at him, mute with terror and appeal. He was used to that look; he had seen it for twenty years on human faces and he had never once felt pity. It was a rare thing to seize a noblewoman, though he had carried off gentlemen before with the *lettre de cachet*. He wondered idly what this one had done, as he tested her bonds and made sure she could not move. Offended the King, annoyed the Du Barry . . . she had as much hope of mercy then, as any of the wretched prostitutes and thieves he had dragged off to prison or the gallows. He tilted her head up and looked at her again; her eyes were closed. She must have fainted. He pulled the hood of her cloak over her head until it hid her face, wedged her unconscious body in the corner, and then banged on the coach wall. It began to move forward, slowly at first and then with increasing speed as they left the wood and came out onto the Paris road. He blew out the candle and settled back to doze for the rest of the journey.

The Governor of the Bastille was in bed when the turnkey summoned him. He got up, yawning and grumbling and dressed hurriedly. What a devilish hour to be woken up; his bed was warm and he shivered as he pulled on his coat.

"The devil," he muttered again. "The devil, why must they bring someone in at this hour! Riveau, you damned fool, why didn't you leave it till morning?"

"The police say it's an important prisoner, sir. They want to deliver him personally."

"Bah!" He began the long walk from his apartments down the icy stone corridors to the prison section, the turnkey holding a torch ahead of him. "Some cutthroat I suppose . . . wait till I see him!"

He came into the small room where prisoners were received and entered in the fortress records, and their personal belongings and all means of identification taken away from them. Two officers of the city police were waiting for him, holding a shrouded figure between them. He knew one of them and he turned to him irritably.

"Bertrand! What the devil is the meaning of this? Getting me out of bed at this hour? Who have you brought here?"

The governor was surprised to see the prisoner was a woman; when Bertrand left her, the cloak fell open a little and he saw the flash of diamonds. He took the paper from him and read it carefully.

"Ah," he said at last. "Ah yes, I see. You did quite right to wake me. My apologies. I will see that she is entered. Turnkey, take hold of the prisoner. You can go now, gentlemen. She will be safe with us."

He had not seen a *lettre de cachet* for a woman for nearly two years, and the name on this one made him whistle to himself. De Bernard! One of the richest women in France. He'd heard of a magnificent ball given in Paris only a few weeks ago . . . she must have made the King himself her enemy. He gave an order, and the turnkey bent and unfastened her feet; he was an old man with a creased, monkey face and small eyes and he had been a gaoler at the Bastille for forty years. His breath stank of stale wine and garlic and Anne flattened herself as he touched her, releasing her wrists; they were stiff and swollen and her mouth ached from the gag.

"You've been giving trouble," the old man muttered close to her face. "You'll learn not to do that here. . . . Stay silent now till the governor speaks, or I'll put this back." He held up the cloth that had been used as a gag. Women were a nuisance, especially this class; they screamed and raved and wheedled and made the turnkey's life a misery unless he began by being firm. There had been one, once a long time ago — very highborn and with the temper of a wildcat, who flew at the previous governor and boxed his ears when she first came. There wasn't much temper left in this one; he dragged a stool up and pointed to it. "Sit there," he said. "And be still."

For most of the drive Anne had been unconscious; when she came to her senses the coach had stopped at one of the city gates; the door was open a little and she could see the watch peering inside with his lantern. She had not been able to move or make a sound and the hood covered her face. She heard the man beside her whisper something, and the watch answered and slammed the door shut again and the coach went on. This was no ordinary kidnapping as she had at first suspected. The dark little prison coach told her that, so did the behaviour of her guard. He had not touched her or looked at her or tried to rob her. This was official, this horror. Now, sitting on the stool in the bare room, she watched the sleepy man in his rumpled clothes, writing something in a book and referring again to the paper the man who brought her had given him. When he had finished, he looked up.

"Do you know where you are, madame?"

"No," she could hardly whisper.

"Then I will tell you. I will explain to you your position and hope that for your own sake you will be sensible. You are in the Bastille, Mme. Macdonald. You have been sent here by order of His Majesty, to be held incognito for as long as this order remains unrevoked. I do not know what crime you have committed — none is stated here."

"What is that thing?" she said at last, although she knew and still could not believe it.

"A *letter de cachet*," the governor answered. "I think you know what that means, madame? Very well. You must give me your jewels and any money you carry. You must also understand this. I am the governor of this place; what I say is obeyed by everyone. Princes of the blood have learnt that arrogance and rebellion are not permitted here. I used your name just now. It is the last time it will be spoken while you're inside these walls. You are not to mention it to anyone. You are not to try and communicate with anyone. You will receive no letters, no visitors, and there is no use your waiting for either. No one knows you are here and no one will ever know. Is this quite clear? Any breaking of the rules will bring punishment, madame. I advise you not to nurse vain hopes. You will only suffer if you are obstinate. I have given you a number, and by that number you will be known from now on — 713. The name written here does not exist. It is forgotten. You are forgotten. Accept that, and you will find it easier. Now hand me your jewels, if you please."

Very slowly she took off her necklace, unfastened her earrings, and slipped a fine sapphire off her finger. She dropped them into the turnkey's dirty hand. She touched her dress where the lace fell in folds at her neck and felt something hard under the folds. Some sad impulse of sentiment had made her wear the O'Neil's little pin. It was so small that the lace hid it completely.

"I have nothing else. Any money I carried was in my coach."

"Very well. Turnkey, take Mme. 713 to the west tower, to the cell of that number."

"One moment." Anne turned to him wildly as the gaoler caught her arm. "I beg you, I have no clothes, no necessities. Isn't there a woman here you could send to me?"

"There are no ladies in waiting here," the governor said coldly. "You will have to wait on yourself. It won't be difficult, we have no social life to speak of; when your clothes are worn out, we may think of finding you some more. Take her away!"

It was not uncommon for guests to stay the night with the De Louvriers if the hour was very late. No one of the skeleton staff left at the hôtel remarked on Anne's absence the next morning. But by the evening, when there was still no sign of her, Marie-Jeanne went to the comptroller. He was busy seeing that the last of madame's boxes were corded up before the journey to Charantaise. He had never liked her maid; he thought she gave herself airs because of her intimacy with her mistress. He told her curtly that the coming and going of the marquise was no concern of theirs. She would return in her own time. He suggested that Marie-Jeanne mind her own business and get on with packing what was left of Madame's personal belongings.

The day passed and another followed, and now the maid decided that she must take matters beyond the comptroller, but without authority she did not know to whom she should go. The Comtesse de Mallot had left Paris two weeks ago to return to her estates; the Chevalier Macdonald and his wife were at Versailles. In desperation, Marie-Jeanne ordered one of Madame's small coaches, used by her servants when the household travelled, and set out for the palace.

"She said nothing of any change of plan?" Lady Katherine demanded. "How do you know she is not still with the Vicomtesse de Louvrier?"

"Madame, I know nothing but what I've told you," the girl insisted. "My mistress set out for the evening and that was three days ago. She never came back and she sent no word to the hôtel. I don't know what can have happened to her!"

"Does she usually stay away without telling you?" Katherine asked. It seemed unlike her daughter-in-law to stay with friends so close to the date of leaving for Charantaise, but Anne had not been herself in the last few weeks; when they saw her she seemed nervous and withdrawn from them as if she wished to be alone. She looked at the anxious girl standing in front of her and smiled.

"You were quite right to come to me," she said. "I'm sure we shall find a simple explanation for Madame's absence. You had better go back to Paris and carry out her instructions. Leave for Charantaise with the other servants as arranged. I will send a messenger to the Vicomtesse de Louvrier and see if my daughter-in-law is still there. She may even have gone to Charantaise ahead of you; I know how anxious she was to get back."

When the girl had gone, Katherine wrote a note to the De Louvriers, asking if Anne were still with them or if they knew where she had gone. By the time she saw Sir James that evening at the King's reception she had the answer. Anne had left their house three days ago, and as far as they knew she was returning straight to Paris.

"I can't understand it," Katherine said. "Where has she gone? The maid swore she said nothing about going on to Charantaise or making any other visit. She had no luggage with her! Everyone expected her at the hôtel. James, I'm worried! Something must be wrong!"

"Come, my darling, what could possibly have happened to her? If she ware robbed on the road, she'd have got back and reported it . . . the De Louvriers said she was in excellent spirits, didn't they?" He took her arm and pressed it. After thirty years he could not bear to see his wife distressed, "Do you know what I think? I think she suddenly decided to go on to Charantaise. It's on the way. Why don't you do this, and set your mind at rest — go to Charantaise yourself. I promise you, you'll find Anne there."

"I'll go," Katherine said. "I shan't rest till I know where she is; that servant frightened me. I'll send you a message as soon as I get there. I'll go tomorrow morning!"

"By the way," Sir James said, "have you noticed the change in the King? I've never seen him in such a good mood."

"Or the Du Barry in such a bad one," his wife whispered. "Look at her there; she's so downcast she can hardly speak."

"There *is* a new mistress," he said. "I heard for certain from the Duc d'Aiguillon this morning. He and Du Barry's faction are in despair. No one has seen her yet; she's kept in rooms somewhere near the King's with a guard to protect her. He visits her every night and leaves the Du Barry entirely alone. D'Aiguillon is beside himself. If the Du Barry is dismissed he will be ruined. They expect the new mistress to make her appearance openly at any time now."

"I wonder who she is," Katherine said. For the moment she had forgotten Anne. So many people's fortunes depended on those of the Du Barry. If she fell, the unknown woman and her sponsors would set about removing her friends from their positions. The Duc d'Aiguillon had every reason to be anxious. He was likely to be sent to prison.

"No one has any idea," Sir James replied.

"I've heard the most fantastic rumours; someone said yesterday it was a former convent inmate, sent by the Princess Louise to wean her father away from the Du Barry. Other people say she's a protégée brought in by the Duc de Richelieu. But we'll soon know, my love. Luckily we've never been on too close terms with the Du Barry, so we shan't suffer if she's sent away."

"She looks so wretched," Katherine said. "Whatever she is, she's not malicious. God knows what her successor may be like, remembering the Pompadour. I feel really sorry for her!"

He smiled tenderly down at his wife. Proud and unpredictable, it was impossible to tell which way her feelings would be moved. She was genuinely sorry for the vulgar, lowborn mistress in her humiliation and her fear, but she had nothing but condemnation for her own son's failings. In spite of his love for his wife and his unwavering loyalty to her, he sometimes felt a twinge of conscience for his unregenerate son. It was such a pity that Charles had never loved his cousin Anne, or been able to make a sensible compromise when he was married. She could have been with him now, in Scotland, helping to rebuild the life that he and Katherine had left in ruins behind them. Instead, his son was alone in the Highlands and his wife had gone off on her own. They would never be reconciled, and he felt absolutely sure in those few seconds that Charles Macdonald would go completely to the devil if they weren't.

"Go down to Charantaise first thing tomorrow," he said suddenly. "If Anne's not there, send for me. I'll come at once."

The window in Cell 713 was so small and set high up in the wall that it gave only the meanest impression of light; the cell itself was small and very damp. The stone walls sweated, and the bed of foul straw was dank and smelling. Anne had lain on it without moving for so long that the miserable light faded and turned into pitch darkness as the twenty-four hours passed since her arrest. The turnkey had come to her once, bringing a bowl of soup and some bread that he left beside her without speaking. She turned her head away and would not touch the food.

It seemed for that first dreadful day as if she were suspended; nature was being merciful, it eased her slowly through the shock, sparing her the violent hysterics that tore so many prisoners' sanity to shreds as the full realisation of their fate was borne upon them. Anne did not shriek or cry; she lay and trembled as if she had fever, and there was a time during the long night when she lay in total darkness and her mind shuddered as helplessly as her body and came very close to giving way. But the dawn came, and with it came a terrible flood of tears; her weeping rose and fell in the tiny room where so many had suffered and raved and mouldered away until they died, and at last she was on her feet and the shock of what had happened began to pass.

She went to the door; it was small and so low that the turnkey himself had had to stoop when he had brought her through it and pushed her inside. It was thick and black with age and strong as the oak from which it was made. She turned then to the walls; when she touched them, her hands were wet. Near the miserable slit of window she could see marks upon the stone, initials and dates carved crudely by long-forgotten hands. Beside one initial there were two dates, and when she made them out she cried out and shrank away. J.D. 1725-1762. Thirty-seven years. For thirty-seven years a human being had existed in that place, eating and sleeping and losing count of time, with nothing of their life on record but that uneven carving in the stone. The last date was very hard to read; the hand that had cut it was unsteady, whether through age or mortal sickness, only God knew. But for thirty-seven years its owner had been held a prisoner in the same cell. No one had ever got J.D. out; 1762 was the year of J.D.'s death.

Anne sank down on her knees and slowly she began to pray for help, and as she prayed, hope reawoke in her.

"No one knows you are here . . . no one will ever know." The governor's words hummed through her head all through that first nightmare when she lay prone and trembling like an animal in a trap. "No one will ever know." Now her hope grew; she had relations, an uncle in Charantaise who was expecting her, she was rich and important and well known. She could not simply disappear like some poor waif of the Paris streets. . . . There would be questions, enquiries, a scandal. There must be all those things at this very moment, because she had not returned to her hôtel. . . . She got up and smoothed the stained and crumpled dress and went to the door and knocked. After a long time, in which she scraped her knuckles on the wood, the foul old man turned the lock and drew back the outside bolts.

"What do you want?" he said.

"Something to eat," Anne said gently. "And some means of washing myself. I have nothing but the clothes I'm wearing."

"Can you pay?" the old man demanded.

"You know everything was taken from me,"

she answered. There was no use in abusing the creature or making demands. She would not be there for very long. "I beg you," she went on. "See what you can do to help me. I shan't forget you when I am released."

For a moment the turnkey was tempted to laugh in her face and slam the door, but he paused. She was dishevelled and, in spite of the calm words, her voice was trembling; she was nearer hysteria than she knew, but he knew it from long experience. And she was a pleasant one, this prisoner; she bore him no resentment, hadn't even yelled and screamed and disturbed his rest the previous night as so many of them did. He was old and his duties tired him out; if a prisoner robbed him of his sleep, he bore him a long, silent grudge.

"Eh," he said, "so you'll remember me when you're released. . . . There's food over there, I left it with you; what's wrong with that?"

"It is stale and cold," Anne said. She was unaware of it but she had begun to cry; the tears were running steadily down her face.

"Give it here," he grumbled. "I'll heat it for you. There's no more till this evening; one issue a day and short at that for the first month; after that, things may improve for you. If you're good and I speak well of you! Washing water and clothes are impossible." He took the bowl of greasy soup and backed out through the low door. "After a month," he repeated. By his own lights he had been very kind. When he came back his prisoner was sitting on her heap of straw, still crying as if she would never stop, and yet without the noise which so offended him and made the other prisoners in adjoining cells so restless. One was a woman who had been there for ten years; she was the discarded mistress of a minister whom she had later tried to blackmail. She was quite mad by now and sat in her cell humming and sewing bits of cloth which the fortress doctor had allowed her. Other sounds set her off and she had once yelled through the door for a whole day until the turnkey came in and chained her to the wall until she stopped.

"Here's the soup. I'll bring more tonight before the light goes."

She took it from him and her shaking hands spilled some of it. She was very young, the old man thought, somewhere in the twenties, and she must be very pretty in the normal way. Long years ago when he was young, a pretty woman could make life almost comfortable by being nice to him from time to time. He was too old for anything now but food and sleep and a little warmth.

"They can't keep me here," Anne whispered. "It's impossible. I've never offended the King . . . it's a mistake, a mad mistake, meant for someone else. You know they can't keep me here! Don't you know who I am!"

"Now, now!" The turnkey snapped at her suddenly. "You heard the governor. I don't remember the name he gave you then, but I know your number and that's all I'll ever know. Don't tell me who you are, 713, I'm not supposed to know. It's forbidden, d'you hear? The penalty for saying it is right above your head!"

He pulled the door behind him and she heard the grind of bolts and the creak of the key. She looked above her, and saw iron rings stapled into the wall and two wrist irons hanging from them. She edged very slowly along the straw until she could not see them any more, and with the same quivering care she tried to drink the soup. The first mouthful turned her stomach and she sank back, sick and almost fainting. Until that moment, Anne had quite forgotten she was carrying a child.

"Jean, thank God you've come!" Katherine opened her arms to her daughter. Sir James and the old Comte de Bernard were in the library at Charantaise; they had been there for a week, summoned urgently by Katherine after her arrival and they had been waiting for Jean to join them.

"I came at once, the moment I got your letter," Jean said.

"There is no word of Anne," her father said. "I started enquiries in Paris as soon as your mother let me know she was not here. No one has seen or heard of her since she left the De Louvriers three weeks ago!"

"I've been demented with worry," Katherine said. "In God's name, Jean, where is she?"

Jean took off her gloves and unloosened the strings of her cloak. She looked round her at the anxious faces and, to their astonishment, she smiled. "You mean it hasn't occurred to any of you where she is?" she asked.

"No, child, for the love of God why should it? She has simply disappeared!" Sir James almost shouted at her. "If you know something, why didn't you let us know?"

"I thought you'd guess," his daughter answered. "I'm sorry, Papa and Mama, and you, poor Cousin de Bernard. I'm afraid this is all my fault. That's why I came at once, to explain and put your minds at ease. You remember the night of that ball, you remember how we all sat round the poor girl planning to relieve her of my odious brother? I gave her a piece of advice that night. I think you'll find she's

290

taken it, that's all."

"And the advice you gave?" the old comte asked. His voice shook and he seemed to have aged ten years since his niece had disappeared.

Jean came and put her arms around him.

"I told Anne to go to Metz," she said. "I told her to go to Captain O'Neil and forget that she had ever seen my brother. I am certain that is where she is now. And I'm glad! Did you question her maid, Marie-Jeanne — did you think of suggesting it?"

"How could we?" her mother said. "It never occurred to us."

"Is it likely," the old comte asked them, "would she run off with the man like that, without a word . . . ?"

"Send for the girl," Sir James said. "Question her again."

"Now," Katherine spoke calmly to Marie-Jeanne, "now, you are not to be afraid, no one is blaming you; you did everything you thought right when you came to me and said Madame had vanished. . . . Think carefully and keep nothing back."

The maid shook her head, "Madame, I swear I've told you everything. Something has happened to her!" She put her hands to her mouth and began to cry.

"Did the marquise ever mention Captain O'Neil to you before she went out that night?"

Sir James said. "Think, girl, and control yourself. Did she ever mention going away to Metz?"

Marie-Jeanne wiped her eyes on her sleeve and nodded. "Yes, monsieur, she did. I asked her if she had forgotten the captain. Forgive me, I knew how much he loved Madame, everyone in the hôtel knew it. . . ."

"And what did she say?" Jean stepped close to her. "Think back, what was her answer?"

"She told me to mind my own business," the girl whispered. "She said she hadn't forgotten him; she said if she were going there, it was no place for me. . . ."

"You see!" Jean turned in triumph to her parents. "Exactly as I said! She must have made a rendezvous with O'Neil and gone straight on with him, instead of going back to Paris. . . . If I had any doubt, it was because she hadn't taken the girl with her. Now that's explained. There's no need to look any further."

"Oh, thank God!"

Jean had never seen her mother lose the iron control that kept her always in command of herself and the situation. Now Katherine sank into a chair as if she were exhausted. "I've had such nightmares . . . I had begun to imagine she'd been kidnapped, murdered. . . . And all the time she is at Metz!"

"Yes," Jean said quietly, "she is; and at this moment she's probably happy for the first time since you married her to my brother. If you have any love for her, or any conscience for that marriage, you'll leave them alone."

"A lover," the old comte said. "I never thought of that, I never dreamed. . . ."

"How much patience did you think she had?" Jean demanded. "What did you think she'd do — come back here and live out the rest of her life alone? Mama, you told her yourself often enough to look elsewhere and let Charles go to the devil; we all let her know she had our full approval. She took my advice, that's all. As I said, I only hope you'll leave her and the O'Neil in peace; let them work out their own way."

"But the scandal," Anne's uncle objected. "To go and join a serving soldier, a common mercenary. I can't believe it! I don't think the child would ever lower herself like that. . . ."

"You're an old man, my dear Pierre," Katherine said gently. "You're thinking of Anne as if she were a child still, not a woman who's been married to my son for a whole year! Jean's right. I was mad not to think of it immediately. She is at Metz; of course she is!"

"And I think we might all take her advice to her maid," Sir James said at last. "I think it's time we began minding our own business.

When she needs us, Anne will send word." He turned to the maid. "There's no need to fret about your mistress; we're satisfied that she's quite safe."

"But her clothes, monsieur, her jewels . . . she took nothing with her. . . ."

"She'll send for them soon, you'll see," Jean said. "You can go now. Put the servants' minds at rest and try to stop them gossiping. There's nothing to worry about. You know the captain; Madame is in good hands."

"The story will come out," Sir James said. "I've approached too many people, trying to find her. . . ."

"She has gone away to rest," his wife interrupted. "That will be enough. When we drop the matter, everyone else will forget it."

And everyone did, just as she had said they would. There was a little gossip at Versailles when the Macdonalds returned and gave their explanation, and the same conclusion was reached by others as had at once occurred to Jean de Mallot. The marquise had got rid of her husband and, as soon as he had left the country, she'd gone off to join her lover. The enquiries were dropped; the great hôtel was barred and shuttered, and Charantaise remained without a mistress, occupied only by the old comte who withdrew more into himself than usual without his niece to keep him company.

The weeks passed into months; the very name of Anne Macdonald was forgotten in the excitement of the bitter struggle for power between Mme. du Barry and her faction, and the King's new favourite, who was still at Versailles, and whom no one but a chosen few had ever seen.

Only one person remained in doubt and it was a doubt that grew as the time slipped away, and she went to the clothes cupboard and saw her mistress' dresses hanging unclaimed and her jewels still in their casket, and no word came.

Marie-Jeanne went about her duties and was silent; there was no one to listen to her fears. At the end of three long months she was convinced of one thing, and all her peasant obstinacy fastened on it and refused to be shaken. Her mistress had not gone to Metz.

It was the middle of November when she went to the comte with an excuse that one of the marquise's Paris staff was sick and had written, begging her to come. They were close friends, she said — if he would just permit her to go to the city for a week and comfort her. The next morning she set off on foot for the nearest posting station and began the long, jolting journey in the crowded coach with her savings hidden in a purse round her neck. She did not know what she was going to do in Paris or to whom she could go with her suspicions, but the secret of her mistress' disappearance would never be found at Charantaise. The key to it was in the city, somewhere on the road Anne had taken that night, never to be seen again, but first she had to satisfy herself that she was right and the chevalier and his wife and the comtesse and all the great ones were mistaken. At Paris she spent the night in a wretched inn, afraid to sleep for fear of being robbed, and the next morning Marie-Jeanne, who had never left Charantaise till she went with her mistress to Versailles, set out for the Royal Army Headquarters at Metz.

"I've missed you so much," Louise whispered.

She put her arms round Charles and drew him down and kissed him with an avidity that was surprising since they had made love to each other for most of the night. He took hold of her clinging hands and pulled them off; he felt suddenly as if they were creepers entwining around him, fastening tighter and tighter until he suffocated.

He had been back at Versailles for two days and Louise had followed him like a shadow, impervious to snubs and mockery, driven by more than sexual hunger though this was hot and fierce as fire. He had returned, and she pursued him desperately, refusing to admit that he had changed in those three weary months while she waited without a letter from him or a word of news. He was oddly impatient as if he were already bored after the few days at Versailles. When he spoke, his speech was full of names and words she did not understand, barbaric places in his desolate country laid waste by wars, but they were real to him now as they had never been before. She had lost him a little and she knew it, and what she wanted from him most of all was something he would never give her, a tender word, a whisper that he loved her. He moved away from her and lay on his back. He was tired and irritable; he did not want to lie and sleep beside her as they used to do.

"Did you miss me?" she asked. "Or am I being vain . . . I suppose you know I have been faithful to you all these months!"

"I neither know, nor care, my dear," he said. "Leave me alone, woman, for God's sake! I've satisfied you, isn't that enough?"

She sat up, her black hair falling around her bare shoulders.

"You found someone else in Scotland!" she accused. "You go away for three months, you never write to me, and then you come back and treat me as if I were a common whore, good enough for your bed but nothing else!"

"Hasn't it ever occurred to you that that's what you are," Charles remarked. "A whore; highly skilled, I'll admit, and taking a deal of pleasure in it, but a whore just the same!" He looked at her and laughed. "I never touched a woman in the Highlands. Not because I was thinking of you, my dear Louise, but because I had better things to do. Also, our women aren't so generous with their favours. They're surprisingly chaste. You wouldn't understand that, of course." He yawned and threw back the sheets.

She sprang up, facing him, maddened beyond caution by the indifference on his face and the hostility in his eyes. "Chaste, like your wife, I suppose," she flashed at him, unable to control herself. "Or haven't you heard that she's gone to join her lover!" She used the lie, now generally accepted everywhere, as if it were a weapon, and like a weapon she saw it had struck home.

He began to dress, his back turned to her, and for a moment she stood there, half covered by her hair, until the soft, drawling voice remarked: "You're better in the dark, you know. In a year or so, you'll run to fat."

She came at him, one hand upraised, spitting

like a wildcat at the insult. He parried her easily and gave her a single blow across the face that sent her reeling backwards. She fell back against the bed, crouching beside it, one hand to her flaming cheek.

"You unspeakable swine." She choked. "Get out!"

"I'm just about to," he said. He fastened his coat and went to the door. "I'm growing very tired of you," he said quietly. "I shan't come here again."

As the door closed behind him he heard a shrill cry, like that of a hurt animal, and the cry followed him through the door.

"Charles, Charles, come back, come back. . . ."

He walked on down the corridor until he could no longer hear it. That afternoon he went to see his father and report that he had ordered work to begin on what was left of Dundrenan House and appointed a factor from one of the Macdonald clan to supervise the work and tell him how it was progressing. Throughout the interview father and son talked long and soberly of Scotland, and there was something very like harmony between them. But no mention was made of Anne or of the judicial separation which she was seeking when he left France. Sir James was careful not to bring it up; her own misconduct had made such a plea impossible and he had let the petition drop.

When Charles left him, he was whistling softly to himself; he had his duties at the War Ministry to put in order and to pay his respects to His Majesty the King. That should take about two weeks. He was in no hurry before then; when his affairs were settled, it would be time enough to go to Metz and pay his wife and Captain O'Neil an unexpected visit.

"I knew you'd do it," the Duc d'Aiguillon put his arm round Mme. du Barry and kissed her warmly on the cheek. "I knew you'd get him back!"

"It's more than *I* knew," the favourite retorted. Her pretty face was thinner and there were lines of sleeplessness and worry round her eyes. "I had to go on my knees — you never saw such a scene! I wept, I begged, I took a leaf out of the Pompadour's book and sent him a message I was dying. Nothing less would have brought him, I can tell you! I ought to join the Comédie Française after that little performance!"

"You're a genius," the duc said fondly. "I never doubted you."

"Oh yes, you did," she retorted. "You were as sick as a cat, you were so worried. By God, so was I! And when I'd got him alone, I wouldn't tell you what I had to do to make him stay the night. . . . But I know what he likes — the old devil! He was grovelling round me by the time I'd finished. I said to myself — 'Now, you cunning little bitch, whoever you are, now try and match that!' He's finished with her now, that's definite. He told me so."

"You're sure?" the duc demanded. "He promised to dismiss her?"

"On his word of honour." The Du Barry sniggered. "Oh, he tried to pretend it had never been serious, said she was a poor, pathetic child who touched his sympathy. I nearly vomited! There were tears in his eyes when he talked about her. . . . I tell you, we've never been in such danger! I saw De Verier this morning, hanging about the King's apartments, watching me like a cornered rat. *He'll* have to go; the dirty skunk held the candle for them, I'll be bound!"

"He'll go," the duc said fiercely. "He and everyone else connected with the business. When does this girl leave? And where's he sending her?"

"Not to the Parc au Cerf," Du Barry rejoined. "He didn't even suggest putting her there. He wants to do something for her, he said. Of course I was all generosity and understanding. Anything to get her out of Versailles! He's placing her in a convent at Lyons, run by the Carmelites. Can you believe it? He wants to turn her into a respectable young lady, with a dowry . . . it's all arranged, Louis, down to the last detail. It only shows," she added, "how damned dangerous this one must have been. Normally there's not a drop of sentiment in his soul."

"What else did he say about her?" the duc asked. "We've got to know everything, my dear, to make quite sure this doesn't happen again! Where did she come from, who introduced her . . . ? That's what we've got to find out!"

"He said she was wellborn." Du Barry began walking up and down; the nightmare she had been through had sharpened her wits and unsheathed her claws; she paced the room like a cat. It had taken all her experience and cunning to win back the King and even though her domination over him was re-established as strongly as ever she had not yet recovered from the fright he'd given her.

"He said she was an innocent child who had been terribly ill-used, abandoned by her parents. That means she's a bastard, some *grande dame's* throw-off. . . . I have a suspicion, only a suspicion, where she might have come from. . . . One or two things he said make me think. . . . make an enquiry, Louis. When we know where she came from, we'll be on the way to finding out who introduced her. And you can deal with them!"

"Leave it to me," the duc said. He, too, could hardly believe that the chasm had suddenly closed under his feet.

By the evening the news of Du Barry's triumph would be all over the court, and the sycophants would come running back to pay her compliments and prove that they had always been her loyal supporters. But among them, somewhere at Versailles, there lurked the man or woman and the faction which they represented, who had so nearly dragged the Du Barry off her unofficial throne. The girl herself was unimportant; her hold on the King was broken. His shallow sentiment towards her did no harm. She would be no danger in her convent. She must have been a very clever minx; the duc gave her that. All of the King's previous fancies had found their way to the luxurious little brothel in the Parc au Cerf, where His Majesty shared his treasures with a few convivial friends and the Du Barry added to the recruits. This one had done very well for herself.

"We'll go quietly," the duc said. "We'll show no animosity, all shall be peace and light. And at the same time, we'll work, you and I, and we'll find out who did this if we have to burrow under the foundations of Versailles!"

★ ★ ★

"I've brought the surgeon to see you," the turnkey said. He stepped aside and another, younger man stooped through the low door and came to the woman lying on the straw. Her eyes opened and she watched him kneel beside her, setting up a lantern; they were bright with fever and her hands picked at the straw and the folds of her dress.

"How long has she been like this?" the surgeon asked over his shoulder; he laid his hand on the damp forehead and then felt for her pulse.

"Two days," the turnkey muttered. "I had to get permission from the governor to call you and he wouldn't believe me. Said she was shamming. I told him it was Bastille fever. . . ."

"You were right," the surgeon said. "Go out, I want to examine her properly. Don't be alarmed," he said gently to the sick girl. "I am the prison surgeon. Let me see if I can help you."

Anne opened her lips; they were parched and cracked with fever and her clothes hung on her painfully thin body.

"I want some water," she whispered. He nodded; he was a humane man and though experience had hardened him to his male prisoners, some of whom he attended after torture, the sufferings of the women always distressed him and he did what he could to relieve them. After a few moments he looked up into the peaked face, its skin surface shining with sweat.

"In God's name," he muttered, "in God's name, how did you get in here . . . does anyone know you're pregnant?"

"No one," Anne whispered. "I don't even know how far I am; I've lost all count of time."

"About six months I'd say, perhaps more. Lie still a little longer; I haven't finished yet."

He talked on as he examined her; the shape of her swollen body stood out grotesquely against her wasted limbs. As he touched her, she shivered with the deadly prison fever, product of foul drainage and bad drinking water.

"Have you any idea why you're here, or who sent you?" he asked.

"I think I know now who sent me."

She turned her head away and the tears began to roll down her cheeks. After hope died, the terrible suspicion grew in her mind and took hold, strong as a poisonous weed. The King was not her enemy, nor the Du Barry; she had only one person in the world who hated her, only one enemy capable of sending her to such a fate. Charles had obtained the *lettre de cachet;* Charles had sent her to a living grave so he could have his mistress and enjoy her money in peace. There was no other explanation. Once she believed that, she began to lose the will to live. He was clever, he would see no trace of what had happened was left behind her in the world outside. He would know how to silence even those who loved her who might ask questions. That's why there was no news, no visit from the governor telling her she was released. Her husband had sent her to the Bastille; he would see she never got out of it alive. When she fell ill with fever and the horrors of vomiting and shivering began, she lay back on her soiled bed and prayed that God would let her die. She wanted the child she bore to die; each time she felt the little movements, growing stronger every week, she touched the place and begged that God would take the tiny life and never let it draw a breath in the surroundings where its mother lay.

"My husband sent me here," she said, and the surgeon started. She put out her hand and touched him. "Don't give me medicine," she whispered. "I beg of you, have pity. Leave me alone and let me die. Let us both die."

He did not answer her, because he had heard that plea made many times before, and obstinately true to his profession, he had ignored it and tried to keep the unwanted flame alive.

There was no point in telling the poor woman that as far as he could see, her wish would be granted in spite of whatever he could do.

"Now listen," he said gently. "You mustn't despair. This child makes you a special case. I'm going to see the governor now and tell him. And I'm going to get you a trestle bed and some clean linen if I have to bring them in myself. I'll get my wife to come and see you. She's a kind woman, and she'll help you." As he went to the door and banged for the turnkey to open it, Anne heard him swearing to himself.

The governor was not responsive to appeals for extra food or what he angrily termed "luxuries" for his prisoners. He listened in stony silence while the surgeon told him that No. 713 was desperately ill with the fever and likely to die. When he added tersely that she was also six months pregnant, the governor lost his temper.

"What in God's name am I supposed to do?" he shouted. "I'm sent these people in any condition, not a word of explanation, not a warning, and then they die on me and I have that on the record, as if they weren't well treated! This is the last straw . . . a damned aristocrat is brought in here with an order of the highest secrecy and you come and tell me she's pregnant and dying as if it were my fault!"

"It will be your fault," the surgeon snapped, "unless you let me do my best for her. Have you seen that cell and the conditions she's been living in for the past four months? It's not fit for a dog, let alone a woman in that state . . . I want a bed for her, and blankets, and permission for my wife to visit her, and clean clothes and decent food! I insist on it! Leave her as she is and you'll be guilty of murder!"

"Beds," the governor sneered. "Linen next, I suppose, and pillows? What do you think this is, a palace?"

"No," the surgeon said, "I think it's the worst prison in the whole of France. The shame of it cries out to Heaven. There's not a system in the world that would have a woman brought in here and shut up without trial and left to die. . . . That's what I think of the Bastille and that's what I think of the government that supports it. Put that in your report when you record the woman's death!"

"That's treason," the governor yelled back; he felt better, having found someone with whom to quarrel. His position was intolerable; he hated it and yet he could not imagine himself doing anything else. He fought the surgeon at every step but he wouldn't have known how to keep his sanity without him.

"That's treason to the King!"

"To hell with the King," was the reply.

"And damned he'll be, for signing things like your 'order of the highest secrecy'. . . . It won't go on forever, I tell you that! The people will rise one day!"

"I'll report you," the governor threatened, enjoying himself thoroughly; they had been playing the same game for years. "You'll end up as a prisoner here yourself for this!"

"Do what you please." The surgeon understood the game and played it with increasing recklessness. "Just give me the bed and get that pesthole cleaned out. I'm going to try and save that woman's life, and keep her child. And by God, it's going to need a miracle!"

The Duc de Richelieu had arranged a firework display on the Ile Enchante; it was his personal welcome to Mme. du Barry on her return as undisputed favourite, and he estimated that the entertainment would cost him more than thirty thousand livres. But it was a small price to pay for assuring her that he was not responsible for the intrigue which had failed.

The unknown girl had left Versailles in a carriage with the blinds down, escorted by three of His Majesty's musketeers, one of whom reported that he had taken his passenger to an exclusive convent outside Lyons where the daughters of the aristocracy were educated and prepared for life in society. He also said that he had seen the lady as she alighted, and he assured his audience that she was as beautiful as an angel and appeared in the best of spirits. The King had been generous and the Du Barry was not vindictive; the abandoned bastard sold into the house on the Quai d'Orée had kept her promise to Louise; she had not remained a prostitute for long, and she had accepted her dismissal with a meekness that delighted the King; he dreaded women who made scenes. The brief bedroom candle was put out and the royal protégée settled down happily with the excellent nuns. When she left her convent three years later, the superior had arranged a place for her in the household of a rich and pious lady at Toulouse.

Twenty years later she returned to Paris to stand trial before the Revolutionary Committee of Public Safety, as the widow of a baron and the mother of two sons who had fled to fight with Austria against the Republic that had seized control of France and put its King, Louis XVI, and his Queen, Marie Antoinette, to death. The baroness died with great dignity as befitted an aristocrat of her station, unlike the terrified woman, shrieking for mercy, who was dragged out to perish on the guillotine for the crime of being the Comtesse du Barry, only forty-eight hours before.

But there were no shadows over Versailles that night; the Grand Canal was thronged with boats, the magnificent royal barge was illuminated like a fairy ship with lights in coloured lanterns and the King sat under the awning on the poop deck, with the Du Barry beside him, glittering in turquoise and silver lace, and in radiant spirits. She adored a firework display; at some of the grander set pieces she clapped her hands and laughed like a child. The King patted her hand and smiled contentedly. His conscience was at peace; there was no conflict to disturb him, and he felt he was fortunate indeed to possess the memory of his delicious little companion of the past weeks and to have exchanged her without fuss for the indispensable, enchanting Bacchante at his side.

A large diamond necklace glittered round her exquisite throat; when he remarked on it, she giggled mischievously. The fireworks from Richelieu, the diamonds from the chancellor, De Maupeou. . . . What gift did he intend to give her, to make amends for having strayed? The gift was in his cabinet at the palace, a diamond as large as a pigeon's egg, with the delicate shade of a budding pink rose. There was not another like it in the world.

He only smiled and whispered that she

would have to wait and see; it might be that he had thought of something. . . .

Louise and the Comte de Tallieu were seated side by side in one of the barges, watching the fizzing, glittering display shoot up like exploding stars into the cloudless evening sky. At each cascade there was a murmur and a hiss of wonder and excitement from the crowds upon the water and lining the canal banks. Rockets soared upwards and flashed out into a spray of multicoloured, blazing lights, enormous set pieces whirled and sparkled on their frames, and the smell of the powder drifted across the water. The scene was as light as if it were day.

"How much longer is this going on?" Louise whispered. She was cramped from sitting on the narrow bench; by the leaping light of the fireworks her lovely face was pinched and hard. She had not seen Charles since the morning he left her room, saying he would not return. She had not seen him and her desperate letters were unanswered. She did not sleep and she ate hardly anything, but she did not believe, because she could not, that he had really left her.

"Not much longer," the comte murmured. "Why aren't you enjoying it, my dear? It's very pretty!"

"You're not enjoying it either," she retorted. "You're on edge. What's wrong with you tonight?"

"Travelling makes me nervous," he said under his breath. "And I can see the time has come for me to travel. I'm going to pay a visit to my estates . . . I've neglected them too long."

"You're running away!" She turned to him fiercely. "Your part of the plot failed and now you're running off. What for? Does anyone suspect you; tell me, for God's sake, you're not alone in it, you know!"

"I know," he whispered. "Stop pinching my arm, you fool, people will notice."

"They might think you've changed your ways and gone to bed with me instead of those revolting boys," she flashed at him maliciously. The dark eyes glared murderously at her and she could have sworn that under the rouge he actually turned red.

"Be careful," he said softly. "Sweeten that bitter tongue or keep it still, unless you want me to start wagging mine a little. . . ."

"You daren't," she said. "We both know that. We're in each other's power, so don't let's quarrel. I'm overwrought these days; I apologise. Why are you leaving Versailles?"

"Because the word is that D'Aiguillon is taking a hand in the matter now; he's curious to know the means by which our little protégée was introduced. He's had the worst fright of his life and so has the Du Barry. They're not going to let it rest at getting rid of the girl. Once questions are asked, and they're bound to start with De Verier, it's safer to be out of the way. I'm not afraid, my dear; don't think that. You and I were small fish indeed in this particular pond. Much smaller than I ever let you know. Some of the greatest names in France involved themselves with His Majesty's sleeping habits, and we very nearly won. I don't think D'Aiguillon will discover anything; De Verier will keep quiet. The girl gave nothing away — she was clever, incidentally — angel face and innocent eyes . . . she kept that horrible old satyr on a string for weeks and got herself a pension and an honourable discharge. . . ." For a moment he giggled, but the darting eyes were anxious and the malicious smile vanished a second later.

"I'm going because I think that when they start upturning stones, it's wise not to be found hiding under one of them. If you take my advice, my dear, you'll plead sickness and do the same. A month or two in the country; it may nearly kill us, but it'll be healthier than the Du Barry's vengeance if she finds out what we did!"

"I can't leave now," Louise retorted. "Do you think I took that risk just to go off to the country as soon as Charles came back?"

"He isn't finished with you then?" the comte said softly. "The rumours have been going round, you know. . . ."

"We've had a quarrel," she answered. "We've had them before; it's nothing. He'll come back to me, he always does. Anyway, I wouldn't dream of leaving unless I can persuade him to come with me."

"That's unlikely; I heard he was very occupied at the Ministry. Curious how he's changed since he came back from Scotland. They tell me he's working quite hard now. He's anxious to go away again."

A brilliant fan-shaped exhibit flared on the bank of the île, shooting cascades of golden stars from its crimson perimeter, and there was a murmur of admiration and delight from all around them.

"That loutish Vicomte de Renouille is a friend of his, isn't he?" the comte went on.

Louise nodded, watching the fireworks. Letters were useless; she would have to dispense with the last of her pride and go to him herself and get him back. The decision gave her the first feeling of happiness she had experienced for weeks.

"*He* said to somebody the other day" — De Tallieu's voice was silky in her ear — "that Charles was planning a trip to Metz. Sh!, my dear, control yourself." He laid his finger to his lips and after a moment Louise turned back in her seat; her fan snapped in her hands with a sound that made De Tallieu jump, as if she had fired a tiny gun.

"I don't believe it," the words came out unevenly; he thought that she looked quite wild. "He's not going to look for her. You're just saying that to torture me." He smiled and shook his head. He had paid back that jibe about the page boys; he always paid his debts.

"He's going to kill the Irishman — that's all De Renouille said. I think it's true; it's in character. If I were you, Louise, my friend, I'd take a trip to the country. . . ."

"He'll never find out," Louise said. "He'll never find out where she is or what happened to her."

"No," the comte agreed. "That's one certainty. No one mentions a *lettre de cachet*. She is gone forever."

"Four months in that place" — Louise was almost speaking to herself — "and carrying a child . . . for all we know, she's probably dead."

"Quite probably," De Tallieu said. He leant back and applauded; the display was over, and as soon as the royal barge left its moorings, the whole fleet would begin sailing back behind it to Versailles.

At the end of the journey the crowd disembarked, slowly and awkwardly, the women almost losing balance in their heavy court dresses as they stepped ashore where their carriages were waiting. It would take nearly half an hour to reach Versailles from the point where the barges were moored. In the middle of the surging crowd, noisy and assertive in its race to get to the coaches and back to the palace, the comte turned to Louise, and made her a low, if slightly mocking, bow.

"This is as good a time as any to say farewell," he said. "I am leaving tomorrow — my estates can't wait another day without me. I'm sorry I can't persuade you to do likewise."

"I'm staying here," she said. "Where Charles is; he won't go to Metz — I'll see to that. Goodbye, my dear comte. Shall I write and tell you what is happening here?"

"Er — I think not," he smiled. "You'd only make me pine, and that would never do. I give myself a month or more . . . until then, most charming lady, *au revoir*. Meeting you," he murmured, "has been an *unforgettable* experience."

The next morning he had left Versailles. The same evening the Duc d'Aiguillon consulted a list his secretary had prepared for him during the past week. There were several names on it; the last and least illustrious was that of the Comte de Tallieu.

"Another rat is deserting, is he? — and a particularly nasty rat. We'll keep a note of you, my dear comte. Normally, wild horses wouldn't tear you from Versailles. You've had a hand in this affair. . . ."

# Chapter 8

The wife of the surgeon at the Bastille was called Marguerite; it was a name that did not suit her, denoting as it did, a bright and dainty flower, whereas from childhood Madame had been plump and mousy, with a placid nature and a kindly unimaginative soul. Only such a woman with such a temperament could have survived living in the fortress with her husband, as shut off from the diversions of the civilised world as if she herself were a prisoner. She had no children and the frustration had dried her into middle age while she was still in her thirties. Now, her nondescript hair was very grey and the round pleasing face was lined and colourless; she looked more tired than usual because she had been nursing the woman who was dying in the West Tower for two days and nights without sleep or rest.

The girl was sleeping now, almost lost beneath the blankets Marguerite's husband had provided for her, and laid to rest in a clean plank bed that was raised up from the straw that harboured fleas and dirt. While the fever burnt away her life, the six-month foetus stayed intact and visibly alive; placing her hand upon the swollen body, Mme. Marguerite marvelled at the resistance of nature. Not till the mother died would that separate soul give up its tenure; she shook her head and covered the girl up, and yawned.

It would not be long, her husband had said she would be gone by morning. Poor thing! Marguerite's motherly heart was touched by the youth and the helplessness of the sleeping girl; you could see the ruins of great beauty in the sallow face. In the worst extremities of that particularly revolting illness, she had remembered to thank her nurse and murmur apologies for the trouble she was causing. Many times during the long vigil, the older woman had wondered how her patient came to be in the Bastille, what frightful vengeance had pursued her and her helpless unborn child and sentenced them to such a fate. She was no criminal; nor would her infant be a bastard. The ravings of delirium told Marguerite a great deal about the dying girl; the pain and the reproaches flowed out of her at this unknown Charles, this inhuman monster whom her own husband said the girl had named as responsible for her arrest. She stirred and the tired eyes opened; for the first time the expression in them was quite lucid. It was often so when the end was near. Marguerite was glad; there was something she wanted to ask the girl before she died; it had troubled her conscience. When they had changed the ragged dress for a clean nightgown from her own wardrobe, she had felt something in the neck; she had the little sapphire pin which had been hidden there in her right-hand pocket now. She leant forward and smiled at Anne. "Would you like a drink of water?"

"No."

She had to bend very low to hear the whisper. Anne closed her eyes again. She wanted nothing except death, and death was very near. She would have stretched out her arms in welcome had she the strength left; she had no fear of her rescuer, only longing and impatience at his delay in coming.

"Don't go to sleep, dear." Marguerite touched her gently. "Open your eyes like a good girl; there's something I want to show you." Anne made the effort to please her. "This is your pin, isn't it? I found it in your old dress. . . ."

It was her pin; she had forgotten it completely. It winked at her with its small bright-blue eye in the light of Madame's lantern. Where had she got it . . . ? Her memory refused its office for a moment, and then a face came to her, handsome and gentle, with eyes the same colour as the stone in the pin. She felt his arms around her and his voice in her ear, and her own tears falling because she did not love him and was sending him away. Francis O'Neil.

"I love you, I've always loved you . . . come away with me to Metz."

She had refused him because she loved that other, and that refusal, and that misbegotten passion for a pitiless fiend had brought her to the cell in the West Tower and to the point of death. The baby stirred and she started at the movement in her womb. Time and sickness had erased so much; she had been conscious of nothing but pain and fever and agonising convulsions. Even before she fell ill there were times in the eternity of the days when she forgot her own identity. Now, the pin in the other woman's hand flashed at her like a tiny light. Poor, sad little jewel; the last gift of a ruined and tragic family to their son and that son's gift to her. Something wet travelled down her cheek; she was crying without knowing it. The woman bent over her again.

"Don't be distressed," she said quickly. "I didn't mean to upset you. Poor child, I didn't know what to do with it. I daren't leave it with you. . . ."

She could have kept it; the girl might well

have given it to her in gratitude. . . . But it would still be theft and she knew it.

"I'll have to give it to the governor," she said. "I wanted you to know I didn't keep it."

"No!" To her surprise the heavy eyes grew wild and Anne made a helpless movement to sit up, but then fell back; she was too weak to raise herself. "No," the quavering voice implored her from the bed, "don't give it to him. . . . I beg of you. It's my last wish. . . . Come closer."

Marguerite bent to within a few inches of her face. "I'm listening, child, speak slowly. I'll do what I can to help you. . . ."

"I know. You've been so kind." She hardly knew what she was saying, another voice filled her ears, a voice full of tenderness and prophecy — "If ever you need me, send it back and I promise I'll come to you. Even out of the grave. . . ."

Death, defeat, anonymous burial inside the walls of this hell upon earth; her spirit had reached out for all those things. Now, suddenly, she shrank away, making a physical movement of revulsion. Her child moved again. With a great effort she composed herself.

"I have nothing and no one in the world," she whispered, "but long ago someone who loved me gave me that. Send it back to him for me."

Marguerite nodded. "I will — but without any message. I can't say who it's from or where it came from . . . you know that, don't you?"

Anne nodded. "Just send it," she whispered. "Please send it; promise me. Captain Francis O'Neil, the Royal Army at Metz."

"I'll do it for you." The woman patted her shoulder. She wouldn't tell her husband. If she sent it anonymously to this captain, there could be no harm and she could keep her promise to the dying girl. A daughter of her own could have been just the prisoner's age.

"Captain O'Neil at Metz. I'll send it, I promise you."

Anne closed her eyes and smiled. When Francis got the pin, he'd know she was in danger. He would come back to Paris and begin to look for her. When she opened her eyes a moment later, it seemed as if some of the shadows in the room had gone.

"Please," she murmured. "Some water now. I'm thirsty."

An hour later Marguerite rapped on the cell door for the turnkey.

"Send for the surgeon."

"Ah! She's dead then?"

"No, she's sleeping. I think her breathing's deeper. He'd better look at her before I doze off."

"I don't know why you don't go to your

bed," the old man grumbled. "She won't last the night. I've seen strapping men die of it within the week."

He went off, grumbling to himself, down the passage. All this fuss over a miserable wisp of a sickly girl and an unborn brat. She'd be better off dead; there was that much pity left in the corner of his soul to wish that the busybodies would let her go in peace.

Two days later the surgeon made his report to the governor. Four prisoners had died, two of them from old age, a third after interrogation, and the fourth was a young man who had succumbed to damp and semi-starvation after a mere nine months' imprisonment. The prisoner in Cell 713 was better; he announced it with triumph and his old enemy glared across the room at him.

"She's been more trouble than the rest put together," the governor snapped. "You damned well don't take such good care of me, or my staff when we're ill! I'll keep an eye on you, sir, and this pet of yours. I'll have that bed out of there as soon as she's able to get up!"

"That we'll see," the surgeon said. "And it won't be for many, many weeks yet. And my wife will continue to visit her — with your permission!"

"Get out!" the governor barked at him. "I'll

put in a report about you yet. By God I will! I'll get me a surgeon who does what he's told!"

A week later Anne was able to sit up; Marguerite brought her food made in her own kitchen and poured the turnkey's cup of fetid drinking water into the chamber pot. She had smuggled a brush into the cell and she brushed the tangled hair into some semblance of order.

"You're getting better every day," she said. "Eat this now, it'll give you strength. My husband's so pleased with you, my child, he says it's a miracle!"

"Perhaps it is," Anne said. She swallowed the broth with an effort. "Madame, did you do what I asked you . . . did you send that pin for me?"

"Ssh! Be careful, that old devil lurks outside the door. If he heard anything, God knows what would happen to me, child. Yes I sent it. I thought you were going to die and there didn't seem to be any harm. But you mustn't mention it again. Not even my husband knows."

"God bless you," Anne touched the plump hand and the older woman squeezed it.

There was no harm in a little hope, and she had lived among the desperate for long enough to almost smell hope when it was there. She had sent the pin anonymously and that was dangerous enough. But it was worth the risk to see the poor girl smile and make an effort. She had only three months left before the child was born and that was something even the surgeon didn't care to think about. But his wife had been thinking of nothing else. When the inevitable happened and the mother died, she would take the child herself. It would be a comfort to the girl to know that at the end, but Marguerite was careful not to mention it; she had grown extraordinarily fond of her.

"Finish that up now, and I'll go. My husband says you must sleep as much as you can. I'll try and slip in for a minute this evening. Remember, don't touch the water, whatever you do!"

When she had gone, Anne lay back and pulled the covers over her. Francis would come to Paris and find her. He must come, before the child was born. The next moment she was fast asleep.

The officer commanding His Majesty's fourth company of musketeers at the Royal Camp at Metz had been on horseback since dawn, watching his men carrying out a complicated battle manoeuvre on the hills outside the city. He was not pleased with the result, and he had already visited his displeasure on his captains who were instructed to convey it to the lieutenants and through them to the musketeers themselves. The finest fighting force in the French Army, the colonel grumbled to himself, and they had shown themselves lazy and spiritless in the manoeuvre. If it had not been for the outbreak of dysentery following the plague three months ago, he would have ordered systematic flogging to put a little discipline into them. But his ranks were thin; the two terrible diseases — coupled with the ever present scourge of armies, the White Plague as they called syphilis — had already caused the town of Metz to be evacuated, and the civilians were only just creeping back. There had been no new cases for two months, and the infection was past, but it had left the garrison depleted in numbers and unwarlike in temper.

The colonel had settled down with a bottle of wine and begun yet another angry letter to the King's Minister of War, Monteynard, in Paris, listing his requirements and demanding that this time some notice should be taken of his complaints. He needed more men, more officers, and an outstanding sum in back pay. It was useless to write; no one in the damned palace cared what became of the army until it was time to send it off to war; then miracles were expected and punishments levelled on its commanders if they were not achieved.

When his junior captain came to the door, he barked at him irritably.

"What the devil are you doing! I'm not to be disturbed!"

"My apologies, sir. I tried to tell you when you came back from the manoeuvre but you were too busy — there's a woman waiting to see you. She was here yesterday and she's been waiting all day today. She says it's important and she won't go away. Will you see her for a moment? She's outside in the passage now."

"What woman?" the colonel threw down his pen. "Who sent her, idiot, what does she want? Don't you know anything before you come in troubling me?"

"She wouldn't say, sir. She only says that it's important; she was asking for Captain O'Neil. I thought you might want to have a word with her."

"Ha, why didn't you say so before? Send her"

Marie-Jeanne came in and stood awkwardly in the doorway, looking uncertainly at the big red-faced man sitting at a table in his shirt sleeves. He had thick dark brows which met above his eyes in an unnerving scowl. The scowl deepened as he saw that the woman in her plain cloak and thick shoes was only a servant.

"What do you want?" he demanded. "Come

in, girl, and close the door. What can I do for you?"

"I am looking for Captain Francis O'Neil, monsieur."

"Who are you? Your name, for God's sake, I haven't got all night to waste on you — I'm busy! State your business!"

"I am Marie-Jeanne Ducro, monsieur, maid to the Marquise de Bernard of Charantaise. I've come from Paris. Monsieur, where is Captain O'Neil?"

"What do you want with him?" he asked her. The frightened colour was fading from her face; she looked pinched and grey with tiredness. The colonel was not naturally ungallant, even to women of the lower classes.

"There's a chair there, sit down. You needn't be afraid of me; you're not a musketeer!" He gave a grimace that was meant to be a smile. "Paris is a long journey. Why have you come to Metz?"

"I'm looking for my mistress, the marquise." The words began to flow from her; she was so nervous and so weary that she stammered.

"She's disappeared, monsieur; I'm looking for her . . . I thought I might find her with the Captain. But she's not in the town and no one seems to know anything about her . . . I'm sorry to trouble you, but I can't

330

find the captain either. Is there a lady with him? I beg of you to tell me!"

"I'm sorry; that fool outside should have told you. There is no lady with Captain O'Neil. There never has been one since he came to my regiment. He died of the plague four months ago."

"Oh my God," Marie-Jeanne's eyes filled with tears. "Captain O'Neil is dead. . . ."

"Unfortunately, yes. He was one of my best officers in the short time he was with me. I grew fond of him; he had become my friend."

"And the marquise never came here, never visited here?" Marie-Jeanne whispered. "You are quite sure, monsieur?"

"Certain. He had no relatives, no friends outside the camp. I still have his personal belongings; I didn't know to whom they should be sent."

"I knew it," Marie-Jeanne said slowly. "I knew she wasn't with him. They were all wrong and I was right. Oh, God, monsieur, where is she?"

"Not here," the colonel said gently. "There's nothing I can do to help you find her. Why did you think your marquise had come here — was she the Captain's mistress? You needn't hesitate with me; I've had ladies join my officers before. It often happens."

"The marquise was married, monsieur."

The little maid wiped her eyes. "To the worst husband in the world. Captain O'Neil loved her; he wanted her to run away with him, to come here with him. She refused, monsieur; when she disappeared from Paris, without a sign or a word, everyone thought she'd gone to him at last. Everyone except me."

"I see." The colonel shrugged; little pieces of the puzzle his dead officer had left behind were falling into place. No women, no letters, the restlessness at peace-time soldiering. And in the end the filthy plague made off with him. The colonel gathered his emotions and spat furiously into the corner.

"When you find your mistress," he said, "you had better give her these . . ." He was pulling out a drawer in his table and he threw down a small packet, wrapped in a leather pouch. "His papers, a medallion he wore, one or two small things. Oh, and this came for him a month after he died. I opened it in case there was a letter, but there was nothing in it, not a word to say who sent it! You'd better take this too."

The sapphire pin that she had fastened in Anne's dress the night she vanished lay in the middle of the colonel's palm.

"That's Madame's," she whispered. "He gave it to her . . . she was wearing it. . . ."

"Excellent." The colonel stood up and

yawned; he had forgotten the letter to the War Minister. It was too late to finish it now, and he was too experienced to send it in its present form with all the curt passages unaltered. It would have to be rewritten in the morning, as all such letters usually were. He had half a bottle of wine to finish and then he was going to bed.

"Excellent," he repeated. "Here, take this package and the jewel. They're all that's left of him, poor fellow; I can't think of anyone better than your mistress to take charge of them. Duvivier!"

The captain opened the door. "Show the girl out; send two men to escort her from the camp and into Metz. And no incidents, you understand? She's under my protection. Farewell, girl. Take care of what I've given you. And tell your mistress when you find her that she was a fool to let him go. There are damned few gentlemen like O'Neil!"

Marie-Jeanne had been very frugal with her savings; she spent the night on the floor of a respectable inn in Metz itself, refusing the price of a bed. The next morning she argued fiercely with the owner of the posting house and finally agreed upon the fare for taking her to Versailles, using his fastest horses, with changes on the road.

Now she had proof for Lady Katherine and

the Chevalier Macdonald that Anne was not at Metz and never had been, and the very jewel she wore at the De Louvriers had been sent to a dead man in a mute appeal for help.

"When are you leaving, Charles?" The Vicomte de Renouille was walking through the *grands appartements* with his friend, and both were on their way to the King's levee. It was a great privilege to watch the King dress and prepare for Mass, and only those who were prepared to go there early, while His Majesty was still asleep, could hope to get a place. Neither Charles nor the vicomte were hurrying; a token attendance was required. They had been waiting on the King for over a year and he had never addressed a word or directed a glance at either of them.

"The day after tomorrow," Charles answered. "It's taken much too long to get my business finished at the ministry; I wish to God I could resign the post. It bores me to death!"

"Does that include the charming baroness," his friend enquired. "After all, she got it for you. . . . Have you really tired of her?"

"Sickened would be a better word," Charles said coldly. "Never permit a woman to make scenes, my dear Victor; they always make one too many. She had begun to bore me; lately she irritated me. That was enough. I'm finished."

"And there were tears?" the vicomte grinned. He had long forgiven Charles that blow in the brothel; he admired him and he feared him too much to bear a grudge.

"A few," Charles shrugged. "Let's change the subject, it bores me as much as she does."

She had sought him out a few days previously and caught him by the arm, refusing in agonised whispers to be shaken off. She was dressed and painted for one of the endless court receptions, her face hollow-cheeked and her black eyes burning as if she were ill. She had begged him to come back to her; the abjectness of it revolted him. And her closeness revolted him too, as much as it had once aroused his passion, so it repulsed him with equal violence. And he had told her so, his face a few inches away from hers, and watched the insults cutting her like stab wounds from a knife until the tight hand on his arm fell loose and she stepped back, her painted mouth twisting in pain. He was done with her; done with the clinging arms, the clever, eager body, the agile, grasping mind in which there was not one soft or gentle instinct. He had a furious desire to knock her down and crush her as if she were some kind of reptile. He told her that, too, before he turned his back on her and walked away.

"And when you get to Metz?" De Renouille

asked. "You're sure you know what you're doing?"

Charles turned towards him as they walked; the vicomte was an easy-going, pleasure-loving young man who found it impossible to take anything seriously. He was surprised at the expression on the other's face.

"Do you suppose I'm going to let that fortune hunter make off with my wife! I tell you, Victor, no one takes anything away from me — even if I don't want it . . . I shall kill him."

"And your wife — what will you do with her . . . ?"

"Believe me" — his voice was very casual — "when I have finished with her, no man will ever look at her again."

The entrance to the royal apartments was crowded with people; there was a crush of spectators inside the antechambers, and even members of the public, admitted at all times to the palace to see their monarch live his tightly regulated life, were standing in groups near the door.

"That's odd," the vicomte said. "If your wife is in Metz, isn't that her personal maid over there, the one who was always with her? Look, the girl in a brown cloak . . . no, wait a moment, where the devil are you off to . . . ?"

But Charles had left him; he was pushing

his way towards the maid. Renouille shrugged. It was Charles's business and it was wiser not to interfere. He went into the levee with the rest.

"Now," Charles said, "where is your mistress? What are you doing here without her?"

Marie-Jeanne gazed up at him in terror. He still had her by the arm in the same fashion as he had dragged her away from the King's room and into a deserted corridor. He had pulled her into a window with her back to it, and his grip tightened until her arm was numb.

"You're hurting me, monsieur, let go!"

"Answer me," he said. "Where is she?"

She had paid off the post chaise and made her way through the palace to the royal apartments where she had hoped to find Lady Katherine or Sir James. She had almost fainted with terror when the Macdonald came upon her.

"I don't know," she whispered. "Monsieur, my arm is breaking. . . ."

"Don't lie to me, or I'll break it properly."

"I'm not lying, monsieur, I swear to God. . . ."

He was the last person in the world she had meant to tell, but suddenly the strain was beyond bearing. She burst into tears and at last he let her go.

"I'm looking for your mother, your father, anyone who can help me! Oh, my God, monsieur, perhaps you'll listen to me, no one else would . . . Madame has disappeared!"

"From Metz?" he asked her slowly, calmly now.

"From Paris, nearly five months ago! She went out to visit the Vicomtesse de Louvrier and she never came back . . . monsieur, she vanished! Everyone supposed she'd gone to Metz, to join the captain, but I didn't believe it . . . I knew Madame. I've just come back from there myself. She isn't there; she never went there."

She paused, trembling. "Captain O'Neil is dead; he died of the plague months ago. His colonel gave me this." She showed him the sapphire pin. "It was sent to the captain a few weeks ago; you don't know what this means, monsieur, this pin!"

"Explain it to me," Charles said quietly. He was no longer angry, he felt strangely cold as if a chill had passed over them both.

"He gave it to her," the maid said. "She told me he made her promise to send it to him if she ever needed him. He was dead and buried when it came, but it shows, monsieur, it shows I was right! Something terrible has happened to her, she's in some dreadful danger!"

"And there's been no word, no clue?"

"Nothing, not since the night she drove away from the hôtel. We were leaving for Charantaise a few days after; I thought she might have gone straight there. I told your mother and she came down to the château with your father and your sister. It was your sister who said she must have run away with the captain. But when the weeks passed and there were all her clothes, her jewels, and not a letter, nothing . . . I couldn't bear it any longer. I went down to Metz myself to make sure. She was wearing that sapphire pin the night she vanished!"

"How very fortunate I found you," he said slowly. "I was going to Metz myself tomorrow. . . ." He took the little jewel and turned it in the light. "There was no message with this, no sign who sent it?"

Marie-Jeanne shook her head. "No. Believe me, Madame sent it, wherever she is. . . . Do you believe me, monsieur? For the love of God, will you help me to find her?"

"Yes." Charles put the pin in his pocket. "Yes, I believe you. I, too, thought she had run away. But not now, Marie-Jeanne, not now. Something has happened to her. I think the time has come to find my mother; she is the one to go to, now."

★ ★ ★

"She hadn't an enemy in the world," Katherine insisted. "It's impossible! If she'd been taken for ransom there'd have been a demand for money. Oh, how could we have been so blind? Five months without a word and we did nothing." She avoided looking at her son.

"She's still alive, or she was, when this was sent," Charles said. "Now, my dear parents, I suggest we stop making excuses and set about finding her!"

"Why this concern from you?" his mother demanded angrily. "If you'd behaved like a proper husband, she'd have been safe in Scotland with you. I said she hadn't an enemy. Well, I'd forgotten you . . . you were the only one who hated her, the only one who ever hurt her!"

"This is no time to quarrel," Sir James interrupted quickly. He had been watching his son and he saw what the angry eyes of his wife did not; under his dark skin he had turned pale and a nerve worked in his cheek. "I didn't think you'd care what happened to Anne," he said, "but I'm glad I'm wrong. We all care; let's be united upon that. What are we going to do? I questioned the police in the beginning and they knew nothing, there'd been no robbery reported, her coach was never found. They even inspected the road to De Louvrier's house and found nothing to suggest that she had been abducted."

"But abducted by whom?" Katherine cried out. "For what reason?"

"By someone who knew how to keep it a secret," Charles said. "Someone at Versailles or in Paris, someone who knew her movements. Father, could I be alone with Mother for a moment?"

He had never asked a favour of her in his life; he did not know how to begin; he only knew that if he were to do it, it must be done without witnesses. When he was alone with his mother, he hesitated. They had never talked of anything that mattered; all his childhood he had been in awe of her and then in flagrant rebellion. But without her, he was powerless and he would have to say so.

"I was going to Metz to kill O'Neil." He began to pace the room as he spoke. "I thought she had betrayed me. I don't know what I meant to do to her, I was so full of hatred. And jealousy." He looked into the beautiful face, set with hostility and suspicion, and recklessly he continued. "Mother, whatever I did in the past, whatever you think of me, you must believe one thing. I want to see Anne safe at Charantaise again. And I want her back, if she'll come. If you want me to go on my knees and beg, I will. Work with me now, and not against me, and we'll find her!"

"I loved her as if she were my own child," his mother said slowly. "I left things alone because I thought she was safe and happy with a man who'd care for her. Someone who'd protect her against you. God forgive me. For all we know, we may be too late to help her now."

"Find out where she is," her son said. "Go to everyone you know of influence . . . ask them. The answer must be here at court. You'll find it out."

"Yes," she answered, "you're right, my son." It was the first time he had ever heard her call him that. She left her chair and now she walked the room while he stood still. "And there's no need to go very far. There's one person at Versailles who can find out anything. Luckily, she liked Anne: I think she likes me. I'll go to the Du Barry."

Charles came close to her. "Today," he said. "Now."

She nodded. "As soon as I can get an audience. But there must be no talk about it, nothing to warn Anne's enemy that we're suspicious. We'll send the maid back to Charantaise to wait. And you must say nothing, pretend that nothing has changed, you understand. Now you must leave it to me."

He came up to her and held out his hand. After a moment she put hers into it, and then

Charles brought it to his lips and kissed it.

"You go to the Du Barry, Mother. When you know where Anne is, or who has harmed her, the rest is up to me. I'm still her husband."

"If I didn't know you so well," Katherine said, "I'd think you loved her."

"If I didn't know myself," he said, "I'd think so too."

"Well," the Duc d'Aiguillon demanded, "what did she want?" He had been waiting impatiently while the Du Barry received the wife of the Chevalier Macdonald.

"Her daughter-in-law has disappeared," the favourite said. "You remember — the one there was all the scandal about some months ago, the Marquise de Bernard. She wants me to find out what's happened to her."

"Bah," the duc shrugged. "That's no concern of ours. I hope you fobbed her off!"

"I said I'd do my best," Du Barry answered. "It all sounds very strange to me. . . . Who'd want to make off with her . . . ?"

"I've been talking to De Verier," he interrupted. "Don't you want to hear about it, or have you forgotten that little business with the King . . . ? For God's sake, let the Macdonalds find their own runaway. I've been with him for an hour, questioning, threatening. . . ."

"And what did he tell you?" Du Barry said. "Nothing, I'll swear. He's as cunning as a snake! He knows everything, but you'll never get it out of him!"

"I got this much out of him," the duc retorted. "He says a woman brought the girl, but he says he didn't recognise her. He said she was veiled."

"He's a liar," Du Barry spat out. "Veiled be damned! Of course he knew her, he knew all about it! What else?"

"Nothing, absolutely nothing. If he weren't the King's confidant, I'd have him taken to my house and asked again with something to help his memory!"

"We daren't," she said. "We daren't touch him without the King's permission. He knows that. Do you think it's true about the woman bringing her?"

"Yes, I'd swear it was. You know the old maxim — tell a little of the truth to cover up the rest — I was watching his eyes; he wasn't lying about that! But we still don't know where the slut came from. . . ."

"I think I do," Du Barry said. "I'm going there tomorrow to find out. And you might do me a favour, and see if you know anything about the Marquise de Bernard. I promised that poor woman and I like to keep my word. It sounds like a *lettre de cachet* to me."

"A *lettre de cachet?* Wait a moment, my dear, wait a moment. When did this woman vanish?" The duc's brown eyes were darting everywhere, as a thought flashed into his agile mind.

"Five months ago. It was thought she'd run off with a lover. But he's dead and she never reached him . . . why?"

"Five months ago that girl came to the King," D'Aiguillon said. "Five months ago exactly. And you don't get a *lettre de cachet* for someone like a De Bernard for nothing. I'll make enquiries for her, my dear, don't worry. Just you find out who brought the girl in, that's the first thing. . . . It's just possible, just barely possible, that there's some connection here."

The sinister doorkeeper at Mme. Grand-mère's house bowed so low that his greasy head almost touched the floor. He knew very well who the small, masked lady was, with her escort of liveried servants, though it was nearly a year since she had paid the house a visit.

He set the one chair in the dingy room for her to sit upon and wiped the seat with his hand. The Du Barry wasted no time.

"Stop fussing, man. Send for Mme. Grand-mère, I'm in a hurry."

"At once, Highness, at once. . . ."

When the old woman came in she swept her distinguished client a low curtsy. Du Barry took off her mask; there was no need to keep up the pretence that she was incognito; she and the dreadful proprietress knew each other far too well.

"What can I do for you, Comtesse? I wish you'd given me a little warning, my stocks are low just now."

"I haven't come to buy," the Du Barry said. With a grimace she sat down on the chair and sniffed at her muff, exactly as all the ladies did when they came there. Unlike the ladies, she made a face.

"Pooh, how this place stinks! Don't you ever open a window?" Madame made a gesture expressing her apology and said nothing. The comtesse had not come to buy. Her eyes were bright and they flickered round her: she seemed nervous. With a connoisseur's appreciation, the procuress decided that she grew prettier with time. She reminded her of the exquisite and fantastically expensive ornaments one saw in the exclusive Paris shops, from her shining red-gold head to the tips of her pattened shoes.

"If you don't want to buy, what can I do for you?" she said.

"You can give me some information. Mme.

346

Grand-mère, I'm in trouble. I need your help."

"Anything," the old woman said quickly. "You've been a good customer, Comtesse, I'll do whatever I can for you. What is it, what do you want to know?"

"Five months ago someone introduced a girl to the King," Du Barry said. "She almost got me out of Versailles. She's gone now, but I want to know who found her and brought her to him. I can't risk it happening again, you understand. There's just a chance this girl was one of yours. Think back — five months ago. . . . Did anyone come to you at that time, someone you'd never seen before, a woman perhaps? Did she make a purchase?"

"A moment now. . . ." Madame scowled, trying to remember.

Many had come and gone in five months; she'd sold some boys, a few girls, including the savage little gipsy to a gentleman who liked them spirited and wild. She had known all of them, all except one, the one who took that passive blond girl from Lyons. . . . That buyer was a stranger and she had never come again. She remembered it all now, the woman's nervousness, her willingness to pay, even the outrageous price — fifteen hundred louis — And no wonder, if she was buying for the King.

"Did you ever see the girl, Comtesse? That would be a help."

"Never," Du Barry answered. "But I had a description of her, after she was sent away. Very blond, angelic looking. The King did well by her; no Parc au Cerf for this one! He gave her a dowry and sent her to a convent to be educated. It makes me sick to think how close she came to staying on. . . ."

"Blond," the old woman said. "That's right, I had a girl like that about that time; blue eyes, pretty, if you like the type. I sold her too, five months ago. And the buyer was a woman I'd never seen before. She said she wanted something special, a virgin, refined . . . you know the sort of thing. She paid a huge price for her and never made a murmur. I'll swear it's the same one!"

"I thought so," Du Barry leaned forward, her lovely little face as hard as stone. "Have you any idea who this woman was? I've got to find her, Mme. Grand-mère. I've got to know who's behind her, who's working against me. Think, for God's sake! I'll pay you well, don't worry."

"I never saw her before or since," the old woman said. "She wore a mask, like they all do. But there was something . . . wait! She paid me and I saw her hands. There was a ring on one finger, I remember noticing it.

Two hearts in rubies and diamonds, and a diamond stag above them. Very unusual, that's why I noticed it at the time. But that's all I can tell you."

"It's enough," Du Barry stood up. "I know a woman with a ring like that. I've never seen another like it. Two hearts and a stag; you're sure?"

"Absolutely, Comtesse. That's it; I was born in the country, you know. I can tell you, the little beast was a stag made in diamonds."

"I'm very grateful to you." The Du Barry drew on her mask. "Here, there's five hundred louis in that bag. If I need someone, I'll give you time to look around before I come."

"How is the King?" the old woman asked. She put the bag of money in her skirt. "In good health, I hope?"

"Too good!" Du Barry laughed. "He drives me hard enough! One thing more; if you get any more callers and you suspect they're buying with His Majesty in mind — send word to me first, will you? I shan't forget it."

"I promise, Comtesse," Mme. Grand-mère gave a wink, and her grotesque red mouth turned back in a travesty of a smile. "You can rely on me. Believe me, if I'd known where that brat was going, I'd have strangled her first!"

As the Du Barry went out of the house,

the old woman gave a silent whistle. That girl — that spiritless milksop had almost ousted the Du Barry — Madame felt suddenly angry at the deceit the minx had practised on her, hiding her talents under that submissive mask. A clever, ambitious little bitch, cunning as a snake . . . she'd look at the quiet ones with new eyes after this.

"Madame. . . ." Louise's maid put her head round the door, she approached her mistress cautiously, for the baroness' temper was uncertain in these days; she ate little and slept badly, and when the girl annoyed her, she boxed her ears or threw things at her. It was all the fault of that cursed Macdonald; Marie often found her mistress crying and she was shocked at the effect upon the baroness of his leaving her. She was such a proud woman, so contemptuous of weakness, so well able to take and discard a dozen men, until this one came into her life and then walked out of it. Indirectly, he had made Marie suffer too, and she could not forgive him. Louise de Vitale had aged twenty years since he abandoned her.

"Madame, you will be late for the hunt. . . ."

Louise was dressed in her habit; her gloves and riding crop lay on the table beside her, her horse was waiting in the stables, and the

King would leave the palace in half an hour. Everyone was expected to be mounted and waiting for him.

"I'm not going," Louise snapped at her. "My head's aching. Go away, girl, for God's sake!"

She couldn't face the hunt; she found it more and more difficult to lead the incredibly strenuous life at court and to maintain a pretence that nothing was wrong, when her mind and body were wracked with longing and despair for Charles; she dreaded seeing him and yet perversely looked for him in every corner of Versailles. And Fate was cruel, for even in the milling crowds she often found him, saw him talking to others, dancing in the evenings with other women until her heart almost burst in her breast. He would be following the King's hunt today. Charles had not taken another mistress; her shameless enquiries had established that. They had also exposed her to the ridicule of a society which found her position peculiarly amusing; it was so unfashionable, so bourgeois to be jealous and eat one's heart out for a man who no longer wanted one. People sneered at her openly and the men, who tried to begin an intrigue with her, shrugged and went elsewhere when she refused them. More and more she had begun to think of the absent De Tallieu's advice; life

351

at Versailles was empty and bitter as long as Charles was there and apart from her. She felt unbearably bad-tempered and ill.

That morning Louise had made up her mind and written to the Royal Chamberlain, asking the King's permission to retire to her estates for a few weeks where her affairs were in disorder. If she went away, it would give her time to recover, time to think and make some plan, however wild, to get Charles back again. Thank God De Tallieu was not there to see her suffer; the situation would have amused him enormously. But thank God, most of all, that the woman who had taken Charles away from her was ignorant of her triumph. That was Louise's only consolation. Anne was paying for her victory in some foul corner of the Bastille, abandoned and forgotten as if she were dead. She might have died months ago; Louise exulted at the thought of that; she addressed frightful prayers, full of hate and blasphemy to the God in which she did not believe, that Anne and her child were already in their grave. He might love Anne still. He might have struck *her*, Louise, who cared for him, and taunted her and left her, but he would never, never see his wife again or know his child.

"Marie!" The door opened again.

"Yes, madame?"

"We shall be leaving for the country at the end of the week. I need a rest. You can begin by seeing to some of my baggage."

"Yes, madame. Shall I help you change now, if you're not going out?"

"I'm not going anywhere," Louise said. "Except to bed. I haven't slept for a week."

The Du Barry was late for her appointment with the Duc d'Aiguillon; she came to his apartment still in the dress she had worn that afternoon when she followed the King's hunt; her face was flushed and her feathered hat askew.

"I came as soon as I could," she explained. "He was in such a good temper, he made me get out of the coach and watch him cut the stag's throat. . . . Ugh, I felt as sick as a cat!"

D'Aiguillon smiled and patted her hand. "Be thankful he still loves you," he said. "Clever, charming creature . . . sit down and get your breath." He bent over and kissed the warm, pink cheek. They were still lovers, but their opportunities were few. "What did you find out last night?"

"I found out who brought that damned girl to Versailles!" Du Barry said. "I was right, she did come from Mme. Grand-mère's and De Verier wasn't lying when he said the introducer was a woman. And do you know

353

which woman? Can you guess?" He shook his head.

"No," he said softly. "Tell me."

"My friend," the favourite said. "My amusing little friend who sat down and played cards with me the other night — no wonder she lost every sou, she must be half out of her wits with fear that I'll find out. . . . Louise de Vitale, that's who it was! The dirty, scheming. . . ." She gave vent to a flood of gutter language until the duc winced.

"Enough, enough," he said. "We know what she is, my dear. And now I've news for you. I hear from the chamberlain that the lady is planning to visit her estates!"

"Oh, is she!" Du Barry swung round. "Thinks she'll escape, does she? Well, by God, she's going to answer a few questions first. . . ."

"She is," he agreed. "And what we couldn't ask De Verier, we'll be able to ask her. But I'm puzzled; why should she turn against you, what did she have to gain?"

"God knows," Du Barry said. "She's not important, she's not involved with anyone like the Richelieus or the ministers. . . . And still she let herself be used, found that girl, brought her to the King's bedroom! She had a reason, but I'm damned if I know what it was. . . ."

D'Aiguillon did not answer; his mind had

been working while she talked, fitting the new pieces into the puzzle, making a little more of the picture. The baroness had been the mistress of Charles Macdonald, whose wife had so conveniently disappeared. That was a clue, but it was not important. That would be extracted from her along with what he really wanted to find out, the names of those who worked with her, the ones who had approached the King's confidential valet and through him, the King himself. They were the enemies he must discover, if they were not to strike again at the Du Barry and at him.

"I'm going to give a musical evening," he said suddenly. "At my house. A small party for just a few friends. And you're going to invite the baroness before she leaves Versailles."

Du Barry looked at him, and after a second's pause she smiled.

"You couldn't question De Verier there, but you can question her," she said. "I'll make it a musical evening for her."

"Don't worry, my dear," the duc said gently. "Mme. Louise will make the music for us. And by the way, I think she'll throw some light upon that missing marquise. Ask her for tomorrow evening and make it a command. She'll have to come."

"She will," the Du Barry said. "Normally, I don't like your methods, but this time it'll be a pleasure! I wouldn't miss it for the world."

Louise had been tempted to refuse when she received the Du Barry's invitation; her dresses were packed and most of her jewels, and she was anxious to leave Versailles. The peace and security of her neglected country estate seemed the most desirable thing in the world. So much of her zest for life had been drained out of her in the last few weeks that she felt old and intolerably tired. She needed rest and quiet and time to think. She would find some means of enticing Charles back to her. Her necessity was so great that it must surely breed invention. When she came back to Versailles again, it would be in triumph, more beautiful than ever, with her lover at her side once more.

As she made the journey to the duc's house that night, Louise lay back against the cushions in her coach. She felt increasingly confident. It was almost her last evening at Versailles but it was unthinkable to refuse an invitation from the duc and the Du Barry herself. She might even enjoy it. Her coach drew up before the entrance; torches blazed at the doorway and two lackeys came running down the short flight of steps as her own postillion climbed off his perch at the back of the coach and opened the door for her. He handed her down the steps and she followed the lackeys to the door of the house.

In the hall, one of the duc's servants came forward, bowing low, and took the baroness's velvet cloak. She paused by a tall gilt mirror and examined herself quickly. Her yellow silk dress was a little creased by the journey; Louise shook out the skirts and half turned once more. She looked very handsome, but undoubtedly tired; that fool Marie had put on too much rouge, it made her look haggard. She opened out her yellow fan and walked towards the door where another lackey waited. It occurred to her that the house was unusually quiet.

"Am I very early?" she demanded. "Haven't the other guests arrived?"

"Not yet, madame." The servant stared back at her blankly. He had been in the duc's service for many years; the staff had been specially chosen for duty that night. "But His Grace and Mme. la Comtesse are waiting for you."

The salon was empty when she went in; at least it seemed so until a voice spoke softly just behind her, and Louise whipped round with an exclamation of surprise.

357

"Welcome, my dear baroness. How charming of you to come!"

The Duc d'Aiguillon was standing behind an armchair, and in the armchair the Du Barry was seated, fanning herself idly. Louise came forward and smiled; she curtsied to her host.

"You startled me, monsieur; forgive my confusion but I thought I was alone. Mme. la Comtesse . . . how delightful you look, as always."

The Du Barry gave her a strange smile; her eyes glittered like points of steel.

"You were always a great flatterer, Louise. Such a great flatterer and such a true friend."

"I fear I must be very early," Louise said.

"Madame," the duc said gently. "I'm afraid you're the victim of a little joke. You're going to be our only guest this evening."

Louise laughed; it was a light laugh ending on a slightly nervous tremor. There was something frightening about these two, the handsome man leaning so relaxedly on the chair, above the lovely woman. She had seen the Du Barry most days for the past three years and she had never seen that expression in her eyes before.

"I'm very honoured then," Louise said. "But why should you choose me?"

"Because we're going to play a little game," the duc went on. "It's called question and answer. We're going to ask the questions, madame, and you're going to give the answers. It's a most amusing game — you'll enjoy it."

The Du Barry leant forward; she shut her fan and threw it aside. "You brought that girl into the King, didn't you? You went to Grand-mère's and bought that little bitch and played procuress to Louis, didn't you?"

Louise looked at her and then back to the duc; she felt suddenly very cold as if she were standing in an icy draught.

"I haven't any idea what you mean," she heard her own voice saying and it sounded absurdly level, almost contemptuous in contrast to the terror which was creeping over her.

"I brought no girl near the King. I'm afraid I don't understand your game, monsieur. And I don't think it's very amusing. You will excuse me, I shall need my coach at once!"

"Oh, no you won't!" Du Barry sprang up then, her hands on her hips in the attitude of the Parisian streetwalker. She opened her mouth and swore at the woman in front of her. And then she turned to the duc.

"We've wasted enough time — she won't tell us the truth of her own will. Downstairs with her!"

Louise heard him clap his hands and saw the look he gave behind her. She managed to scream once before the two menservants smothered her in a blanket and carried her out through a door in the tapestried wall.

"Now," the Duc d'Aiguillon said once more, "we will resume our little game, madame. We want to know all about your intrigue to replace Mme. du Barry. We want to know about the girl — who suggested her — who arranged that the King should see her, and who directed the whole plan. Names, madame, dates, everything useful which comes to mind."

The cellar was in darkness except for one end where a pair of resin torches blazed in their sconces against the wall, illuminating the figure of a woman fastened to it with arms outstretched, her dress cut away to the waist.

A few feet away, a man bent over a brazier, working a hand bellows on the white-hot coals, where a branding iron was heating. There were other instruments close at hand; a device for crushing the fingers, a cross-shaped stretcher festooned with ropes and pulleys where the obdurate were racked until every joint was dislocated in their bodies, and the scourges and pincers which were the ordinary tools of the professional torturer.

At the back of the small cellar Mme. du Barry was seated comfortably on a chair where she could watch the interrogation. The duc himself was standing to one side of Louise; he had taken off his coat. He looked into the white face, distorted with hatred and terror.

"Why did you do it, eh?" he said. "What did you gain from betraying madame?"

She gave a violent jerking movement against the wall.

"I know nothing!" she said. "Nothing!"

"Very well." The duc lifted his finger to the man at the brazier.

"Apply the iron to her breasts."

It was past three in the morning and the great sprawling palace was in darkness; here and there a few lights burned, some of the hundreds of royal servants were still cleaning and preparing the rooms for the next day; lovers kept their trysts in corners; a few late gamblers were making their way down the dark corridors to sleep; and Sir James Macdonald, his wife, and his son were waiting in an anteroom for a summons from the Comtesse du Barry.

The warning had come to them during the evening after the King had retired to bed. It was a short note, delivered by a lackey, and it told them to wait for the comtesse, adding that it might be far into the night. Charles had been pacing the room, opening the door, and looking out into the empty corridor, while his parents passed the time playing cards. A servant had brought them some wine, but that was finished long ago. Nobody had spoken for some time. Charles went again to the door and pulled it open; he almost knocked down the lackey who had been about to come through it.

"Chevalier Macdonald?"

"Yes," Sir James sprang up.

"I have a message from Mme. la Comtesse du Barry. She asks you all to wait on her in her rooms immediately. I'll take you there."

Sir James took his wife by the hand. "Be calm," he whispered. "It will be good news."

Katherine did not answer, she only nodded and held on to him. He did not believe it, nor did she. As she passed her son, they exchanged glances, but said nothing. They had little to say to each other, but much of the hostility between them had disappeared. Friends they could never be, but they were enemies no longer. They followed the lackey down the corridors and down the main staircase to the Du Barry's apartments on the first floor.

The favourite was very tired; she lay back on a chaise longue, her shoes had been kicked off, and stretched her beautiful arms above her head and yawned. Louise de Vitale had been very, very obstinate. Du Barry had stayed in the cellar below the duc's house for nearly two hours and by that time her vengeance was satisfied and she felt faintly sick. She had gone back upstairs and left the duc to finish questioning the baroness; she had seen enough.

She looked at the three people standing in front of her and wondered why she hadn't let the matter wait till morning. It was not going to be pleasant, and all she longed for now was to take off her corsets and go to bed. But she had kept her promise.

"Chevalier, Lady Katherine . . ." she gave a cold glance at Charles. What the devil did he care about his wife, at this eleventh hour . . . ?

"I have found out where your daughter-in-law, the marquise, is. Lady Katherine, I should sit down if I were you."

"Where is she?" Charles came close to her; she saw that the hands clenched at his sides were trembling.

"Your wife is in the Bastille, monsieur. She was taken there nearly six months ago with a *lettre de cachet* signed by the King. Don't interrupt me! I'm as tired as the devil and I want to get this over. It's been a long night, I can tell you!"

"Oh, my God," he heard his mother say. "The Bastille — oh, my God!"

"Why," Charles said slowly, "how . . . who did it?"

The Du Barry considered him angrily.

"Your mistress, Louise de Vitale. She was the one who brought that little whore to the King and De Verier got a signed paper from him. The order was made out against your wife and she was abducted and taken to the Bastille. All for the love of you, monsieur. Quite an achievement, if I may say so. Louise didn't want you to find out your wife was pregnant."

She looked into the ashen face of Katherine Macdonald and back to the man standing above her. Except that his dark skin had turned grey, his face was like a mask. "None of you knew about it? Well then, that's why the baroness got rid of her. I've heard it all only a few hours ago. From her own lips."

"Where is she?"

Charles asked the question very quietly. His eyes made the Du Barry shiver. "Where is Louise? I'm going to kill her," he said. "Very slowly, and with my own hands. Madame, you haven't answered me, where is she?"

"She came to the Duc d'Aiguillon's house this evening," Du Barry said at last. "It was a trick to make her speak; I'd found out she had procured this girl for the King; we wanted to know more. The duc and I confronted her but she was obstinate, she denied everything. The duc had her tortured, monsieur, until she

364

confessed, but too late to save herself. She died on the rack. I saw most of it and I promise you, she paid for what she has done to your wife. . . . And now, there's nothing more to tell you." She yawned. "I've kept my word, I've found out where the marquise is; now I must go to bed."

"Wait, wait," Katherine came forward and before the Du Barry could get up, she fell on her knees before her. "It can't be left at that . . . she must be rescued, the King must release her!"

"Madame," the Du Barry spoke gently; she liked the older woman and it distressed her to see her crying at her feet. "The King does not know she is in the Bastille. That's the art of the *lettre de cachet;* he never knows whose name is written on it. He never wants to know. I'm sorry for you, for all of you. But there's nothing anyone can do for the marquise."

"You can go to the King, madame," Sir James broke in. "You can beg him — explain what happened. . . ."

The Du Barry shook her head. "I have done many things with the King, Chevalier, but even I haven't tried to recall a *lettre de cachet* to his mind. I wouldn't dare. I told you, I'm sorry. But there's nothing more that anyone can do for your marquise now. Officially she doesn't exist."

Then Charles turned to his mother; he held out his hand and lifted her up. "No more now, Mother; Madame is tired. We're very grateful to you," he said to the favourite. "Now at least we know where Anne is. I don't expect you to go to the King, madame; I know how tactless it would be to mention a *lettre de cachet* to the one who's signed it and sent a human being into prison without trial, without appeal. I don't expect you to say anything to him about it. But in the morning *I* shall go to His Majesty and demand my wife's release. Come, Mother. Your servant, madame." He bowed very low to the Du Barry; though the pale, glittering eyes were fixed upon her, she knew he didn't even see her.

"If you do that," she called out after him, "you'll likely join her there! I warn you!"

At the door he turned, and now the burning look was focused on her.

"What better place can a man be, madame, than with his wife and his child?"

In the beginning, as some of her strength came back, Anne used to lie in bed and watch the window in the wall; it was her only means of trying to assess the time, her only measure of night and day as the light faded. At the start of her convalescence, Marguerite had brought her some needles and thread and some pieces of linen to make shifts for the baby; it would help to pass the time and keep her occupied, but she insisted that the turnkey must not find her sewing. The governor was still threatening to take away the trestle bed and stop her privileges.

Anne did as she was told and sewed in secret for the baby, but now the little clothes were put away, hidden beneath the paillasse. She had no interest left in anything, for at last her hope had died. The weeks had gone by, until two months had passed since the pin was sent to Francis at Metz and there was no word or sign that he was coming. The cell enclosed her like a tomb, and though she was well enough to walk slowly round the tiny room, Anne spent hours lying on the bed, staring at the damp stones above her head, for now she had lost interest in the window too. Night and day were of no consequence; nor was time, because there was only a little left. The child was strong and active; each movement caused her agony because it showed the vigour of the pitiful unborn that had no hope either.

What would become of it, if it survived . . . ? She closed her mind to that; fear for the child was the only thing that could arouse her now, and she dreaded anything that brought back memories or responsibility. She was a dead woman who would soon be buried. Sometimes she put her thin hands over her womb and wept, without making any sound, but most of the time she lay inert, wide-eyed and withdrawn on her bed, the food untouched beside her, not even turning her head when the turnkey came in and took it away.

The old man had not been unkind; according to his lights he had shown this particular prisoner a great deal of mercy. He could have complained to the governor about her special treatment and urged him to take away the wretched bed, and forced the fetid water and foul prison food upon her, but he had held his tongue, grumbling bitterly all the time. She had never given him a moment's trouble and she would soon be dead. On the rare occasions when women had given birth in the fortress, they had all died of infection and neglect, and if the child was born alive, the executioner strangled it. This one would be more fortunate; he had gained that much from the surgeon's wife; she meant to take it for herself. Watch for the first sign of restlessness or pain, she told him, and then send for the surgeon. In the prisoner's condition it could begin at any time. . . . He unlocked the door and came over to the bed; the girl lay still as usual, her eyes open, not seeing or hearing anything. It was a common phase among prisoners; with some it lasted for years, while others lingered on for a few weeks and then quietly died.

"You've eaten nothing," he said, as he said every day. She turned her head very slowly.

"I'm not hungry, thank you."

She always thanked him, but the voice was slow and faraway as if it was an effort to speak.

"What waste," he grumbled, taking the plate away; there was a little meat and some rice on it, the daily ration sent in by the surgeon's wife, and a cup of fresh water. Most days the turnkey ate it himself.

"You have no pains?" he asked her, staring suspiciously into the sunken, jaundiced face. She shook her head. "Call out if you feel anything," he said. "I'll hear you. Call out at once, understand?"

"I will," Anne whispered. "Will the surgeon come?"

"If he can," the turnkey muttered. "You're not the only one here, you know. He has other things to do besides deliver you. . . . His wife will be here anyhow. She's got an interest in you, after all."

"She's going to take my child," Anne said flatly. "If it lives."

"Aye," he said. "Nobody does anything for nothing in this world . . . it's all she's waiting for. She'll be in some time today to see you, I daresay."

He went out, locking the door behind him

and shooting the thick bolt into place. He would be sorry when this one died. God knew what kind of troublemaker would be sent to the West Tower in her place. He settled down on his stool in the dim passage and began to doze.

"You're going to the King," Jean said. "Let me go with you!"

"No," Charles said again. "No one is going with me."

"You think you'll move him," his sister said. "You must be mad . . . the only chance might be with a woman. I'll weep, I'll go on my knees. . . . Let me come with you, I might be able to help!"

"You will mind your own business," he answered coldly. "Anne is my wife, and she's my affair. It's through me she's in the Bastille, and by God, I'll be the one to get her out of it."

Jean turned away from him; her pretty face was pale and there were shadows under the eyes, from tears and lack of sleep.

"What a death that creature De Vitale died," she said. "And all to keep you. She must have been insane. It's a pity you were ever born! Oh, my God, when I think of Anne in that place I could go mad. And she was pregnant too, and never said a word!"

"Don't speak of that," he told her fiercely. "Don't you suppose I'm nearly out of my mind thinking of her, thinking of the child too? I'll get them out in time if I have to tear the walls of the place down with my own hands!"

As the result of Katherine's pleading, the Du Barry had done them one last favour; she had managed to find out from the Governor of the Bastille that Anne was still alive, and it had taken all the duc's influence as well as her own to get him to admit that much.

"She has probably miscarried," Jean said. "In a way I hope she has. . . . What time is it, Charles, isn't it nearly time to go to him?"

"Five minutes more," he said. "Don't worry, my dear sister, I shan't keep His Majesty waiting."

The King was in his anteroom in the *petits appartements,* standing by the window with his back to the door when Charles was shown in. He heard the name announced and still he did not move; one of his hunting dogs was beside him and he stroked its head and let it lick his hand. He had not wanted to give this young man an audience, but the Du Barry had wheedled him against his will. She was difficult to resist these days; wicked, laughing, lascivious little enchantress. He had only to think of her to smile, and relent.

When he turned round; Charles dropped on

his knee. He wanted a position, the King supposed wearily, or money, or some favour. He supposed it would be easier to grant it than upset the sunny humour of his mistress. She was in a strangely demanding mood these days, primed by that arch intriguer D'Aiguillon, but the King was too tired and his happiness too precarious to refuse her anything. He had been free of depression for weeks; it was worth a few orders for banishment, even the loss of two ministers to keep the shadows in his mind at bay. Only the day before he had signed an order exiling the Comte de Tallieu to his estates for life and levying an enormous fine upon him because Du Barry said he had offended her.

"You asked me to receive you privately, M. Macdonald. What do you want of me? You may rise and approach."

Charles stood up and came towards him; the King's dark eyes watched him warily with a glint of hostility in them.

"I have come to ask Your Majesty for justice." Charles spoke calmly, and he held the King's look without faltering.

"There is always justice in my kingdom," Louis said icily. "Explain."

"My wife disappeared from Versailles six months ago, sire. I have only just discovered where she is. She is a prisoner, and I need your order for her release."

"Where is your wife, monsieur?" The voice was flat and cold. "And what was her crime?"

"She committed none," Charles said. "She is in the Bastille, under a *lettre de cachet*. You alone can rescind that order, sire, and right a most terrible wrong. I beg of you, on my knees; have her released at once."

The King did not answer immediately; he said something under his breath and the dog moved away and lay down, watching him. He took a small pinch of snuff and sneezed into a lace handkerchief.

"No one is in the Bastille without cause, monsieur," he remarked. "If your wife is imprisoned there by the means you suggest, then she must deserve to be. You have been misinformed."

"My wife is there because of a woman's jealousy. She obtained the order of arrest from you. I know that beyond doubt."

"You know a great deal too much."

Louis said it in the same flat tone, but now the black eyes were narrowed and angry. "You contradict me, monsieur. You say you have come here to ask for justice. Justice has apparently been done. If I signed an order for your wife's arrest, then I wished her to be punished. I have not changed my mind. I have no intention of changing it. Your petition is dismissed!"

"But, sire, you didn't know . . . you didn't know who it was for — if you will let me tell you what happened, the injustice and horror of it. . . ."

"I neither know nor care," the King's voice cut in. "Those who are in the Bastille are there at my orders. I remember nothing about your wife and I advise *you* to forget the whole affair. Do not persist, monsieur, I warn you! You have gone far enough. Page, show Monsieur out — the audience is over."

He turned his back on Charles and the double doors were opened for him to back away and leave. For the first time in his life, Louis felt the touch of an inferior's hand upon his arm and he was so surprised, he jumped.

"My wife and unborn child are in that prison, sire." Charles said it very softly. "Now I warn you; I'm going to get them out!"

He bent his knee again and then backed out towards the door. In the anteroom he came face to face with the Du Barry, the duc a few paces behind her. She didn't even trouble to ask what had happened.

"I told you you were wasting your time. I hope to God you didn't anger him!"

"I told him I'd get her out in spite of him," Charles said. "And I meant it. I'll go further; I'll kill anyone who tries to stop me!"

He pushed past her without a word. For

a moment the Du Barry paused and looked after him. Then she smiled at the duc and shrugged. "Arrogant fool," she said. "I'll have to stop the King from having him arrested now. Why do you let me get myself involved with all these people?"

"I can't stop you," D'Aiguillon said gently. "You're incurably interfering and you have the kindest heart in the world. Go in and pacify him."

# Chapter 9

"No, I don't think any of those will do; show me something else, something much better."

The little jeweller raised his brows and shrugged; the gentry were notoriously difficult to please and he had spread out the finest pieces in his stock for the gentleman to see. But still he and the lady with him shook their heads and asked for something better, always something better. They did not strike the merchant as having the wealth to indulge their tastes, but he had done as they asked. Now he had begun to give up hope of making a sale at all.

"I have shown you everything, Excellencies," he said. "This necklace." He picked up a collar of blazing diamonds. "Rings, this magnificent brooch. . . . If you were buying for the King, you couldn't ask for better!"

"We are buying for Mme. du Barry," Jean de Mallot said. "And you haven't shown us anything that will please *her*."

The little man's brown eyes opened wide

with surprise and then half shut as he began to smile; he reminded Charles and his sister of a monkey. "Excellencies, why didn't you say before . . . the Du Barry! Ah, this must be expensive then, but something different, something unique. . . . One moment! One moment!" He put his jewels away, sweeping them into a black velvet bag and carried them into the back room.

Bribery was the last resort, but nothing was left to Charles now except the hope that he could please or tempt the favourite into helping him once more. Her intervention had averted his immediate arrest, but none of his parents' powerful friends at court, not even his own minister, to whom he went for help, offered the slightest hope that the King would change his mind and order Anne's release. Everyone gave the same advice. Accept the inevitable; it may just be possible to get the child if it is born alive and save it. But for Anne herself, there was no hope. Even his mother gave up at the end of fruitless pleadings and enquiries; she broke down and wept and the sight shocked him; even she, so indomitable in her efforts, believed that all was lost. But Charles would not accept it; there was one hope, one last link with the King that could give him all he needed to rescue his wife. And that link, that hope, was the Du Barry. No, he interrupted his parents when they interposed, no, she wouldn't ask for Anne's release. He wouldn't expect that of her. All he needed was one thing, and she alone could get it for him. He needed a letter to the governor so that he could get into the fortress. That was all. The rest he must accomplish alone.

He had sold everything he possessed, his jewels, including, ironically, the diamond pin Louise had given him; his horses; he had borrowed under promissory note on his estates in Scotland from everyone who would consent to lend him money, and he had collected nearly a hundred and fifty thousand livres with which to buy a present for the Du Barry.

"He won't have anything," Jean whispered. "We've seen the best. My God, Charles, we've been to every jeweller in Paris! Are you sure we shouldn't compromise and take the necklace. . . ."

"No," he said obstinately. "She has a dozen better. Wait and see what he brings out. De Renouille said he always does this until he knows the buyer is determined on the best. . . . Ah, at last!"

The merchant folded up the black cloth on which he displayed his jewels and in its place he spread a white one. He looked up into the worried face of the young woman with red hair, and from her to the dark man. They were very anxious; they would perhaps pay more than he judged they could afford. Indeed, they'd have to, if they were going to find anything beautiful and rare enough to tempt the richest woman in France. He took out a small box and opened it between his hands, and laid what was in it in the middle of the white display cloth.

"There, Excellencies," he said softly. "There is something Mme. du Barry will appreciate."

After a moment Charles picked up the single jewel that lay like a gleaming coal upon the dazzling white. It was a pearl, a pearl as large as a pullet's egg, shaped into a perfect pear and absolutely black. It hung on the end of a plain chain connected by a single black diamond as a mount. It was incredibly beautiful. Its dusky surface gleamed with a flawless patina, its sides were smooth and without the slightest crudity or bubble. Charles passed it to his sister; Jean held it swinging to and fro for a moment in the light.

"A week ago I was approached by a gentleman acting as agent for the dauphine," the merchant said. "But the price was too high. If you can buy it, I think Mme. du Barry will appreciate it even more when she knows that Marie Antoinette wasn't able to afford it. . . ."

Charles put it back on the table. "How much?" he said.

"One hundred and seventy thousand livres, Excellency. There isn't another pearl like that in the world. It came from Constantinople, from the collection of the sultan. I'm not even making a profit at that price!"

"Too much," Charles said. "I have only one hundred and fifty thousand livres to spend. I'm not haggling with you; if you asked me a million and I had it, I should take the pearl and pay you. But I have only that much money and no more. One hundred and fifty thousand."

The merchant shook his head. "My regrets, Excellency. If I were to rob myself, and say that I would take a hundred and sixty-five, what good would it do?"

"Say a hundred and sixty," Jean said suddenly. "And we'll take it. I'll raise the ten thousand," she said to her brother, "but I can't do more. Here." She unfastened the diamond and ruby brooch she wore and a fine matching bracelet and laid them down beside the pearl. "These will make up the price. But if you don't take it, we're not going to haggle over another sou!"

The little man took up the brooch and examined the stones in it; he did the same with Jean's bracelet. Both pieces were part of the De Mallot heirlooms, and the rubies were of superb colour.

"Why should you do this?" Charles asked her. "He'd have taken my offer. . . ."

"No, he wouldn't!" his sister snapped. It was impossible to be in her brother's company without quarrelling with him, even when she was trying to help. It would always be so, even though they were closer than they had ever been because of their efforts to rescue Anne.

"I'm not doing it for you anyway," she added. "I'd sell the clothes off my back to help Anne."

"In that case, I won't thank you," Charles said. "But I'll redeem them for you later. Well?" he demanded of the merchant. "Make up your mind, or give back the jewels."

"One hundred and fifty thousand livres and these two items." The merchant put away his magnifying glass and smiled at them.

"The great pearl is yours, Excellencies. You won't regret the purchase, I promise you. There isn't a woman in the world who could resist such a stone. Madame will be very, very grateful."

On their way back to Versailles, Jean asked to see the pearl again. Charles unwrapped the box and opened it; the dusky lights gleamed and shimmered, reflected by the darker brilliance of the rare black diamond.

"I wonder if he told the truth," she said. "I wonder if Marie Antoinette did make enquiries for it . . ."

"What does it matter as long as Du Barry thinks she did? She'll wear that pearl and flaunt it in front of the dauphine and imagine she's scored over her. The effect will be the same."

"If she gets you a pass into the Bastille, what good will it do you? It won't take you to Anne, nothing can do that. . . ."

"All I need is to get in," he said. "I can't breach the walls alone or storm the gates. But once inside it, I'll find Anne. And I'll bring her out. Pull on the cord and tell that fool to whip up the horses!"

"They're tired," his sister said. "You're an impatient, inconsiderate devil, Charles."

"I want to give her this tonight, if I can," he said. "Hasn't it occurred to you, my dear sister, that time is very important . . . or don't you realise that Anne must be at the end of her term by now. . . ."

There was a reception for the Russian envoy from the Court of Catherine the Great arranged at Versailles that evening, and the presentation was to take place in the Galérie des Glaces, that fantastic hallway of mirrors and silver, large enough to accommodate the huge crowds of people. Three thousand wax candles burned down its enormous length; the tables and ornaments were all made of silver, magnificently chased by master craftsmen; the ceiling was splendidly decorated with allegorical paintings depicting the triumphs of the great Louis XIV in his war with Holland, and two exquisite Savonnerie carpets reflected, overhead, in their design and colouring the paintings of Charles Le Brun. There was a sweet, slightly pungent smell of oranges from the fruit trees that were spaced between the windows in their silver-mounted tubs, and members of the Swiss Guard and the King's gentlemen at arms were at their posts by the superbly gilded and decorated doors.

The Galérie des Glaces was one of the triumphs of Versailles in an age when glass was still a luxury; its priceless mirrors reflected a scene of opulence and display that impressed itself deeply on the mind of the envoy of Catherine the Great of Russia, whose own court was accounted lavish by any standard. He was even more impressed, though he forbore to mention it officially, by the beauty and elegance of the French King's official mistress, a tiny, fragile creature as graceful as a bird, her colouring as delicate as that of a Sevres figurine; she was wearing a dress of shimmering white silk and one of the largest and finest black pearls he had ever seen hung from a simple chain round her neck.

He found her captivating and the King pleasant enough, though inclined to be morose, and he came away from the reception with the impression that the much vaunted beauty of Marie Antoinette was overrated; she was too haughty and her manner too unyielding to please him. He had to admit that her complexion was brilliant and her eyes very blue. As it was his duty to report the meanest items to his Empress as well as the most important, he added that the rivalry between her and the Du Barry was as keen as ever. The dauphine had apparently suffered a slight on account of the pearl which the King's mistress was wearing. He ended his report with a eulogy of the virtues and modesty of his own imperial mistress, by comparison with the ladies of other royal houses, and made sure of his own interests by humbly enquiring about the health of the Empress' favourite, Potemkin. The reception at the Galérie des Glaces was a success for everyone but the discomfitted and jealous dauphine, Marie Antoinette.

But the most rewarded of all those who attended it was Charles Macdonald. He had been standing in the background, watching the Russian envoy and his retinue of servants and attendants make their way down the gallery from where the King and his ministers had received them, when the people ranked in front of him suddenly moved away and he found himself standing face to face with the Du Barry. Her face was flushed and her eyes shone; one dainty hand fingered the glowing pearl that hung from her neck, and she made a gesture with the other that sent everyone near them out of earshot. Charles bowed to her.

"Your servant, Comtesse."

"I want to thank you," she said quickly, "for this magnificent present. Did you see her face, did you see it when I came in with this round my neck . . . I thought she was going to fall down in a fit! Oh, my dear monsieur, I was so sick of you and your family pestering me that I nearly sent the box back without opening it! But I'm delighted — overjoyed! I want you to know you haven't wasted your money either. I'll do the favour for you, whatever it is, because of what this evening has meant to me!"

"I'm glad you like it," Charles said quietly. "And I thought the dauphine was so angry she was going to leave the reception at one moment. It's not the pearl's triumph, madame, it's yours. Only you could wear it as it should be worn. I think she realised that too."

"She's choking," Du Barry said. "When I

think of how she's snubbed me, humiliated me. . . . Do you know what I think I'll do, monsieur?"

Charles shook his head; he managed to keep the attentive smile on his lips while she continued excitedly, but it was slowly turning to a strained grimace. The hours since he sent the gift had seemed as long as every year of his life while he waited for some word or acknowledgment. It was his last chance; if the jewel was not good enough or the Du Barry was in a capricious mood, he would never get within reach of Anne.

"I'll send it to her as a present," Du Barry declared. "That should embarrass her; that should make it impossible for her to go on ignoring me. . . . let me know in the morning what I can do for you, monsieur, and I shall do it with pleasure. As long," she added more seriously, "as it isn't to get your wife released. You know I can't do that!"

Charles took her hand and kissed it. She noticed suddenly how lined and thin his face had become. He was still a very handsome man if one liked that sardonic, mocking type.

"I'm not asking you to get anyone out of the Bastille, madame," he murmured. "Just get me a pass so that I can get in."

She took her hand away and looked at him, her head a little on one side.

"You're mad, you know. Very well, I'll get D'Aiguillon to get you a pass. You'll have it before the end of the week. Tell me something — why were you such a swine to your wife before? I'd have thought you'd be thankful she was out of your way and taken damned good care to keep her there. I don't understand you at all."

"It's not surprising, madame. I'm only just beginning to understand it myself. Men are often very cruel to women when they find they're in love with them against their will. You'll let me have the pass in two or three days' time, then? I'm deeply grateful to you, believe me."

"I promise you'll have it. And I hope you succeed in whatever you're planning, but please don't tell me; I'd rather not know. I hope she hasn't had her child yet."

"I hope so," he said. "But it doesn't matter. Her life is all that matters to me now. Good night, madame. Whatever happens to me, I shall always thank you."


"I must say," the Comte de Mallot said gently, "it's nice to see the family so united!"

Jean's husband made her a little bow which she returned with a grimace. All Paul de Mallot's relatives were gathered together in the small château owned by Sir James Macdonald. It had been thought wiser not to hold this particular conference anywhere inside Versailles for fear of being overheard. What a curious family they were, he thought, looking from one face to the next. Lady Katherine, so beautiful and so determined; few French husbands would have put up with her for a moment, but Sir James was besotted still, and he was formidable enough with a past reputation that was stained and brutal. Paul dearly loved his own wife; he had grown accustomed to the gusts of temper associated with red hair and Scottish blood, he had forgiven her for much that was wilful, extravagant, and foolish, but he could not do otherwise. He loved her, and in spite of that one stupid episode, of which the silly girl thought he was ignorant, he knew that she loved him. It was typical of Jean to sell her jewels to help her sister-in-law Anne. It was equally typical that she abused her brother mercilessly and accused him of being responsible for the whole tragedy. What was stranger still was the calm with which Charles bore her reproaches. Paul de Mallot had never liked him; on the few occasions when they met in previous years, he had always regarded him as an unprincipled, heartless scoundrel, and resisted the temptation to box his ears and call him out, because he was by then married to his sister. But

Charles had changed. Much of the old mocking attitude remained; he would always convey an insult whenever he opened his mouth and there would always be people who resented it, but the callousness which had made Paul hate him seemed to have gone. At last he had shown some evidence of human feeling for someone besides himself. He had aged ten years since the night he learnt what had happened to his wife.

"It's very good of you to involve yourself, Paul," Sir James said. "But we feel we need your help."

"But in anything," the comte said. "All you need to do is ask!"

"My son has a plan to rescue Anne from the Bastille," Katherine said. "It seems incredibly dangerous to me, and he will need the luck of Heaven to succeed with it. Charles, you had better explain to Paul and let him tell us what he thinks."

"I have a map of the fortress," Charles said. "I also have a pass signed by the Duc d'Aiguillon to see the governor on a private matter. Nothing could be attempted without this pass. But I have it. I can get into the Bastille, my dear brother-in-law, and then it will be up to me to get out again, bringing Anne with me. This is where I shall need you."

"Go on." The comte nodded. "It sounds

quite mad to me, but go on. What am I to do?"

"Come to the outer gates with me in a carriage and wait, that's all. If I have difficulty in getting away, or manage to get only Anne through the gates, there must be someone in command to take her into hiding. And en route, two pistols will be better than one, if we're followed. Will you come with me?"

"Of course." Jean's husband shrugged. "A coach journey, a little wait, another journey . . . it's nothing. Of course I shall come. I thought you were going to ask me to strangle the gatekeeper. . . ."

"*I* shall do that, if I have to," Charles answered shortly. He looked at his sister. "Don't worry, I shan't bring Paul into any danger!"

"Not unless you get captured on the road," Jean retorted. "Then he'll be tried with you and lose his head, that's all. I'm content he should go; Anne must have someone to protect her in case anything happens to you."

"She also needs a woman," Katherine said. "No, Jean, not you, we've had this argument before. Nor me, unfortunately. We're both too conspicuous. I've asked Annie, my son, and she says she'll go in the coach with you and take care of Anne on the journey. She'll look after her like a child."

"She's not afraid?" Charles asked her. "She

understands what it could mean if I fail?"

"Don't underestimate a good Scotswoman," his mother said. "Annie faced worse dangers with me than anything you're talking about!"

"Perhaps," her son said. "I've always felt you exaggerated your adventures, Mother. I don't think you can compare a Highland raid with being broken on the wheel, and that's what they will do to Annie if she's captured helping a state prisoner escape. I'm very grateful to her. Anne will need her."

"And now your plan," Paul de Mallot said. "What do you propose to do to persuade the governor to release a prisoner to you and how do you expect to get her past the gate? I confess I'm fascinated to know. I don't think I shall ever see you again, my dear Charles, once you've gone into that place!"

"My plan is simple." Charles grinned with a flash of his old insolence. "Extremely simple, because I haven't got one. I'm going to the governor and I'm going to put a pistol at his throat and make him take me to my wife. I'm prepared to kill him, and, indeed, anyone else who shows resistance. But once I'm with her, I have no idea how we shall escape. But something will come to me at the time. I'm confident."

"You're insane," his sister interrupted.

"But the devil looks after his own. I think you'll do it!"

"So do I," Sir James said. He walked over to his son and held out his hand. "I had a brother," he said. "He was killed before you were born, Charles. This is just the sort of enterprise he would have loved. Hugh Macdonald was afraid of nothing. You're very like him, I think. You'll rescue Anne. God go with you."

He put his arm around his son and kissed him, but he did not look at his wife. After thirty years he had made peace with his dead brother. Katherine left her chair and came close to her son.

"When are you going?"

"Tomorrow," he said. "I've arranged for a plain coach and two changes of horses on the route we'll take. We shall drive towards the coast, to Le Havre. I can get a ship from there and we'll be safe in Scotland in a week. Don't worry, Mother; I'll be a father to my family and my Highlanders yet! Isn't that what you always wanted!"

"I know what I want now," she said slowly. "I want to see you safe. If she's dead, Charles, when you get there, promise me one thing — promise me you'll leave the fortress quietly and do nothing to betray yourself. . . ."

"If Anne is dead," he said quietly, "I have

nothing to leave it for. Pray for me that I'll succeed. You never know, it might do some good."

"I'll pray," she said. "We all will. Annie will be ready to go to Paris with you tomorrow morning. Good night my son."

It was growing late and the light in the cell was fading; Marguerite got up from beside the bed and patted Anne's hand.

"I'll go now, my child," she said. "You go to sleep. You must reserve your strength, you know."

She smiled into the haggard face; the girl's listlessness disturbed her. How could she summon the effort to give birth to her child alive when all she wanted was to lie back and slide into death? In spite of her kind heart, Marguerite felt angry with her; she was so afraid of losing the precious baby through the mother's apathy and despair. And how infinitely precious that unborn child had already become to her . . . she had made a beautiful layette for it, and there was a cradle ready in her attic room. For all these months she had nursed the girl and protected her, and nagged at her husband to visit her daily, just so that she could live long enough to have the child and give it into Marguerite's keeping. Marguerite was so excited now, as the time for the delivery came and overlapped by a few days, that she went round her house humming to herself, and took out the tiny vests and gowns and caps a dozen times a day. She would have been horrified to realise that she had no personal interest in the mother at all by this time; the child had become an obsession with her. She was quite ready to tear it out of Anne's arms if she made any protest. She bent over her again.

"You're sure you have no pains," she asked. "No discomfort? Call at once when they begin; I'll be with you immediately."

"I'll call," Anne whispered. "Good night, madame."

She shut her eyes, waiting until the cell door was closed and bolted. She had come to dread the visits of the surgeon and his wife. He was kind in his brusque way, but she sensed that the force behind him was the driving maternal instinct of his wife, and his wife she dreaded most of all. She had no wish to live; indeed, there was not the slightest hope of it, but something in her cringed before the bright eyes and greedy expectancy of the older woman, so anxious to gather her poor infant to herself, so indifferent to how she suffered or what became of her as long as she gave away her child. Illogically, because it was ungrateful and she was in no position to complain, Anne sometimes wished the child would die with her. She did not want the other woman to have it, and she could not have given a coherent explanation why.

For that reason, when the first pain came she turned slowly on her side and tried to sleep, refusing to admit that she had felt anything. It was very dark now; the cell was as black as a pit. She was lying on her back, very still and rigid and she tried to count during the long intervals between the pains. It was endurable; she needed nothing and no one; she lay like an animal, alone and waiting, and the turnkey slept on his stool in the passage outside. For three hours Anne passed through the first stages of a long and painful labour without making a sound.

The governor had dined very well that evening; he was in a good humour, which was rare, and had even begun discussing the possibilities of retirement with his wife. They would live in the country, he declared, and enjoy the life of gentlepeople once again. It was all very well to receive a confidential post like this, but the responsibility was out of all proportion to the salary, and the surroundings sapped the spirit. His wife was not a talkative woman; she had lost the art through ten years of living in the Bastille, and her husband disliked interruption when he felt expansive. She nodded her head and agreed with him, and thought wistfully of having a garden where she could grow flowers and vegetables, without the fortress walls shutting out the sunlight. She was sewing in the small drawing room after dinner and the governor was dozing over a book, when their maidservant announced a visitor.

The governor sat up irritably, all his mellow humour gone.

"What visitor, you idiot? Don't you know the time?"

"It's a gentleman, Excellency; the chief porter admitted him. He has a letter to see you; he says it's very important."

"Ah, bah!" The governor got up and began buttoning his coat. "No peace," he grumbled. "Never any peace in this place. Go to bed, my dear. I'll see the fellow in my office over the way. God knows what he wants. . . . Why can't these people come in the daytime?"

With the porter lighting the way ahead of them with a lantern, Charles followed the way which Anne's captors had taken seven months ago, carrying their helpless prisoner; he climbed the steep steps that turned sharply against the angle of the walls, and even here the stones glistened with damp and the pervading smell of cells stank in the nostrils. He stooped to pass through the door into the governor's room, and stood where Anne had stood, facing the table and the man who sat behind it, glaring irritably at him.

"It is very late, monsieur," the governor snapped. "I was about to go to bed. What can I do for you?"

His visitor wore a long red cloak, but gold embroidery gleamed on his coat, and the fine lace at wrists and neck bespoke a gentleman of means. The dark face and light, contemptuous eyes were also aristocratic. This must be some person of importance. The governor decided he had better offer him a chair. The porter bad withdrawn and they were alone.

"I have a pass, giving me authority to see you," Charles said. "I have it here." He threw the note signed by D'Aiguillon on the table.

The governor decided that this was indeed a nobleman. The way he tossed the paper at him, as if he were a servant, made him sure of it. He read the few lines very quickly, saw the duc's name at the bottom of the letter, and then made his visitor a bow.

"What service can I do you, monsieur?"

Charles moved closer to him; he smiled.

"You can tell me how Mme. Anne Macdonald, Marquise de Bernard, is faring in your charming prison."

The governor stared back at him; his face was set and blank and he gave a quick glance

397

downwards at the hand bell on his table.

"We have no prisoner of that name here," he said. "Is this what your business is? I'm afraid you've been misled. There are no names here, monsieur, no marquises. I do not discuss my charges; they belong to the King."

"There you are mistaken," Charles said gently. "This particular lady belongs to me. She is my wife." The fold of his cloak fell back and the muzzle of a pistol appeared on a level with the governor's eyes. "Don't touch that bell, Excellency, or I'll blow your brains out. Sit down!"

The governor sat back slowly and let his hands rest on the table; with difficulty he looked away from the small, black mouth of the pistol and into the tense, savage face of the man who stood above him. "You're being very foolish, monsieur. That pistol won't help you. You'll lose your life for this!"

"Ah, no," Charles shook his head. "It's you who will lose yours. Unless you tell me where my wife is, and then are good enough to take me to her. . . . Speak man, I'm in a hurry!"

He touched the cold muzzle to the centre of the man's forehead and the governor's eyes blinked.

"I need my records," he said. "They're in the chest over there."

"Well, get them then," Charles murmured.

"Come, take care."

The pistol was now touching the back of the governor's neck; it stayed there like a cold kiss while he sorted through the ledgers and files and came to the book in which he had entered Anne's name so many months ago. They went back to the table, Charles standing so close to him that their two shadows on the wall merged into one.

"She is in the West Tower," the governor said. "Cell 713." He read some notes further down. "She is pregnant, she has been ill, the surgeon attended her. She has been well treated, not disciplined or deprived of privileges. . . . Can't you be satisfied with that monsieur? She is as comfortable as if she were at home. . . . Put down that weapon and I promise I'll overlook the whole incident. You can go out the way you came, monsieur, and I shan't stop you. I understand a husband's feelings. . . ." He made a sympathetic grimace. "But this is not the way to help Madame — be sensible now."

"I'm being very sensible," Charles answered. "West Tower, Cell 713. Take out pen and paper and write an order releasing Madame into my custody."

The governor glared up at him; he had been pale and sweating with fear; now he turned red.

"I'll see you damned first," he barked. "By God, I hope they give you to me for this — I'll stretch your limbs for you, I'll have the tongue torn out of your head! Go to hell . . . you'll get no paper signed by me!"

He had not expected a blow and it caught him unawares across the face. The man who had struck him leant almost on top of him and now the mouth of the pistol was pressing hard into his throat. He saw murder in the narrow, pale eyes and he shrank back. Never in all his life, not even during military service, and a short campaign, had the governor come so close to death. He swore, and drew out a sheet of paper and scribbled a few lines upon it; his hand shook so hard that he made a blot on his signature. The pistol sank deeper still into his neck until he was forced to twist his head upwards to escape it. In those few seconds Charles satisfied himself as to what he had written. "Good," he said. "Now get up. We're going to the West Tower." At the door he struck the governor once again upon the face.

"I don't have to tell you what will happen if you make a move or give a sign," he said very softly. "I'll put the ball through your spine, Excellency, and you'll take as long as any of your poor tortured wretches to die, I promise you. No signals now, no tricks! Just take me to the West Tower. If you even stumble, I'll kill you!"

They passed out of the door and the governor turned and closed it behind him; they began the steep descent down the winding stairs and at the end of them a shadow moved; it was the porter, waiting to escort Charles back to the main gate. "Dismiss him," he whispered. The governor nodded. The porter would have to be sent away, but if he could even give a signal, make some grimace of warning, there would be others, turnkeys, someone along the route to the West Tower.

"I shan't be watching you," the voice said in his ear. "I'll watch his face, that's where I'll see if you've betrayed me; anyone else we see too, remember. And if they even twitch an eyebrow, I'll pull this trigger."

The governor stopped at the end of the stairs and without hesitation and in a normal tone, told the porter to go back to his post. They went on their way again, down through the open doorway and across a small cobbled yard; Charles was beside him now, the hand hidden by his cloak, prodding the pistol into the governor's back.

"The West Tower," he snarled at him once. "Don't try to turn east, my friend, I know the compass!"

The governor did not answer. All his adult

life he had been in command of men; on his
father's small estates, in the army, and in the
latter years as Governor of the Bastille. Even
with the pistol jabbing at his spine, he was
unable to surrender completely, and though
he was in many ways a tyrant and inhuman,
he was not a coward.

"I'll take you to the West Tower," he snarled.
"But much good it'll do you. . . . Do you think
you'll ever escape from here? Do you think
that writing a piece of paper like that is all
one needs to take a state prisoner out of the
Bastille? You'll find out, by God! Here's the
West Tower now."

"Go in," Charles said. "And remember what
I said. One move, one look from anyone we
meet and I'll blow your spine in half. Come
on!"

They went past the turnkey on duty at the
wicket gate which he unlocked for them and
Charles heard him fastening it again; the governor mounted the first steps of the long, steep
spiral which wound up to the top of the tower,
broken by small landings where a turnkey kept
guard over the three cells cut out of the walls.
They went by three such landings, and three
blackened doors, serrated by huge bolts, and
at each stage upwards the governor identified
himself.

Over his shoulder, he jeered at Charles.

"Not so easy is it? Try passing any of them without me and see how far you'll get!"

Charles did not answer, for the governor had stopped at the third landing and an old man was coming towards them, holding a lantern. The lined old face peered at them suspiciously; in spite of his age, the turnkey was still broad-shouldered and his arms were thick with muscles. He must have been a giant in youth. When he saw the governor he pulled off his greasy cap and bowed.

"Good evening, Excellency. All the prisoners are quiet. There's not been a squeak out of 713 so far." There was a look in the governor's eye that troubled him but he could not decide what it was. He glanced long and hard at the man standing behind him and saw nothing there to excite suspicion; the expression on his face was bored. The turnkey supposed it was some government official or court messenger who had some secret business with one of the prisoners.

"Open 713's cell," the governor said. "We want to have a look at her. Quick, man!" Even without turning, he could sense the tension in the man with the pistol and he grew frightened again for a moment. This was not the time to give the warning; he must wait until the cell door was open and the man was off his guard for a moment.

Down below, a carriage waited outside the fortress' main gate. It was plain and well sprung, the kind of coach the middle classes hired for journeys when they did not possess equipages of their own; the coachman wore no livery, though he had been in the service of the De Bernards since he was a boy in his teens.

The old comte had sent him up from Charantaise as being the most reliable and devoted of Anne's servants. He would do what he was told, without asking a single question and he could handle horses better than anyone on the estate. The comte had also insisted on sending Marie-Jeanne to help care for his niece; she had made her way to the first posting station on the coach road and would be waiting there. Inside the coach, Paul de Mallot took out his watch and swore.

"Nearly an hour," he said to Annie, who was perched on the seat opposite. "My God, will they never come?"

"How long are we to wait?" she asked him.

"Until they come out," he answered. "Or until there's a commotion. If we see guards running out of those gates towards us, we whip up the horses and fly for our lives!"

"Do ye think they'll get away?" Annie asked him; she spoke in English which the comte understood better than her accented French.

He looked across at her in the dimly lit coach and shook his head.

"I doubt it, it's never been done before. No one escapes from the Bastille, Annie, it's impossible. It would need an army to get Anne out. I don't think we'll ever see M. Charles again"

"Who would have thought it?" Annie muttered. "Of all people, him going in there to risk his life for the marquise. I'd have sworn he was as bad as any of the murdering Macdonalds, and I know how bad they were, sir, I can tell ye that!"

"Except for your master," the comte corrected her, and she nodded.

"Aye, except for him. But it's taken me half a lifetime to forget what he and his family did at Clandara Castle before he ran off with Her Ladyship. Master Charles would have been at home with all of them, don't doubt it."

"Love changed Sir James," Paul de Mallot said. "It may do the same for M. Charles if he gets the chance. But if he's not out of that gate with the marquis inside half an hour, we can give them both up for lost!"

As the turnkey pulled back the bolts on the cell door and unlocked it, Charles whispered to the governor.

"You go first."

The turnkey went in before them, holding his lantern up and the governor stepped unwillingly after him. He had a quick glimpse of the bed in the corner and the figure of the woman lying on it as the yellow lantern light fell on her in a sweeping arc. It was the last thing he ever saw because the butt of Charles's pistol caught him on the back of the neck, breaking the vertebrae. He fell dead with a grunt of pain. It was so quick that the turnkey lost the initiative; he saw the cell door bang shut and then the governor fell against him almost at the same moment when he gave a shout, but it was too late. They were enclosed in the cell, inside the thick walls, and the pistol was pointing at his face. He swore furiously and raised one hand as if to strike at Charles.

There was a cry from the corner of the room, a low moan of terror and pain and it almost gave the turnkey his opportunity because for a fraction of a second Charles turned to where it came from, and the turnkey sprang at him. The pistol shot cracked out and echoed round the walls; it seemed as loud as a thunderclap. The old man staggered, blood pouring from his shattered face, and then he fell like a tree, the lantern crashing down. Its light did not go out; It was cushioned by the foul straw and Charles picked it up and righted it quickly. There was another cry, very faint this time, from the bed, and he brought the lantern over to it and fell on his knees. At first he thought he had been tricked, and that the woman staring up at him was a stranger. Her lips moved and the eyes, sunken with pain and weakness, gazed at him in terror. A faint whisper told him that this was indeed his wife.

"Charles . . . I'm going mad. Charles, is it you . . . ?"

He took the skeletal hands in his and held them to his mouth; for a moment he could not speak. The dirty sheet that covered her exposed the grotesque pregnancy; the rest of her body was wasted until the bones in her arms and shoulders stood out under the skin. The blue eyes were all that remained of the woman he had known; the sallow face, hollow-cheeked and pitifully thin, the long hair falling over her, were like a disguise.

"Oh, Anne," he said at last. "Anne, my love, what have they done to you. . . ."

"I've lost my mind," she whispered, more to herself than to him. "Or I'm really dying. You sent me here, didn't you . . . ? Have you come to gloat . . . ?"

She turned away from him and cried out again, hiding her face in the mattress. "They mustn't know," she said wildly, "they mustn't know the baby's coming. I don't want them to take it! You're not to tell them, do you hear!"

He lifted her upright, very gently, and felt her convulse in his arms.

"Oh, my God," he said slowly. "This is the end. Hold on to me, my love, try not to make a sound. Is the child really coming?"

"Yes," Anne said; he held her close to him, cradling her. "The pains are worse. I don't understand this . . . are you really here, or am I dreaming it . . . ?"

"I'm here," he said fiercely. "Don't be afraid; I've come to get you out. Wait, my darling, stay quiet for a moment."

He went back to the bodies lying by the door and bent over them. The governor's neck was broken and the turnkey was dead. Charles took the keys out of his belt, and dragged the two of them away from the door.

"Anne," he said gently. "Anne, listen to me. Can you stand?"

"No," she said. "No. You've killed the turnkey." Her voice trembled. "What have you done?"

"Don't trouble about it," he said. "Stand up! You must! Stand up!" He lifted her off the bed; she was limp and heavy and she sagged against him, but she was able to support herself.

"We're going to escape," he said. "Do you

understand, we're going to get away from here. There's a coach waiting outside to take us to safety. You're going to be all right, you're going to walk out of this place and no one," he whispered into the distraught face so close to his own, "no one is going to take our child away, if you can just hold on a little longer!"

He held her for a moment, giving her time to rally her strength. It was some time since that pistol shot and nobody had come; the walls were very thick and they must have deadened the sound. Everything had gone well until that moment; he had reckoned on everything except finding Anne in labour. He raised her head and made her look at him.

"You'll have to walk," he whispered. "Do you hear, Anne, you'll have to walk down the stairs and past the turnkeys and out through the wicket gate, even if you have a pain, you've got to keep on walking. If you falter or fall, it'll ruin everything. We've got to get away before anyone thinks of looking for those two. Here, put this on."

He slipped off the cloak he wore and unfastened another, smaller one that had been hidden underneath it. He pushed her long hair back from her shoulders and made her stand unsupported while he put the cloak over her and pulled the hood over her head. It covered her from head to foot.

"Now," Charles said, "we're ready. We're going out and down the stairs. How long between the pains?"

She shook her head. "A few minutes, ten perhaps . . . I don't know. Charles, why don't you leave me and escape . . . we'll never get out without being stopped. I'm lost anyway now. . . ."

"God damn it," he blazed at her deliberately, hating himself because she winced. "Do you think I've risked my life getting in here just to walk out alone? Where's the De Bernard courage I used to hear so much about? Stop snivelling, woman, and come on!"

He took her arm and walked her to the door; he unlocked it with the keys taken from the dead gaoler and then they were out in the corridor. He locked the cell behind them. By the light of the torch burning at the head of the staircase he saw that Anne was crying. He bent down and kissed her on the mouth.

"Be brave, my love," he said softly. "It won't take long."

They passed the first two landings without incident; at the last one the turnkey called out to him. "Hey there! Where's His Excellency — who's that with you?"

"A prisoner," Charles barked over his shoulder. "Ask the governor if you want to know; he's coming behind us!"

Then they were down the last few stairs and he had an arm round Anne as if he were dragging her against her will. The gatekeeper peered at him suspiciously, holding his lantern up; it shone on the tear-stained face of the woman and he recognised the man who had come in with the governor not long before.

"Here," Charles said, "His Excellency's following later; he's got business with one of the others upstairs. Here's my authorisation." He held out the governor's note and the man bent over it.

"Pass through then," he said.

Charles put the paper back in his pocket and pulled Anne after him. "Come on, damn you," he said.

He had seen by the gatekeeper's eyes when he bent over the note that he couldn't read. They were in the courtyard then and the stars were bright in a clear sky above them; he squeezed her gently, and at the same moment he felt her steps dragging and the way her body stiffened and arched with pain under his arm. The temptation to stop and hold her, even to make the last part of the journey, carrying her in his arms, was so great that for a moment he almost succumbed to it. But it would have been fatal; a sick prisoner, a woman being taken out of the fortress, showing signs of imminent childbirth, was bound to cause acute suspicion. The guards at the gate would delay them, asking questions, and meanwhile the inquisitive turnkey in the West Tower would wonder why the governor was so long and go upstairs to look for him. If that note committing Anne to his custody was going to get them through the main gate, then it must do so quickly. He forced her on across the cobbled square, and down the side path leading to the governor's quarters. They were in sight of the main gate.

"Charles," she moaned. "Charles, I can't do it, there's another coming. . . . They're coming quicker."

"You mustn't stop," he said. "If you falter now we're both lost, and the child too. Hold tight to me and don't make a sound. We're coming to the main gate now!"

There were two guards on duty at the gate; one scrutinised the papers and faces of those who came and went and the other operated the mechanism which opened the small door set in the massive outer doors and controlled the drawbridge. They had seen this man come in alone; as he waited, holding a woman at his side, the guard read the governor's note very carefully. "This is an order to release the prisoner in Cell 713, West Tower, into the custody of M. Macdonald, the holder of this authority." The governor had signed his name at the end of the line, above the blot of dried ink that had formed when his hand shook as the muzzle of Charles's pistol pressed hard into his throat.

The guard read it twice, and Charles saw Anne raise a hand to her mouth and he knew it was to stifle a groan of pain; her body was quivering with the intensity of the spasm.

"Well," he demanded, "isn't the paper in order? Isn't that His Excellency's signature?"

"It seems so," the guard said. "You're taking the prisoner into your custody. . . . Doesn't look too happy about it, does she?" and he laughed.

The tension was broken then; the second guard grinned and went over to the lock mechanism on the door.

"No," Charles answered. "But a few months' stay here has tamed her down. She'll give me no more trouble now."

It was not unknown for a ward to find herself in the Bastille for a short period, where money or estates were in question and her legal guardian wished to break her spirit. Recalcitrant wives, unwilling to yield their inheritance, even sons and daughters who exasperated their parents, were disciplined into obedience by a few weeks' sojourn in the fortress.

The little door swung open and Charles

stepped through it, holding Anne by the hand. "Come on, my dear," he said. "There's our carriage waiting over there."

He heard the door shut and their feet echoed on the planks of the drawbridge. Below them the moat reflected the starry night sky. He walked as fast as he could force Anne along, but as they came to the end of the drawbridge and the edge of the road, she gave a cry and began to sink to the ground. If anyone was watching them from the main towers of the Bastille, and there were always watchers, it was too late to worry about them now. He swung her up in his arms and ran to the carriage. He saw Paul de Mallot jump out and come to meet him; they didn't have time to speak. They lifted Anne inside and sprang in after her; at a shout from the comte, the coachman whipped up his horses and the carriage bounded forward, rocking wildly on the rough, cobbled street, and raced down it towards the main thoroughfare and the coast road.

The turnkey on the first landing in the West Tower went to the stairwell and peered up again; he lifted his lantern and swung it upwards, lighting the worn steps. There was no sign of the governor coming down — and no sound. The turnkey decided he had waited long enough; there was something strange about the governor staying on so long after letting the man take his prisoner out without him. He picked up the light and began to climb the stairs. At the landings above he called out to the turnkeys on duty.

"Is His Excellency with you?"

And the answer was the same. "He's not here. He hasn't come down again."

At the third landing the man paused, searching for the turnkey who should have been on duty. He went to the door of the first cell and called out. "Are you there, Excellency?"

A feeble shout came through the door: "There's no one here but me, and the rats!"

He called through to the next prisoner and got a howl of abuse in reply. At the third door, where the woman had been kept, he banged and shouted in vain. There was nowhere else the governor could be; they had reached the top of the Tower. And where was the turnkey . . . ? He turned and ran down the staircase to the wicket gate. The gatekeeper had a master key that fitted all the cells, but it was only used in grave emergency. Five minutes later they had opened the door of Cell 713, and in the semidarkness, they tripped over the dead body of the governor, lying on his back with his mouth and eyes wide open, his head lolling awkwardly on his broken neck.

Moments later the shout went ringing through the West Tower: "Escape! Escape! Sound the alarm!" And the hopeless wretches in their black cells dragged themselves to the doors and listened. From behind some of them there came weak cheers of encouragement.

The warning bell began to toll out, chiming its message over the fortress roofs and towers; the doors jammed shut leading to the drawbridge, and the drawbridge itself began to rise, closing the buildings off completely from the outside world. The deputy governor came running from his bed, and the governor's wife was by this time weeping over her husband's body where it had been laid out in his house. There was little confusion, because the deputy governor was a retired officer and he reacted with military alertness.

Twenty minutes after the discovery of the two dead bodies in the West Tower the drawbridge came down again and a troop of thirty soldiers under the command of the deputy's nephew, rode out of the Bastille and set off in the direction that the fugitive's coach was seen to have taken.

"She can go no further," Annie said. She held Anne in her arms, cradling her head against her breast as if she were a child, and on the other side, Charles held on to his wife's hands. Paul de Mallot stared out the window; pain distressed and horrified him. Every few moments now, his sister-in-law cried out; Annie had to shout to make herself heard.

"We'll have to stop," she insisted. "She'll have the child any moment with all this jolting!"

"We can't wait till the posting inn," Charles said. "It's half an hour or more from here. Paul, isn't there a house nearby?"

"I can't see anything," the comte said. "And anyway, who'll take us in at this hour of the night . . . ? We'd best pull up the coach off the road and let Annie do what she can."

"And let Anne die?" Charles demanded. He rubbed his wife's hands between his own; every moment or so he kissed them, leaning over her to whisper encouragement. "Look for some lights and we'll stop. I've enough money to pay for attention. If they won't listen to money, they'll listen to this!" He touched the pistol in his belt. He bent over Anne again. "Be brave, my love," he said. "We'll find somewhere safe for you soon now. Hold on to me."

He wasn't sure whether she heard him; in the half darkness of the coach, her face was a white blur; often she shut her eyes and surrendered to the pain, and cried until he felt as if his heart would break because he couldn't help her. And they carried another passenger besides pain and fear; Death was in the carriage with them, waiting to carry off the mother or the child — or both. The Dark Midwife hovered round the bed at every birth but its presence was very close to all of them now.

"There's a house, up there, to the right!" De Mallot called out. He pulled on the coachstring. "Turn off there, where the lights are!"

The coach slowed up and made the turn off the road onto a rough track; its pace was very slow now because the path was pitted with holes. Even so, it lurched and bounced on its springs and at one moment the whole carriage sank on one side and hung as if it were going to turn over. But the coachman was an expert driver; he pulled his horses round and righted the coach; they picked their way up to the gates outside the farmhouse, and moved slowly through them, drawing up in front of the door. Dogs were barking from the house and from the outbuildings; a moment later the front door was unbolted and a man came out in his nightshirt, carrying an old firing piece, with a large wolf-hound beside him.

De Mallot jumped out first.

"For the love of God, monsieur," — Charles

heard him say — "give us shelter and help. My sister-in-law is inside there, in the last stages of childbirth. I saw your lights and came here for help. She can't go another yard!"

"Pauline!" The farmer turned towards the house and yelled. "Pauline, come out here and bring the lantern — it's all right, they're not thieves!"

A few moments later the carriage door opened and a woman swung the light inside. It fell on Anne, supported by Charles and Annie, and in a sharp voice the woman said, "Jesus!" Swiftly she added, "Carry her into the house — and by the look of her you'll need to be quick! Pierre! Take this light and hold it!"

The farmer and his wife stood aside as Charles came down first, carrying Anne in his arms.

"In here," the woman said. "Hurry up, monsieur . . . you come too, madame," she called to Annie. "There's no other woman in the house except me. Pierre, see to the gentlemen, and put some water on the stove!"

"I'm very grateful to you," the comte murmured. "Is there anywhere we can put the coach for the night?"

They were inside the house by then; Charles had carried his wife up the stairs and Annie had disappeared after him. The farmer looked at the aristocratic gentleman with suspicion. They had stopped at an isolated farm in the middle of the night, with a pregnant woman who looked as if she was dying anyway, asking for shelter, and it was obvious he was anxious to hide the coach.

"Who is pursuing you, monsieur?" the old man asked simply. "If you want help from us, then you'll have to tell the truth. You're no ordinary travellers; people of quality don't take their ladies out onto the road when they're so near the time. You may as well tell me, monsieur. What is that lady doing with you and who is she?"

"Her identity is not your business," the comte said quietly. "It will be better for you not to know who any of us are. But I'll tell you this; we're fugitives, and madame has just been rescued from prison. It's certain we are being pursued by now; that's why I wish to hide the coach. If we are caught, it will mean death for all of us, including madame and the child. If they come here looking for us, you will do well to plead ignorance. Hide us, and you'll be well rewarded. If you decide to betray us, I promise you madame's husband will find a way to kill you both!"

"Eh," the old man said. "That's clear enough. Since I've let you in, there's not much I can do but keep you hidden, at least until you can take madame on the road again."

"Just let the child be born," the comte said. "That's all we ask for the moment. I'll go out and put the coach into one of your barns. With any luck, we haven't been seen coming in here."

"Go out, monsieur." The farmer's wife turned brusquely to Charles. "There's nothing you can do for her, you'll only be in the way!"

"I'm going," he said. "In a moment."

Anne lay on the bed in the couple's own room; tallow candles cast a yellow light upon her. She looked very small and wasted, her face half hidden by the pillows, the dark, damp hair drawn back from her face. Charles bent over her, and stroked the forehead which was sticky with sweat; as he did so, her eyes opened. A moment before she had shrieked in agony; now she lay like an exhausted animal in the short interval between the final birth pains. "Charles . . ." The tiny whisper cost her a tremendous effort. "Are we safe . . . ?"

"Yes, my darling heart, we are. You're going to have the child now. You've been so brave, so good. . . ."

For a moment he faltered. He had never cried in his life and his pride forbade him to do so then, but for a second or so he could not speak.

"You've got to be brave now and then it'll be over. We'll have our child and we'll be together, you and I. Promise me you'll be strong and not afraid. I want you well and safe, both of you. . . ."

"You didn't send me there," she whispered, her voice trailing off. "I thought it was you . . . I wanted to die so much. . . . Thank God you came — Go away now, please go away —"

"Come on! Outside, monsieur!" The farmer's wife almost pushed him through the door; behind her he saw Annie at the bedside. "We'll call you when it's over!"

He caught the woman by the sleeve. "Will she live?" he said. "Tell me, do you think she'll live?"

"God knows, monsieur," she said and shrugged. "I don't like the look of her. I warn you, you may well lose the child anyway. But we'll do our best for both of them."

# Chapter 10

The captain of the horse troop from the Bastille had divided his forces into two; he dispatched ten men and a noncommissioned officer on the road back to Paris, though he felt it was unlikely that the fugitives had gone in that direction. There would be an extensive search of the city, and the police would soon get to hear of strangers being hidden, especially one in Anne de Bernard Macdonald's condition. It was unthinkable that any member of their own class would shelter them. The King's anger would have frightful repercussions on anyone involved in the affair.

The captain led his remaining twenty men at a brisk canter down the road which the coach had actually taken; there were a few scattered houses on the way but there was no means of approach for a carriage across the fields which separated them from the road, and at one inn where he stopped, a thorough search revealed no trace of the escaped prisoner or her rescuers. It was a very dark night, and the captain cursed as he rode; it was impossible to see wheel tracks without stopping and examining the road on foot, and this meant a further loss of time. If he was right, and he had great confidence in his own judgment, then the quarry were speeding for the coast as fast as they could go, there to disappear in any one of a dozen little ports until a ship could take them out of France. He was very anxious to catch the man who had killed the governor; it would advance his own promotion along with that of his uncle, and he was a very ambitious young man.

At a bend in the road he saw what Paul de Mallot had seen two hours before; the farmhouse standing back behind its gates at the end of a rough track, and a single light burning in the upper window.

"Draw in!" he shouted, and the troop pulled up. "Examine the ground here for wheel marks."

One of his men dismounted, and peered at the serrated path, which was dry and pitted with holes. Mud would have told him immediately if anything had turned in there, but not a drop of rain had fallen all day.

"I can't see anything, Captain. There are ridges and marks everywhere. . . ." He walked a distance farther on and came to the spot where the coach had almost overturned.

"There's a big rut here, sir, but it could have been made a week ago!"

"Could a coach come up here, eh?" the captain asked. He had ridden up behind the soldier.

"Possibly, sir. I wouldn't like to try it."

"All the same," the captain said, "I think we'll pay the place a visit. Follow on!"

A few moments later there was a loud knocking on the door of the house and the dogs began to bark furiously for the second time that night. The captain had to knock again, harder still, and shout before someone shuffled up to the door and opened it a crack.

"Who's there . . . ? Go away or I'll shoot!"

"Open in the King's name!"

The farmer stood in the doorway, his old fowling piece cocked in his arm, the house dog snarling beside him. He was in nightgown and nightcap, and he grumbled sleepily as he stepped aside to let the officer come in.

"What's the matter . . . what the devil's going on! It's past four in the morning — I've only another hour to sleep!"

"We're looking for an escaped prisoner," the captain explained. "A woman and a man, perhaps more than one man. The woman is pregnant. Have you seen them?"

"Ach," the old man said. "How would I

see them at this hour — the whole household is in bed!"

"Did a coach pass, do you know, or stop here for anything?" The captain watched him closely. His senior trooper moved nearer the old man and the dog gave a low, fierce growl of warning.

"No coach has been here," the old man said sullenly. "I've told you, we've seen and heard nothing!"

"In that case," the captain said briskly, "you won't object to a search. Sergeant, take ten men outside and look in the barns; you, Grissot, take another five and begin looking through the house. I, sir," he added, "will accept a glass of wine from you. Then I will go upstairs and have a look round for myself. For your own sake, I hope you've been telling me the truth!"

The sergeant and his ten men began their tour of the barns and outhouses; there was only one lantern available and that gave a poor light. In the smaller buildings there was nothing but farm implements, and stores of grain; in the big open barn near the house there was a mountain of hay and two guard dogs on chains which leaped at the searchers, snarling and snapping. They gave a quick look into the stables to make sure that no one was hiding in the stalls with the horses. There was not a sign of anything; they came back and took up positions in the courtyard, yawning and cursing, because they would have to ride on.

Inside the house the captain finished his glass of wine and looked from the farmer to his wife who had been summoned downstairs and had given exactly the same answers to his questions as her husband. If anything, she was more sleepy and more sullen. The soldier Grissot put his head round the door.

"We've searched upstairs, sir. There are only two women up there in bed."

"My niece," the farmer's wife said, "and my husband's sister. They live with us."

"I think I'll have a look at them," the captain said. "I thought you were alone here? Show me the way, Grissot!"

He went up the narrow stairs, and behind him the old couple followed, holding each other's hand. "The old woman's in here, sir."

Grissot opened the door, and held up his lantern. A figure on a trestle bed in one corner dragged the shabby blanket to her chin and glared at them, a nightcap pulled down to her eyes. *"Mordieu!"* she said, and lay down again, grasping the cover as if she expected them to tear it from her.

"Eh," the captain nodded. "The sister. Move on, Grissot!"

When the door shut behind them Annie lay

427

rigid, listening. She heard them go on down the passage, their heavy riding boots thumping on the bare boards, and then they stopped outside the door of Anne's room. The captain saw a young girl sitting up in bed, her brown hair hanging loose; she blinked in the light and made the same gesture with the covers as the old woman in the next room; she held them up to her and stared in terror at the captain and his sergeant. Immediately, Pauline pushed past them and hurried over to the bed. She sat on it and put her arm around the girl, holding her close.

"Don't be alarmed, my child," she said. "They won't hurt you. They're looking for some criminals." She glared at the soldiers like an animal defending its young. "My niece is ill, don't frighten her. . . . There, there, my dove, they only want to look inside; they'll be gone in a moment!"

The girl clung on to her, her blue eyes gazing at the captain as if she expected him to spring upon her. It was a natural assumption for any young girl of the peasant class to make when confronted by the military. In his youth in the army the captain had enjoyed one or two amusing evenings at the expense of people like these when his duties called for a search or the requisitioning of food. They were all the same, stupid as oxen, stubborn and cun-

428

ning as foxes when it came to hiding their money or telling lies to the authorities. He gave the girl a contemptuous look. She was thin as a reed and obviously sick. He turned his back on her and went out.

"There's nothing here," they heard him say. "Collect the men, Grissot, and we'll ride on. They'll have stopped somewhere. We'll find them!"

The old woman put her finger to her lips and squeezed Anne's shoulder as a warning not to speak. They stayed silent until the house door banged and they could hear the clatter of the horses as the troop remounted and began to ride out of the courtyard towards the gate. Anne sank back against the old woman and closed her eyes.

"They've gone!" The old man came into the room and hugged his wife. She had recovered herself by then and she gave him a push. "Of course they've gone! I heard them. Quick, go down to the barn and dig those gentlemen out from under the hay before they suffocate!"

"The baby," Anne whispered. "Where is she . . . ?"

"Wrapped up in the cupboard, madame," Pauline said triumphantly. "And sleeping like a little angel. She never made a whimper! You were very good too! Eh, if they'd come half an hour ago, those pigs!"

The coach had been hidden under mounds of hay, and Charles and Paul de Mallot were concealed inside it with the coachman. Their horses were unharnessed and stabled with the farm animals. The farmer had hidden everything very well; so well that it was as hot and airless as an oven in the coach, and the three men crouching inside it were almost stifled. They had still been clearing the towels and water jugs out of Anne's room when the troop stopped on the road, attracted by the light that burned in the upper window. Pauline and Annie between them had worked like furies, hiding the evidence of the birth, hiding the newborn baby in the linen cupboard as the first knocks sounded from below. Now Annie came rushing into the room, fully dressed in her travelling clothes, with the old woman's nightcap askew on her grey head.

"Och, madame, madame," she cried, bending over Anne. "Are ye all right now? Where's the wee one? Take her out of that cupboard woman, for the love o' God, before she comes to harm!" That one exclamation with which she had greeted the intruders was the only French she dared trust herself to speak, and there were half a dozen better ones in honest Scots she would have sooner used to them. Anne opened her eyes and tried to smile.

"She doesn't understand a word," she murmured. "She's bringing the baby now. I'm bleeding again. . . . Annie?"

"Yes, my lamb." Annie bent down close to her, one wrinkled hand smoothed her forehead as if she were a child. "What d'ye want . . . ?"

"Where's M. Charles . . . ?"

"Och!" Annie shook her head. She would never understand the ways of her own sex. Love turned their brains, for certain. She made a great effort and concealed her disapproval.

"I'll go and get him for ye."

It was the farmer's suggestion that they should hide in the coach until daylight, when anyone approaching from the road could be seen a mile or more away, and it was the insistence of Paul de Mallot that had made Charles agree to leave the house without knowing if the child was born.

"How do we know you can be trusted?" he had demanded of the old man. "How do we know you won't betray us when we're buried alive in that coach. . . . By God, if you do. . . ."

"You can trust me, monsieur, because you can trust my wife," came the answer. "She's not the woman to betray that poor girl upstairs or her infant. We've had two of our own and lost both. Get outside and hide yourselves. If

431

you've been followed, they'll be here any moment!"

The three men had hidden in the stuffy, suffocatingly hot coach for the best part of an hour when the troop of horses came into the courtyard. It had needed all the strength of Paul de Mallot and the coachman to hold Charles still, inside their hiding place, while the searchers were at work; he had been like a maniac for fear that they would discover Anne and take her away while he stayed in safety.

When the hay was dragged away, it was the farmer himself who opened the door and held the lantern for them as they scrambled out.

"They've gone," he said. "You'll be safe for a while now."

"My wife?" Charles demanded. "Is it over?"

"Over an hour or more," the old man said; he turned and shouted after him into the darkness, but Charles was already running to the house.

"It's only a girl, but she's healthy!"

Annie met him in the hallway; she raised her eyebrows for a moment at the wild figure, dishevelled and decked with pieces of hay, and stepped in front of him.

"Ye've a daughter, M. Charles," she said. "And Madame is not too bad now, bless her. She's been asking for ye." She gave him a look that expressed a full twenty-seven years of disapproval. "God knows why!" she added, and then she stepped aside.

"She's dark," Charles said. He pushed the edge of the wrapper back from the tiny head, showing the fuzz of inky hair; the little girl yawned and settled with a birdlike movement closer into the shelter of her mother's arm. Anne glanced down and smiled.

"She's like you," she whispered. "She's so small, poor little mite. Promise you'll take care of her."

She had not looked at Charles for some moments after he came into the room and Pauline gave her the child to hold and then left them together. She had asked for him, but now that he had come she felt unspeakably weary and drained; all she wanted in the world was to sleep, and her longing for it was very near that fatal yearning she had felt in the Bastille when death was very close.

In the panic when the soldiers came, the two older women had been forced to move her while they hid the signs of the birth, and she had suffered a heavy loss of blood. She was no longer in pain, but there was a shadow round her mouth that had nothing to do with the light in the room. The child was born and it was safe; it felt very warm next to her side.

Her own body was quite cold. The same chill was on her hands and cheek; Charles felt it when he kissed both, and a spasm of fear flickered through him like a shaft of lightning. He gazed at the pale face, sunken and sallow as if her skin had turned to wax, the heavy lids were closed over her eyes as if they would never open again, and it came to Charles then that in spite of everything that he or anyone could do, his wife was going to die.

"Anne! Anne!"

She was drifting gently and the sound of her name was like an echo, as if he were calling her in a dream.

"Open your eyes! Look at me. . . . God damn you, woman, do as I say!"

Instinct made her look at him, blinking to bring him into focus; she saw the dark, angry face a few inches away from her, the light eyes blazing with command. The tears were running down his cheeks.

"If you go to sleep now," he said, "you'll die. Do you hear me, you'll die! I love you, Anne. I want you; don't shut your eyes again. . . ."

"I'm so tired," she whispered.

"I know," he said, and now his voice was gentle again and he held her close, pressing his cheek against hers. "I know, my darling. But you mustn't give way to it. Listen to me.

434

I love you. Does that mean anything to you now?"

"It meant everything to me, always," she said. "It was all I ever wanted. I thought you hated me; I thought you got the *lettre de cachet*." The words were trailing off again and desperately he persisted.

"Now, you know I didn't. I thought you'd run off with your Irishman to Metz. I was going down there to kill him, I was so jealous. I love you, Anne. I loved you long before, but I wouldn't admit it. I didn't know how. Try to forgive me for what I did to hurt you. Anne, I beg of you, fight it, don't slip away from me now. My heart will break if I lose you."

With a great effort she looked up at him and raised one hand to touch his face.

"There's nothing to forgive. I love you; nothing could change that. And I'm happy now, believe me. Nothing matters except that I'm with you at last, just as I always dreamed of being. Safe and loved by you. . . . Take good care of the little girl for me."

"I'll take care of you both," he said. "I'm taking you home to Scotland; we've done with France, you and I and Mistress Macdonald there. And when you're well and strong, my love, and the good Scottish air has healed you, I'll tell you how you came to be in the Bastille and how I came to get you out. When you're safe at Dundrenan, it will seem like a hundred years ago."

"It seems like it now," Anne murmured. She felt a little warmer in his arms and she was loath to let him go. The baby made a tiny sound, and she smiled. The past seemed very unimportant; nothing mattered but her love for him and the knowledge of his love for her. She listened as he talked on of the Highlands, and felt sad for a moment because she knew she wouldn't be going with him.

"Hold me," she said softly. "Just for a few moments more. I'm really going to sleep now."

When he looked down at her, her lips were smiling.

A week later, a small boat set out from Le Havre to make the long crossing through the Channel and up the North Sea to the port of Leith. She often combined a little smuggling of French silks and brandy to the Scottish coast on her trade runs; the captain was quite sure he carried an equally dangerous cargo when he accepted the gentleman and the baby and their young servant, but he had been well paid to take them aboard and take his ship off its usual course. He gave up his own cabin and the gentleman, who was never seen to smile, settled the maid and the child in it and slept below decks himself.

Throughout the voyage the captain kept to his bargain and avoided all other ships. Five days later he landed his passengers at Leith and did a profitable trade with his contraband among the Scottish merchants. He never made another journey because the French customs arrested him on his return.

Across the sea, Charles and his infant daughter stayed with Marie-Jeanne in Leith until the child was strong enough to make the long, slow journey through the Highlands to the glen of her ancestors at Dundrenan.

As a result of what the French customs officers discovered about the passengers who had sailed to Leith, a King's commissioner paid a visit to the Château de Bernard at Charantaise, and silently inspected the new tomb of the last marquise, which was inscribed simply — ANNE MACDONALD and the date. The commissioner took his leave without asking any more questions and the affair was soon forgotten.